Dead Dukes Tell No Tales

Sass and Steam
Book 3

Catherine Stein

Copyright © 2021 Catherine Stein, LLC.

All rights reserved. No part of this book may be used or reproduced by any means, graphic, electronic, or mechanical, including photocopying, recording, taping or by any information storage retrieval system without the written permission of the author except in the case of brief quotations embodied in critical articles and reviews.

This is a work of fiction. Names, characters, places, and incidents are products of the author's imagination or are used fictitiously. Any resemblance to actual events or persons, living or dead, is entirely coincidental.

ISBN: 978-1-949862-27-0

Book cover and interior design by E. McAuley:
www.impluviumstudios.com

To Aarisa, for always loving my bonkers plots and finding my plot holes before they get too big.

1

England
January, 1906

'I AM VERY SORRY TO INFORM YOU of the death…' No, no. Not dramatic enough. 'I am *immeasurably* sorry to inform you of the *tragic* death of His Grace, the sixteenth-and-three-quarters Duke of Hartleigh.'"

"Twelfth, Daddy. You're the twelfth duke."

Clifford Kinsley, who, much to his dismay, was now apparently the *twelfth* Duke of Hartleigh, set down his pen and turned in his chair to face his seven-year-old daughter.

"How do you know that?"

Lola shrugged one shoulder, the movement setting her jet-black curls bouncing. "I counted the pictures."

"Pictures?"

She pointed across the study to where a pile of ghastly, faded portraits leaned against the empty bookshelves. "Those pictures. They're old dukes or something. There's ten pictures there, plus the big statue outside. Eleven. Are you going to get a picture made, Daddy?"

Cliff grimaced. "God, no."

"Miss Wallace says you're not supposed to say 'God' all the time. She says I should say 'goodness' if I say anything."

"Who the hell is Miss Wallace?"

Lola shrugged again. "That lady who's here to watch me. I think she's a teacher, but they called her a word I don't know. It sounded like 'government' or something."

"Governess."

"That." She stuffed her hands in her pockets.

"Don't drop spiders on her."

Lola pulled her hands out and turned them palms up. "No spiders."

"Good." Cliff pushed his spectacles more firmly onto his nose. "I'm sure you're as frustrated with all this as I am, but we both should remember that the people who work here didn't ask for this any more than we did. We should be nice to them."

Her little head bobbed in agreement.

Cliff glanced at the door. It was closed, but who knew whether there were servants lurking outside. This place was crawling with people. At home it had always been just him and Lo. And that's how he liked it.

Since his arrival in England, he'd been surrounded at almost all times. A driver had met him at the train station and driven him to this massive house, apologizing for its small size and unsuitability. Only later had Cliff discovered this was a "dower house," intended as a residence for the old duke's widow. The still-larger house across the gardens was meant to be his home. Apparently it had been sold off due to some questionable point of law. He owned the land, but not the house. Cliff remained baffled by the entire thing.

Fortunately, the dower house included this cozy, if sparsely furnished study. And when he retreated here, no one intruded without knocking. It was the closest thing he had to a refuge at the moment.

He glanced again at the door and lowered his voice. "We

won't be here much longer. Soon the twelfth duke will be dead and you and I will start a new life in California."

Lola skipped over to him and climbed into his lap. "What's it like in California?"

"I don't know. I've never been there."

"I want to go home to Chicago. I miss the city. I miss the lake." She nuzzled against his chest, and Cliff pressed a kiss into her hair.

"Me too, baby. Me too. You'll like San Francisco. It's right on the ocean."

She straightened up, frowning at him. "I don't like the ocean. The boat made my tummy sick and it was *so* long."

"Maybe we'll take an airship this time."

Her eyes widened. "Ooh, like a sky-pirate ship?"

Cliff winced. Lord save him from pirate-loving little girls. "More like a naval ship. Very clean. Organized. I'll make sure to buy you a telescope and you can learn about air currents and steam engines."

"And how to sword fight?" She made a slashing motion with her arm, smacking him on the side of the head.

He grunted and lifted her off his lap. "Not around me. I don't want to die for real. Now go back to your toys. I need to finish brainstorming ways to kill the duke."

She slashed the air. "Swords!"

"We have to disappear, Lo. Something like drowning in the ocean or falling into a bog."

"Hmm." She plopped on the ground beside her dolls, and for a few minutes, Cliff thought that was the end of it.

He scribbled about half a page of mostly worthless notes. Honestly, he didn't have anything better than the bog. Set upon by thieves in London would spark a search for a body. For a duke they'd probably dredge the whole damned Thames. "Washed out to sea while fishing?" he muttered. He probably owned some sort of boat, and it was probably full of holes.

"Daddy? Can it be pirates?"

For the love of God.

"Babe, there really aren't that many pirates."

"The lady next door is a pirate."

"What?" Cliff knew nothing about the woman who lived in the former Hartleigh mansion, except that she was rich. He'd never even seen her. "Don't be ridiculous."

"It's true."

He shook his head. "Pirates don't live in giant ducal houses in the Middle of Nowhere, England."

Lola hopped up, clutching her favorite doll to her chest. "It's true, Daddy. I saw her. I was playing outside and she was practicing with her sword and slicing things up, and she saw me and did this." Lola put a single finger to her lips. "She was secret pirate practicing."

Cliff fought not to roll his eyes. "I don't think she's a pirate, Lo, but maybe we'll walk over tomorrow and pay her a visit." It couldn't hurt to get to know his neighbor a bit. People would take it as a sign he was growing accustomed to this whole duke thing. Put them at ease. Make them more likely to believe him truly dead when he vanished without a trace.

And with luck it would quash Lola's absurd pirate talk. After her constant buccaneer chatter throughout the agonizingly long ocean voyage, he really didn't think he could stand much more of it.

Lola bounced in place, clapping her hands. "Ooh, ooh! Can we really, Daddy? You'll see! She's a real pirate! I promise!"

He sighed and ruffled her hair. "If you say so, babe. Now let's get you to bed. It's getting late."

Cliff walked Lola upstairs to the bedroom she'd claimed as her own and helped her prepare for bed. Before she finished buttoning up her footed blanket sleeper, he popped open the metal plate in the center of her chest that protected the delicate workings of her biomechanical heart. Nestled among brass tubes and copper pipes, a small fuel tube filled with precious luxene glowed bright green.

"Fuel looks great," he said, then gently pressed the plate closed so it once again meshed snugly with her skin.

"Next time we refuel, can I do it all by myself?" Lola asked.

"You may, but only with supervision." He buttoned her up, tucked her into bed, and kissed her goodnight, wishing for the millionth time they didn't need to have these conversations.

Never would he forget his terror when the doctors had discovered the defect in Lola's heart. He'd consulted dozens of specialists before choosing the biomechanologist who had crafted her life-saving device.

He trudged back down to the study. When he'd set out for England, he'd hoped the prestige of his new title might be of benefit to Lola. He'd thought perhaps it would give him access to a substantial, unadulterated supply of her rare and expensive fuel. Or give him a connection to top scientists, who might have better and safer alternatives to power her biomechanics.

Instead he had debts, a house full of people who thought him strange, and a neighbor his daughter believed was a pirate.

Cliff sank into his seat at the desk. He had no real work, no real purpose, just this unmitigated mess of an inheritance. He tapped his pen on the paper, then wrote, *Kidnapped by pirates and thrown overboard.*

The sooner Hartleigh died, the better.

2

Sabine gingerly lifted her foot off the crushed object, pulling her skirt aside to see what she'd inadvertently stepped on.

What did I ruin this time? A mummified bird? A taxidermied squirrel? The egg of an ancient creature?

Whatever it was, it had crunched.

"Ah. Nur ein Heißluftballon." She bent and picked up the remains of the model, its balloon flattened and its wicker basket in pieces. She tossed it into the large metal waste bin she'd dragged here for just this purpose.

This room was the worst yet. Models, gadgets, and artifacts—some of which she couldn't even hope to identify—littered the floor. Every flat surface was strewn with objects, papers, and a thick layer of dust. No wonder everyone called the late Duke of Hartleigh "mad." She'd been here a month, and she'd been through less than a quarter of his bizarre and unorganized collection.

Sabine picked her way to the window seat, pushed aside a pair of tarnished candlesticks, and plopped down onto the worn cushions. Outside, a few flakes of snow drifted from the sky. Pretty. Fortunately, from this view she could see neither the marble statue of the old duke in a toga and laurel wreath nor the pyramid-shaped mausoleum in which he had entombed himself behind the dower house.

A knock sounded on the door.

"Come in," Sabine called, rising from her seat and again attempting to cross the room. She wondered what the carpet looked like beneath everything.

"Hey, Captain, there's…" Hawkes paused and straightened his shoulders. "My lady, you have a visitor. Shall I bring him here?"

A part of her wanted to laugh at his stuffy, affected mannerisms. With his long, sandy hair whipping around his shoulders, and the wicked scar across his left cheek, he was as unbutlerish as a man could be, even in his fine suit, but he'd thrown himself into the role with such enthusiasm that she didn't dare do anything that might discourage him.

"Here?" She stepped over a metal and brass contraption with no discernible function. "Only if he's come to haul away trash."

"Er, I think he's the duke from next door. He left a card."

Sabine hopped over a few more things and took the small rectangle from Hawke's thick fingers. The sturdy, cream-colored paper stated its owner's name and business in a clear, no-nonsense typeface.

Clifford J. Kinsley
Kinsley Metals
Scrap Collection & Recycling
Chicago, Illinois

So this was the mysterious American duke. She'd been too busy working to pay a visit to her new neighbor, but she had seen his little girl playing outside.

"Scrap collection? Hmm. Perhaps he *will* haul away my trash. Show him into the, um… music room, please."

Hawkes executed quite a nice bow for a man who had until two months ago been a pirate. "Certainly, my lady."

Sabine made her way down the blessedly empty halls to the music room and took a seat at her favorite of the four pianos. Her fingers skimmed across the keys. Perhaps she would hire an instructor someday and learn to play. It seemed a pleasant sort of activity to take up in her retirement. And she had always had nimble fingers.

She'd left the door standing open, but Hawkes knocked anyway.

"His Grace, the Duke of Hartleigh," the butler intoned, imparting the words with gravitas fit for a king. "And Miss, uh—"

"Lola Hartleigh," the girl declared, bounding toward Sabine and thrusting out a hand. "I'm practicing my new name. H-E-A-R-T-L-E-Y."

"Lo, it's a title, not a name," the duke said. "I don't think that's how it works."

Sabine's eyes lifted to study him as she shook Lola's hand. Father and daughter shared the same black-as-night hair and the same prominent nose, but where her eyes were dark and her skin olive, he was pale. His light-colored eyes were partially obscured behind a pair of spectacles with oval-shaped lenses set in a bright red frame.

Eyeglasses as a fashion statement? Interesting. Sabine automatically adjusted her own plain spectacles.

"Also, it's H-A-R-T. It means deer," Hartleigh clarified. "And leigh is L-E-I-G-H for some ungodly reason."

The girl's brow furrowed. "Shouldn't it be Hart-le-guh, then?"

"It's one of those weird words, like 'through.'"

"T-H-R-U. Through. Why is that weird?"

Hartleigh pulled out a cloth and wiped his spectacles. "Uh,

you know what, we'll have a spelling lesson another time. Let's meet our neighbor first." He gave Sabine a half-smile and a little shrug. "Sorry. She's at a curious age and I usually indulge her with explanations for just about everything." He extended a hand. "Clifford Kinsley, with an L-E-Y. Pleased to meet you."

"Sabine Diebin." His grip was firm, his hand warm against hers. "And for the curious…" She smiled at Lola. "Sabine has an E at the end, in the German way, not an A as you would spell it in English."

"Sa-been-ah," Lola pronounced carefully. "With an E."

The duke's dark brows crinkled slightly. "Isn't Diebin German for a lady thief?"

Sabine rocked backward in shock. "You speak German?"

He held his thumb and forefinger about an inch apart. "Ein bißchen."

Lola tugged urgently on her father's coat until he bent over to hear her whisper. He frowned and shook his head emphatically. He hoisted the girl up onto one of the other piano benches, then took a third bench for himself.

"So," he said. "You must be very fond of music."

"I am, but I'm afraid I don't play. These instruments came along with the house. The previous owner lived to be very old and gathered a massive collection of things during his lifetime. I'm still sorting through it all. Well, all but the few things that were moved to the dower house before the sale."

"The leftovers of the Mad Duke." He huffed a little laugh.

"Yes. I understand you run a scrap collection business? Perhaps I could employ you to haul everything away."

"I *was* in the recycling business." His mouth tightened into a hard line. "Now, unfortunately, I'm a goddamned duke, if you'll pardon my French."

Sabine tried not to laugh. She really did. But he was so delightfully, blunt-spokenly *American*.

"Has your new title destroyed your ability to pluck valuable bits from the rubbish?"

He adjusted his spectacles, assessing her with a steady gaze. His eyes were an icy blue, like the glacial caves in the Alps—quiet, still, and eerily beautiful.

"I don't expect it has, no."

"Since we are neighbors, maybe you would like to lend your expertise and help me straighten out this mess of a house? As payment, you may keep what you wish of the saleable items. After I have taken any that are of interest to me, of course."

Hartleigh folded his arms across his chest. "Why, may I ask, did you purchase this house and all the items in it if you didn't want them?"

"I do want them. Or, rather, I want some of them. There are items in this collection, purchased long ago, that are of great interest to me, if only I can find them in the mess."

"So you're a collector yourself, then."

She chuckled. "More of a treasure hunter."

"See, Daddy?" Lola grinned at her father. "I told you!"

"You told him I was a treasure hunter?" Sabine asked.

"No. I told him you were a pirate."

"Oh, God." Hartleigh put a hand to his temple. "I'm so sorry. Pirates are her new favorite thing. The trip across the ocean was very long, and we'd just read *Treasure Island* together…"

"Please, don't apologize."

He leaned so far forward he rocked the piano bench onto the front two legs. "No, I must. I'm sure there's some way I could have better explained that you don't call your new neighbor a pirate, even if she does collect treasure, and…"

"But I *am* a pirate," Sabine said. "Haven't you heard of the infamous La Capitaine? I am she."

Hartleigh gaped at her. "I, uh…" Before he could stammer a coherent word, the piano bench slipped, sending the peculiar new duke tumbling to the floor with a resounding crash.

3

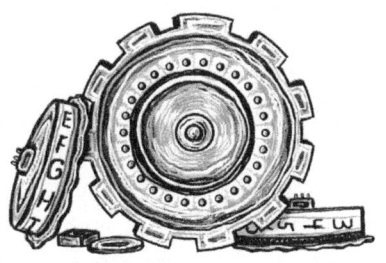

"Ow! Fuck!" Cliff rubbed the back of his head, which he'd somehow managed to smack on the damn piano bench. "I mean, 'drat.'" He wasn't sure what was worse: that he'd injured himself, that he'd displayed his supreme clumsiness in front of his new neighbor, or that he'd just taught Lola yet another bad word. This whole duke nonsense had him swearing like a… pirate. Shit.

"Daddy? Are you okay?"

"Fine." He winced.

Miss Diebin offered a hand to help him up, but he waved her away. He struggled to his feet, noticing all the other places that now smarted. His elbow. His shoulder. His ass. He righted the piano bench, but didn't sit. He wasn't going to go through that again.

"Sorry about that."

La Capitaine, or whoever she was, smiled at him. "Quite all right. It could happen to anyone. I didn't mean to startle you. I thought my identity was common knowledge."

Maybe it was, but Cliff hadn't had any opportunity to gather common knowledge since arriving in England.

He'd barely been out of his house. The duke business was overwhelming. First, he'd had to learn what the hell a dower house was and why it was shameful that he was living there. Then he'd had creditors pounding on his door and random people begging him to use his own hard earned money to clean up someone else's mess, all in the name of a family he knew nothing about.

"Right," he said. "So, you're a pirate."

He would never have guessed, just looking at her. She was the very picture of ordinariness. Medium height, with medium-brown hair and medium-brown eyes. A simple, modest dress in an unpretentious mauve color. Round, wire-rimmed eyeglasses. If he'd passed by her on the street, she would have been just another pretty face in a sea of pretty faces.

Her lips twitched, as they had done so many times during the course of their conversation. It distracted him, that twitch. It made him stare at her mouth and wonder if she always hovered on the brink of laughter, or if he was the cause of her amusement.

"A retired pirate, actually."

"I see."

"Keeping busy by digging for random treasure." Her lips didn't twitch this time, and she glanced away at the word "random." So. She was on the hunt for a specific treasure. Intriguing.

"And sword fighting in the yard," Lola added.

Miss Diebin smiled again. Tiny dimples appeared in her cheeks. "Staying fit and healthy is always important. I recommend regular exercise, plenty of sleep, good nutrition, and relaxing hobbies."

"I thought all pirates drank to excess and lost their teeth from scurvy," Cliff replied.

The twitch returned. Was she laughing at him, or did his words bring her genuine pleasure?

"This is the twentieth century, Your Grace. The freedom of

the skies gives us access to the entire world, including regular fresh fruits and vegetables. But, yes, pirates do drink a lot. What do Americans like to drink? Scotch? Brandy? I have a fully stocked liquor cabinet, and I'd be happy to offer you a drink."

"Nothing, thank you. We should let you get back to your treasure hunting. It was a pleasure to meet you, and if we can do anything to assist you in your efforts, please let me know."

Oh, no.

Why had he said that? He had enough troubles without adding a potentially dangerous and curiously interesting woman to the mix. Especially one who probably thought he was a buffoon.

She beamed and her dimples grew larger. "Wonderful! Thank you very much." She turned to Lola. "I'll think of a special project just for you and send a secret message when I need your help."

Lola's eyes widened, and she bounced gleefully. "Thank you, Miss La Capitaine!"

Cliff frowned, a mix of happiness and apprehension bubbling inside him. Finally, he'd met someone here who accepted and befriended Lola—and she was a self-professed thief and pirate.

"You're very welcome, Miss Kinsley." Miss Diebin's eyes met Cliff's again. Had he really thought those eyes ordinary? They were large and luminous. Riveting.

"And thank you for visiting, Your Grace. I'm happy there are no hard feelings over my purchase of your ancestral home."

"Right." As if he could even contemplate living in this hundred-room palace. He'd thought his twelve-room home in Chicago spacious. The dower house had three times that many. The day they'd arrived, Lola had asked if it was a hotel. "I'll, uh, show myself out."

"Oh, no, let me."

Miss Diebin led the way down the hall, past rooms

crammed with junk. She was right. He could make good money here. He tore his eyes from the piles, resisting the urge to dive in and start sorting. If he really wanted to get back to work, he needed to develop a concrete plan for killing off his ducal alter-ego.

He stopped in the middle of the hall. Lola and their hostess turned to frown at him.

"Before we go, Miss Diebin, I have one question for you." The words came out before he could stop them.

"Yes?"

Don't ask. Don't ask. Just mutter some apology and go home.

"Uh, do you, by any chance, have any experience with murder?"

4

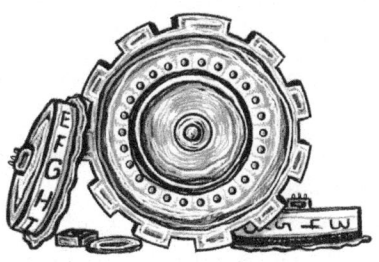

Cliff didn't notice when he smashed his shoulder on the doorframe, nor when he let out a brief yelp of pain. Only when a concerned female voice asked, "Are you quite all right, Your Grace?" did the experience begin to register.

Wonderful. He still cringed every time he thought of how he'd embarrassed himself in front of Sabine Diebin two days prior. Now it seemed he would be putting on a similar show in his own home.

"Uh..." Cliff stared at the quartet of ladies taking tea in his parlor, all blinking up at him with worried frowns. His shoulder hurt, now, dammit. He walked into door frames, tables, and other large obstructions on a regular basis, and usually he simply kept going without a second thought.

"Yes, yes, fine," he babbled. "I'm, uh, sorry to interrupt. I believe I have the wrong room."

The ladies laughed.

"Don't be silly, Hartleigh." Her Grace, the Duchess of Hartleigh—widow of the previous duke—addressed him with a casual wave of her hand, as if she'd known him all her life and not less than a week. "You're exactly where you belong. Sit down and let me introduce you to these lovely ladies."

"I prefer to stand, thank you. I have business to attend to and can't stay more than a moment."

The duchess glared at him. Younger than Cliff by several years at least, she nonetheless carried herself with the worldly superiority of an established matriarch. She had ideas for the dukedom, and expected Cliff to embrace them. Today, apparently, she meant to marry him off.

He bowed over each woman's hand as the duchess made introductions, but paid no attention to their names, or the details of their families that she imparted. A few polite phrases, some forced smiles, and he'd leave.

In the midst of some utter fabrication about how enthusiastically he had undertaken his family duties, he glanced up at the ceiling. Right above the tea-sipping ladies, a pair of two-inch clockwork spiders dangled precariously from the chandelier. The "web" they perched on had been constructed from assorted bits of string and looked to be rapidly unraveling.

"Oh, no," he muttered.

"What was that, Duke?" the duchess asked.

"Uh…" What could he do? If he lunged for the spiders, he'd look unhinged and startle his guests. If he let them fall…

He hesitated too long, and the first spider plopped down into one woman's hairdo. She shrieked and clawed, trying to dislodge the creature. The second spider fell a moment later, landing in a second woman's lap. Unlike her screaming companion, she rose, calmly shook out her skirts, and lifted her foot to smash the offending arachnid.

"No!"

Cliff dove for the spider, knocking the poor woman right off her feet. She came crashing down atop him, smothering him with her skirts and driving the air from his lungs, but the delicate mechanical creature was safe. Cliff wriggled free and climbed to his feet.

"Sorry about that." He plucked the second spider from the other woman's hair. "These are my daughter's pets and they're very special to her. They have their own names and everything. I'll just go return them. Excuse me."

He turned and hurried from the room.

The duchess found him half an hour later, sitting in his study and staring dejectedly at the mountains of correspondence, much of which was dated before the Mad Duke's death. If only he'd handled his request to Sabine Diebin better. Her hulking butler had all but thrown Cliff out of the house, even as he'd tried to explain what he meant. He'd ruined Lola's only friendship.

"That was appalling!" Her Grace shouted, slamming the door behind her in a refreshingly un-duchess-like fashion.

Cliff only shrugged. "Accidents happen."

"Those were your three best prospects! Astoundingly wealthy women with families eager to move up in the world."

"Attaching oneself to a dukedom burdened with debt is hardly moving up in the world. You can take my word for it."

She threw up her hands. "Americans! You have no idea how things work here, do you? Now you've embarrassed yourself, insulted a trio of fine, marriageable women, and probably heaped yet another scandal onto our already massive troubles! And then you brought that child into it!"

Cliff crumpled whatever paper sat on top of the pile. "Her name is Lola. She's seven years old and she likes spiders, pirates, and playing dress-up."

"That may be, but she can't remain here. I've made a list of excellent schools…"

"Toss it in the fire. It'll save time."

Something soft bounced off the back of his head. He turned to find a crumpled piece of paper sitting on the floor behind him. He bent to retrieve it.

"Your list?" It amused him that he'd made her so angry she'd balled it up and thrown it at him.

"Read it."

"No." He walked over to the fire and tossed it in, watching

the flames flare up and consume it. "Lola stays with me." No way in hell was he sending her anywhere. She wasn't old enough yet to handle the fuel for her heart on her own. And he'd be damned if he'd trust some stranger to do it.

"You can't flaunt your bastard in front of all society!"

Cliff stalked toward the duchess. "Do not call her that."

She stood her ground. "It's the truth. Who even is her mother? Some shop girl or farmer's daughter, no doubt."

"Actually, these days she's the owner of a notorious brothel in New York City. Doing rather well for herself, last I heard."

The duchess pressed both hands to her face. "Dear God, you're a disgrace to the dukedom."

"Good. Pass it on to the next person. I'll go back to Chicago."

"There is no next person. You have to marry and you have to produce an heir. You refuse to use your money to buy back the house and pay off the debts, so the wife you choose must be an heiress. It's the only way to save us all."

Her hands dropped to her sides, and in the brief moment before she schooled her features, Cliff caught a glimpse of true fear and sorrow in her eyes.

"Look, I'm sorry your late husband left you with such a mess, but I had nothing to do with it, and you can't simply force me to straighten it all out. The money from my business is for Lola, to provide for her future. No one touches it. I have no intention of marrying anyone, no matter how rich she is. You'll simply have to find another way. Sell off more of the property."

"There's nothing left. All the lands, all the other properties were sold off months or even years ago. The house was sold to that pirate woman just before your whereabouts were discovered. This is all that remains." She waved her hand around the study. "This house and the land surrounding the two houses. You own nothing else."

"Actually, I own several warehouses, a recycling plant, and a pretty house with a view of Lake Michigan." *That I can never return to because creditors and hopeful future duchesses would hound me for the remainder of my life.*

"Sell them."

"Not yet." If he sold his business and his house, it would extinguish the last tiny spark of hope that maybe he could find a way home. Even as he planned to fake his own death and forge a new identity, that spark still lingered. *Home.*

"If you do nothing, we will be forced to sell all we have left. Your entire household will become unemployed. I will have nowhere to go, nor will Luella."

"Who?"

She heaved a sigh. "My companion."

Right. Duchesses employed companions to hang around and be their friends, or something of that sort. Strange people, these British nobles.

"Ah. Well, she could get a new job. *You* could get a job. Teach finishing school. You'd be good at that."

Her eyes filled with tears. "I'm a disgrace to my family," she whispered, and fled the room.

"Dammit." Cliff sank back into his chair. He hadn't meant to make her cry. She'd probably been reared from birth to be nothing but a duchess, and then her family had married her off to some bizarre old duke. No wonder she was scared and upset. He'd have to apologize. He was willing to work with her on some sort of solution. Hartleigh didn't have to die right this minute.

There would be no compromising about Lola, however. She was his family. She was his life. They stayed together, no matter what.

He poked through the papers for a few more minutes before coming to a decision. Leaving his coat hanging on the back of his chair, he walked outside, breathing in the brisk January air. The wind stung his cheeks and the cold cut straight through his shirtsleeves. Nothing like the winds of Chicago, though. He missed snow. He missed the ice that built up on the lake. He jogged across his ducal gardens and rapped on the door of the Mad Duke's former home.

"Captain's angry at you," the butler said, waving Cliff inside, regardless. "She's fought battles, but she's no assassin."

"I didn't mean to imply that she was. I'll explain everything, if she'll see me."

"There's only one way to find out. Follow me."

Cliff followed the burly butler deep into the house, where he was shown into a room filled floor to ceiling with mechanical contraptions. He broke into a grin. This was even better than anticipated. He could make this work.

"Miss Diebin," he said, tilting his head to peer at her through the empty belly of what might have been a life-sized, metal grizzly bear. "Clifford J. Kinsley. Scrap metal dealer. I have a business proposition for you."

5

Sabine stepped around the large metal beast and met the duke's smile with her stern captain's look. "A business proposition," she echoed. "Does this mean you would like to haul away things like this?" She banged a fist on the bear, which rang with a hollow *thunk*.

"I could get good money for that. Lots of saleable metal, excellent condition."

He was serious. Pleasure bubbled through her, despite her lingering annoyance from their disagreeable parting the other day. Clifford Kinsley had the skills she needed to sort through this disaster. Without him, her search could drag on indefinitely.

"You're welcome to it," she replied, "*if* you think you can restrain yourself from insulting me again?"

The duke cringed. "I'm sorry about that. I completely bungled things. What I intended to ask was if you knew of useful ways to murder a man." He pushed up his glasses and rubbed his nose. "No, that doesn't sound right, either. Let me explain."

"Please do," she answered dryly.

Hartleigh looked around the room, as if hoping for a place to sit, then shrugged and turned back to Sabine. "This dukedom I've inherited… I don't want it. I never wanted it. I'm being bombarded with silly rules and debt collectors and people who think I ought to hide my own daughter away and pretend she doesn't exist. To be blunt, the duke needs to die. I was hoping that in exchange for my services here…" He waved a hand at the messy room. "You might be willing to assist in faking my demise."

"Ah." *That* she could do. Sneaking and deception were weapons in any good pirate's arsenal. "I may be able to devise some plan."

"Excellent." He grinned at her again, ice blue eyes sparkling. It was unsettlingly endearing, that grin. "Here's my proposal: I clean this house for you. I will sell off any scrap of value, dispose of anything worthless, and so forth. I'll make sure everything is properly catalogued, so there's no danger of accidentally discarding whatever treasure you seek. When the sorting is done, or you've found your treasure, you will then arrange for myself and Lola to disappear and, if necessary, help us arrange anonymous transportation to California. I want this done in such a way that no one will come looking for us. Do we have a deal?" He extended a hand.

Fake a duke's death in exchange for her treasure? Sabine could accept that. She shook his hand. "Deal. You can even keep the money from the sale of the scrap."

"Wonderful. I can begin right away. What are you looking for, if I might ask? A treasure map? It would be helpful to know so I don't miss anything potentially important."

"Not a map. A cipher."

One black eyebrow arched. "Oh?"

"I have a very valuable text written in code. The key to deciphering it is somewhere in this house. I intend to find the key, decode the message, and claim the treasure."

"A modern-day pirate. Scientific and logical. I approve."

She inclined her head. "Thank you. How long do you anticipate the cleanup to take?"

Hartleigh scanned their surroundings. "Dozens of rooms, each like this? One month."

Sabine burst out laughing.

"That wasn't a joke," he said. "One month and I'll be done."

She only laughed again.

Sabine heaved a sigh, setting more papers atop the stack. Two weeks later, and now Hartleigh was the one laughing. Or, he would be, if he ever paused long enough to enjoy the fruits of his labor.

The duke wielded organization and efficiency the way Sabine wielded a blade. Fifty rooms had already been emptied, the contents sorted into papers, metals, other salvageable materials, and trash. The ballroom now housed thousands of potentially valuable items awaiting appraisal by experts. She'd eaten in her dining room last night for the first time ever, and now had half-a-dozen bedchambers available for guests. Not that she expected anyone to come by aside from the duke and his daughter.

Hartleigh worked twelve-hour days, much of the time with Lola at his side, teaching by example. He mixed fun tasks with challenging ones, pushing her to learn while still leaving her the freedom to play and explore.

Sabine cringed, thinking of her own father. He'd taught her only two things: how to fend for herself and not to trust anyone. Lola was lucky, but also vulnerable. Someday she'd find herself all alone, forced to make her own way. Would she have the skills to survive, as Sabine had? Or would she fall victim to the machinations of men who saw her as no more than a commodity?

Sabine glowered at the papers she had examined today.

Nothing. Another code deciphered, another accounting of random antiquities purchases. Sometimes it seemed half the duke's papers were written in code. At least most of what she'd found were simple alphabet shifts. Easy to decode. After weeks of this, she was beginning to doubt the veracity of the document that had brought her here. What if it was no more than a shopping list?

Nein, she scolded herself. Men had killed for that letter. Redbeard himself had employed a code-breaker in an attempt to read it. Its value was no fiction. It would lead her to her treasure.

If only she could find the key in this epic disaster of a library.

A knock on the door prevented her from moving on to the next unhelpful bit of correspondence.

"Tea, Captain?" Hawkes inquired, entering the room holding a tray with a steaming pot, two cups, and an array of snacks.

"Yes, please. Set it down there." Sabine waved at the single empty table in the room. She still wanted to laugh at Hawkes' determination to do everything a proper English butler would, but she couldn't deny that she found the afternoon refreshments beneficial. Sorting through old maps and papers was shockingly exhausting.

"Here you are, my lady. Shall I ask the duke to join you?"

"Please. I'd like to hear his latest progress report."

The butler bowed and departed, leaving the door open. Sabine poured herself a cup of tea and returned to her work. She *would* find her treasure, no matter how long it took.

She was in the middle of scanning yet another Caesar cipher when the duke's now-familiar American accent sounded from the doorway.

"You wanted me?"

Sabine looked up. He leaned against the doorjamb, his sleeves pushed up to his elbows, wearing neither tie nor waistcoat. The combination of his words and the untidy state of his smartly-tailored clothing conjured up visions of other, more intimate ways a handsome man might become so rumpled. She wouldn't mind doing a bit of rumpling, especially if it meant getting a taste of those generous lips.

Don't be ridiculous, Sabine. He's not your type.

And those were not at all the sort of thoughts anyone ought to have about a neighbor with whom she had a business arrangement. It had been too long since her last tryst, apparently.

"Hawkes made tea," she replied, gesturing at the refreshments. "Help me eat these biscuits and tell me how today's efforts are progressing."

"Slowly." Hartleigh walked to the table and poured himself a cup of tea. He took a seat across from Sabine. "The master bedchamber looks to have been the duke's dumping ground for old, obsolete, or broken projects. Mechanical contraptions piled to the ceiling, tangled up with one another. I'm trying to get them apart, in case any might be worth more intact, but I've already had a couple things almost fall on my head. I might be giving up soon and just demolishing everything."

"Feel free. I can't imagine you'll find many books or papers there, but if you do, you know where to find me."

Hartleigh nodded. "I'll put them in the small study. This room doesn't need anything else brought into it." He plucked a biscuit from the tray and chewed silently for a moment. "So, have you come up with a plan to murder me yet?"

Sabine glared at him. "Stop using that word. I'm no murderer. Life is a fragile and precious thing. I would never take it so casually and coldly."

"Fine. Have you arranged for Hartleigh to meet some untimely end in an entirely accidental fashion that you have nothing to do with?"

"Why do you speak of yourself in the third person?"

He snapped a biscuit in half. "I don't. Hartleigh is the duke." He dropped one half onto the plate. "I'm Cliff Kinsley."

He dropped the second half. "Two different people." He scooped up both halves and popped them into his mouth.

"Two halves of the same cookie. You may split them apart, but they came from one whole and they're meeting the same end."

Cliff/Hartleigh gulped down half a cup of tea and rose. "Thanks for the food. I'll be getting back to work."

"You can't expect to kill Hartleigh and walk away from his world without another thought. All this," she waved a hand, "is part of who you are now. The past stays with us, whether we like it or not. You won't get away from it."

His blue eyes hardened. "Watch me."

She let him go, shaking her head. He was asking for trouble. Faking his own death was a path fraught with risks, and could easily leave him in a worse situation than he found himself in now. But he seemed determined, and if that was the cost for his assistance in finding her treasure, so be it. She'd uphold her end of the bargain. But she'd take no responsibility when things went wrong.

Sabine was dusting the last crumbs of biscuit away when Hawkes again knocked on the door.

"Her Grace, the Duchess of Hartleigh," he announced.

A buxom blond woman in a gauzy blue gown glided into the room, her brows knit together in a look of suspicion. "Where is Hartleigh?" she demanded.

A duchess? Is Hartleigh married?

Sabine studied the intruder for a moment, trying not to let her surprise show. The woman was in her mid-to-late twenties, at best guess. She wore no obvious cosmetics and minimal jewelry, but her gown looked to have been crafted by a skilled hand and was decorated with elaborate embroidery and fine lace.

"Well?" The duchess tapped her foot irritably. "He's here, isn't he? I am informed that he's here all day, every day, and I've had quite enough of it. He has duties to attend to, and it's unseemly for him to waste his time fraternizing with a lady pirate, even if she is a national heroine. Where is he? Is he off doing unspeakable things with her right at this minute? Well? Speak up, girl. You must know something. Who are you, the pirate's housekeeper, or a new governess for Hartleigh's bastard child? That dress is too fine for a chambermaid."

Sabine studied her plain green dress. A housekeeper? No housekeeper could afford a dress this well made. Simple and functional didn't make it any less fine than the duchess' fancy attire. A duchess who was an English aristocrat, through-and-through. Definitely not the wife of an American businessman.

"You must be the widow of the Mad Duke," Sabine surmised. She'd known the woman existed, but had imagined her to be far older and more sedate. Was she only behaving so imperiously because she thought Sabine to be a servant? Or was this simply how duchesses were?

"A fine way to speak of the dead!" the woman scolded. "I'll be speaking with your mistress about you. Where is she? It's time I met the woman who stole our rightful property."

"*I* am Miss Sabine Diebin, better known as the privateer La Capitaine."

"You?" The duchess visibly flinched. "You look like a schoolteacher, not a pirate. And you don't sound French."

"I'm not. I'm German. What do you want with Hartleigh?"

"What do I want? I want him to stop wasting time. I want him to do his duty. I want this house back."

Sabine shrugged. "I'll sell it for a reasonable price once I'm done with it."

"Well, that's something. Where is he?"

"Upstairs. Working. Earning money so he can afford to buy this house." In truth, Sabine had no idea what Hartleigh intended to do with the money he earned from this venture. Probably use it to help him move to San Francisco if his fake death plan succeeded. But the duchess didn't need to know that.

"Working?" The duchess sighed. "He's so terribly *American*. I really don't know what to do with him."

Sabine's mouth twitched as she fought a smile. "I'll take you to see him. He's digging through machines. He deals in scrap metal, you know."

The duchess made a little huffing noise, but followed Sabine without protest. "You've improved the place," she said sometime later. "Some of the rooms look usable. I never lived here, you know. He filled it with his junk and did his experiments, and I left him to it. He probably *was* mad, I suppose."

"Mm-hmm. Harleigh should be just—" She rounded the corner and nearly collided with him.

"Miss Diebin!" He staggered backwards, juggling a large, rectangular wooden box studded with gears, screws, and other mechanical bits. When he finally recovered, he clutched the box to his chest, gasping in relief. "You startled me."

"There you are, Hartleigh," the duchess said. "Enough with whatever this nonsense is. It's time you came home. I'm taking you to a ball in London in three days, and I expect you to be prepared. We will find you a wife this time, even if I have to drag you around the dance floor myself."

Hartleigh didn't even look at her. His eyes were locked on Sabine, shining and eager. "I found it! He'd hidden it in a corner, behind heaps of broken things."

Sabine frowned at the box. "Found what? What is it?"

He turned the box and flipped it open. The top half of the machine was a jumble of gears, knobs, and switches. Rows of mechanical keys bearing the letters of the alphabet lined the bottom. Half-a-dozen steel wheels, inscribed with more letters, sat stacked in one corner. A bit of faded paper dangled from a small slot in the side.

"It's a cryptographic apparatus," the duke replied, in a voice choked with awe. "He wasn't insane. He was a genius."

Sabine reached out a hand, letting one finger brush over

the smooth, metal keys. A shiver of joyful terror raced through her. Was this it? Her treasure, at last?

"This will decode my document?" She almost whispered it, afraid to shatter the dream.

"Type in the letters and the solution will print out. It appears to need new ink and new paper. And I believe the wheels need to be placed in these slots, in the correct order and rotated to the correct positions." Hartleigh pointed at four semi-circular slots above the keyboard.

Sabine's excitement faded. "But how do we know which wheels to use, and how to place them? There must be hundreds of thousands of possibilities!"

Hartleigh closed the box and turned it on its side. A small, brass plate surrounded a hole that looked to require a clockwork key. Scratched into the metal were the words, *safebox – London*. "I assume the old duke had a bank?"

Sabine's mouth curved into a broad smile. She turned to the duchess. "You say Hartleigh is going to London for a ball?"

"Yes. Whether he wants to or not."

"Excellent. I'm always being invited to these things. I think this time I'll go."

6

"I can't do this."

The whole room was staring at him. The whole room had been staring at him since he'd walked through the damn door twenty minutes ago. Cliff toyed with his cufflinks. They were diamonds. Enormous, ostentatious diamonds. What kind of snob wore diamond cufflinks? The duchess claimed they were family heirlooms. Cliff wanted to sell them and swap for something less ridiculous.

Her Grace took hold of his elbow. "Everything is perfect. All you need do is smile. A thirty-year-old, unmarried duke? People are salivating."

"So I'm a piece of meat. How reassuring."

"The choicest of cuts, I assure you. Your American past has everyone talking, and you look especially handsome tonight, now that you're properly attired. The eyeglasses, though…"

"I can't see without my glasses. I have terrible astigmatism in both eyes. If you think I walk into things often now, you should see what happens if I take off my eyeglasses."

"Yes, yes. I suppose it can't be helped. We'll see about getting you something less obtrusive. One of those rimless pairs, perhaps."

Cliff gritted his teeth. "I like the red."

"Why must you be so difficult?"

"I'm here, aren't I? I think you should be happy."

"I am relieved, certainly. You've been pleasantly agreeable to *most* suggestions. Now, who shall we choose for your first dancing partner?"

Cliff's gaze darted back and forth, taking in the brightly lit ballroom and the couples gliding and twirling in time to the music. His cufflinks fit right in. Everything sparkled, from the highly polished floor, to the glittering chandeliers, to the gems and beads sewn into the ladies' dresses.

I'm just a fancy bauble on display. Help me.

"I can't dance," he blurted.

"Nonsense."

"No, truly. I can't dance. I don't know the steps, I have terrible balance, and no rhythm."

"Not even a waltz?"

"I can almost polka. I grew up next door to a family from Germany. They taught the whole neighborhood to polka."

"Close enough. We'll pair you with the Danbury girl. She won't know the difference."

"Fine."

Put on a show. Make them believe you're okay with this.

Easier said than done. Cliff followed the duchess through the crowd and forced a smile throughout the introductions. Miss Danbury giggled at his accent and intentionally dropped her handkerchief.

"I'm living in a farce," he muttered as he bent to retrieve the square of cloth.

Any moment now, some newspaper man would jump out and cry, "Surprise! You're our newest featured story! Tell us, how does it feel to be dragged from your home and thrust into a world of gilded opulence?"

"Do you enjoy dancing, Your Grace?" the girl tittered.

"I—"

He lost his train of thought when he caught sight of Sabine Diebin striding into the room as if she owned it. An unadorned black corset covered her high-necked, long-sleeved white top. A puffed skirt of black velvet fell to the floor in the back, but was cinched up in the front to reveal knee-high, military-style black boots. Simple, elegant, powerful. The other ladies, in their gauzy, bejeweled pastels, with their pinched-in waists and thrust-out chests, looked gaudy by comparison. Sabine was a perfect slice of obsidian atop a pile of dusty, unpolished quartz. She also, Cliff noted with pleasure, still wore her wire-rimmed spectacles.

A hush fell over the room. The music faded, the dancers freezing in place to stare.

"It's *her*," Miss Danbury gasped. "The savior of the royal family! She's real and she's *here*." She fanned herself vigorously. "And she's so piratical! You can see her legs! Oh, heavens, I think I'm going to swoon."

"There's a sofa right over there." Cliff pointed. "Go sit. Please excuse me. I'd like to go greet my friend."

"She's your *friend*?" Miss Danbury collapsed in a theatrical heap.

"Bravo, young lady. You'd make an excellent Juliet." He struck out across the room, ignoring the glare from the duchess. Was he supposed to have caught the girl? Probably he'd just insulted another heiress. Tragic.

"Your Grace," Sabine greeted him, her mouth hitching in that now-familiar half-smirk. "Fancy seeing you here."

"Indeed." He nodded his head slightly, because apparently dukes didn't bow to anyone except the king. Not that Cliff had any intention of ever bowing to an English king. Not when his country's very existence began with rebellion against such a monarch.

She took hold of his arm, as if they really were old friends eager to catch up. "I cased the bank," she whispered. "It's vulnerable. I think we can break in tonight. Did you learn which box is his?"

Cliff turned to stare at her. "You're seriously planning to rob a bank?"

"Thief is in my name," she pointed out. "And that treasure is invaluable to me. I could use your assistance as a lookout. Are you in?"

"I'm the man's only heir. I've already gathered the necessary paperwork. I can stroll in tomorrow and take whatever I want."

"Ah." Her smile waned. "I suppose your way carries less risk. Though part of me had hoped you would be unsuccessful."

"And planned for it, clearly."

"Your obvious distaste for your new position in life made me question your willingness and ability to gain anything via your title."

"A fair point." An elbow jostled him and he stumbled. Music began to swell. "Uh, we appear to have wandered onto the dance floor."

"Lovely." Sabine turned toward him. "Shall we?"

"I can't dance."

"Neither can I. We'll fake it." She nodded her head at the smartly dressed man who had bumped them and his tall, graceful partner. "Do what they do."

"Right."

Cliff took hold of her hand and struck a pose that looked vaguely like that of the other couples. Three steps in, he stepped on Sabine's foot, then turned the wrong way and narrowly missed a collision with another couple. They half-ran back into position and tried again, only to slip and crash into one another.

Sabine's fingers clenched on his coat. She let out a very unpiratical giggle. "You really are terrible."

"I know." He gripped her tightly and spun them around in a circle entirely at random. "I'm not even certain which of us is leading."

"I don't know, but I'm having fun."

"Are pirates allowed to have fun?"

"We do whatever we want." She yanked him in the opposite direction, neatly slicing between the other dancers. "What about dukes?"

"They're boring, as far as I can tell."

"Then I'm glad I will save you from being one. Tomorrow we'll get that key and hopefully the instructions for the machine. Then we'll set out to find my treasure and you and Lola can vanish. Tonight, we dance."

They spun, bumped, tripped, and whirled until the music stopped, leaving them in the center of the dance floor, breathless and laughing. Cliff made an inelegant bow, no longer caring that all eyes were on him. "It was a pleasure, my lady."

Sabine curtsied, gracefully. "Yes it was, Your Grace. I will see you tomorrow, first thing in the morning." She turned and departed, not looking back.

Cliff abandoned the dance floor, looking for a drink. After that performance, no one would be wanting to dance with him, thank God.

"You're a bold one, Hartleigh."

Cliff turned toward the voice. The dapper man he'd bumped into on the dance floor—several times—held out a glass of amber liquid. Cliff accepted the drink. He wasn't bold. Sabine was the bold one. He preferred to be off alone with his work, not having to deal with people.

"Barton. Marquess of." The man raised his own glass and took a drink. Blond and handsome, with pristine clothing, he was the very picture of a bored, indolent aristocrat. "I'm impressed. Not only did the reclusive La Capitaine appear at this ball, but it appears she came here only to speak with you. And you didn't hesitate to cause a scandal with her in the middle of the dance floor."

Cliff took a swallow of the brandy. No, he hadn't hesitated. Sabine had no expectations of him other than he do his part to assist her treasure hunt. To her he was simply Clifford J. Kinsley, scrap dealer, and that made her the closest thing he had to a friend.

"You make it sound sordid," he said blandly.

"It was. The woman showed off a good inch of bare skin above her boots. Is she your mistress? She's no beauty, but she's a fine choice if you're trying to continue the legacy of the Mad Duke and scare off potential brides."

"She's my neighbor. Just a friend," Cliff replied, uncertain whether to acknowledge the insult. Sabine *wasn't* a beauty. She was an ordinary sort of woman. Or should have been. Yet something about her always caught his eye, and the eyes of others if they were willing to acknowledge it.

"Ah, yes. Friend." Barton chuckled knowingly.

There was no point explaining. Cliff wasn't going to so much as hint about their business arrangement. And he didn't mix business with pleasure. He didn't mix anything with pleasure, in fact. He bought it when he needed it, and that was the end of it.

"What would you say to a game of billiards?" Barton asked.

"I play billiards about as well as I dance."

"Excellent! I'll win a fortune off you, then."

"I'm afraid my fortune consists solely of portraits of my dead ancestors, so I will have to respectfully decline. I think I'll mingle and chat with some of those potential brides."

Barton frowned. "Isn't that what you're trying to avoid with your pirate friend?"

Cliff only smiled. Barton's comments had sparked an idea for a new plan. Perfectly scandalous one minute and perfectly normal the next. Let people think madness ran in the family. When the Mad Duke Junior went missing, no one would come looking.

7

Sabine plucked the mechanical spider from her teacup and poured herself a fresh cup. She handed the spider to Hartleigh, who passed it on to Lola. Sabine didn't have much experience with elegant hotel dining rooms, but she doubted clockwork arachnids made many appearances. She glanced around at the primly-dressed patrons at the other tables, but no one seemed to have noticed. Most of the people here had their eyes glued to their morning papers.

"Lo, can you please put Ralph away?" the duke sighed. "That's the third time he's gotten loose in a single breakfast."

"Daddy, that's Mary-George! Ralph has the little brass eyeballs. And I can't make her stop. She got wound up all the way and she flips herself over." She set the spider on its back and it thrashed its little legs until it flipped right-side-up, then began to march down the table. "See?"

"How many spiders do you have?" Sabine asked.

"Six. Ralph, Mary-George, Mary-Sue, Billy, Wolfgang, and Peg. Peg used to be called Sally, but she broke a leg and now limps like a pirate with a peg-leg."

"Interesting." Sabine would have to ask Hartleigh where he'd purchased the spiders. Perhaps she could commission a hive of wasps or a nest of ants. Swarms of mechanical insects could be an interesting and unexpected defense, and easily stored in a relatively small space. "Ooh, maybe little termites with tiny drills for mouths," she said aloud. "I could scatter them on an enemy ship, or maybe dump acid-spitting ones into an engine."

"Enemy ship?" Hartleigh narrowed his eyes at her. "I thought you were retired."

"It always pays to be prepared. Speaking of which, are we prepared to storm the bank?"

Lola hopped up from her seat, stuffing the still-wriggling spider into the pocket of her pinafore. "Treasure hunt!"

"I object!"

Sabine turned to the newcomer. "Good morning, Your Grace. How lovely that we're all staying at the same hotel."

"It's not lovely," the duchess lamented. "It's awful. Have you seen the papers?" She sank into the chair beside Sabine.

"I haven't, but Hawkes informed me that we are featured prominently."

The duchess splayed the paper on the table. "'The Duke of H,' as if we all don't know who that is, is termed, in a single article, 'erratic,' 'uncivilized,' 'clumsy,' and 'oddly charming—for an American.'"

"They called me charming?" Hartleigh leaned back in his chair in a way that made Sabine fear he might tip it over.

"Lady Lumfeld took a liking to you. But it can hardly make up for your 'indecent behavior on the dance floor with a woman of questionable reputation,' or the way you 'left an ailing young lady fainted on the floor, in a shameful display of unmannerliness.' Since you followed it up with perfectly polite and cordial discourse, everyone thinks you're out of your head. Or that you deliberately acted out in an attempt to win the favor of a mysterious pirate woman, which also suggests possible madness."

Hartleigh rocked his chair precariously, not seeming to notice he was doing it. "They called your late husband mad. Why should it bother you?"

"He was a peaceful, quiet eccentric."

"I'm usually a peaceful, quiet person. Aren't I, Lola?"

"'Cept when you knock things over."

He stopped fidgeting and straightened his chair. "Right." He rose. "Please excuse us, we have an appointment at the bank."

The duchess stared up at him, her pale gray eyes wide and pleading. "Please no more scandals."

"We're only visiting a bank," Hartleigh replied. "What could go wrong?"

"Never say that," Sabine scolded, the moment they were out the door.

"Say what?"

"'What could go wrong?' Something can always go wrong, and if you say that, it's sure to happen."

"That's superstitious nonsense."

"Sky pirates are the heirs to the pirates of the seas, and sailors are known for their superstitions. I believe in luck, Duke, and I don't need you bringing misfortune into my life."

"They're only words."

"They're tempting fate."

"Fine, fine. I apologize. Many things could go wrong and I hope none of them do."

"Thank you."

The banker who met them was a jolly man, with round, rosy cheeks and a shock of bright orange hair. He also, apparently, did not read the papers.

"So you're the new duke." He pumped Hartleigh's proffered hand. "Excellent. Excellent. So pleased to meet you. Brought the whole family along, did you? Wonderful. I'm sure you'll find everything in perfect order, and I hope you'll consider putting some of that splendid American money into an account with us. We love to work internationally, you know. We'd be happy to set up some investments, and perhaps handle the dowry for the lovely young lady here."

"What's a dowry?" Lola asked.

"Money set aside to see to your needs when you grow up and marry," the banker replied.

"Oh, I'm not going to get married. Daddy says only naive fools get married. Naive means like you don't know a lot."

"Er... uh... I see. Um, if you would all follow me, please."

Sabine bit her lower lip. *Scandal one, Duke zero.*

The banker ushered them into a small room with a single empty table and two chairs. He motioned for them to sit and departed, returning a few moments later with what looked like a wooden treasure chest from a storybook.

"Here you are. One box, straight from our vault. That's all the late duke kept here, I'm afraid. When you've finished, please let me know and we can return it to the vault, or you may arrange to take it with you." He left once more, closing the door behind him.

Lola bounced in delight and rushed over to look. "It looks just like real treasure!"

Hartleigh unfastened the latch and lifted the lid. "The real strongbox is inside." He lifted out a metal box the size of a loaf of bread and placed it in the center of the table. The wooden chest he set on the floor for Lola to play with. "Here you go, babe. Have fun."

Sabine eyed the plain steel box. A combination lock of three small, numbered wheels blocked her from the contents.

"Well this is simple, at least," Hartleigh said, flicking the first wheel with one finger. "We can flip through the numbers until it opens." He set all the wheels to zero and pushed on the latch.

The box erupted in a blast of heat and smoke.

8

S<small>MOKE</small>. F<small>IRE</small>. P<small>AIN</small>. The searing agony spread across her chest, clawing its way beneath her skin, slicing through her flesh, tearing her apart as she lay helpless on the cold, wet planks. This was death. This was how it felt to have your life stripped from you. An instant that stretched into years. A sudden end that lingered for eternity.

"Daddy!"

The terrified voice of a child jerked Sabine from the horrors of her own memories. No heat, no fire, but thick smoke filled the room, choking her, paralyzing her with fear. The blast had knocked her from her chair, and she lay on the floor, her eyes watering, her limbs refusing to respond.

The door opened.

"Good God, what happened?" The hazy figure of the banker waved his arms, trying to clear the smoke.

"Daddy!" Lola shrieked again.

Scheiße! Hartleigh had been directly in front of the box. If he died, what would become of his spunky little girl?

"Doctor," Sabine gasped. "Fetch a doctor. Hurry! Lola, crawl out the door. I'll help your father."

Sabine crawled toward the shadowy form of the fallen duke, her arms and legs obeying at last. Her fingers brushed against his arm, and he twitched. A deep, hacking cough echoed from his chest. Not dead. Thank God.

"Hartleigh." She shook him. "Hartleigh. Cliff. Can you hear me? Can you move?"

He coughed again, then groaned.

She tugged on his jacket and he rolled toward her. "Come on. You can do it."

Footsteps pounded toward them. More dim figures blocked the doorway, and a shower of icy water rained down on them. Cliff jerked and sat up.

"Jesus Christ! What the hell was that?"

Sabine shoved him toward the doorway, and they both crawled into the hall, sucking in lungfuls of fresh air. A sobbing Lola flung her arms around her father.

Cliff stroked her hair and hugged her close. "I'm all right, baby. Everything's all right."

He didn't look all right. A goose-egg was forming on his temple, his spectacles were askew, and a trickle of blood ran down his right cheek. Small burn marks peppered his once-fine suit coat. He was lucky to be alive.

"We've doused the fire!" a man declared triumphantly. The steel bucket he had used to dump water all over Sabine and the duke dangled from his hand.

Sabine peered into the slowly-clearing room. She didn't think there'd ever been a fire. Whatever little sparks had been released during the explosion had died quickly, else they'd all be more badly burned. What she could see of the room appeared undamaged.

Bank workers darted here and there, opening doors and windows, fanning away what they could of the smoke. The moment it was clear enough to see, Sabine climbed to her feet and went to inspect the carnage.

A few tiny singe marks dotted the table surrounding the

remains of the steel safebox. The top had been blown into several chunks, which lay scattered across the room. Hartleigh's injuries must have come from the flying shrapnel. Sabine peered into the box. It was empty, save for a few charred bits of paper.

My treasure! She flattened both hands on the table, fighting the panic, willing herself to breathe. *Stop. Think. There should have been a key.*

A quick scan of the room came up empty. The explosion hadn't been powerful enough to vaporize a key. The trap had been designed to deter, not to kill.

She picked up the broken box, held it up to her ear, and shook it. The faint rattle of metal on metal came from somewhere inside. A false bottom. Of course. She spun the combination wheels and pressed the latch on the now-disarmed box.

As the duke consoled Lola and attempted to explain the situation to the bank staff, Sabine continued on, trying number after number. Several hundred later, the latch clicked, and the bottom of the box popped open. A small puff of smoke rose from the secret compartment. Sabine fanned it away to reveal a mangled key and more charred paper.

"No! Damn you, Hartleigh, why did you have to try to open it without even stopping to think?"

"Excuse me?" The duke stormed into the room, Lola clutching his sleeve. The lump on his temple had grown larger and uglier. He was steady on his feet, though, and his ice-blue eyes were clear. "Just how was I supposed to know it was booby trapped?" He touched the bruise on his forehead and winced. "And I believe *I* was the injured party here."

Their rosy-cheeked banker rushed into the room, along with a slender man carrying a medical kit. "Did you say you are injured, Your Grace? I've brought a doctor."

Hartleigh waved the men away. "I'm fine. Could we have a moment alone?"

"Oh, yes, of course." The banker bowed. "Please excuse us, Your Grace." He stepped out, shutting the door behind him.

Hartleigh frowned at the closed door. "It's really strange to have people bowing and leaping to fulfill my every request."

"Oh, you'll get used to it," Sabine scoffed. "Give it another few weeks and instead of asking for privacy you'll be puffing up your chest and saying, 'Leave us,' in your deepest, most lordly voice."

"I don't have a lordly voice. And I intend to be gone in another few weeks. That's *your* part of the bargain."

The bargain. Right. She'd been so caught up in her excitement over the treasure, she'd almost forgotten he was anything but her assistant. And she didn't really blame him for triggering the trap, but lashing out felt better than crying over the loss.

"I'll uphold my end," he said. "I'll keep going through the house. We'll find more information. Maybe another key. Maybe another machine. Who knows, maybe your treasure is even in the house."

"Very well. Let's go. At the least, I can change out of these damp clothes." She pocketed the mangled key. It was better than nothing.

Hartleigh took the wooden treasure chest for Lola, and they all walked out to the waiting carriage, amid a flurry of questions from the panicked banker and concerned doctor regarding His Grace's health.

The duke's personal carriage was a gilded monstrosity, pulled by two enormous mechanical dragons that may have been intended to resemble the Pegasus. Hartleigh summarily dismissed the banker and the doctor, climbed aboard, rapped on the ceiling, and ordered, "Home!"

Sabine shook her head. He was fooling himself if he thought he couldn't or wouldn't be a proper duke.

She stared out the window, trying not to sulk. Hartleigh was right. She had other options. She could employ a codebreaker.

Keep searching. Perhaps the machine hadn't even been intended to decrypt her message in the first place.

"Daddy, Ralph is stuck," Lola complained. "His leg got wedged inside the treasure chest."

Hartleigh took the box and looked inside. "Yeah, he got into a little crack, it looks like. I think I can wiggle him free. Just a little... Whoa."

Sabine's head snapped up. "What?"

"I think this slat opens up. As if there's something inside." Hartleigh dropped Ralph into Lola's lap and held the box out to Sabine. "Would you like to check for traps, Madam Pirate?"

She ignored the snide remark and took the box without a word. She deserved a bit of censure for yelling at him earlier. Now they were even.

She poked and prodded all around the loose board, feeling for anything unusual, but only the single spot responded to her touch. Nothing to do but try. She removed her dagger from beneath her skirt, jabbed it into the crack, and popped the board open. In a small hollow lay a winding key and a folded slip of paper.

Lola hopped from her father's side to sit by Sabine. "Is it a treasure map?"

"I think it's a note," Sabine replied, unfolding the paper. She adjusted her spectacles and read, "'If you are reading this, then you are my long-sought heir and my wife has deemed you of sufficiently good character to entrust you with the secret of the treasure chest.'"

"She was supposed to tell me about this?" Hartleigh gingerly touched his forehead once again. "Goddamnit. What else does the note say?"

"He talks a bit about why he hid the treasure."

The potential of the Heart of Ra to be weaponized makes it too dangerous to reveal to the world. If, however, you should have need of it for a truly honorable purpose, the encrypted directions will reveal the location.

"Then he tells us the key is for starting the machine. Insert it, turn it two full rotations to the right, make certain that the paper and ink are loaded, the moving parts are lubricated, et cetera…" Sabine flipped the note over. "Oh, hell."

"What?"

She read again. "'In order to prevent decryption of the directions by unscrupulous parties who may happen upon my Sphinx device, I have hidden instructions for the placement of each rotor in separate locations. The first can be found at the convent of Sainte-Marie de l'Aurore, concealed inside the reliquary of Saint Felicula.'"

Hartleigh pursed his lips. "It looks like you'll have to hunt for your treasure after all."

"Yes," Sabine sighed, half in relief, half frustration. Only days ago she'd had no idea whether she'd ever decrypt the document or whether the Heart of Ra was real. Now she had confirmation that it existed and had completed the first step along the path to retrieval.

Still, the length of that path was disheartening. The longer she took, the more time her enemies had to discover her plan and come after her. She was relatively safe in England, where she had the backing of the king and the government, but in most parts of the world she was considered something between a nuisance and a wanted criminal.

Lola tugged on Sabine's sleeve. "Miss La Capitaine?"

"Yes, Lola?"

"Can I come with you?"

Sabine looked across the carriage into Hartleigh's eyes, sharp and blue behind his thick lenses.

He nodded once.

She grinned back. "I think it's time we make some funeral arrangements, don't you?"

9

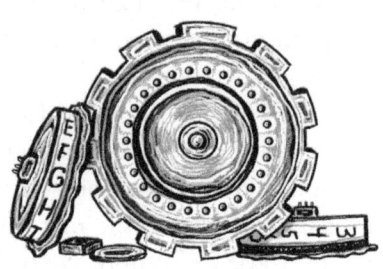

Lola sat on the edge of her bed, legs dangling well off the floor. She looked so tiny, perched there on the massive old bed. None of the rooms in the dower house had been intended as a child's bedroom. Another pang of homesickness for their pretty house in Chicago stabbed at Cliff's chest.

Lola carefully slotted the syringe full of luxene into her fuel tube, then looked up at him for approval. Cliff checked the placement of the syringe and gave her a nod. She depressed the plunger, sending the glowing green fuel streaming into her mechanical heart.

"Did I get it all?" she asked.

"Yep."

She passed him the empty syringe and popped the cover back into place. Cliff helped her button up her shirt buttons.

"Nice job, Lo. Pretty soon you'll be able to do it all yourself. You're good for another week. Hopefully by then we'll be in San Francisco, looking for a new house with a view of the ocean."

Cliff cleaned the syringe and stashed it in the fuel kit, checking that the luxene bottle was properly sealed against leakage. The eight-ounce bottle was already half empty. At half an ounce per week, he'd need to buy more before the winter was out. Even a two-month supply didn't feel like enough. Nothing ever felt like enough.

Lola gripped the doorknob with both hands, looking back at him with wide-eyed expectation. "Can we go now, Daddy?"

Cliff tucked the fuel kit into his shoulder bag. "Go ahead. But walk, don't run. If you smash something rushing to get there, you'll be stuck here until it's cleaned up."

She yanked open the door and leapt out into the hall with a whoop of joy. Cliff grimaced. He still had a lingering headache from yesterday's incident at the bank, which was probably a bad sign. Not that he could do much about it other than lay down and rest. And he could do that just as well on an airship as he could here.

Sabine Diebin's pirate ship hovered in the middle of his garden, its oblong, midnight-blue balloon swaying slightly in the chilly wind. The dark-stained, wooden hull resembled a seventeenth-century sailing ship, complete with portholes and shuttered openings that could potentially conceal cannons. It was smaller than Cliff had expected, perhaps sixty or seventy feet in length and as tall as a two-story house. His mental picture of her commanding a full score of rough, angry pirates was apparently a bit exaggerated.

Lola ran toward the ship, waving a stick she'd scooped up off the ground, overjoyed at the fulfillment of all her pirate dreams. Damn, but he loved her. He couldn't imagine loving anyone or anything as much as he loved his baby girl. He hitched up his bag to keep it on his shoulder, patting it to feel the fuel kit inside. Her health and safety were first priority.

"Hartleigh!"

Cliff sighed, slowing his pace. "Duchess. How kind of you to come see us off."

"Where do you think you're going? The debts are still

unpaid. The papers are making a mockery of you. You can't go running off like this."

Cliff folded his arms across his chest. "I'm the Duke of Hartleigh. I can do whatever the hell I want."

"No, you can't. You have obligations. Duty to your family name."

He glared at her. "Excuse me if I don't want to take the advice of a woman who can't even be bothered to warn me of dangerous traps."

"What?"

"The treasure chest?"

Her aristocratic brow crinkled. "What treasure chest?"

"The one with the hidden key. And the booby-trapped strongbox inside. Your husband entrusted you with the secret, and you were supposed to tell me. But apparently I'm not respectable enough."

"I have no idea what you're talking about."

"Your late husband. Did he or didn't he leave information that was to be passed on to me?"

Some of the fire went out of her usually-bright eyes. "He left dozens of notes, most of which made no sense whatsoever. He was… not his usual self in the last months of his life."

Her genuine sorrow dampened Cliff's anger. "I'm sorry. I can tell you cared for him."

"I did. He was a kind man and very good to me."

Cliff nodded. He couldn't pretend to understand how a sixty-year age difference could make for a satisfactory marriage. But, then again, his own views on the institution were cynical enough that he wasn't certain there even was such a thing as a satisfactory marriage.

"Well, I'm sorry for your loss. It will not, however, prevent me from traveling to France. This is my chance to take Lola on an airship and show her another new country. I'm not going to pass up the opportunity. We'll be back in a few days."

We'll be "dead" in a few days. Swept out to sea, perhaps. The convent is near the coast.

An odd, guilty feeling fluttered in his belly. He didn't want the duchess cast out of her home with only the clothes on her back.

She'll be fine. I'll have Sabine send all the money from the sale of the scrap and antiquities we sorted straight to the duchess.

"Why do I doubt that?" the duchess muttered to herself.

Cliff pretended he hadn't heard. "Excuse me. I need to see that our luggage has all been loaded." They weren't coming back. Nothing important could get left behind.

The only access to the ship besides ropes and winches appeared to be a single ladder dangling from the deck to the ground. Lola scampered up it so quickly Cliff thought his heart might stop. He waited at the bottom, both hands free, ready to catch her if she fell. When she was safely aboard, he slung his bag across his body and started up.

The ladder swayed as he climbed, tipping this way and that with each step. His knees and elbows banged against the hull, sending jolts of pain up and down his limbs. How the hell did anyone do this on a regular basis? No wonder pirates drank all the time. Pain relief. At least the bruises distracted from the headache.

"Welcome aboard, Duke."

Cliff steadied himself with a hand on the rail. "Captain," he replied.

Sabine wore one of the simple dresses that made up her everyday wardrobe, but she'd topped it with a dashing military jacket in the same dark blue as the ship's balloon. A leather tricorn hat sat atop her brown curls. She smiled at him. "This is my ship. Die Fledermaus. As of now, I officially outrank you."

Cliff lifted one shoulder. "Okay."

"Allow me to introduce my crew. Hawkes you know, of course." She gestured at the butler, still attired in his tidy

English suit, pointing out features of the ship to a beaming Lola. "Nicole Palmer, here, is my first mate."

"Pleased to meet you." Cliff shook the woman's hand. She was tall, with dark brown skin and a penetrating gaze. Her unadorned, tan trousers and plain, white shirt revealed an athletic figure well-suited to shipboard duties. Cliff expected she could handily kick his ass if she ever tried.

"Nicole does most of the piloting and oversees almost everything else," Sabine continued. "Do what she says. Her husband, Ben, is our engineer." Sabine pointed at a lanky man busily working on one of the engines, a pair of goggles obscuring his face, and mysterious tools strapped all over his body. "They both hail from Jamaica, so the rule on board is if they don't complain about the cold, you'd better not, either. Right, Jules?"

"La Capitaine wounds me, monsieur," the Frenchman said to Cliff, tossing his chin-length, white-blond hair. "She knows it is a rule I break all too often. But, you, of course, are our guest. We will give you every comfort during our travels. I am the navigator. I will see us safely to our intended destination. In this particular instance, I am delighted to escort you to my homeland."

Cliff shook the man's hand, trying not to stare at the canary yellow embroidered waistcoat that looked like something from the court of Marie Antoinette. Maybe it was. For all Cliff knew, the crew had once looted an old French castle.

"This is my personal ship," Sabine explained, "and she flies easily with no more crew than this. In the days before I retired, I had two other, larger ships with crew members from even more countries. So if you hear anyone speaking Chinese, Spanish, Russian, Icelandic, or any other language, that's where it came from. Mostly we all know the curse words."

Cliff made a vague noise of agreement, not certain how to reply. What he wouldn't give to wake up at home in Chicago thinking, *Dukedoms and pirates? What insane sort of dream was that?*

He stayed up on deck while the ship ascended, walking about with Lola and reminding her of the dangers of climbing while flying until she began to roll her eyes. Twice he stumbled over coils of rope because he was too busy watching the world fall away beneath them to look where he was going.

The air grew even colder as they rose, and the crew donned thick coats and gloves. Lola wrapped herself in a borrowed fur and marched around bellowing orders to an imaginary crew. Cliff plopped himself down near the rail, protected from the wind and shaded a bit from the bright sunlight. The pounding in his head had grown worse, and he shut his eyes briefly.

"You ought to go down to the captain's cabin and rest, Your Grace," Hawkes suggested. "I can keep an eye on the little miss. I'll teach her all the pirate safety rules and if she starts to shiver, I'll bring her down to you."

Cliff hesitated a moment, then nodded. Ordinarily he gave Lola plenty of freedom to play and do things on her own. And a flying airship wasn't much more dangerous than an ocean liner. Right?

He knew he'd made a good decision the moment he settled down in Sabine's sturdy, but comfortable, armchair. His head fell against the back of the chair, his eyes closing again. He hadn't slept well last night, still achy and anxious after the explosion at the bank. He'd be no use to Lola dozing on the deck. Better to nap well in comfort with the assurance that someone was watching her.

Half an hour of sleep revived him, and when he woke he took a bit of time to examine the room around him. It suited Sabine's style. Everything of quality, but nothing too ornate. The chair he sat in and a chest for storage sat opposite a rugged desk and a well-stocked bookshelf. To his left was a tidy bed, built directly into the wall for stability.

The Sphinx device sat atop the desk, its wooden case closed and latched. Cliff walked over to examine it. The key they had found in the treasure chest fit neatly into the slot, but he didn't turn it. He wasn't foolish enough to try any more of the Mad Duke's inventions without proper instructions. He fished out the folded piece of paper that had come with the key, wanting to read the directions for himself.

> *The potential of the Heart of Ra to be weaponized makes it too dangerous to reveal to the world.*

"Heart of Ra?" he asked aloud. "*Weaponized?* What the hell kind of treasure is this?"

Cliff rushed up to the deck, the note in his hand. No way in hell was he going to be part of a hunt for some kind of unspeakable weapon. He'd make Sabine drop him and Lola off at the closest convenient spot, and hopefully throw the damn decryption machine into the ocean as well.

"Explain this," he demanded, waving the note in Sabine's face.

"Calm down, Duke. What's your problem?" She snatched the paper from his hand.

Cliff refused to back down. "This 'Heart of Ra.' What is it?" He jabbed a finger at the paper. "It sounds like a fancy gemstone, but the duke speaks of its potential as a weapon. What is it really? A gun? A warship? A poison?"

"It's a battery."

Cliff's eyes widened in surprise. "What?"

"A tiny but powerful fuel cell. No bigger than my little finger, according to my sources, and they've been correct about everything so far. You've seen those pet dragons that run on luxene?"

"Of course." The small mechanical creatures used power sources similar to the one he and Lola had refueled only that morning. He'd practiced with them exhaustively in the days when Lola had first received the biomechanical implant, learning to make all necessary adjustments for regular maintenance of small devices.

"The Heart of Ra could power one of those dragons for one hundred years."

Cliff reeled. One hundred years? Fuel for a lifetime? The very idea was intoxicating. A battery that small and powerful could change Lola's life. It would free her from any fears that luxene would become too rare or too expensive. It would protect her from suppliers' haphazard quality checks that could result in tainted, weak, or otherwise faulty fuel. It would keep her heart pumping until she was a great-grandmother, surrounded by generations of adoring family. Cliff wanted it so badly his chest ached.

"I see," he replied, the bland words all he could manage without revealing the turmoil now roiling inside him. What would he do to claim the Heart of Ra? Postpone his escape to California? Without a second thought. Betray a pirate? Not if he could help it. He'd pay her for it, once they found it. He'd pay everything he had. Sabine's single-minded pursuit of the treasure was the only question mark. What if everything he had still wasn't enough? What then?

"I don't plan to weaponize it, if that's your concern," Sabine said, staring up at him with her arms folded across her chest. "I believe we have already discussed how I am not a murderer."

"I know. I just… I'm worried for Lola, is all."

"If we stumble into any dangers, I will see that she is protected. The crew can fly her away at a moment's notice."

"Thank you. I'll, uh, go put those instructions away. Sorry to bother you."

Sabine handed the paper back, still scowling at him. "Don't make me regret our bargain."

He shuddered and hurried down to the cabin, plopping himself into the armchair once more.

"Fuck," he muttered.

Apparently he needed new business cards. *Clifford J. Kinsley. Scrap collector. Duke. Treasure hunter.*

10

Dagger, check. Torch, check. Lockpicks, check. Duke…

Sabine stared into the dimly lit cabin, where he lay sleeping in her bed, Lola curled up beside him. Did she really want to bring him along? She could take Nicole instead and not have to worry about anyone making noise or poor decisions.

No. She wouldn't involve the crew. That had been part of the retirement deal. They'd agreed to stay on as her personal crew with legitimate, legal positions. They maintained her ships and flew her place-to-place. Nothing more. Any treasure hunting or potentially criminal deeds would be Sabine's alone.

And sneaking into a convent to break open a reliquary was certainly illegal. Cliff Kinsley would have to do as a partner. He was already involved with her search, and he was the right sort of person to send running for help if everything went horribly wrong.

She crossed the room silently and gave him a gentle shake. He sat up immediately and climbed carefully over Lola. He hadn't undressed, and it took only moments for him to don his eyeglasses, step into his short boots, and pull on his coat. The suit wasn't ideal for burglary, but it wouldn't unduly hamper him either, and she doubted he had anything better.

"You're wearing trousers," he commented when they reached the deck.

"So good of you to notice."

"It's not so dark that I could possibly miss it, and you did walk up the stairs right in front of me."

"Staring at my bum, were you?"

He shrugged. "It's a nice bum. You have nice legs, too."

Sabine chuckled. She liked that forthright manner of his. "Thank you. You're not unpleasant to look at yourself. And, yes, I have discarded my everyday clothing in favor of something that will allow me to climb through a window or over a wall."

"I imagine you're better at that sort of thing than I am, even in a dress. I'll do my best not to muck things up."

"Do as I say and hopefully we'll avoid any trouble."

"Aye, aye, Captain."

The moonlit walk to the convent took no more than a few minutes. The abbess had given Sabine permission to park her ship on the grounds overnight, based on her supposed interest in a monastic life. Dinner and an evening spent in the company of the convent's highly religious inhabitants had been excruciating. Sabine had never been a churchgoer, knew little about religious life, and certainly had no intention of ever giving up all her possessions to live in an uncomfortable little cell. She'd had quite enough of poverty as a child. She'd earned her way out of it and she wasn't going back.

Fortunately, the allure of a pirate repenting all her sins had captivated the nuns. They'd passed the hours telling Sabine exactly why she should pick *this* convent above all others for her holy life of redemption. She'd said little in return.

"The reliquary is in the chapel," she whispered to Hartleigh, pausing in a deep shadow along the convent's outer wall. "The nuns take turns worshiping Saint Felicula's holy bones, or some such nonsense."

"They don't worship the bones, or even the saint," Hartleigh explained. "They're asking the saint to intercede on their behalf or on behalf of others."

"I see."

"My mother was Irish Catholic. I know all about saints."

"Ah." Sabine could count on her fingers the number of times she'd been in a church during her adult life. As a child, churches had been nothing more than easy places to snatch a few coins. "Whatever they're doing, we need to approach cautiously. We will climb through a window here, and I will lead the way to the chapel. You must be absolutely silent."

"I'll do my best."

"If we need a distraction to draw the nun away from the relic, I will signal you. Be your usual self. A man in the convent should cause plenty of fuss. You can run, or chat at her, or whatever you wish while I retrieve the information from the reliquary. Once I have what we came for and have climbed back out the window, you are free to follow any way you wish."

"I'm not certain I like this plan. What if the nuns overwhelm me and I end up in a French prison?"

"Don't underestimate yourself, Duke." Sabine patted his chest, then immediately wished she hadn't. He had a warm, solid, pleasant body, and she didn't need that sort of distraction. She jerked her hand away. "Let's go."

Sabine worked a window open with little difficulty and hauled herself up and over the sill, dropping into the long, dark corridor. Hartleigh climbed after her, sliding through the narrow opening with ease. As they walked the hall, however, he continually drifted off to the right, nearly ruining everything when he banged his elbow on a statue and had to swallow a yelp.

Sabine couldn't understand him. He had a strong, athletic body, and displayed moments of agility. Yet he couldn't walk in a straight line? She took hold of his arm and steered him along.

A sudden snort from up ahead made them both jump.

Pushing Harleigh against the wall, Sabine crept up to the doorway and peeked into the candle-lit chapel. A gnarled, old woman sat in a pew, beads clutched in her hands and her head tipped forward, sound asleep. She gave another noisy snore, barely twitching.

Sabine slipped back to Hartleigh's side. "The nun is asleep," she whispered in his ear. "Stay close and don't bump into anything. No noise."

He nodded and followed, keeping one hand pressed to her back. Sabine applauded his good sense, but his touch and the nearness of his body sent prickles of awareness dancing across the surface of her skin. She fought the desire to turn around and burrow against him. She needed to do something about her recent lack of intimate contact as soon as possible.

The reliquary sat in the center of a recessed nook, cut off from access by a row of stark, wooden kneelers. Sabine paused, considering the best way to climb over without upsetting anything. Before she could move, Hartleigh grasped her about the waist and lifted her over the top, then stepped over himself, his long legs easily clearing the barrier.

Sabine stared at him, turning her hands palm-up in a silent, *What was that?*

He frowned at her in puzzlement, clearly not understanding. He pointed outside the nook, then to where they were standing.

We were there. Now we're here.

That was the logic of a man whose only companion was his seven-year-old daughter. She imagined he picked up Lola all the time, boosting her over fences and into trees. They would have to have a "don't pick up a woman without permission" talk.

Shaking her head, Sabine turned to the reliquary, opening it and examining the contents. An old bone, perhaps from an arm, sat wrapped in a moldering piece of cloth. She lifted it out, unwrapping it, looking for a slip of paper or any other sort of writing. Nothing.

Hartleigh swore under his breath.

Sabine thrust the bone into his hands. He made a strangled noise and fumbled with the relic. She gave him a hard look.

You. She pointed at him, tapped the bridge of her glasses, and pointed at the snoring nun. *Watch her.*

He nodded, grimacing and holding the bone as if it were about to explode. Superstitious nonsense. It had probably come from a sheep.

Sabine reached inside the reliquary, feeling for cracks, loose panels, or hidden latches. The box was smooth and solid. Where were the damned instructions? She closed the door, feeling around the edges, then moving on to the outside of the box. Still her fingers found nothing. No unusual bumps or hollows, nothing that shifted beneath her touch. If it had a hidden compartment, she could see no way in but to smash the thing.

A tap on her shoulder made her whirl around. Hartleigh gestured frantically at the elderly nun. The woman shifted in her seat, her head lifting. She mumbled something.

Scheiße! Sabine shoved Hartleigh to the floor and dropped down on top of him.

II

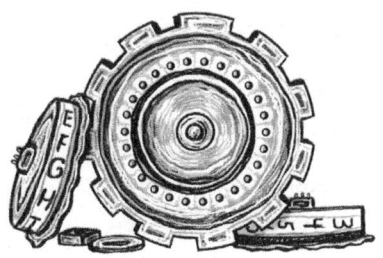

He was going to hell.

Cliff wasn't particularly religious, despite his mother's best efforts. The afterlife wasn't something he usually contemplated. Tonight, however, he was pretty sure he'd earned himself a ticket to everlasting damnation.

Breaking into a convent was one thing. Even opening a reliquary to search for clues was something he could get behind. But desecrating a holy relic?

The bit of cloth was gone somewhere, and pieces of the bone had already snapped off during his dive to the floor. Now he lay on top of the thing, feeling it dig painfully into his side, and what did his brain keep drifting to? The pair of shapely legs wrapped around his thigh and the inconvenient erection they were causing.

He was going to hell.

"Ave Maria," the nun intoned in a voice as stentorian as her snoring.

Dear God, he was going to be trapped here, pulverizing poor Saint Felicula into the dust from whence she came and fending off thoughts of carnal pleasures with a pirate captain, while a little old lady shouted the entire rosary.

Sabine shifted slightly atop him, and he sucked in a sudden breath. Every bit of him hummed with awareness of her. The contrast of the cold floor against his right side and her warm body against his left. The brush of her arms against his chest and his back, as she braced herself to avoid toppling off him and banging into something. The heat of her breath on his neck.

She shifted again, her chest pressing into his arm. Instead of soft, yielding flesh, he felt something hard and inflexible. Was she wearing armor?

"Give me that bone," she whispered.

Cliff squirmed, trying to free Felicula's fragile remains while concealing the other bone that he was aching to give Sabine. His arm wrenched and his head banged against the floor. His gasp of pain was blessedly drowned out by a booming, "Amen!" from the praying nun.

At least the discomfort helped squelch his lust. No mixing business with pleasure. And certainly no sexual entanglements with anyone who might possibly be a friend. He knew better than that, after the fool he'd made of himself with Miranda.

"Ave Maria," the nun began again.

Sabine's hand wormed its way beneath him, found St. Felicula's bone, and worked it free. "Got it," she whispered. She carefully rolled off of Cliff, grasped the bone with both hands, and snapped it in half.

As he gaped in horror, she calmly tugged a tightly-rolled paper from inside the bone. She opened it up and scanned it, nodding.

"This is it. We can go. You distract the nun while I escape, then follow when you can. I'll have the ship ready."

"You... you..." He couldn't take his eyes off the ruined relic.

"It's a fake. Now get ready to—" She froze, listening. The

nun's prayers were fading, her words becoming slurred. A few moments later, she began to snore again.

"That's our chance," Sabine hissed. "Go. Now."

Cliff scrambled to his feet and over the kneelers. Sabine pocketed the note and shoved the broken bits of bone back into the reliquary before climbing after him. Together, they hurried back to the unlocked window and out into the relative safety of the night air. They jogged across the grounds and climbed aboard the ship, where they sagged against the rail, catching their breath.

"I think we'd best depart at once," Sabine said.

"I agree. We'll have a whole convent out for our heads the moment anyone sees what we did to their holy relic."

"Their holy hoax. Obviously the duke agreed with me, because either he hollowed it out to hide the paper, or he replaced the original bone entirely."

"I agree it's not from an ancient Roman saint, but we were still disrespecting the dead."

"What do they care? They're dead. It's probably not even a human bone. Unless he took it from one of his mummies."

Cliff winced. "Oh, God."

"You make a terrible pirate. Much too sensitive. Thank you, though, for your assistance. You performed your lookout duties well. I have the instructions for the first rotor and the location of the next clue, and I'm ready to uphold my end of our bargain. Where would you like me to drop you and Lola, and what shall I tell the world about your sudden and tragic demise? I jotted down a few ideas if you don't have any."

"Actually, if you don't mind, I'd like to help you complete your quest first. It doesn't feel right, leaving after solving only one small portion of the puzzle."

Sabine folded her arms across her chest. "You want the Heart of Ra for yourself, is that it?"

"No," he answered, immediately and truthfully.

"To sell, then."

"Nor that."

"Hmph. Well, you must want *something*, Duke."

"I don't like leaving jobs half-done."

She took her time before answering. "Fine. You can come along. Your help will be useful in obtaining the next clue."

"Why? Where are we going?"

"St. Berhtwald's Hospital, in Brighton. Time to go home, Hartleigh."

Cliff sighed. "Wonderful."

12

"Welcome to St. Berhtwald's," said the smiling woman who greeted Sabine and the duke as they stepped into the bizarrely glittering foyer. What kind of hospital was this? Electric chandeliers? Gilt-framed mirrors? Footmen in matching livery? "How can we be of assistance…" She glanced at the calling card where Hartleigh had hastily scrawled his title. "Your Grace?"

"Only a few questions," he replied.

Hopefully a very few. Lola and the crew waited on Die Fledermaus, ready to fly back home, or wherever the treasure hunt sent them next. With luck, Sabine would have the next clue in her hands in minutes.

"Of course." The woman's smile grew even wider. "I'm sure you've heard that we are the foremost center for recuperation from nervous complaints as well as physical ailments that benefit from our healthy sea air. The strain of your sudden inheritance must be immense, I'm certain, but we will do all we can to see that you receive the absolute best care."

Hartleigh winced. "Uh... Actually, we're not here for a medical issue. We're looking for a vase."

The woman's eyebrows rose into pointed arches. "A vase. I see." Poor Hartleigh. Apparently rumors of hereditary madness had reached Brighton.

"Or maybe a pot?" He glanced to Sabine for help.

"I'm Sonja Cain," she said, offering a hand to the woman. "I am here on behalf of His Grace as an antiquities expert. We are cataloging the artifacts collected by the previous duke, and part of that process involves a thorough check into the provenance and current locations of any donated items. The late duke was not in the best of health when many of these items were sent out, and it is vital that we ensure the correct pieces were sent to the correct places."

The woman's expression didn't change. "I see."

"We're looking for a big Greek pot," Hartleigh told her.

"The Krater of Hippocrates," Sabine clarified.

"We have no Greek antiquities here," the woman replied. "But I can take you to a man who might be able to help you. Follow me, please."

As they walked through the opulent halls, Hartleigh moved close enough to Sabine that their arms brushed together. "She thinks I'm insane," he whispered.

"You're in a mental health facility, asking after ancient pots in order to help a pirate track down a treasure hidden by a dead man who invented bizarre machines."

"Excellent point. Perhaps I *should* check myself in here. Very restful, I understand."

"If it helps us find that vase, Duke, I'm willing to vouch for the depths of your madness."

"How kind of you."

They paused outside a small office, and the woman waved them through the door. "Dr. Standish should be able to answer your questions. Good day to you, Your Grace, Miss Cain."

Sabine walked straight to the desk and offered her hand

to the gray-haired man who sat behind it. "Hello. I'm Sonja Cain, antiquities expert. His Grace has brought me to your facility to inquire after a Greek artifact donated by the late Duke of Hartleigh. It's a large vase or pot known as the Krater of Hippocrates."

The doctor rose and shook her hand. "Yes, I remember the piece. It's no longer here, I'm afraid. The images painted on it of surgeries and other medical procedures were upsetting to our patients, unfortunately."

"Where is it, then?" Hartleigh asked.

"Dr. Willingham took it home for safekeeping. He has a large and well-respected collection himself, so it is in good hands."

"Can we see it? Where does he live?"

Standish frowned. "What? A duke is in town and hasn't yet been invited to Willingham's home?"

"Er, I did only just arrive."

"Of course, of course. He hosts regular parties, you see. Always the very best of society. And, of course, now he's looking for a husband for Miss Willingham. Beautiful, beautiful girl. Certain to marry well. I haven't gone to a party in years, being too much devoted to my work. I'm certain he will show you the artifact if you request, and if you inquire he is likely to even provide an invitation for Miss, uh, Cale, was it?"

Sabine nodded, not caring whether he remembered her false name. "Thank you so much, Doctor. You've been a great help. We'll show ourselves out."

"Yes, of course. I have work to return to. And if you fill out the paperwork that our clerks will provide for you, Your Grace, we will review all your symptoms and come up with a personalized plan for your rest and recuperation."

Hartleigh looked up at the ceiling. "For the love of... I'm not insane, okay? I don't need a beach-side hospital holiday, especially not in January!"

"Of course," Standish replied. "Good day, Your Grace."

"I should have killed him," the duke muttered, once he and Sabine were alone in the hall.

"The doctor?"

"Hartleigh. I should have killed him off and gone to San Francisco and never come back here."

"Why didn't you?"

"The quest isn't over. We haven't found the treasure. But do you have any idea how annoying it is to have everyone think you're mad?"

"Some idea, yes." People made all sorts of assumptions about her, based on everything from the word "pirate" to the fact that she sometimes wore trousers. Occasionally those assumptions were true, but more often than not they were both incorrect and insulting. "Don't worry about it. You'll go to one of this Dr. Willingham's famous parties and behave exactly as a duke should and everyone will forget the rest. I, in the meantime, will find the Krater and retrieve the next note."

"And if he won't invite a madman, no matter the rank?"

Sabine waved a hand. "Don't be silly. We know someone who will make *certain* you get into that house."

"Willingham?" The duchess sighed in delight. She waved Sabine, Hartleigh, and Lola into the parlor, where tea and snacks sat waiting for them. "Oh, Hartleigh, did you see Miss Willingham in Brighton and fall madly in love at first sight? Isn't she a beauty?" She fanned herself. "Truly blessed, that girl, and her father has money by the boatload. Owns hospitals all across England. Oh, Hartleigh, she's perfect!"

The duke stared back at her, stone-faced. "I have no intention of marrying Miss Willingham, whoever she is."

"Oh, nonsense. You'll take one look at her and fall at her feet. Everyone does. Really, you couldn't do better, Hartleigh. Her father has been holding out for a duke, and you're the first one available."

"Because every father wants a madman for his daughter."

"Oh, no one will care about that, even if it were true. My family didn't care that my duke was odd, any more than they cared that he was so very old, and about as likely to give me a child as... well, never mind that. He had the title and the social prestige, you see, and that is what matters. Come, sit down. Have some tea. I'll make all the arrangements. No dancing, this time, except perhaps a very simple waltz with Miss Willingham. Or a walk in the garden, if you can't manage that." Her gaze flicked to Sabine. "I assume you will be attending as well, Miss Diebin? Perhaps you might refrain from dancing with His Grace on this occasion."

"My dancing days are ended, I'm afraid," Sabine replied. She'd be much too busy treasure hunting.

"Perfect. This is just marvelous! Oh, and I have those papers you mentioned, Hartleigh. The ones my husband left for you. Although, I'm warning you, they don't make any sense. I'll have them sent down. Please excuse me, I'm going to tell Luella the news. We'll all get dressed up and go together and have a grand time!" She rushed from the room with a decided spring in her step.

Sabine took a seat at the table and poured herself some tea. Lola scrambled up onto a couch, arranging her skirts as if she were a princess. Hartleigh fetched her a cup of tea and two cookies, then returned to the table to sit beside Sabine.

"Perhaps you *should* marry this Miss Willingham," Sabine jested. "You'd make the whole world happy, apparently."

"Except myself, Lola, and Miss Willingham."

"Ah, but how do you know that Miss Willingham hasn't been sitting at home longing for an American husband who can't dance and comes loaded with debt?"

"The dukedom came loaded with debt. *I* have a perfectly respectable and financially solvent business."

Sabine stirred her tea, though she hadn't poured anything

into it. "Why not pay the debts, then, and avoid the marriage issue?"

"The money I already have is for Lola and no one else. And I don't want to sell the business yet. Not until..." Pain filled his eyes and he looked away. "Not until I'm one hundred percent certain I can never go home again."

Sabine pushed the plate of cookies toward him. "Fleeing to California and taking on a new identity sounds awfully certain to me. Is that why you're still on this treasure hunt? You can't bring yourself to sever all those ties, can you?"

He shrugged and picked up a cookie. "That's part of it, I guess."

A knock at the door made them both look up. "Papers for you, Your Grace."

"Excellent. You can bring them here. Thank you." Hartleigh accepted the papers and spread them across the table. "Let's see what the Mad Duke had to say, shall we?"

Sabine grabbed a few of the papers and began to read. The duchess was correct. Very little of it made sense. Lists of antiquities bought and sold were mingled with random scribblings such as, "Tea's gone cold. Must request new pot."

"Do you think he was trying to catalogue his collection?" Hartleigh asked.

"Could be. Or at least make some attempt at leaving you a list of his possessions. He must have realized too late what a mess he was leaving behind."

"And both his memory and his health were failing."

"It looks that way to me." She flipped to the next paper, munching on a biscuit as she read. "Oh!" A few crumbs fell from her mouth, and she dusted them from the document.

Hartleigh leaned in, his nearness causing that increasingly familiar shivery sensation. "What have you found?"

"I think this is the note about the treasure chest. He apologizes for any confusion, then says, 'The directions for the Sphinx were written at a time when I was in better health.'"

Hartleigh slid his chair around beside hers, bumping shoulders with her once again and not seeming to notice. "It's quite rambling, isn't it? Something about how he constructed the machine and the precise tooling of the rotors. Oh, look there. 'The etched note on the device is a false clue. Don't trust the box.' That's his warning."

"And then several lines later he says, 'Doesn't everyone keep their treasures in a treasure chest?' And then he promptly goes back to listing things he's purchased. Well. No wonder his wife didn't know to warn you. I wouldn't have known what any of that meant, either."

"I never thought she was malicious," Hartleigh said. "She's a good-hearted woman. She truly cares for everyone in this entire household. It's not only her old way of life she's fighting for."

"So you intend for the Heart of Ra to pay off all the debts and solve both her problems and yours?"

"I already told you I have no desire to sell it."

"Yes." Sabine tapped a finger on the table, her lips twisting as she thought. "And you don't seem like a talented liar. Yet you must want something. Something more than delaying the inevitable end of your old life and completing all projects you start."

He moved away from her, scooping up the papers. "I'll read these over again this evening and let you know if I come up with anything new. I doubt it, but best to be thorough. Let's go, Lo."

The girl scampered over to him, depositing her empty teacup on the table and snatching up another cookie.

Sabine shook her head. "I'm going to figure you out, Duke. It's only a matter of time. I've been a thief since birth, and I'll find a way to steal your secrets."

Hartleigh rose from his seat, the papers in hand, and regarded her silently for a moment. "Or perhaps you could share some of your own secrets in exchange for mine. A fair business deal. A partnership, even."

"Pirates don't have partners, Duke. Save your business deals for Miss Willingham. You get a wife, she gets a title."

He put a hand to his temple. "I really should have killed him."

13

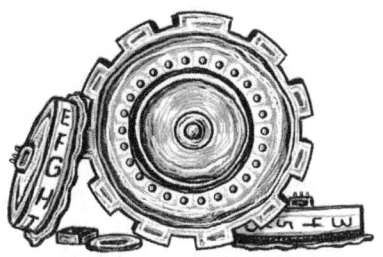

"His Grace, the Duke of Hartleigh."

Excited whispers buzzed through the room, setting Cliff's teeth on edge.

Not again.

His stomach churned with the need to flee. Bright electric lights glittered overhead, illuminating him for the entire ballroom to see. Heads of men and women alike turned toward him. Even the musicians in the orchestra had glanced in his direction. He was a curiosity. A shiny bauble in the center of this shiny room.

A pair of stalwart women flanked him, cutting off any escape route.

"Keep smiling," the duchess urged.

"Remember the quest," Sabine hissed.

The quest. The Heart of Ra. He could do this. He'd do it for Lola. Anything for Lola. He forced a smile and allowed the duchess to lead him around the room, meeting so many people that faces began to blur together.

"Hartleigh. Good to see you again."

Cliff nodded at the man who had spoken. Blond, perfect suit, drinking brandy. "Barton, right?"

"Indeed." Barton lifted his drink. "Ready for that game of billiards yet?"

"Afraid not. I'm supposed to be mingling." *I need to be mingling. Sabine needs time to find the pot. And smash it open, if it's anything like last time.*

Barton laughed. "You're not seriously wife-hunting, are you? Have you given up on the pirate mistress? I thought I saw her walk in with you."

"Miss Diebin isn't my mistress and I don't keep track of her whereabouts."

Barton's hand clamped down on Cliff's shoulder. "You're a terrible liar, old chap. Anyone can see you're smitten with her."

"She's a friend," Cliff said. Again. "Excuse me. I should go, uh, wife-hunt. As one does. You know, duke and all that."

Barton only laughed.

Cliff did his best to throw himself into the role of heiress-hungry nobleman. He spoke as little as possible. Taciturn duke was better than mad duke, and as long as he was polite and didn't try to dance, he thought perhaps he could pull this off. He had only two goals: don't make a scene and give Sabine enough time to find the next clue.

He wished he knew where she was right now. She'd vanished during the agonizingly long introductions, and he'd been watching for her reappearance ever since. He couldn't understand how the rest of the party wasn't murmuring about her absence. An image of the fantastic, bright green dress she'd worn tonight was burned in his mind, and he'd yet to see any other gown in the room that could compare. Long-sleeved and high-necked like all her clothing, it molded to her athletic torso, and the snug, black breeches underneath the short skirt had him once again fantasizing about having those legs wrapped around him.

"Shall we take a tour of the conservatory instead?"

Cliff's attention snapped back to his companion. "Uh…"

"We don't have to," Miss Willingham said. "But I noticed that a look of panic flashed across your face when more dancing was announced."

"Yes." He crooked his arm to escort her. "The conservatory sounds nice."

She was, as everyone had said, an astonishingly beautiful woman. More than that, she was amiable, unpretentious, and intelligent. An absolutely perfect duchess. A good stepmother for Lola, even. Marrying her would be entirely logical and could potentially solve all of his problems.

And he felt nothing. Her hand on his arm was just a hand. Her smile didn't cause a flutter in his chest. He had no interest in finding out her favorite things, hearing about her childhood, or even discovering what her perfect lips tasted like. He wanted to hand her off to whatever titled man was next in line and go back to treasure hunting. Maybe he *had* gone mad.

The conservatory door swung closed behind them. Miss Willingham released him and began to walk on her own through the greenery.

Tropical plants Cliff had never seen before hung from the ceiling and sprang up from the ground, their leaves and branches tangling together and clogging up all but the narrowest paths. The heat was oppressive. Cliff tugged his necktie loose before remembering that he was supposed to look formal and aristocratic tonight. Oh well.

He followed Miss Willingham, for lack of anything better to do. They were deep in the bowels of the massive greenhouse when she whirled around suddenly.

"Will you compromise me?"

"What?" Cliff took an involuntary step backward.

"Oh, you don't have to do anything too terrible. Being caught alone here with me might be enough. Perhaps we could fake a torrid embrace?" She tugged on the top two buttons of her bodice. "I can rumple my clothing enough that it looks as though we were kissing madly."

"Look, Miss, uh, Willingham, you're a lovely girl, but, um, I really…"

"You don't have to marry me."

Cliff's brows drew together. "What?"

"You compromise me. Or propose, if you like. We let people think that we have been inappropriate together. News will go out that we intend to marry. Then you jilt me or I refuse you. Either one. The scandal is immense and I beg my parents to send me to India where no one will have heard of my disgrace."

"O-kay. Why India?"

"For this." She gestured at a rather ordinary-looking green bush. "Tea. I want to grow tea. I've been studying tea processing and cultivation since I was thirteen years old."

"Oh." He took another step backwards, caught his foot on a plant, and toppled into the foliage. "Look, I, uh…" He staggered to his feet, brushing dirt from his trousers. "I applaud your desire to strike out on your own, but I really can't…"

The conservatory door banged open. Cliff turned in that direction, even though he couldn't see the door through the tangle of plant life.

"I'm certain they went this way."

The duchess. Fuck. He started for the door, Miss Willingham close on his heels.

"I know he's a bit unrefined, being an American and all," the duchess continued, "but he truly ought to know better than to go off alone with a young lady."

Cliff turned sharply, hoping to veer into a corner and hide until he could slip behind the newcomers and escape, but as he turned down the next path, he came face-to-face with Lord Barton.

Barton's laughing eyes surveyed Cliff from head to toe. He saluted Cliff with his drinking glass. "Well, well, well. Dirt on your trousers, necktie unfastened, a bit of something green in your hair. Having a tumble in the jungle, were you?" He looked past Cliff to Miss Willingham. "And with an heiress, too. You don't waste any time, do you?" He shook his head and made a tutting noise. "What will your pirate friend think, I wonder?"

Cliff's hands balled into fists. He would punch Barton in his smug-mouthed face if that was the only way out of this greenhouse. Let Miss Willingham deal with the repercussions of her own ridiculous plan.

"What on earth is going—" The duchess' words were cut short by an ear-splitting crack.

An instant later, one of the glass panels in the conservatory roof erupted in a shower of tiny shards. Without a second thought, Cliff flung himself atop Miss Willingham, shielding her from the falling pieces.

Men and women alike screamed as a group of black-clad burglars dropped from the sky, their eyes hidden behind bulbous goggles. Barton took a swing at one of them, missing entirely and nearly knocking himself down.

"Dammit, you made me spill my brandy," he grumbled, gulping whatever was left in the glass.

Cliff nudged Miss Willingham toward the door. "Run," he whispered. "Stay low. I'll try to keep them occupied." He climbed to his feet, looking for something—anything—he might use as a weapon.

Barton threw another ineffective punch, though this one at least landed. "A little help here, Hartleigh!"

Three of the invaders whirled to look at Cliff. With their matching clothing and dark lenses hiding their expressions, they looked like mechanical monsters stomping toward him.

"That one's the duke!" one exclaimed in an entirely human voice.

They leapt at him, crushing him between them and twisting his arms until he cried out in pain.

"We got him! Let's go!"

One of the side windows exploded, and the men dragged Cliff toward the sudden opening. He twisted and kicked, trying to free himself, or at least hurt one of them, but they were built of solid muscle, and each small blow he landed earned him twice what he had dealt.

"Hartleigh!" The duchess' panicked voice rang out behind him. "No!"

Cliff got his head around just enough to see her racing toward him, a potted plant in hand. She hurled it at one of his assailants, then jabbed at another with a garden spade.

"Let him go, you bastards!"

"That must be the pirate wench!" one of the kidnappers declared. "Grab her, too!"

Another man dropped from above, landing behind the duchess and seizing her.

"No! Help!" she shrieked, thrashing in his grasp. "Luella!"

The thug clamped a hand over her mouth and dragged her toward the shattered window. Cliff and the duchess locked eyes. He was certain the terror he saw in hers would be reflected in his own.

Lola! My baby!

What if he never made it back to her? What if they killed him? What would happen to her?

As his unknown enemies dragged him out into the darkness, he offered up a final plea.

"Sabine! Help me!"

14

H*ARTLEIGH WOULD LOVE THIS.*

Sabine turned the probably-not-ancient-Greek pot on its pedestal, examining it from all sides. The images were hilariously gruesome. On one side, a surgeon held up a severed leg with enormous, stylized drops of blood dripping from the end. Opposite, a teacher stood behind a sliced-open corpse, his arms lifted in a gesture of oration. She could understand why the hospital patients may have found it unpleasant, but the affected poses and unrealistic gore simply made her laugh.

Maybe once I find the note I can bring Hartleigh here to take a look. He'll get a good laugh.

She let her hands fall from the pot. Why was she thinking about the duke instead of doing her job? He had his task, she had hers. This was about the treasure. It wasn't some lark and she wasn't here to laugh with a friend. Business.

Pirates don't have partners.

He'd gotten under her skin with his blunt words and his pretty smile and that bit of mystery she couldn't quite puzzle out. Did he really think he could run away from everything? Why did he want to help her? Who was he, really?

Sabine had always liked a good mystery. It was thanks to Sherlock Holmes, after all, that she could read, write, and speak fluent English.

She lifted the krater from the pedestal and set it on the floor, reaching inside and feeling for paper, debris, or irregularities in the vessel itself. The very bottom of the pot had a spongy texture and was softer than the walls around it. She found a crack with her fingernail and pried. A section of the bottom shifted slightly. Perfect.

Pointing her torch into the interior and using her dagger, she removed the soft covering to expose the true bottom of the pot. A folded slip of paper lay waiting for her. She opened it up and read it.

> *Second slot receives wheel number one. The next step can be found inside the Helmet of Einar, which I have donated to the* Illyrian Institute for the Education of Exceptional Young Women *in the Swiss Alps.*

Switzerland. Dangerously close to Redbeard's territory. It couldn't be helped, though. She'd sit down with Nicole and make a plan for getting in and out. If necessary, they could take a wide path and come up from the south.

Sabine returned the pot to its place and adjusted it until it looked more-or-less as it had when she had found it. She would have to say thank you to Dr. Willingham. His confiscation of the artifact had made her job remarkably easy. She started back toward the ballroom, her step light and a smile on her face. Hartleigh would be pleased when she arrived to rescue him from his duties. Perhaps they would dance again after all.

An unexpected noise made her slow, cocking her ear to listen. A commotion rumbled in the distance. The high scream of a woman cut through the jumble of sounds.

"Dammit!" Sabine swore in English. She should never have termed this mission "easy."

She broke into a run, flying into the ballroom to find the guests standing like statues, looks of fear and confusion on their faces. Hartleigh was not among them. Sabine slalomed through the flabbergasted crowd, heading for the screams and shouts beyond.

The conservatory was a riot of confusion. Men and women pushed and shoved, trying to get through the doors as goggle-faced robbers tore valuables from their persons and their clothing. Sabine yanked one man out of the way, threw an elbow up to crush an intruder's nose, and forced her way into the greenhouse.

"Hartleigh!" Good God, how was she supposed to find him in this mess of vegetation? "Cliff! Where are you?"

She kicked another robber and plowed through a bed of ferns, aiming for the center of the room where the glass roof had been destroyed.

"Cliff!" she shouted again.

Goddammit, why did he always seem to stumble into danger? This should have been easier and safer than looting the convent in France. Instead, they'd run smack into a well-organized gang of house-breakers.

A blond man holding an empty drinking glass and weaving slightly stepped into her path. Sabine skidded to a stop. "I recognize you. Where's Hartleigh?"

He waved a hand. "Dukenapped. I tried to fight them off, but..." He shrugged. "You want to pay his ransom, Pirate Girl?"

"Pirate?" One of the robbers raced toward her. "If you're the pirate, who did they take?"

Sabine grabbed the arm of the drunken lord, spinning him into the grasping hands of her pursuer. He hollered, but she didn't bother trying to make sense of his cry. She had a duke to rescue.

A rush of chilly air revealed the shattered wall before Sabine's eyes found it through the maze of flora. She leaped a bush, running for the manufactured exit.

"Get your hands off—" The distant cry of the duchess was abruptly cut off, but it was enough to steer Sabine in the right direction. The villains had a lead on her, but they would be hampered by their unwilling captives.

What are you doing? she wondered. *It's just a ransom. No one will harm them. Don't get involved.*

Her feet paid no heed, racing across the wide street that separated the house from the beachfront where local eccentrics liked to leap into cold water to wake themselves up in the mornings. No hired carriage lay in wait to whisk the duke away. No steam car zipped by, too late to stop. Ahead of her, a group of hazy figures lurched toward the water's edge.

Sabine vaulted over the iron rail that separated road from beach, making no sound as her feet landed in soft sand. A chill of unease ran down her spine. Why the water? Why take your prisoners away by boat when a two-hour ride by car could hide you in the seediest hells of London? Where were they going that a car couldn't access?

She crept closer, keeping low in case she had to dive to the ground to avoid detection. Ahead of her, a large, round contraption loomed up out of the water, the front of it gaping open like a whale swallowing its dinner.

"Toss 'em in," one of the kidnappers said, "and let's get outta here before anyone comes looking."

Sabine skirted a short distance to her right, crawling beneath a bathing cart to watch. The masked criminals shoved their captives up to the mouth of the whale. The duke thrashed in their grip, but he looked to have his hands bound, and the only sounds he made were muffled grunts. Three of the men lifted him clear off the ground and threw him into the machine. Sabine's heart lurched at the heavy thud that ensued.

Damn you, Hartleigh, why can't you ever stay safe?

The duchess followed him into the metal beast, though they tossed her in less forcefully. The kidnappers turned away, scampering off into the night, their role in this apparently complete. The machine creaked, the mouth beginning to close.

Sabine cursed softly, crawling from her hiding place. If that whale was taking them out into international waters, this was far more than an ordinary ransom kidnapping. And if she was correct about who was behind it, she wouldn't leave a stranger to such a fate, much less a friend.

Business partner, she corrected. *No, not partner. Ally. That's it.*

Metal ground against metal as the jaws of the apparatus inched closer together. It was now or never. She sprang to her feet, flew down the beach, and launched herself through the shrinking gap. She landed with a thud on the cold, hard metal of the floor, and she cried out involuntarily. A clank and a shudder, and the gap closed behind her, plunging her into complete darkness.

15

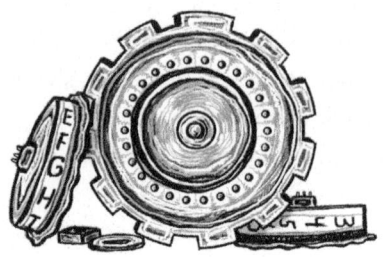

A HAND CLAMPED DOWN on his thigh, and Cliff lashed out, the toe of his dancing shoe meeting flesh. It took several seconds for the startled feminine yelp to register in his brain.

Sabine?

He tried to speak, but the gag choked off all but the faintest of sounds.

"Cliff?" Sabine's voice was no more than a whisper. "Hold still. I'm here to help."

She groped him in the darkness, her hand traveling up his leg, over his buttocks, and all along his back until she reached the ties that held the gag over his mouth. Her fingers brushed through his hair as she worked at the knot, sending little tingles throughout his body. His arms twitched instinctively, wanting to reach for her and pull her closer. He forced himself to lie still.

You're a bonehead, Cliff. She's here to rescue you, not cure you of your obviously far-too-lengthy celibacy.

The gag slipped away and he took a long, deep breath.

"Are you hurt?" Her breath against his ear tickled.

"No. Bruised is all. And I lost my glasses." Not that they would do much good inside this pitch black monstrosity.

"I'll look for them after I untie you." She pulled away, her lips grazing his cheek.

Hell and damnation. Had she just kissed him intentionally? The moment his hands were free, he sat up, running a finger across his cheek where it still burned from that fleeting touch. It had been an accident, that was all. It meant nothing.

Shuffling noises nearby told him Sabine was freeing the duchess from her predicament. Cliff didn't move or utter a sound. He had no idea who might be nearby. If any enemies were listening, he didn't want them to know they'd been freed from their binds.

A sudden light sliced through the darkness. Sabine held a flashlight beneath the top layer of her skirt, the muted beam casting just enough light to allow them to see one another and get their bearings. She turned in a slow circle, pausing to scoop something up off the ground. A moment later, Cliff had his spectacles in his hands. One earpiece wobbled slightly, but they were intact and he could see without straining to focus.

Sabine uncovered the flashlight and pointed it at the wall, making a full circuit of the round chamber in which they found themselves. The walls were smooth, with no apparent openings save for the tightly sealed jaws they had entered through. Cliff placed a hand against the wall. A slight vibration shook the metal, and he could hear the low hum of an engine. He pressed his ear to the wall, and the hum became a clear, steady buzz, like one of those new-fangled boat motors he'd encountered that past summer on the lake.

He straightened up and looked to Sabine, shrugging in a gesture of, *What now?*

Could the driver of this metal monster hear them, if they talked? Did it even have a driver? Did the kidnappers know Sabine was with them? And just where the hell were they going?

The duchess, who sat on the floor in a pool of shimmery fabric, scooted closer to the wall and kicked it hard enough to make an audible thud.

"Let me out!" she shrieked. "You get in here and untie me at once, you loathsome, disease-ridden scofflaws! How dare you do this? Do you have any idea who I am?"

She continued to rant as Sabine moved to Cliff's side. "I don't know if anyone can hear," Sabine murmured, "but I asked the duchess to do what she could to make it sound as if you and she are alone and still tied."

"Sensible. Where do you think they are taking us?"

"To a boat." The tight set of her mouth made it clear she didn't intend to elaborate. "Our best chance to escape is to take them by surprise when this creature opens again. I have a dagger. I'll give you the torch. Shine it directly into the faces of the kidnappers when they look in. I can attack while they're blinded. I'll knot up the ropes into a sort of cudgel that the duchess can wield. Beyond that, we will have to improvise. I have a flare to signal to my crew. It can be seen at least a mile off."

Cliff nodded. Lola would be asleep on the airship, with no idea that he might not be coming back for her. His fingers clenched on the flashlight Sabine handed him. He'd do all he could. And pay a hefty ransom, if necessary.

"Sit down, Duke. We will have some time, yet."

Cliff sank to the floor, Sabine settling beside him and picking up the discarded ropes. He stared at her hands as she knotted the strands with well-practiced movements. In no time, she had a thick, semi-flexible club with a looped handle on one end. She swung it around a few times, then handed it off to the duchess, who had finally quieted from her performance.

Sabine looked at Cliff, pointed at the flashlight and mouthed, *Off*.

He nodded and flicked the switch. No sense in letting the battery drain down when nothing here required light.

Time ticked by, with nothing but the faint hum of the engine and the occasional rocking of the machine. Cliff couldn't even guess whether they were above the water or below. He turned the flashlight over in his hands, adjusting his position every few seconds. No matter how he sat, some portion of his body was uncomfortable.

He shifted again, and his knee came in contact with Sabine's leg.

Move. Back away. Don't make this awkward.

He edged closer. He needed to thank her for helping. For simply being here. Without her, he'd still be lying on the floor, bound and gagged, without even a rudimentary plan of escape. A quick whisper of thanks in her ear would be enough. Just to let her know how grateful he was.

Cliff lifted a hand, trying to locate her in the darkness. His fingertips skimmed the soft skin of her cheek.

"Sabine." Her whispered name was almost inaudible, even to his own ears, but his fingers spoke his message without sound, sweeping up her jaw, caressing the shell of her ear. She leaned into his touch, pressing her cheek into his palm.

Desire pounded through him. He bent toward her, seeking her lips, finding them parted and eager. His hand slipped to the back of her head, his fingers tangling in her hair, drawing her closer.

Cliff heard her sharp intake of breath as his tongue traced the curve of her bottom lip. She had a perfect mouth, and it fit against his even better than he'd imagined. Her hands rose to grip the lapels of his coat, holding him in place, spurring him on.

He tipped his head, angling to deepen the kiss, sinking into her luscious heat. Her mouth was sweet perfection, a pirate's treasure offered up for him to plunder. Each eager little gasp of breath added to the fire in his veins. He wanted to take her, right here in the belly of this mechanical beast. To ride her until he couldn't think any more and this mad longing inside him was all burnt out.

Sabine clambered up into his lap, not breaking the kiss, her hands beginning to rove across his chest, her hips rocking against his. Their passionate embrace had knocked his eyeglasses askew, but he didn't care. Here in the darkness, he was almost willing to toss them aside again. He didn't need to see to devour her. He groaned against her mouth, lost to everything but their melding bodies and tangling tongues.

"For goodness' sake, Hartleigh!"

Cliff and Sabine sprang apart at the duchess' scandalized voice.

"Have you no decency? It might be dark in here, but I can still *hear* you."

Cliff managed only a strangled noise in reply, which was good, he supposed, if anyone were to listen in. Good God, what had he been thinking? What had Sabine been thinking to allow him to kiss her under such circumstances? Were they both out of their minds?

He backed away, his heart still pounding in his chest, his lungs still heaving. The sudden influx of reality hadn't dampened the fire inside him. His body ached for her. His mind was in a lust-induced haze, struggling to form coherent thoughts.

Their mechanical prison shuddered, jerking to a halt as it collided with some outside object with an ear-piercing clang. The vehicle lurched, sending him tumbling. He groped for the flashlight, abandoned during their ill-conceived canoodling session.

The whale swayed, the buzz of its engine replaced by an eerie silence. Back and forth it rocked, until suddenly, with one last bone-jarring thud, it fell still.

Cliff's fingers touched the curved metal of the flashlight and closed around it.

Let's get the hell out of here. Wherever "here" is.

16

Sabine took down two enemies before they ever saw her coming. A third she struck from behind while Her Grace pummeled his face with the improvised rope weapon. The duchess might be haughty and priggish, but she had a fierce spirit underneath.

Cliff grunted in pain, and Sabine whirled around to find him doubled over, trying to twist away from another blow to his midsection. Before she could jump to help him, he hooked one foot behind his attacker's leg and pulled, sending both men tumbling to the ground.

Cliff was back on his feet in an instant. There were some advantages, apparently, to falling down on a regular basis. He aimed her lighted torch at the enemy's face, and when the man turned reflexively away Sabine jumped onto his back, jabbing her knife into his kidneys.

She had no qualms about stabbing these men. This steamship flew the colors of a German cargo vessel, but these were Redbeard's parasites. Sabine had been the man's bane for the last decade. She knew how he operated. There would be no ransom. These men had one mission: to torture Cliff until he confessed everything he knew about the Heart of Ra. She'd be damned if she was going to let that happen.

Hartleigh recovered quickly for a man unused to fighting. He raced down the deck, calling for Sabine and the duchess to follow. He stopped at the rail, where a small lifeboat dangled over the side, and began yanking at ropes and turning winches in a surprisingly competent manner. The duchess didn't hesitate an instant before climbing over the side and dropping down into the boat.

A hand grabbed a fistful of Sabine's skirts. The material tore away easily as she spun clear of the attack. Fools. These sailor boys didn't know La Capitaine. She hit the man solidly in the chest with a booted foot, then slashed across his face with her knife. He dropped to the ground with a howl of pain.

"Let's go, let's go!" Cliff shouted, freeing the lifeboat from the last of its ties and sending it on a rapid descent to the waters below.

Sabine dodged one more attacker, jumping back to avoid the blade of a dagger that perfectly matched her own. The pirate adjusted his stance, feinting with little jabs, trying to pin her against the rail. He was a small man, but quick.

Their blades clanged together. The little shit was faster than she was, but none too bright. She held his gaze and faked retreat, skittering backwards to keep out of reach of his knife. Only when it was far too late did he realize he'd been flanked. The duke grabbed him from behind, hauled him off his feet, and hurled him over the side.

"Sorry, we've got to go now."

Hartleigh nodded at Sabine, and together they scrambled over the rail and dropped down into the boat.

She landed hard enough to leave a bruise or two, but with relative ease. The duke, in typical fashion, crashed in an ungraceful heap, giving a yelp of pain. Even so, he hurried to right himself, grabbed hold of the oars, and shoved off.

He didn't know how to fight and he couldn't walk in a straight line, but he clearly knew boats. He sent them flying away from the ship using only the power of his own body, the muscles in his arms and back flexing so hard that Sabine could hear the seams of his tight evening jacket popping.

A gunshot rang out, and the duchess screamed and dove to the floor, covering her head.

"Get down!" Cliff shouted.

Sabine shook her head, not even turning to look for the shooters. "No. They want us alive. They're only trying to frighten us. Keep rowing. I'm going to signal my crew."

She climbed past him, up to the prow of the boat, and pulled the flare from the pocket of her breeches.

"I thought you said that worked up to a mile!" Cliff called over his shoulder. "How far out do you think we are?"

"I have no idea, but once that ship comes around, you won't stand a chance in hell of outrunning them even with all your manly vigor." She lashed the flare to the prow, pulled the cap off of it, and turned away.

The flare lit with a pop, bathing them in a green glow that in these open waters would be seen farther off than a mere mile.

"Jesus!" Cliff swore.

"Don't turn around." Sabine knelt behind him. "It'll blind you."

"I can tell. It's like daylight." He was breathing hard, but his strokes were strong and smooth, propelling them swiftly across the waves.

The gunfire had stopped, the sailors concentrating on maneuvering the ship for a chase. They would give it everything they had. Redbeard had no tolerance for failure.

Her flare popped again, the color changing to a bluish-purple. Thirty seconds more and it was back to green. The crew would recognize the blinking pattern as hers.

Sabine watched the slowly turning ship, her fingers clenching and unclenching. Helpless. She wouldn't be able to row half as well as Hartleigh. She could do nothing but watch and wait.

"How long for your crew to reach us?" Cliff asked. In the light of the flare she could see the sweat dripping from his dark hair, running down his cheek and neck.

"A few minutes from the time they see us. Can you hold on that long?"

"Do I have a choice?"

"No."

Their only other option left them back on board the steamship, hoping her crew could stage a rescue before the torture could go very far. Or before they decided to kill her and go after the Heart based only on Cliff's knowledge. Would they truly believe she had entrusted anyone in the world with all the relevant information? Maybe they'd kill him and torture her instead.

Then again, Cliff knew everything except the location of the coded document. Far more than she had ever expected to share with anyone. Surely it was no secret that they'd flown in and out of France together. And the newspapers had painted them as lovers.

Sabine rocked back on her heels, putting a tiny bit more distance between herself and Hartleigh's straining body. Why had she been so foolish as to kiss him? Watching him display his strength and athleticism was not what she needed right now. She closed her eyes and imagined him tripping over things instead. No good. She rather liked him when he was clumsy, too.

She just liked him. That was the trouble. She didn't often like people, especially men. She might respect them or get along with them, and perhaps in time that could grow to liking, as with her crew. But to simply *like* someone, just because? She cast about for reasons, but the two that first sprang to mind made her cringe. Cliff was funny and he was sweet. God, she was the softest pirate in the history of pillaging.

"Can't keep this up much longer," he panted. His arms continued pumping, his entire body working with every stroke. He hadn't slowed even a fraction since he'd started.

"They're coming."

Sabine looked to the sky, shielding her eyes from the harsh light of the flare, hoping her words were true. Her dark-blue airship had been made for stealth. With the light disrupting her night vision, she might never see her until she was right on top of them.

"They're going to ram us," the duchess cried, pointing at the oncoming ship. Her voice trembled, and her face was pale with fear, but she didn't cower. Sabine was beginning to like her, too. Maybe retirement wasn't good for her.

An area of stars at the edge of Sabine's vision winked out of existence. Her ship! "They're here! Keep going. If we can avoid a collision for one more minute, we'll be safe."

"One more minute and my arms might fall off," Cliff grunted, but he didn't let up.

Sabine squeezed herself onto the seat beside him. "You take the left oar, I'll take the right."

He put the oar in her hands and slid over to give her more room. She'd been absolutely right that she couldn't row as well as he did, but her arms were strong and rested, and he visibly relaxed with the lessened burden. He counted off as they rowed, keeping their strokes synchronized, setting a grueling pace and trusting her to match it.

The sound of her ship's engine made Sabine's heart vibrate with joy. A ladder unfurled, dangling down nearly to the water as Nicole moved the craft into position. Sabine abandoned her oar, grabbing for the bottom rung.

"Duchess, you first. Then you, Hartleigh."

The duchess scrambled for the ladder and began to climb as best she could in her cumbersome dress. Hartleigh stood, wobbled as the lifeboat rocked in the waves, and fell back onto his seat.

"I can't. I think I sprained my ankle in that fall and I can hardly lift my arms. I'll never make it."

Sabine glanced up at the massive steamship bearing down on them and shoved the ladder into his hands. "Get the fuck off your ass and get up that ladder. There's a little girl waiting for you."

The mention of Lola spurred him to try again. He struggled up several rungs, too slowly to leave Sabine time to climb after him. She leapt onto the opposite side of the ladder instead, threading her arms through the openings and grabbing onto him to keep them both anchored in place.

The airship shot into the air, hoisting them out of danger just as the steamship clipped the rowboat, cracking the hull and starting its descent to a watery grave. Several more gunshots rang out as the pirates made a final, desperate attempt to knock their prey into the water. It wasn't happening. Sabine's grip on Cliff was like iron, and the crew was already reeling them in.

They banged and bumped against the hull on the way up, but with their limbs firmly tangled with the ladder and one another, they survived the jarring trip, and soon had the capable hands of her crew hauling them over the rail. Hartleigh took two staggering steps, then crumpled.

"I hurt everywhere," he moaned.

Sabine gave a single nod of thanks to her crew. There would be time enough later for proper gratitude and briefing. "To the closest Haven. And quickly."

"Aye, aye, Captain." Nicole and Jules said together, then sprang for the controls.

"What's a Haven?" the duchess asked. "Are you taking us back to Brighton?"

"Not a chance in hell. Someone in England set us up. It's not safe. We're hiding out and forming a plan of action."

"What?" She put her hands on her hips. "Unacceptable. You will take me home this instant."

"Duchess, on this ship, you do as I say."

"You can't do this to me! What will everyone at home think?"

"Probably that you're dead. Hawkes, please escort Her Grace down to my cabin to rest. But see that she doesn't wake Lola."

"Aye, Captain."

Sabine walked over to where Hartleigh still lay on the deck and sat beside him. "Well, Your Grace, looks as though you're getting your wish after all. The duke is dead. Long live the duke."

"There is no next duke. The duke is dead. The end. Right up until Her Grace the duchess goes home and reports that I am, in fact, entirely alive."

"Well, the plan still has a few kinks to work out."

"Or maybe not. Maybe I'll just die here on the deck, unable to move."

"You're being silly."

"I'm not. I'm in horrible pain."

Sabine leaned close to his ear and whispered, in a voice serious as death itself, "Duke, you have no idea what horrible pain is."

He sat up, wincing and rubbing his sore limbs. "Perhaps not. But I do hurt a lot."

She laughed. How did he manage to make her do that so often? "You were splendid tonight. I'll be sure to tell Lola how strong and brave you were." She pressed a kiss to his lips, sinking into the taste of him for a few glorious seconds before her brain seized control from her addled senses.

She shoved herself to her feet and hurried off to help with the ship, not looking back. He could find his own way to a bed for the night. Alone.

17

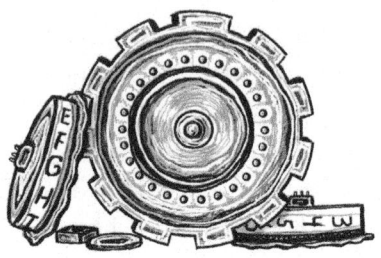

"This tea is substandard, the food is terrible, and I haven't even a proper table at which to eat it."

Cliff gazed across the cabin at the duchess, still her lofty self, even with her hair unbound and her dress a wrinkled mess. "You have the desk. That's good enough." He took another bite of the perfectly acceptable bread and cheese he held in a simple dish on his lap.

"I have no brush. I have no change of clothing. No one on board who knows the least thing about assisting a lady of my station. This is intolerable!"

Cliff rolled his shoulders. His muscles still ached this morning, and putting weight on his left foot sent shooting pains up his leg. Better than last night, though, so he wasn't complaining.

"She's not going to take you home, regardless of how much you rant, so I'd suggest you try to make the best of it."

The duchess glared at him. "Make the best of it? Luella will think I'm dead! The world will think you're dead and the title will sit empty! The king might confer it on some secret illegitimate child of his!"

"Horrifying," Cliff replied dryly.

"She will be tossed out with *nothing*."

"Everyone can go live in Sabine's house. She's not using it. She can send a telegram."

"The house will go to whomever receives the title. I'm certain of it. Parliament will make it so. It's only through the fault of some questionably written documents that it was sold in the first place. It ought to be entailed along with the land."

"Pretend I'm a clueless American and I don't know what the word 'entailed' means."

"It means it goes with the title, Hartleigh. To the next male in the line. It can't be sold, can't be given, only inherited."

"Great system. I'm shocked we rebelled against it."

"Why couldn't there have been a French relative," she moaned. "I might still have to deal with pirate-kissing, but at least he might appreciate a noble lineage."

Pirate-kissing. Oh, God, what a bad decision that had been. Cliff had no idea what he was going to say to Sabine now. *Sorry about that? That was really great, but we shouldn't do it again?* Or could he simply pretend it hadn't happened?

Never kiss a friend. Never kiss a business partner. Or a sort-of-friend-sort-of-business-partner. Stop wanting to kiss her again.

"Well, Duchess..." Cliff paused, tilting his head to study her not as a rank, but just as a woman. Young. Proud. At once strong and vulnerable. "You know, I don't even know your name."

"Of course not. Why would you? You have no need of it."

"Actually, I think I do. I'd like to know you as a person, not as a title. Let's start over." He set his plate on the floor and crossed the room, extending his hand to her. "Hi. I'm Cliff. It's a pleasure to meet you."

She frowned up at him, unmoving. He was moments away from admitting defeat when she sighed and shook his hand. "Amy."

Cliff lifted her hand and kissed her knuckles. "Good to

meet you at last, Amy. I will let you know the moment our fearless captain deems it safe for you to return home."

He released her hand and left, taking what remained of his breakfast with him.

Up on deck, Lola sat breaking her own fast in the middle of a circle of ex-pirates, her eyes shining as she listened to Sabine recounting last night's adventure. Cliff glanced around as he walked toward them. The ship had been tucked neatly into a grove of tall trees, hidden from view and miles from any city. He guessed they were somewhere in Europe, but their surroundings told him nothing specific.

"And he rowed and rowed, as hard as he could, while I signaled to the crew," Sabine was saying. "It was dark and cold and waves splashed us and the pirate ship was heading right for us, going faster and faster, but your father kept on going. Then, suddenly, the airship appeared in the sky above us, dropping a ladder and flying us to safety just as the pirate ship splintered the rowboat into a million tiny pieces."

"Wow."

Cliff limped toward them, wincing when Lola hopped up and rammed into his battered body.

"Daddy, Miss La Capitaine says you're a hero."

"I just did what I could to help."

"When do I get to help?"

Never. "Maybe when you're older, kiddo. Why don't you take a break from pirates and go down below to see Duchess Amy. She doesn't have anything to wear, so maybe you can help her look through Miss Diebin's things and you two can play dress-up."

"Nothing I own will fit the duchess," Sabine replied. "She is tall and curvy and I'm..." She made a chopping motion with her hand to indicate *flat*.

Cliff shook his head automatically. She wasn't flat. Her breasts were small, perhaps, but they were perky and round beneath her tight-fitted evening gowns. Or was she smaller than she looked beneath her protective armor? Twice, now, he'd bumped up against a hard surface while embracing her. One of these days he wanted to feel her without anything in between.

No, no, no. This needed to stop. *Stop thinking about her alluring dresses. Stop thinking about her leg-hugging trousers. Stop thinking about her laugh and her mouth. Stop thinking about* her.

"Walk the deck with me, Hartleigh, if you can," Sabine said. "We have plans to discuss."

Cliff hobbled along beside her, trying to put as little weight as possible on his injured ankle.

"Leg bothering you?"

"It's not terrible," he replied. "But not good, either. No running for a few days would be helpful, if you think we can manage it."

"Stop here." She paused along the rail, giving him a chance to lean on it and rest the foot. "This is private enough."

"This is about the next clue, I assume? You found the Greek pot?"

"I did, with little difficulty."

"And?" He started to lean toward her, eager to hear her news, then caught himself. He needed to maintain distance. This was business.

"The next artifact is something called the Helmet of Einar. It's located at the Illyrian Institute for the Education of Exceptional Young Women."

"The what?"

"It's a school in Switzerland. Very expensive. Very exclusive. Not only do they need to be filthy rich, but the girls also have to meet very exacting standards of both intellect and physical fitness. My father used to joke that if I brought home enough money he would send me there." Sabine turned away, staring out into the forest. "For a time, I actually believed him."

Her voice was flat, but not so much that she could hide the pain. Cliff had to restrain himself from reaching out to hug her.

He couldn't imagine what could possibly compel a father to be so cruel to his own child.

"He should have saved his pennies," Cliff replied. "You'd have been admitted in an instant."

She spun around so quickly that he flinched and almost lost his grip on the rail. Her soft, brown eyes were wide and full of sorrow—a glimpse of the lonely girl she must once have been. He braced himself, thinking she might kiss him again, knowing he wouldn't be able to pull away if she did.

Then a calm settled over her features and she straightened her shoulders. "I like to think that's true. It will be interesting, seeing the school of my childhood dreams. I hope I won't be too disappointed. Real life never lives up to our imaginings, does it?"

"No. It doesn't. Tell me more about the school. What can we expect there?"

"The Institute occupies a former medieval castle high in the mountains. It sits up on a rise above the local village. These days pupils are flown in and out by airship, but it's said that in the first days of the school the arduous trek to reach the castle was the proof of a student's physical fitness."

"I feel bad for the students who trudged all the way there and then were denied."

"I feel worse for those who never reached the castle."

Cliff cringed. "Okay, so castle in the mountains. We have an airship, fortunately. What's your plan? Drop from above and break in?"

Sabine folded her arms across her chest, her eyes flicking upwards behind her polished lenses. "Break in how? Through the massive, barricaded front doors or through the windows too small to climb through? It's a castle, Duke. It's built to keep people out."

"Okay, knock on the front door, then. 'Hi, I'm the Duke of Hartleigh and this is the notorious pirate, La Capitaine. We're here to plunder your treasures. May we come in?' Why is your nickname in French, by the way?"

"They say French is more passionate than German," she scoffed, tossing her long braid over her shoulder. "I called myself Die Kapitän, but I was flying mostly in and out of France, Spain, and the British Isles. People got it wrong, and it stuck."

"Have you considered changing it back?"

Her lips twitched. "I enjoy the shock and confusion on the faces of people when I shout at them in *passionate* German."

Cliff laughed. "I believe that. Sehr gut, meine Freundin."

Her lips flattened into a thin line. "Not friends. Business associates."

"Right." *Business associates who kiss passionately. For fuck's sake, Cliff, what have you gotten yourself into?* "So, uh, breaking in? What's the plan?"

"Lola."

"What? No!" Cliff stumbled backward, grimacing as he stepped with the injured foot. "No way. Have you forgotten that I was kidnapped *yesterday*? Those people could be following us from England, despite your little hiding places." He waved a hand at the thick forest surrounding the ship. "No way in hell am I letting Lola get involved in any of this. Not happening."

Sabine stepped toward him, staring up into his eyes. "It's the only way, Duke. They won't allow adults in. We won't get through the doors without a child. She's a perfect candidate for the school. They will allow her in at least for a day or two to meet the faculty and take the entrance examinations. She can either find the clue for us or open a door and let us in during the night. She will be thrilled to help, and you know it."

"No."

"Do you want to find the Heart or not?"

"I do. But nothing is worth risking her life over. I refuse to involve her, and that's final. End of discussion. Find another way."

"All of life is a risk, Hartleigh. She'll be as safe in that castle as anywhere in the world. Probably safer than on the ship."

Cliff spun around and stormed off as best he could on an injured leg. Sabine followed, easily matching his stride.

"She can do this. She would *love* to do this. What are you really afraid of? That she'll decide school sounds wonderful and leave you?"

He stumbled. No, he hadn't even considered that, but now that Sabine said it he suddenly began to second guess his fury every time the duchess—Amy—had even hinted at the idea of boarding school.

"Her safety comes first," he replied.

"Then enroll her at the school. She'll be behind castle walls and surrounded by a circle of like-minded people. How much safer can you get?"

Cliff shook his head, aiming for the stairs to the cabins below. He'd find Lola and they could read a book or play a game. Something. Anything. "I can't. I won't. She's all I have."

"Well, you've had seven years more than some of us ever get."

Her words were so harsh that he spun around, once again compelled to soothe her, but she was already walking away, her stride purposeful, her shoulders back and head up. Needing no one.

18

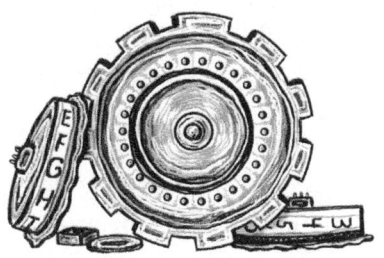

"Good afternoon, Your Grace." Lola dipped into some ridiculous facsimile of a curtsy.

Cliff raised an eyebrow. "What happened to, 'Hi, Daddy,' or 'Avast, ye scurvy dog'?"

"Miss Duchess Amy says I need to practice my princess manners because we're going to visit a castle. Did I do good?" She gazed up at him expectantly. Even here in one of the more sheltered spots on deck, the cool wind still whipped through her long, dark curls as the airship zipped across the skies of northern Italy.

"Um…"

"She says the castle is a school that teaches girls to be leaders. Like queens, I guess. 'Cept I can't be a queen when I grow up because I'm not really a princess. But you're a duke. So what does that make me?"

"Nothing, dear," the duchess said. Cliff turned around to glare at her. "You are Miss Kinsley. Only children born in wedlock can have a title."

"What's a wedlock?"

"Marriage, dear. Your parents must be married."

Lola put her hands on her hips. "Well, that's stupid."

You tell her, babe.

Amy walked toward Cliff and Lola, her aristocratic presence undiminished by the loose men's shirt and trousers she'd grudgingly adopted.

"That's why this school would be so very good for you, Lola, dear," she said. "It's the sort of school that produces female explorers, doctors, engineers, athletes. It can give you a place in the world that the irregularity of your birth would otherwise deny you."

Lola blinked up at her in confusion.

"Look, Amy," Cliff cut in, deliberately ignoring any sort of title or honorific. "She's not going away to school. She's only seven, and I don't know anything about this place."

"Don't be absurd. It's perfect for her. I should have thought of it immediately. It is *the* school for parents who want their daughters to make a statement in a man's world. And since you refuse to be discreet about your youthful mistake—"

"Lola was *never* a mistake."

Amy waved a hand. "Technicalities. Now, I've formulated a plan where you, Miss Diebin, and Lola will go to the school for a week or so. That should give you time to realize that it is perfect for your daughter. In the meantime, the crew will fly me home to England."

"So you and Sabine are conspiring against me, is that it?"

"Don't be silly. I asked where we were headed, and when she told me I knew it was all meant to be. You get a school for Lola, that pirate woman can do whatever it is she's heading there to do, and I can return home where I belong."

"She won't let you leave," Cliff predicted.

"Nonsense. And when you've finished, you can come home free to do your duty."

"My duty is to take care of my daughter, and abandoning her at some bizarre castle school is not the way to do that."

Lola grabbed hold of his jacket. "But we're going to visit,

right, Daddy? We're going to go inside the castle and look for secret passages and dungeons and things?"

Cliff looked past her, at the distant mountains ahead, growing ever larger as the ship neared its destination. He couldn't wait to arrive, and dreaded it at the same time. Nearly two days, now, he'd been on this ship, and he was beginning to go stir-crazy from lack of anything to do. Amy had taken over Sabine's personal cabin, and he'd spent the last two nights on a narrow bunk above a snoring Frenchman.

Sabine refused to suggest a different plan for retrieving the next clue, and his own lack of knowledge about the place left him with no other options to suggest. They'd barely spoken since their argument, communicating instead with irritated glances.

Worst of all, he was beginning to suspect that Sabine was right to think Lola would be at least as safe inside the castle as on the ship. Certainly no kidnappers would be barging in the way they'd done at the party in Brighton.

And he had to find some way in. The whole purpose of this treasure hunt was to get that battery for Lola. He wasn't going to give up on it.

"Daddy?"

"Sure, babe, we'll visit. Why don't you practice your curtsy again for the duchess? I need to talk to Miss Diebin for a moment."

Sabine stood at the helm, flying the ship, a pair of goggles protecting her eyes and her hair once again pulled back into a practical braid.

"A word with you, Captain?"

"Are you going to be civil now, Duke? Or did you simply wish to argue again?"

"I want to know about the men who tried to kidnap us. Do you know who they are and what they want? Will they be coming after us again? I can't make rational decisions without knowing everything. I don't expect you to confess all your deepest, darkest secrets, but I'm asking you to work with me. I told you Lola's safety takes priority, but I can't be sure I'm doing the right thing when I'm completely in the dark."

She stared at him a long moment, her expression unreadable behind the goggles. "Let me get one of the crew to take over and then we'll talk down below."

Cliff nodded. "Good. Thanks."

A short time later, they stood together in Sabine's cabin, the door closed. Sabine clasped her hands behind her back.

"You know that I have a coded document detailing the location of the Heart of Ra."

"Yes."

"I stole it."

Of course she had. She was a pirate, after all.

"From my sworn enemy," she continued. "A man who wants me dead. The infamous pirate Redbeard."

Cold fear washed over Cliff. He'd heard the name Redbeard, and it had always been in connection with ruthlessness and brutality.

"And now he's after me too," Cliff guessed.

Sabine didn't need to answer.

· · · ⚙ · · ·

"So you are the notorious Duke of Hartleigh."

The spry, gray-haired woman whisked into the room and took a seat at the head of the large, rectangular table, motioning for everyone to sit. Candles flickered overhead, the play of light and shadow across the stark castle room making Cliff wonder if he had somehow stepped back in time.

He helped Lola into a too-big chair and then took a seat beside her. "I don't think I'm 'notorious,' but I am the duke, through some outlandish accident of birth."

The woman chuckled. "As blunt as the papers say. Though I must admit, the emphasis on your Americanness had me expecting you to look more like a cowboy."

"I grew up in the city. The closest I've ever come to riding a horse is watching them pull the milk truck through my neighborhood as a boy. And even those were replaced by carriage dragons by the time I was a teenager."

"Ah, of course. Allow me to introduce myself. I am Klara von Arx, headmistress here at the Institute." She looked toward Sabine, who had taken the seat directly across from Cliff. "And you must be the legendary lady pirate La Capitaine."

Sabine smiled, but the expression was tight and no dimples appeared in her cheeks. "Like the duke, my reputation is apparently exaggerated."

"Oh, I doubt that. Now, tell me about this energetic young lady who brings you here."

Cliff nudged Lola. "Go ahead and introduce yourself, Lo."

Lola clambered down from her seat and made her ridiculous curtsy. "I am *Lady* Lola Kinsley from Chicago. My daddy is a duke and now we have a big house in England and maybe we can't go home. I want to be a pirate when I grow up like Miss La Capitaine. It's a pleasure to meet you." She curtsied again and scrambled back into her chair. "Oh, and I'm seven years old and my birthday is March fourth, so I'll be eight soon."

"A good age to begin your schooling," the headmistress said, her chin bobbing slightly. "Since your father has brought you here, I assume he has done his research, but would you like me to tell you about our school and the things our students learn here?"

"Yes, please."

Lola listened wide-eyed as Headmistress von Arx detailed the curriculum. Bits and pieces of the conversation stuck in Cliff's mind. All students learned English, French, and German. They could choose a variety of artistic and athletic pursuits. The faculty was half men and half women to foster a comfort with and expectation of intellectual discourse with both sexes.

The particulars mattered less to him than the overall

impression. Would Lola be safe here? Would Lola be happy here? His various options warred in his brain, none seeming to hold an edge over any other. He tried to weigh the relevant details, one at a time.

An enemy of Sabine's who calls himself Redbeard is chasing us.

He would kidnap me for information. He would surely take Lola hostage to get me to confess all I know.

This castle seems secure from what I have seen of it.

If no one knows she's here, she'd be even safer.

I wouldn't be able to help her refuel her biomechanics, and I would have to leave her a huge supply of luxene.

If she's with me, I will know she's safe.

Sabine knows Redbeard and how he operates. Staying close to her is better than trying to go anywhere alone.

She's the one who stole the coded document from him in the first place.

Maybe I should just give up on getting the Heart of Ra and run off to San Francisco like I'd intended. Disappear. Change our names. Let Sabine and Redbeard fight it out.

No. He couldn't do that. From what Sabine had told him, it seemed that Redbeard would stoop to any low to take the Heart for his own personal weapon. If Cliff could play a part in preventing such a thing from happening, he had to do so.

As much as he understood the previous duke's reasons for hiding the device, he disagreed with the decision. Someone could stumble upon it by accident. Someone else could invent the same sort of thing. Better to share the invention with the world. How many other people like Lola could benefit from the technology? And knowing that it was out there would allow people to be aware of potential weapons and take measures to prevent their creation or protect against them. If Redbeard alone could make such a weapon, no one would be able to react until it was too late.

All throughout dinner, the same arguments played in his head, getting him nowhere. He had to find the Heart of Ra and protect Lola, but no best strategy presented itself. His anxiety rose alongside Lola's excitement, and by the time they set off for a tour of the school he was ready to run through the castle, just to shake himself out of the stupor. Anything to end the cycle of self-doubt.

"Are you okay?" Sabine's arm brushed his and he jumped. "You look pale. And nervous." Her eyebrows twitched. "I don't think the castle is haunted."

Cliff managed only a half-hearted laugh.

"I attempt humor for you and it still doesn't help?" She sighed. "I'm regretting telling you about Redbeard. You've been quiet and unhappy ever since."

"No, I'm glad you told me. I'd rather know. I'm just feeling like I did back when Lola was a baby. As if I have no idea at all how to take care of her."

He forced himself to scan the walls of the classroom they had entered. A suit of armor stood in one corner, with an antique sword mounted on the wall nearby. This was the third room with such a display. He leaned close to Sabine.

"Maybe we can locate that Helmet of Einar during this tour," he whispered. "Then we can head off to the next clue at once and get to the treasure as soon as possible."

"A nice thought, but I wouldn't count on that. I don't expect to see more than a fraction of the school."

Two rooms later, the tour ended.

"When do we get to see the secret passages and dungeons?" Lola asked.

"We do not have either of those things here at the school," the headmistress replied.

Lola's face fell. "Oh."

"But I hope you like what you have seen so far."

"I like that it's old and creepy."

The headmistress looked at Cliff, who answered with a shrug.

"The next step in the process will be for Lola to sit for the examinations," Headmistress von Aux explained. "We need to assess her current knowledge, the pace at which she learns new things, her physical fitness, and her ability to interact with both adults and children. In order to achieve the clearest results, we space the examinations out over three days. This gives her time to rest between each evaluation, and for us to observe her comfort with the school environment."

"Okay. Is there a guest room of some sort where we can stay during this process?" Maybe they hadn't found the helmet yet, but if they could sneak around at night, there was a good chance they could still find it before morning.

"Lola will stay in a student dormitory with other girls near her age. Parents must lodge outside the castle walls. There is an inn down in the village that will accommodate you."

"But…" All his hopes of finding the next clue quickly or even of deferring his decision crumbled.

Sabine touched his arm. "Sorry, Duke," she murmured. "I'd pick another way if I could."

She'd been right all along. Without Lola's help, they'd never find the artifact.

"She's never been away from me overnight," Cliff explained, feeling for the first time a truly over-protective father.

"This is the first time away from home for many of our girls," the headmistress replied. "Rest assured, very few are upset by the separation."

Probably because most of the girls were from families where the parents hardly knew their children. They were more likely to miss their governesses.

"And you are allowed to return during visiting hours in the afternoon to see how the examinations are progressing," the headmistress continued. "Of course, should any problem arise, we would contact you at once."

"Ah." Cliff's fingers clenched involuntarily. Was he really going to do this? Was there no other choice? "We'll, uh, have to discuss it for a moment as a family so I know she knows exactly what's going on and where I'll be, but otherwise, yes, she can stay the three days."

"Of course. You can take what time you need in the room where we dined, and when you are ready, we will see about your luggage and your rooms."

"Thank you." He trudged along to the dining room, his hands shaking.

"If I stay here for three days, does that mean I have to stay here forever?" Lola asked suspiciously.

"Come on in here and I'll explain everything," Cliff promised. "You're going to get to do some important big-girl things these next few days."

His fate was sealed. He'd just involved his daughter in a pirate's treasure hunt.

Goddammit. I'm a horrible parent.

19

Tonight was the night. Yesterday, after leaving Lola at the castle, Sabine and Cliff had practiced creeping through the halls of the village inn and along the quiet streets. The duke had done well at moving silently, despite his tendency to drift while walking. What he lacked in natural grace, he made up for with a dogged determination. Sabine respected that.

A clock in the distance chimed midnight. Perfect. They'd paid another visit to the castle this afternoon and received a detailed update from Lola. Time to move ahead with the plan.

Sabine slipped into the small bedroom Cliff had taken at the inn, closing the door softly behind her. The room was identical to her own, save for the trunk with his things. A simple bed, a washstand in the corner, and a lone window with a view of the empty streets outside.

She held out a small, rounded piece of leather dangling from a narrow cord. "Put this on."

"An eyepatch?" He turned it over in his hands. "Are you trying to turn me into a pirate?"

Sabine tapped her foot impatiently. "Must you question

everything I say? And keep your voice down. No one is supposed to know I'm in your room."

Cliff made a short, sniffing noise. "The entire village thinks we're lovers, and half of them think you're Lola's mother. They probably *assume* you're in my room."

"Fine. Feel free to make all the sex noises you'd like."

The eyepatch slipped from his grasp and he fumbled and flailed, managing to do nothing but ram his elbow into the wall.

"Ow." He bent to retrieve the eyepatch.

"Hopefully everyone will think that was the bed banging against the wall."

Cliff grimaced. "Will you stop with the sex talk? I really don't think this is the time."

Sabine leaned against the door, placing her free hand on the hip that now jutted out. "Embarrassed, Duke?"

"No. But… We're just friends. All that—inside the whale thing—was a mistake. Correct? We were a little frenzied from the dark, and the touching."

Sabine's entire body heated from the memory of that kiss. She couldn't even remember the last time she'd been kissed like that. Maybe never. She'd been so out of her head that night. Had circumstances allowed, she would have laid herself bare for him without a thought to the consequences. What a disaster that would have been. No more kissing.

"Let's go. Time for a more rewarding nighttime activity. Keep the eyepatch over your left eye until I tell you to switch it."

She expected the castle to have areas of greater and lesser darkness. Having one dark-adjusted eye and one light-adjusted eye would make their search faster and safer. Particularly with someone as accident prone as Cliff.

Sabine opened the door, closing it and locking it as silently as possible behind them. The snow squeaked beneath their boots as they walked the narrow, winding road leading up to the castle. Hartleigh shivered, clutching the lapels of his coat together to block the wind. Once again his suit was inappropriate for their outing, but he didn't seem to own any other sort of clothing. Sabine had chosen trousers, a simple shirt, and her warmest jacket. The cold still cut through her clothing, but she refused to acknowledge it.

"Here." She stopped Cliff with a hand to his arm, pulling away quickly to avoid any further mentions of kissing. She pointed up the rocky slope at the wall above. "That's the easiest point of entry. If we climb here, we should be able to get over the outer wall."

The wind had swept the jagged rocks bare of snow, making their climb an easy one. Hartleigh had no difficulty keeping up, and with Sabine's advice to only move one limb at a time he didn't even stumble.

"Ready for a boost?" Cliff asked when they reached the base of the wall.

Sabine gave a nod, and he picked her up, lifting her high enough to scramble up on top of the wall. She unwound the rope she'd tied around her waist, dangled one end down to him, and dropped into the castle to find a place to secure the other end.

A growl behind her made her jump. A fanged mechanical beast the size of a large dog prowled toward her, its crystalline eyes glinting in the moonlight.

Sabine sprang into action before the creature could attack, leaping up onto its back and lashing the rope to a hind leg. Her own grip plus the weight of the dragon would be enough to support Cliff as he climbed. She gave the signal tug on the rope and slipped from the guard dragon's back.

The mechanical animal lunged, still growling, only to tip over when the rear leg didn't move as expected. It lay on the ground, thrashing, trying to right itself and failing. Not especially smart, these dragons. More to intimidate than anything, she guessed.

Cliff dropped down from atop the wall, staggering backward when he spied the guard dragon.

"What in hell is that thing?" he hissed.

Sabine untied the rope and the creature at last picked itself up.

"Wolf, maybe? The head is dog-like, but the body a bit too round, and its feet are ridiculously wide and flat, but that may be for walking on the snow."

He backed slowly away from it. "It's hideous and it's snapping at me."

"They're only for show. Follow me. Lola's door was this direction."

Sabine and Cliff made their way to the small gate beside the castle's chapel, skirting a second guard dragon with feline features and spikes on its back. Cliff tapped out the prearranged code on the door and they waited.

A tingle of anxiety ran just beneath her skin. As Captain, she delegated tasks on a regular basis, but only to adults who had proven their competence. Tonight she had to rely on a child who had never done anything of this sort. Sabine had to remind herself of what she'd done at Lola's age. She'd brought in nearly all the household money. She'd kept herself fed and bought her own clothing. Old before her time.

The clank of the heavy bolt unlatching made Cliff jump beside her. A moment later the door creaked open. They slipped inside, and Sabine closed and latched the door with a great deal more finesse than Lola had opened it.

Lola immediately wrapped her arms around Cliff's middle. "Sorry I was noisy. It was heavy."

He hugged her back. "You did good. Show us what you've discovered."

She looked up at him. "Do I get a pirate eyepatch too?"

"I'll give you this one when we're all done. Let's go." He put a finger to his lips to quiet her, and the trio started off through the dim castle halls.

Lola led the way deep into the castle, whispering details on the relevant areas. "Dining hall. Lots of armor on the walls. Library. No armor, but lots of stuff. It's like a museum. Classrooms down this hall." She dashed up a set of stairs, silent on her bare feet, her nightgown swishing around her legs. "More classrooms that way, and down here are the dormitories."

Cliff walked her to her door and kissed her goodnight. "You did great, babe. Get some sleep. We'll see you tomorrow."

With Lola safely back to bed, Sabine nudged Cliff toward the classrooms. If they were anything like the rooms on the tour, they were unlikely to contain anything too extraordinary, but it was worth a quick investigation.

She slipped into the first room, reaching behind her eyeglasses to slide her eyepatch from left to right. Cliff followed her lead. The classroom had none of the low-burning oil lamps that lit the halls, but the old pirate trick allowed them to see well enough to navigate the space and confirm that it contained no ancient helmets.

Room after identical room, they continued, finding nothing. The dining hall was, indeed, full of armor, but none of it looked the least bit Scandinavian. Sabine shook out a few helmets, just to be thorough.

"The library?" Cliff asked, adjusting his eyepatch and opening the door. Even in the darkness he hadn't bumped into a single thing this evening.

Sabine nodded, following a few steps behind. He walked quickly, without drifting. Peculiar.

The library could have been decorated by the Mad Duke himself. Books and curiosities lined every wall, with more objects and art in display cases scattered throughout the room. A number of items had been set carefully in the center of tables beside notebooks and drawing implements.

"Looks like they actually study some of these artifacts," Cliff murmured, picking up a broken chunk of crockery and examining it.

"But no helmets. We may have to look inside of things." She grasped his shoulders and turned him to look the direction she wanted. "That chest beneath the window."

On closer examination, the chest was more accurately a padded bench, as long and wide as a grown man. Sabine tapped the side of it with her toe and it made a hollow sound. The top didn't lift off, but a moment of running her fingers along the edge found a latch. She unhooked it and opened the bench to peer inside. Empty.

She had just begun to lower the lid, when the echo of approaching footsteps made her jump.

"Every time," a disgruntled voice griped in German. "Something disrupts the guard dragons, and they make me walk the whole damn castle. A strong wind could disrupt those dragons! Worthless things. They ought to be sold for scrap."

The scrap man himself was already stepping into the hollow bench. He pulled on Sabine's arm, and she climbed in after him, not seeing any better option. She pulled the lid down over them, hearing the latch fall into place.

Not this again.

How many times was she going to end up lying atop him or crammed into some small dark space beside him? Outside their tiny prison, the night watchman stomped around the library, still complaining to himself, but his words hardly registered. Her traitorous body had robbed her of all her senses, shrinking her world to the rise and fall of Cliff's chest beneath her, the warmth of his body, and the strength of the arms that had wrapped around her.

She inhaled sharply, her nostrils filling with the scent of ordinary soap. No fancy fragrances or smelly hair pomades for this duke. Sensible and unfussy. She liked that about him.

The door to the library banged closed, but Sabine didn't move. *Get up,* she told herself. *Get back to work. Stop indulging your ridiculous, lustful urges.*

"I'm beginning to think you enjoy being on top of me," Cliff whispered.

Actually, she wanted to be under him. On a bed. Clinging to him so tightly that her nails dug into his skin as he pounded into her. For now she shut him up with a kiss.

His tongue plunged between her parted lips, sparring with hers, tasting, teasing, setting her aflame. Their eyeglasses clinked together. His hands roamed down to her backside, cupping her buttocks, rocking her against the stiff bulge of his erection.

To hell with everything. They hadn't found the helmet tonight. They'd have to make another attempt tomorrow. Better to give up and return to the inn, where they could finish this in a bed.

Cliff broke off the kiss suddenly. "Something's poking me." He shifted this way and that, his arm sliding off her to search for the offending object. "There. Not sure what—" His words turned into a stifled yelp as the ground gave way beneath them.

20

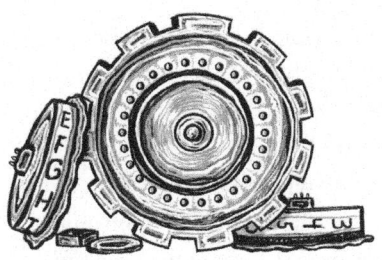

"Goddammit." Cliff rolled over, trying to assess the damage. His ankle had almost recovered from his fall the other day, and now he had to go tumbling down some hidden staircase into total darkness. Even the eyepatch didn't help down here.

Gingerly, he tested his arms and legs. All working. More bruises to add to the collection. It was a very good thing he was going to stop kissing Sabine for certain this time, because if they ever got naked, they'd just be a mess of purple and yellow. Were there any spots on him she'd be able to touch without it hurting?

He sat up, looking around, but the darkness was absolute. In the unnatural silence, he could hear his breathing and the roar of blood past his ears.

"Hartleigh." Sabine whispered his title in a sharp, commanding tone. "Are you hurt?"

"I don't think so. You?"

"You cushioned my fall. Flip your eyepatch. I'm going to use my torch."

Cliff moved the eyepatch and adjusted his spectacles. Her

light clicked on, illuminating blank stone walls and an empty chamber with a single archway leading out.

"Lola's dungeons?" he asked.

"Perhaps. But why would the castle builders hide the entrance?" Sabine shined her light up the stairs at the hinged bottom of the storage bench. "Could it be something that was done during renovations? There may be an ordinary entrance somewhere else, but this one is clearly meant to be secret."

He struggled to his feet. Ow. More bruises for certain. "Maybe they wanted to keep students out."

"Then close the whole place off."

"Maybe the faculty wanted to continue using the rooms."

"For what purpose? Dungeons aren't warm, sunny, useful sorts of places."

"Storage?" Cliffed shrugged. "Maybe we'll find the helmet down here in a pile of junk."

"You're absurdly optimistic, did you know that? More likely we'll stumble into danger and have to fight or flee."

He rubbed a sore spot on his arm. "Thanks. I feel much better now."

"One of us needs to be sensible." She angled the flashlight at the passageway. "Shall we explore?"

He gave a nod and followed her into the dark hall. The corridor ran only a few yards before ending at another staircase—wider than the first and fully visible, thank God. It twisted down in a spiral, the steps disappearing into the darkness. Slowly Sabine and Cliff descended, around and around, at least two full stories deeper into the mountain, by his best estimation.

"Not especially practical for storage, is it?" Sabine said dryly, starting down the long hall at the base of the staircase.

"Make fun of me all you want," he retorted. "I intend to continue believing that we *will* find the helmet and complete this next step. To think otherwise is to give up, and I'm not doing that."

That half-smirk he liked returned to her lips. "I do admire your tenacity. You may actually succeed at faking your death after all. Though I expect you'll go through many both literal and figurative stumbles to get there."

"That's life. Trip and fall, get up, keep going. I've never been one to lie around waiting for help."

"Neither have I." She placed her hand on a simple wooden door that didn't look especially dungeon-like. "Shall we?"

Cliff looked directly into her liquid-brown eyes and gave her his best wicked smile. "Sure. What could go wrong?"

She poked a single finger into the center of his chest. "You. Are. Evil."

"Simply trying to keep pace with my pirate partner."

She turned away, testing the door handle and slowly pushing into the room. "Pirates don't—"

"Have partners. Yes, I remember." He moved closer, peering over her shoulder to see into the room. "So what's… Damn. Was the Mad Duke here?"

That was a bit of an exaggeration, he supposed. The room was crowded, certainly, but enough space had been left to allow him and Sabine to walk between the large steel and brass objects that filled the chamber.

"Pieces of some larger device," he mused, running a hand over a smooth piece of metal.

"How do you know that?"

Cliff grinned. "This is my profession, Captain. I've disassembled so many broken machines I could do it in my sleep. There is no joint, hinge, splice, or fastening that I haven't seen. This here…" He touched the cylindrical end of one piece. "Fits into that hole, there." He pointed. "This unfinished end is probably meant to be welded to another piece when the machine is constructed. Put together, I'm guessing this thing would be wider than the room."

"Can you guess at what it is?"

"Maybe if I could lay all the pieces out and look at them.

They would have to be hauled outside, one-by-one, and assembled outdoors."

"Not something the students here would do, I don't imagine."

"Don't know. Maybe older girls who want to be engineers?"

Sabine gestured back at the door. "No helmets here. Next room."

The room across the hall was more of the same. Large pieces that may even have been part of the same machine as those in the first room. They glanced around quickly, then moved further down the hall.

"Well." The beam from Sabine's flashlight traversed the third, much larger room. "This is where they make the pieces."

Cliff walked the room, examining the workbenches and tools of the underground engineering laboratory. The room was clean, highly organized, and fully-stocked. Small tools hung from pegboards on the walls. Large tools had their areas marked out with painted lines on the floor. Projects in progress sat up against the walls or rested neatly in the center of workspaces. Against one wall, a cabinet of narrow drawers held notebooks, schematics, and other drawings. A few sketches had been tacked to the wall above. The plan in the center caught his eye.

"Oh, fuck."

"What?" Sabine rushed to his side. "What did you... Scheiße."

"Does that, or does it not look like the machine that kidnapped us?"

He didn't know why he'd bothered to ask. The round chamber with its gaping jaws and fin-like propulsion system couldn't possibly be anything else. The small sketch in the corner showing a mechanical arm lifting it onto a ship only confirmed his initial assumption.

"Scheiße," Sabine repeated.

"Agreed. Someone at this school is manufacturing

mechanical monstrosities, possibly using students as unwitting, unpaid workers. And Redbeard is a customer."

"Or an employer. His permanent home is in the Schwarzwald, at most three hours away by airship. He's the criminal king of all of southern Germany and even moving somewhat into Austria-Hungary. Why not Switzerland, too? For all I know, he owns this school."

"Jesus Christ." Cliff whirled away, racing for the door.

Sabine jogged after him, grabbing his shoulder. "Hartleigh, where are you going?"

"I'm getting Lola out of here, right now."

"No, you can't. If we do that, we lose our chance to get the helmet."

"Fuck the helmet. Redbeard probably already has it. We're screwed. I'm leaving and taking Lola with me."

Her hand clamped hard on his arm. "He doesn't have the helmet. Whatever his connection to this place, he doesn't know about the Sphinx or the clues. All he knows is that we're searching."

"If anyone at this school is in his pay, then he knows we're here. He might not know what we're looking for, but he'll be coming for us. I won't leave Lola here all alone, and that's final." He shook himself from her grip and walked off, not knowing how he'd navigate in the dark if he walked out of range of her flashlight. It didn't matter. He was leaving. Now.

Sabine ran to keep pace with his furious strides. "I'll stay."

Cliff stopped so suddenly that she crashed into him. "What?" He turned to look at her.

"I'll stay here with her. I can easily sneak into the dormitory area. Closets, trunks, under beds—the hiding places are endless. I'll stay with her overnight. You return to the village, make certain our things are packed and put my signal light out on the roof so my crew knows to stay in the area after their next fly-by. If anyone asks after me, say I'm ill and sleeping and don't want to be disturbed. I'll make certain that both Lola and I are ready to depart tomorrow when you arrive for visiting hours."

"And what if you haven't located the helmet?"

"Then we'll improvise."

"And if something happens during the night?"

Sabine's eyes narrowed and her jaw tightened. "I will guard your daughter with my life," she vowed. She drew the dagger she wore at her hip and ran a finger along the edge until a bead of blood welled on her skin. "You have my solemn blood oath."

Cliff reached for her hand, wanting to tend to the small wound, but she dodged his touch, sticking her finger into her mouth and thrusting the dagger back into its sheath. He let his hand drop. She didn't need him. He had to remember that. More and more often, though, he seemed to be needing her.

"Okay," he agreed. "I'll go back. You watch Lola. Tomorrow we get that helmet and get the hell out."

"Good." She pointed the flashlight in the opposite direction from the way they had come. "Let's see where the hall leads. There must be an entrance large enough to move the machine pieces out. I would bet there's a hidden door right in the side of the mountain. You'll probably find yourself mere steps from the village."

"Now who's being optimistic?"

"Realistic, Duke. You'll slip out the secret entrance, go back to the inn, and rest up for tomorrow. Everything will be fine."

"Yes, very realistic."

"It will be fine," she repeated, her voice hard as iron. "I'll make it so."

21

From her cramped hiding place in the corner, behind a suit of armor and two pots overflowing with ferns, Sabine munched on the cheese she'd stolen for lunch and watched. Just like old times. Though Lola was an unusual sort of mark.

Most of the students had abandoned the sitting room, reluctantly rising from the leather chairs and plush couches to return to their classrooms. Lola lingered behind, wandering slowly, examining the tapestries hanging from the walls.

The guard dragon Sabine had roped the night before limped into the room, its damaged rear leg slightly misaligned. Not as tough as it looked, apparently. It made a low, growling sound, but Lola bounded happily toward it. She looked it over, then patted its head and began to stroke its back.

"You're such a cute dragon!" the girl exclaimed. "Can I ride you?" She slung a leg over, positioning herself in the center of the creature's back. It shook, trying to toss her off, but Lola's excellent balance kept her in her seat. She giggled and patted the dragon's head again.

"Step down, Miss Kinsley." The headmistress approached,

and Lola slid to the floor with a sigh. "This is one of our guard dragons, and he is here for repairs, not for fun. He's been having problems all night, it seems."

"What does he guard?" Lola asked. "Treasure?"

"Of a sort. He protects the castle from intruders, keeping all you girls safe."

"That's not as exciting." She ran her hand along the dragon's back. "You should make him growl meaner. He's too cute to be scary."

"You like machines, Miss Kinsley?"

Lola shrugged. "I like the animal ones. I miss my spiders."

"A school is no place for pets, I'm afraid, but if you are interested in dragons, we do teach engineering here. Most people think women shouldn't be engineers, but we would like to change that outdated attitude."

By building giant machines in a dungeon laboratory? Sabine had to stop herself leaning forward for a better view.

"Tagget Industries hires girls," Lola said.

Von Arx blinked in surprise. "Ah…"

"Daddy said so. He says he's not sure if he hates Mr. Tagget because he once sold bad luxene that could've been dangerous, or if he admires him because he doesn't care what a person looks like, or if they're a boy or a girl, he just cares if they're good at their job."

The headmistress collected herself. "I can see you and your father have had excellent conversations regarding your future. Are you rested from the morning examinations? I would like to take you to the science room to take the engineering test. You're a bit young, but I'd like to see what you can do regardless. We are always looking for mechanically-minded girls."

Sabine's muscles tensed. Was that what this school did? Seek out girls with an aptitude for automechanology and use them to build machines for the criminal market? She couldn't imagine any leader with sense would involve girls in secret projects and then release them back to their families and friends. Someone would talk. Which meant that most likely they were indoctrinating the girls from a young age with the intent of including them in the secret projects when they were both well-trained and fully committed to the cause. Rearing them to be criminals.

Because a laboratory hidden inside a mountain couldn't be anything but illegal. If the machines were meant for legitimate customers, they'd be in plain sight. Advertised to the world to proclaim the talents of the women who constructed them. Doing what Klara von Arx claimed the school wished to do.

Lola and the headmistress departed, leaving the limping guard dragon to be wrangled by an unhappy servant. The moment the room was empty, Sabine darted from her hiding place and hurried toward the classroom wing. She'd stolen a school uniform and braided her hair into two looped plaits, the way many of the older girls wore it, but the disguise wouldn't withstand any close interaction. The more she kept completely out of sight, the better.

She couldn't stray too far from Lola. No little girl deserved to be lured into the criminal life Sabine had grown up in. Especially not a sweet, smart kid with a father as devoted and loving as Cliff.

Hartleigh, she corrected herself. This intimacy of first names had to stop. She wasn't going to let herself get duped by his kind words and protective inclinations. His love for Lola was mucking with Sabine's head. It called to that lonely little girl she'd once been, yearning for someone to love her and protect her. But she'd long since grown up, relying on no one but herself. Better to go it alone and know where you stand than to trust someone and endure their betrayal.

The hall leading to the classrooms had no good places to hide. Sabine moved down the corridor, clutching the large book she could use to shield her face if anyone happened by. She pressed her ear to each closed door until she heard the voices of Lola and the headmistress.

Sabine waited just long enough to be certain they were truly doing an examination, then headed upstairs to the dormitory. If they followed the morning's pattern, von Arx would send Lola up to rest after the exam. Lola would play with the toys provided for the younger girls or maybe read a book until she grew bored and wandered off to explore.

Sabine swiped a pillow and concealed herself under Lola's bed, seizing the opportunity for a nap. After Hartleigh had left through the secret mountain exit, she'd spent hours retracing their steps, rechecking the rooms, looking for anything they might have missed. She'd examined every helmet in the whole damn castle, but had come up empty.

The possibility that Redbeard might have learned what she was after and gotten to it first made Sabine's skin crawl. She fell into an uneasy sleep, where past and present worries commingled in a confusion of disjointed dreams.

Lola's voice woke her. "I'm not tired."

"Your body may not be," said an unfamiliar voice. Sabine peeked out from behind the curtain of bedding. An older student was ushering Lola into the room. "But the examinations are hard work for your mind."

"It wasn't hard. It was fun. I got to take apart a machine and build a bridge out of sticks."

The older girl was unmoved. "Headmistress always insists we rest on examination days. You can play with the toys if you don't want to sleep."

"I'm bored of dolls." Lola moved her hands as if to stuff them into pockets, but the school uniform had none. "Is there sewing stuff?"

The older girl walked to a chest of drawers, removed a box and handed it to Lola. "You can make a doll a new dress instead. Someone will come to fetch you when your father comes to visit. Don't wander off this time. They won't let you in the school if you can't obey the rules."

The girl left without another word, closing the door firmly

behind her. Lola opened the sewing kit, selected a piece of cloth, and cut it to the size she wanted. After half-a-dozen failed attempts, she finally threaded a needle, then began stitching the crooked square of cloth to the outside of her uniform skirt.

Sabine grinned. The headstrong girl was making herself a pocket. A terrible, ugly pocket with loose, uneven stitches. It would probably fall off the first time she tried to put anything heavy in it. She'd be reprimanded and told to remove it the moment any of the faculty saw it. The pocket of a true pirate princess.

Sabine let Lola finish her project, catching a few more moments of rest before whispering her name.

Lola's head jerked up. "Who said that?"

Sabine poked her head out. "Good afternoon, Miss Kinsley."

"Miss La Capitaine? Why are you under my bed?"

Sabine put a finger to her lips. "We must talk very quietly. I've been hiding in the castle, waiting to talk to you."

"Is Daddy here, too? Did you find the treasure?"

"No and no. Your father should be here soon, but we didn't find the right helmet."

Lola's mouth turned down in a sad little pout. "Oh. Does that mean I have to stay here another day? I'm bored. They won't let me explore by myself, and I don't like these clothes." She turned to show off her pocket. "But I fixed this dress a little bit. I wish I had my spiders. I can't put the real ones in a pocket because they just crawl away. Did you know there are lots and lots of real spiders in castles? I have a big box full of them. There's even a giant one in a cage in the science classroom. I named him Lucas. Did you look in *his* helmet?"

Sabine's eyebrows arched. "A giant spider with a helmet?"

"Well, it looks like a helmet. It's all banged-up and old looking and it was stuck in the cage on its side. Lucas crawls inside it and hides."

Sabine scurried out from beneath the bed. "Show me."

"Right now? But there's girls in the classroom. They came in to do school things right after I did my machine test."

"I want to leave the moment your father arrives, and to do that, we need to look at that helmet. If the classroom is full of girls, we'll need a distraction. Just how many spiders do you have in that box?"

Lola fetched a box from the shelf that held her possessions. "This many." She flipped the lid open for just an instant. What must have been one hundred or more spiders crawled over all sides of the box and atop one another. "I'll let them go later. I promise. I know Daddy won't let me bring them home."

"I think we should let them go now." Sabine lifted her schoolgirl skirt and withdrew her watch from the pocket of her trousers. Nearly the top of the hour. Classes would be changing soon. "If we do this quickly, we might even be able to find our treasure before your father arrives. But we need to go now. Bring those spiders and pretend I'm one of the older girls sent to show you around."

Sabine and Lola hurried down to the classroom wing, waiting outside the science classroom until the door opened and students began to exit. They pressed close to the crowd. Sabine kept her head ducked to hide her face and shielded Lola from view with her body.

"Now," she whispered.

Lola flung a handful of spiders up into the air. Several girls shrieked as arachnids rained down on them.

"It's only a spider," a more level-headed girl commented.

Lola threw another handful.

"They're everywhere! They're falling from the ceiling!"

The group erupted into chaos. Arachnophobic girls screamed and ran, batting at their clothes and pawing at their hair, while other girls and one overwhelmed teacher struggled to calm them down or shoo the spiders away. Girls from nearby rooms also began to run and shout, as their schoolmates barreled into them.

"Don't hurt the spiders!" shouted one girl who seemed to have the same affinity for the creatures that Lola did.

Sabine pointed to the doorway, and Lola dumped the rest of the spiders on the floor.

"They're coming from the classroom!" Sabine cried in German, pitching her voice as high as possible to sound young and terrified. The last of the girls fled, and she and Lola slipped inside and shut the door.

Sabine grabbed a table and dragged it in front of the door to temporarily prevent anyone entering. She was betting heavily on this helmet being the one she needed, but she'd searched everywhere else. If this failed, she would have to resort to begging and bribery.

"Here." Lola grabbed Sabine's arm and dragged her across the room to a large terrarium full of wilting greenery and a chunk of tarnished gold something.

"That's a helmet?"

"Yeah. Look down from the top." Lola climbed up on a chair and lifted the mesh top off the terrarium. "Or I can just pull it out." She reached into the cage and removed the metal object. Cracked and dented, the Norse-style helmet brought an ear-to-ear grin to Sabine's face. Lola tipped something out of the helmet before handing it over.

"This is promising."

Sabine turned the helmet over in her hands, examining it both outside and in. One of the side pieces that protected the ear and face was badly cracked. She grabbed hold of it, tugging and flexing until it came off in her hand, sliding free from a thinner strip of metal underneath.

"Almost as if it were meant to do that," she murmured.

The clue had been scratched directly into the metal: *5. Cat mummy. Hunterian.* Sabine committed the message to memory, then drew her dagger and scored the metal until the words were obliterated.

"Time to go, Lola. Let's grab your things and go meet your father. If anyone questions why I'm here, we are saying he sent me to sneak in and prove the school was unsafe, and now he won't allow you to stay."

She nodded and slipped something black and fuzzy into her makeshift pocket. Sabine didn't ask. Lola could take whatever she wanted from this school. Only the clue truly mattered.

Sabine pulled the table away from the door and listened before opening it. The noise had died down. The girls had presumably been herded off to class, and no one had yet tried to enter the science room.

Sabine and Lola stepped into the hall, walking briskly toward the staircase. They had nearly reached it when a woman dressed in the austere ensemble of a teacher stepped out from a nearby doorway. Sabine froze in recognition.

"Well, well," the woman said, smirking as she drew a revolver from a hip pouch. "If it isn't little Sabine the thief. Papa is going to be so disappointed in you."

22

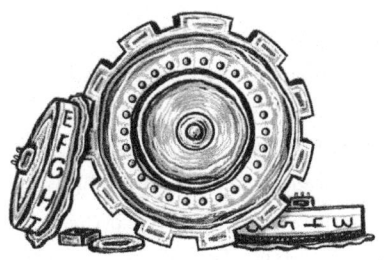

Cliff smiled at the girls skating circles on the small ice rink in the castle bailey. He hadn't been skating in ages. This winter he had been too occupied with unexpected duke business to take Lola out on the ice.

Next winter. We'll make up for it.

He stiffened. Did it ever get cold enough in San Francisco for ice skating? Probably not. Damn. Maybe not next winter after all. He needed to start accepting that his life would never be the same. They'd be okay. Lola would have the Heart of Ra and never have to worry about fuel again. They could always travel north to go skating.

Cliff glanced at the unmoving guard dragons that flanked the main doors. Powered down for the day, they looked like ugly statues. Neither were the ones he and Sabine had encountered the night before. He shivered. The sooner he was done with this school, the better.

Despite Sabine's insistence, he'd hardly slept. He'd circled the village three times before the urge to storm the castle faded enough to let him return to the inn. Then he'd spent another hour packing their things. *Her* things. She'd only had a small bag with two changes of clothes, but he'd had to move them from the drawer to the bag. He'd had his hands on that sexy, emerald green corset and her tiny, powder blue knickers. Cliff had spent far too long thinking about those knickers. Small enough and light enough to be comfortable beneath trousers. Practical, though still feminine. He was dying to see what she looked like wearing nothing else.

Packing her clothes had demolished his resolve to stop kissing her. When he had finally slept, his dreams had contained an alarming mixture of running from enemies and erotic encounters in dark locations. The moment they were back on the airship, he intended to pull Sabine aside for a talk. He would tell her, in a perfectly calm and rational manner, that he didn't see any reason for denying their mutual attraction.

The *'don't get involved with a friend'* rule rattled around in the back of his head, but he pretended he couldn't hear it.

He would suggest they find a quality hotel with a nice bed and spend a pleasant night together. They'd no doubt both feel immeasurably better the next morning. Sating their physical needs would help eliminate any distraction those desires were causing during their treasure hunt. It was all highly logical, he told himself.

"Welcome, Your Grace."

Cliff's brows knitted together. Why was the headmistress herself greeting him in the front hall? A man dressed in the simple, brown garments of a farm worker or manual laborer stood beside her. A castle caretaker, perhaps, or security guard?

Another shiver ran through him, this one racing out to the very tips of all his limbs. Was this man the guard from last night? Did he somehow know of Cliff's trespass? Or worse, had Sabine been caught?

The door banged closed behind him and he jumped. From somewhere in the distance came the sounds of raised voices and running feet. Something was wrong. The hairs on his arms stood up. His heart thumped out a rapid rhythm. *Fight, flee. Fight, flee. Fight, flee.* He couldn't move.

"Follow me, please." Despite the polite phrasing, the headmistress' words were every bit a command.

Several seconds passed before Cliff's feet finally obeyed him and started moving. His mind raced even as his body plodded, turning over possible scenarios. Von Arx led him past the visitors' room where they had dined that first evening, her hired muscle trailing behind. She opened the door to an austere office space, uncluttered and simply furnished.

"Is there some problem?" Cliff fought to keep his voice even and to relax the clenching muscles of his body.

"Please, sit." The headmistress gestured at a chair, but Cliff shook his head.

"No, thank you. I'd rather just get to the point so I can see Lola."

Please tell me she dropped a spider in a teacher's lap. Tell me she's been climbing the suits of armor or playing pirate with antique swords. Tell me she's unfit for this school and you want me to take her away immediately.

"I've declared the examinations finished. I am giving Lola a place in the Institute."

His heart skipped a beat. "I'm afraid we are no longer interested."

"You may not be, but we here at the Institute are extremely interested. She will excel here, and be sheltered from your current difficulties."

Cliff pressed a fist to his belly, where his stomach was twisting in knots. "No. We're leaving. Excuse me."

He spun to leave, but the guard's meaty hand clamped down on his arm. "The lady is not finished speaking."

"You don't understand, being a man," von Arx continued. "There are few opportunities available in this world for women of brains and talent." Her voice rose, growing louder and more impassioned. "This school will allow your daughter a choice:

strike out on her own after graduation, or join a confederation of women dedicated to creating a new order where their abilities will see them rise to be the rulers God intended." She flattened her palms on her desk, leaning toward him, her eyes gleaming with furious intensity. "She has the potential. She can be one of us."

What the hell? Was she trying to raise a generation of female dictators? Was everyone mad?

"This isn't the sort of environment I want for her. I'm sorry. We'll be leaving now." He tried to shake himself free of the guard's grip, but the man held fast.

"That will not be possible," the headmistress replied, her voice calm but determined. "We have visitors today who wish to speak with you. And with your pirate friend, who I assume is here somewhere? You needn't worry about your daughter. I promise we will take better care of her than you possibly could."

"Over my dead body," Cliff snarled.

Von Arx shook her head. "Seems a bit extreme." She looked to the guard. "Becker, please escort His Grace off the premises. There have been quite enough disruptions for the day. Our guests can speak with him outside. If he cooperates, I may allow him to say a farewell to the girl."

The big man hauled Cliff out the door. Cliff raised a hand to take a swing at the man's face, but a second thug waiting in the corridor lunged, grabbing him around the middle and knocking his arm aside.

"Let me go, goddammit!"

Cliff squirmed helplessly, outnumbered and outmuscled. He thrust his hand into his coat, fumbling for the signal flare the crew of Die Fledermaus had given him when they'd picked up his belongings that morning.

"I won't let you kidnap my daughter, you bastards!"

One of the men snatched at the flare, but Cliff was faster. He yanked the cap off with his teeth, squeezing his eyes shut. The flare popped and sparked and both Cliff's captors screamed. Cliff jerked and twisted, kicking out and thrusting with his elbows, hitting any flesh he could reach. He hit one of the men with the flare, and the man howled in agony.

Blinded and in pain, the men lost their grips, and Cliff broke free. He tore down the hall, holding the flare behind him to protect his own eyes. He ran to the front gate, heaved the door open, and hurled the flare as far out into the bailey as he could. He prayed the crew would see it.

"Lola!" he shouted, spinning and racing back into the castle, past the public spaces and into the areas he and Sabine had explored during the night. "Lola! Sabine!"

He shouldered his way through a disorderly cluster of girls. The word "spider" jumped out from the multilingual confusion of chatter. Lola.

"Have you seen a little girl?" he asked. "This tall? Wavy black hair? Ein kleines Mädchen?"

Several girls shrugged. Two girls pointed in opposite directions. Cliff swore and ran.

"Sabine! Lola!"

"Daddy!"

Cliff wheeled in the direction of the cry. The library! Good God, if they were taking her down the secret passage and out the side of the mountain…

Never!

His legs burned, new pains shooting up from the ankle that had yet to entirely heal. He crashed through the library doors, darting around tables, smashing into chairs and not caring. A few steps from the entrance to the dungeon laboratory, Sabine stood with Lola in her arms, her body turned to shield the girl from harm. Beams of lamplight glinted off the polished barrels of three revolvers aimed straight at them.

Cliff staggered to a halt. "Let them go. Take me." The guns didn't waver, but eyes turned in his direction. "I'll give you anything. Money, jewels, whatever you want. Just let them go free."

The oldest of the three villains, a woman in a navy blue schoolteacher dress who looked near to Cliff's own age, turned to point her gun at his heart.

"Ah. The duke himself. I thought Papa was sending men for you, but we all know that we ladies are the true brains of the organization. Ist das nicht so, Schwester?" She glanced at Sabine, her teeth baring in a feral smile.

Sister?

The translation clashed with his reality. Not Sabine. Never Sabine, who guarded his baby with her own life. She would never be one of them. He took a step toward the gun, refusing to cower, despite his racing heart and his trembling hands.

"Let them go," he repeated.

"Release the girl, Dieben," the woman said to Sabine. "Von Arx wants her for a student, and we have no use for one so young. We only want you and your American lover."

"He's not my lover," Sabine snapped. She pressed Lola to her chest. "And I trust your word about as far as I can piss."

"Not your lover?" The woman's eyebrows arched. "Has the little slut grown picky?"

Sabine cursed at her in a language Cliff didn't even recognize.

"Well, then." The woman nodded at her two companions—girls in their late teens, wearing the uniforms of the Institute. "Since he's so inconsequential…"

Cliff was moving before the words "shoot him" were out of her mouth. He plowed into the schoolteacher, sending her flying into Sabine and Lola as gunshots whizzed over his head.

Lola screamed. Cliff dove for her, catching her around the waist and pulling her against his chest. Sabine and the enemy teacher grappled on the floor, the gun trapped between their two hands. Cliff rolled away from the melee, shoving Lola behind a large, upholstered armchair.

"Go!" Sabine shouted. "Get out! Leave me!"

"Are you out of your fucking mind?" Leave her? In the hands of a castle of murderesses?

Another gunshot rang out, the bullet slamming into the carpet inches from his leg. He scrambled behind the chair with Lola. The sounds of knuckles smacking flesh mingled with grunts of pain.

"Damn you, Duke, get the hell out!"

Out. Their only chance.

I'll be back for you.

Cliff gathered Lola in his arms and darted for the next possible shelter—a lectern he'd overturned on his way in. He dove behind it. The dictionary it had held lay splayed on the ground, its pages bent and crushed. Cliff's eyes fixed on the exit. He had a clear path except for a single curio cabinet that was probably filled with priceless antiques.

"Not as priceless as our lives," he whispered. "Hold tight, babe."

He sucked in a single, deep breath, bit his bottom lip, and sprang. Legs churning, he streaked through the room, knocking the cabinet aside with his right shoulder. The pain didn't even register. Glass shattered and artifacts went flying. Cliff hit the door with the same shoulder, crashing into the hall before setting Lola on her feet.

"Daddy!" she wailed, tears streaming down her cheeks.

"I'm here, Lo. I'm here," he babbled, yanking oil lamps down from the walls. "I'll keep you safe."

He kicked the hall carpet into a wad in front of the door and smashed the lamps atop it. Flames raced across the fabric, flaring up as the fibers caught fire. Cliff scooped up Lola and began to run again.

"Sabine!" she cried.

"We'll meet her outside," he promised. "The library has a secret exit."

The only exit, until his pile of oil-soaked carpet burned out. He'd meet her at the other side, even if he had to run down the mountain to get there. The enemy needed her alive to get to the Heart. That was what mattered. They couldn't harm her. She would be safe.

The front gate still stood open from when he'd tossed the flare out, but the blinding multicolored light had died out. A large shadow slanted across the sunlit flagstone steps. Cliff stepped out and looked up. Die Fledermaus hovered above the castle, her engine purring a beautiful song of rescue. A metal basket attached by chains rested on the ground, awaiting cargo. Half a dozen rough-looking men circled, kept at bay by a pair of spiked mechanical arms that sprouted from the cargo hoist. Ben Palmer, Sabine's engineer, stood inside the basket, manipulating the arms like a puppeteer, his brass gloves attached to the machine with a series of wires.

"Duke! Climb aboard!"

Ben cleared a path for Cliff and Lola, and they scrambled into the basket.

"Go!" Cliff barked. "To the other side of the castle. They'll be bringing Sabine straight out of the mountain."

Ben kicked something and the cargo hoist zipped upward, knocking Cliff onto his ass. The mechanical arms retracted.

"Nice design."

"Thank you. Where's the Captain? What happened?"

"Some woman. Talked about 'Papa' and called her 'sister.' She had a couple of helpers and they had her at gunpoint, but they want information from her."

Ben took his turn swearing. In Spanish, Cliff thought, or perhaps Portuguese. "Bastards never give up, do they? Don't worry. We've gotten her out of worse."

By the time Cliff and Lola were on deck, Nicole had maneuvered the ship up and over the castle, dropping down toward the outskirts of the village and the secret entrance.

"Right there," Cliff said. "Where those pink-gray rocks meet in a sort of a V."

"I see it. Hawkes, you ready?"

The butler-pirate stood at the rail, a rope tied around his waist that looped through a series of pulleys, ending in Jules' hands. The Frenchman gave an experimental tug, easily lifting his crewmate off the ground. "Rig's set."

Cliff peered down at the rocks, his arms tight around Lola, who watched with worried, but now dry eyes. A section of the mountain shifted. Bits of dirt and grass seemed to melt away as the entrance doors swung inward. Sabine stepped out, the three enemy women at her back, still clutching their pistols.

Hawkes leapt over the side of the ship, hurtling toward the ground at a pace that looked terrifyingly out of control to Cliff. Hawkes snatched Sabine right off the ground, flying back upwards as Jules hauled on the rope. The engines roared and the ship shot toward the sky. Jules gave one final yank, and Sabine and Hawkes cleared the rail.

Lola ran to Sabine, flinging her arms around her neck. "Miss La Capitaine! I was so scared!" The tears began to flow again, and Sabine stroked Lola's hair gently.

"You were such a good, brave girl. Thanks to you, I found our treasure."

The treasure. Cliff flinched. The Heart of Ra. The replacement for Lola's fuel tube.

Lola's luxene. Oh, my God.

"Stop!" he commanded. "Go back. I have to get Lola's things."

"What?" Sabine leapt to her feet. "Don't be a fool. Redbeard could be on us in an instant. He must have a ship hidden nearby." She looked at Nicole and Ben. "Full power. Burn all her fuel, just get us to safety."

"Aye, aye, Captain," the first mate replied, flicking several dials on the control panel. Her husband ran to work on the engines.

Wind roared in Cliff's ears as the airship tore away from the castle. Somewhere inside of him, generations of aristocratic ancestry had apparently been lurking. He drew himself up to his full six feet and stalked to the helm.

"Go back to the castle," he ordered, sounding every bit the duke he had never wanted to be. "Now."

Nicole ignored him.

Cliff reached for the wheel. "I'm turning this goddamned ship around."

She punched him.

23

Sabine had to say this for Hartleigh: he wasn't one to surrender to physical pain. He wasn't one to surrender to anything, really, despite his usually mild temperament. The duke—for he was fully a duke in this moment—stalked toward her, blood trickling from his split lip, blue eyes flashing with icy fury. The very antithesis of mild.

"Turn the ship around."

Sabine had faced down many a furious man in her time, most of them armed, some who even wanted to seize her ship. Never before, however, had she entered into such a confrontation without even the slightest bit of fear. Instead she felt... aroused.

The unwelcome and unexpected reaction fueled her own anger. She curled her fingers into fists, hating that she wanted to kiss Hartleigh as much as slap him. Hating that she wanted to fling herself into his arms and surrender. To just once not need to be the all-powerful captain.

"You have no power on this ship," she snarled, her face so close to his that he had to wipe a drop of spittle from his cheek.

He only leaned closer. "You are putting Lola's life in danger. Turn the goddamned ship around."

"Danger? There are murderous pirates back there! *That's* danger."

"She could die, do you understand me? Turn. The fucking. Ship. Around. Now."

"Explain yourself."

"I don't have time for a fuc—"

"Miss La Capitaine?" Lola interrupted, pulling on Sabine's arm. "Daddy wants my fuel. See?"

The little girl had unbuttoned the top of her uniform dress, revealing a metal plate in the center of her chest. She opened it, pointing at the small tube partially filled with glowing luxene. Sabine's own heart hummed unnaturally in her chest.

"I have a machine in my heart," Lola explained, as if it were nothing out of the ordinary. "It needs luxene every week. I'm not scared, but Daddy is always worried that I will run out."

The cold mountain air sliced through the fabric of Sabine's clothing, stinging the flesh on her right side. The left side felt only the pressure of the wind. Damaged. Artificial. A constant reminder of failure. She rarely noticed the contrast anymore, except in times like this when everything came flooding back.

"Ben should have a few ounces of luxene among his engineering things." The voice belonged to Sabine the captain, who saw problems and fixed them. Patched them up like her patched-up body. "And when we next stop, I will buy you a gallon jug to replace what was left behind." She looked back up at Cliff. He still loomed over her, but the anger had faded from his face. "Acceptable?"

He gave a curt nod. "I want to see the luxene. To be certain." He reached for Lola, tugging her dress closed. "Lo, it's freezing up here, you can't be all exposed like—" He jerked back with a yelp. "What *is* that?"

Lola scooped up the fuzzy creature that had crawled out

of her pocket. The spider was as large as her hand, black and hairy, with small red stripes on its legs.

"His name is Lucas. He's a spider." She pressed the animal to her chest. "I think he's cold. His cage was supposed to be kept warm. I picked him up when we were finding the treasure. But then you almost squashed him when you were carrying me. I was so scared you were going to squash him."

Cliff blinked several times. "Right. Why don't you head down below where you can both be warm? Maybe find a bucket or something to put him in. Introduce him to his mechanical spider siblings. I'll check on the luxene and then come down, okay?"

Lola looked for a moment as if she might protest, but then she shivered. "Okay."

Cliff watched her disappear down the stairs before turning to Sabine. "You found the helmet?"

"I did." Sabine folded her arms across her chest, studying him. He had calmed, but his resolve remained in the hard set of his mouth and his unflinching gaze.

I don't like leaving jobs half-done, he had said. Liar.

"You want the Heart of Ra for Lola." It was so obvious now she didn't need to ask, but she wanted to hear him confirm it.

"Correct."

"And what of *my* quest for it?"

"I'll pay you whatever you think it's worth. Whatever you ask."

"And if I told you that it's priceless and not for sale?"

"Then I would have to take it from you." He touched his split lip. "As you can see, I'm willing to defy you."

"Sorry about that," Nicole called. "Ship policy. There's no tolerance for mutiny. Never challenge the captain's authority."

"I'll make certain I'm standing more than an arm's length away next time I do it," Hartleigh replied.

Nicole laughed. "I like him, Captain. You can keep him."

He's not mine to keep.

But neither was he going anywhere anytime soon. Not when they had a treasure to find.

The Heart of Ra. The power source she'd coveted since learning of its existence. Lola's revelation left her conflicted. She'd worked for this. It's what she did. Worked to drag herself up. To make her life better. And now a seven-year-old girl had bared her metal heart and left Sabine wanting to sacrifice. Wanting to be a protector again. She knew that path. That way lay pain.

"This way. I'll find you the luxene."

She led him down below without another word. It took her no more than a minute to locate the fuel in the bottom of Ben's tool chest. She handed Cliff the bottle and turned to climb up to the deck.

"I'm sorry."

His unexpected apology made her freeze.

"I shouldn't have tried to command your crew. I overreacted and I apologize."

Sabine turned slowly. "Apology accepted. You had your reasons. And I should thank you for helping the crew rescue me."

"You helped Lola. I owed you. Now we're even. You want to tell me who those women were and why that one called you sister?"

"Not especially, no." Old pains and old betrayals. She'd never be free of the past, but she wasn't going to dwell in it.

"Perhaps another time."

"Yes."

No.

She neither wanted nor needed a confidant. Her business was hers alone. She'd tell him no more than was necessary.

"Well, how about the helmet?" he asked. "What was the next clue?

"Wheel number five. It said, 'Cat mummy. Hunterian.' Does that mean anything to you?"

"Afraid not."

"We'll figure it out."

"I know."

Their eyes locked. His were as sharp as the alpine air. And he was so close. Had he stepped closer or had she? A bit of rough air and she'd rock right into him.

"Because neither of us is giving up on this, are we?" she asked.

His head dropped toward hers. "Not a chance."

Sabine swayed closer.

The door to her cabin flew open, startling them both so badly that Cliff slipped and banged into the wall behind him.

"Oh!" the duchess exclaimed. "Sorry to interrupt, but that girl has a… a *thing*, and she's letting it crawl all over. I can't stay there."

"I should go," Cliff said, waving the hand with the luxene bottle. "Make sure Lola's okay after what happened." He stepped through the doorway, then looked back at Sabine. "We should talk later."

"Yes."

"You two ought to find better locations for your kissing," the duchess said to Sabine when the door closed behind her. "In a bedroom, perhaps?"

"We weren't kissing." *Yet.* Sabine started up the stairs. Amy followed right on her heels. She was in a skirt again, though Sabine had no idea where it had come from. Maybe the crew had let her out long enough to go shopping in the village, to placate her after Sabine's refusal to let her return home.

"It's not ideal, his having an inappropriate lover," the duchess continued, "but I'm sure we can arrange things so he can still marry Miss Willingham. You won't mind, I hope?"

Sabine reached the deck and turned around, putting her hands on her hips. "We're not lovers."

The duchess arched the most perfect skeptical eyebrow

Sabine had ever seen. A slightly pointed bow of pure disbelief. *You are fooling even yourself,* that eyebrow said.

"And, yes, I would mind if someone had professed an intention to be with me and then married someone else. That is why I avoid romantic entanglements."

Amy laughed. "Oh, my dear Miss Dieben, allow me to explain something about these things. I fell hard, at seventeen, and my affections have never wavered. You don't choose passion of that sort. By the time you realize you've stumbled into it, you're too deep to get yourself out. You and Hartleigh look at one another like lovers do. You argue like lovers. You share secrets like lovers. That sizzle between you will become a conflagration and you won't be able to quench it."

Sabine's jaw tightened. "Then we will simply have to put out the fire before it starts." She spun on her heel and walked to the helm, where Nicole stepped aside to allow Sabine to fly the ship.

"Have you decided on a destination, Captain?"

"We're heading to Paris. I think we all need a day about town." She and Hartleigh most especially. Something had to be done to quash their mutual lust. "And I have plans."

24

"Sorry."

Cliff looked back down at the ground, trying to concentrate on watching where he was walking. That was the third time he'd bumped into Sabine since they'd left the ship. She was going to think he was doing it on purpose.

Truth was, he was too easily distracted by the sights of a new city. Motorcars and carriages pulled by ornate dragons rumbled by in equal proportions. Elegant ladies and gentlemen of leisure strolled the pavement, showing off their winter furs and the latest French fashions. Cliff glanced up just in time to see a woman pass by wearing a two-foot-wide hat that looked to have been decorated with a whole ostrich.

"Where are we going?" he asked.

"Number Seventeen."

"Helpful. An address?"

"Very good."

Cliff shoved his hands into his coat pockets. "Look, I don't have to go along with whatever scheme you've got cooked up here. If you're not going to confide in me, I can go back to the ship. I don't like leaving Lola behind."

"Lola will have a wonderful time. Nicole and Ben decided years ago not to have children of their own, and instead they dote on the children of others. You heard their plan to design a cage for Lola's spider. She'll be enthralled and you'd only be in the way."

"Fine. But when we get to this Number Seventeen, can we take a minute for an actual conversation? We still haven't really talked about this… whatever it is between us."

"I'm taking care of it. We're almost there."

Cliff looked up at the building beside them. The small blue number plate affixed above the door gave the address as number eleven. At least his curiosity would soon be appeased.

The plaque above Number Seventeen was larger than usual, with a neat red border and rosettes carved in relief in each corner. The simple brick facade looked like any other building on the street, and the interior was hidden behind plain, opaque curtains.

"A brothel?" Cliff guessed.

Sabine grinned. "Ah, he is more worldly than he appears."

Cliff frowned down at her. "Haven't I told you who Lola's mother is?"

"No, but now I'm intrigued. Tell me."

"Miranda was a parlor girl at a popular Chicago bordello. We took a liking to one another, and she became my mistress for a time. After Lola was born, Miranda moved to New York with all the money she'd saved and a plan for her future. She now owns an exclusive gentlemen's club. Her ladies cater to the elite of American high society."

"And here I thought you were the type to passionately romance a farmer's daughter or the girl next door."

"You're not the first to make that mistake." He paused outside the brothel door. "Honestly, I'd rather we just rent a hotel room."

"You'll enjoy it here. Trust me."

Cliff shrugged. If nothing else, he was curious to see what

these infamous Parisian pleasure houses looked like on the inside.

Sabine ushered him through the door, into a sumptuous foyer with a bubbling fountain, frescoed walls, and a mosaic floor reminiscent of a Roman bath. Not that Cliff had ever seen a real Roman bath, but he imagined this room had a similar ambiance. Sparkling opulence. Gilded debauchery. He preferred the simple, no-nonsense establishment he'd frequented in Chicago.

"La Capitaine in the flesh!" exclaimed a man attired in evening dress, with a red cummerbund and bow tie. He carried a thick binder tucked under one arm. "It has been forever! Welcome to you and your handsome friend. Come, tell me what we can do for you today."

Sabine motioned for Cliff to follow as the host led the way into a lavish parlor. Large, gold-framed mirrors accented the flocked wallpaper. Light glimmered from chandeliers dripping with crystals. All throughout the room, men and women in various states of undress lounged on sofas, cushions, or plush armchairs.

"Welcome to Number Seventeen," Sabine said.

"You've been here before, I take it?" Cliff asked.

"Yes. Whatever your tastes, they have something to suit you. They specialize in fantasy rooms. I don't recommend the airship room. The swaying is nauseating and not at all like a real airship. But there are many other choices. A forest room with fake trees and carpeting made to resemble grass, a theater room with rows of seats where they will play opera music in the background, a prison for those who like to be subdued…"

"Um, no."

"Even a pirate room that resembles a ship. Pick a room, pick a companion or two. I'll pay, since this was my idea."

The maitre d' flipped open his binder to reveal an array of photographs. "Allow me to present our menu. We have photographs of every room to assist in your selection, as well as images of the lovely men and women who work here."

Cliff's gaze drifted from the page of naked women up to Sabine's face. "This is really your plan? We whore it up for a while and then magically we're not attracted to each other anymore?" He almost laughed, the idea was so ludicrous. All the women in the whole building couldn't make him stop wanting her.

She crossed her arms and narrowed her eyes at him. "It's clear we have both been too long without intimate companionship. We satisfy our physical needs and then that constant urge will go away."

Now he did laugh. "It won't work."

"Don't be ridiculous. Of course it will work. It's just sex, Hartleigh. It's a basic human desire and it simply needs to be sated."

"In many cases, that may be true. But this…" He gestured between the two of them. "It's different. It has to be the two of us or we won't be satisfied."

"How could you possibly know that?"

"Because it was different with Miranda."

Sabine sniffed. "Yes, well, she's obviously very talented. And probably a raving beauty."

"She's pretty. But that's not why it was different. It was better than what I'd had with others. No one else could match it. Because we were friends. We had affection between us. Fun. Mutual enjoyment of one another's company aside from the purely physical. A different sort of intimacy."

Heads around the room had turned to watch and listen, but Cliff didn't care. There was something oddly satisfying about arguing in front of a dozen whores and their customers. Only with Sabine could this ever happen to him, and he liked that. They were like the setup to some peculiar joke. A duke and a pirate walk into a brothel…

"I'm not having any kind of intimacy with you, Duke."

Sabine poked him in the chest. "That's the entire reason for being here. We're both hungry for sex, and working together puts us conveniently close. Look around. The women here are gorgeous. What do you prefer? Tiny and wasp-waisted? Voluptuous? If you like my body shape, I'm sure there is someone of that sort. No sense in settling for an ordinary woman when you have an array of professionals to choose from."

The maitre d' held out his picture book again, but Cliff waved it away. He scanned the room for a moment. A few of the women waved, blew him kisses, or made suggestive gestures. Happy to join in the show, he guessed.

"Sorry, I still prefer you. And nothing about you is ordinary."

The longer he knew her, the more tiny things he noticed about her. The way sunshine on her hair highlighted threads of darker and lighter brown. How clear her eyes were. Like glass. A man could read things in those dark, expressive eyes. Her sardonic mouth. Cliff had long ago determined that it never curved evenly. One side or the other was always higher. Her little half-smiles were adorable. Her full grins were heavenly.

And who could compare with her to-die-for body? The simple dresses she wore were only modest at first glance. Today's green top and brown skirt hugged her athletic figure, displaying perfect, round breasts and nicely flared hips. If she turned around, he was certain to get a fine view of her curvy bottom. He'd been fantasizing about her legs since he'd first seen them wrapped in snug trousers.

"Why are you staring at me like that?" Her voice had lost much of its arrogant swagger. He would have said she was squirming beneath the intensity of his gaze, but Sabine didn't squirm. Did she?

"Like what?" he asked.

"Like I'm... a raving beauty."

"Because you are."

"I'm not beautiful, I'm dangerous."

Cliff couldn't stop a smile from spreading across his face. "Dangerous can be beautiful. Tigers are beautiful. Jagged mountain peaks are beautiful. Lightning is beautiful."

"Embrasse-le!" cheered a woman wearing a corset and nothing else. "Kiss him!"

Sabine turned away. "Enough nonsense. All our adventures have played with your head. If you want the fantasy, pick a girl and use the pirate room."

"We also have a desert isle room with sand on the floor if you'd like to be marooned at sea," the eager host added, holding up his book to show off the room with its ocean-painted walls and taxidermied birds dangling from the ceiling.

"No, thank you."

"Pick anything, Hartleigh," Sabine sighed. "It doesn't matter what."

"I pick *you*. In a nice hotel room. No gimmicks, nothing fancy. Just the two of us enjoying what we really want."

"Don't be foolish."

Cliff's shoulders tensed. Her words echoed that tiny voice in the back of his mind. The one that said he was asking for trouble. What made him think he could become involved with Sabine without letting things go too far?

I'm older now. I know better. I'm over silly childhood fantasies. One time is all we need. A good, long afternoon where we can revel in the wild passion, have some fun, explore one another. That will be enough.

"It's not foolish," he said aloud. "It's perfectly reasonable."

"Well, it's not the plan. We're taking care of this my way. Let me see that photo book."

Cliff sank down onto one of the circular cushions as Sabine flipped through the brothel's illustrated menu. "Do as you like. I'll be waiting when you're done and still unsatisfied."

Her head snapped up to look at him. "What do you mean you'll be waiting? You're going to sit there doing nothing?"

"I'd rather go back to the ship, but I also don't want to become lost in an unfamiliar city. I can wait."

Sabine glared at him, her jaw clenched. "The plan won't work if you don't participate. You'll still be eyeing me and touching me."

"I won't touch you if you don't want me to."

"Just have some fun, Hartleigh. Please? I promise you this will solve the problem."

Cliff rose to his feet. "Is that all I am to you? A problem?" Apparently he was a fool after all, for assuming his feelings of friendship were reciprocated. "Please excuse me. I think I remember the way back to the ship. Enjoy your afternoon."

He strode toward the exit.

Never get involved with a friend. Even in your imagination.

25

"Now, now, chérie, you aren't going to let him run off so easily, are you?"

The woman who had spoken eased out of her chair and glided across the room with effortless elegance.

Sabine nodded in greeting. "Madame Séverin."

The brothel keeper gestured toward the foyer. "Well? Go on, then. Go fetch your American."

"Why does everyone insist on referring to him that way? He's not mine."

"He would have been, if you hadn't pushed him away."

"He left of his own accord. It's not my fault he won't listen to reason."

Madame Séverin chuckled. "It must be frustrating for you, to have found someone who will not obey your commands."

Sabine's brows narrowed. "Plenty of people don't obey my commands."

"And who are they? Enemies. Adversaries. People you can fight or shut out from your life. But this American of yours, you want him in your life. I can tell because of the passionate way you respond to him. You should have accepted his offer. I expect he will pleasure you quite thoroughly."

"The way he handles things, he won't be pleasuring anyone but himself. He's completely ruined the plan." Sabine heaved a sigh. "I'll have to think of a different tactic. Perhaps hire a woman to go to him. That might work better, especially if we choose just the right lady. I will consult with you soon on the matter. Now, though, I ought to track him down before he stumbles into a sewer."

Sabine nodded to Madame Séverin and headed for the foyer, but froze in the middle of the archway when she caught sight of Cliff walking back into the brothel. He pulled up short.

"Sabine. Sorry. I got halfway down the block and realized I had no idea which street we'd turned off of. I guess I was looking at the ground then."

Madame squeezed past Sabine and grasped Cliff by the arm. "Welcome back, darling boy. I am Madame Séverin, the owner of this establishment, and I'm so happy you did not run off after all. I have just the place for you. We upgraded the pirate room only a month ago. You will love it."

"That's very kind of you to offer, but I'm only here to wait for Sabine. Don't mind me. I'll amuse myself by wandering around and admiring the erotic artwork."

"You must at least let me walk you about and show you some of the rooms. La Capitaine has yet to make her choice, so she will accompany us and chat as we walk, won't you chérie?" Madame's free hand gripped Sabine's arm. "Never mind the photographs. I know the boys here better than any picture can convey. Now tell me, what are you in the mood for?"

Nothing. No one. She wasn't in the mood at all. Hartleigh's contempt for her plan had squelched any desire to be here. She was ready to return to the ship, alone with a drink and a mystery novel.

"Lean or muscular?" Madame asked. She led them up an ornately carved staircase and into a long corridor.

"Neither," Sabine replied. "I like strong men, but not bulging."

"Ah. And tall, of course. I remember that about you."

Cliff stared at the series of lurid frescos that lined the walls. Sabine couldn't tell if he had taken a real interest, or if he was simply avoiding looking at her.

"Tall, strong, but not bulging," Madame Séverin mused. "I have a lovely redhead who pretends to be a Scotsman. He might suit you."

Sabine shook her head. "No, thank you."

"A blond, perhaps? Or dark-haired? Yes, I think dark-haired is best. Now what about eyes? A fiery woman like yourself will want a vivid pair of eyes. Any color preference?"

Cliff glanced at Sabine, only for an instant, but it was enough to cause a flutter in her belly. Blue like ice. But hot as molten steel.

"No," she said.

"Ah, here we are," Madame announced, throwing open a door. "The pirate room. Does it meet your approval, Capitaine?"

Sabine peeked inside. Soft, electric lights lit the room, displaying wood-planked walls made to resemble a ship's hull and nautical-themed decor. Several thick ropes ran floor to ceiling—a sort of pseudo rigging. The bed that filled much of the space appeared sturdy and comfortable. A chest at the foot of the bed stood open. Sabine couldn't see everything inside, but she spied a wooden sword, a feathered hat, and what may have been a velvet coat. She inched closer.

"So, blue eyes, you said?" Madame asked.

"Yes, blue," Sabine replied distractedly.

"Wearing red eyeglasses and a dark gray suit?"

Sabine whirled around. "Wait, what?"

"I've found the perfect man for you. Here he is." Madame Séverin pushed Cliff through the doorway. He stumbled, crashed into Sabine, and toppled to the floor on top of her.

The door slammed closed. "Have fun, darlings!" Madame's voice called from the hall.

"Sorry," Hartleigh mumbled. "I didn't expect her to shove me at you."

Sabine gripped his coat, her hands frozen when they should have been pushing him away, keeping him tight against her. She fought the urge to spread her legs and let him settle between her thighs. She moistened her lips, staring at the bow curve of his kissable upper lip. This wasn't the plan.

"Are you wearing armor again?" he asked. "Even at a brothel? And why is it only on the one side?"

His arms twitched, and she imagined him sliding his hands over her to cup her breasts, one cold and hard, the other warm and supple. Would he be horrified? Intrigued? Ambivalent? Her fingers relaxed and she pushed at him.

"Get off," she commanded.

"I would love to, sweetheart, but you insist you don't want me." He rolled away, and the loss of his weight above her made her stomach sink in disappointment.

Hartleigh rose to his feet and walked over to look at the box of pirate props. He plopped the feathered hat down on his head. "How do I look? Dangerous and dashing, I assume?"

"Ridiculous."

He hefted the wooden sword. Intended as a child's toy, it looked absurdly small in his hand. He slashed at the air in possibly the worst display of swordsmanship she'd ever witnessed.

"Would you stop waving that thing around?" she groused.

"Why? Afraid I might thrust it into you?"

Sabine stalked up to him, caught his arm in mid-swing, and disarmed him before he had time to protest. "Enough with the sex jokes."

He delved into the box again, pulling out a stuffed parrot that he set on his shoulder. The stupid feathered hat flopped down over his forehead, shading his eyes.

"Can you believe this, Polly? I make a perfectly innocent remark and she misinterprets it with her deliciously wicked mind." Hartleigh made a fake bird squawk. "Pretty lady. Wicked mind."

"You are completely out of your head."

"Come on, Sabine." He tossed the bird back in the trunk. "You don't want to fuck me. Fine. But I'm sure Madame will want us to pay for this silly pirate room, so we might as well have fun with it. Relax. Play."

"Play." He *had* lost his mind. It was the only explanation. "Spielen."

"I know what the damn word means, Hartleigh."

He pulled off the pirate hat and those blue eyes bore into her. "Do you? Because I get the sense that your childhood wasn't hugs and roses."

She folded her arms across her chest. "I survived."

"You did. Admirably. And I think you deserve at least a little bit of what you missed out on. Now, do you want to pretend you're my sworn enemy storming my ship, or are you the governor's daughter who I'm holding for ransom?"

"I'm the captain." Sabine strode across the room, eyeing the ropes that ran up the walls. Perhaps if she removed her spectacles they might actually resemble a ship's rigging.

"That's not how this works," Cliff sighed.

"We're in the midst of a terrible storm. Waves crash against the hull, tossing us up and down. We're struggling to pull down the sails before they're ripped apart."

A smile tugged at his mouth. "Is 'pull down' a technical term?"

"I command airships, okay? They don't have sails."

She yanked on a rope, expecting it to cause the floor to tilt or set the bed rocking, like the hanging bed in the airship room. A jet of water shot down from the ceiling, slamming into the right side of Hartleigh's face. He let out an indecorous yelp.

"What the hell was that?"

He looked so funny standing there, dripping, his eyes wide with shock. Sabine laughed. "The storm, apparently." She tugged on another rope and water spurted out from a second hidden nozzle. It splashed at Cliff's feet, splattering his boots and trousers. Another laugh escaped her lips. She might have called it a giggle except she wasn't the sort to giggle. Definitely not. She reached for a third rope.

He darted toward her, his hand clamping down on her wrist. "Oh, no you don't. It's *my* turn to get *you* all wet."

Sabine shivered. His tone hadn't suggested innuendo, but her body went as hot as if he'd whispered huskily in her ear. The heat of his fingers singed the delicate skin of her wrist. Dammit, why was he standing so close to her? The slightest movement and…

She wobbled, just a bit, and her back collided with his chest. She heard the hiss of his sudden inhalation, felt him twitch against her. His grip slackened, but he didn't move.

"Sabine," he breathed.

Do something. Step away from him or yell at him. Move, dammit.

"Sabine, tell me you don't want this and I'll go away. Or tell me you do and I'll kiss you until neither of us can see straight."

"We already can't see straight. Eyeglasses, remember?" Her voice was low and breathless. Why? Why did he make her melt like this? Why did she sink into him with every word he spoke?

His lips found her ear. "I remember. Yours are simple. Pretty. Shall I awkwardly slide them off you while I nibble right here?"

He sucked on her earlobe and her body surrendered. He made her laugh and tremble at the same time and she had no defense against such a tactic. Maybe he was right. Maybe she needed *him* to slake her lust.

Her fingers dropped from the rope and she turned to kiss

him, winding her arms around his neck. The collar of his coat and part of his right sleeve were soaked through, but he didn't seem to notice anymore. He moved toward the bed, pulling her along with him, not breaking the kiss.

Sabine drifted across the room, too intent on the hungry, insistent pillaging of his tongue to heed where she was going. The backs of her legs collided with the bed and she would have fallen onto her rear if it hadn't been for his arms around her.

"More?" he asked. His lips skimmed across hers. "Please say yes."

"Yes."

"Thank God." He lowered her to the bed and straddled her, his thighs pressing against hers as he bent to nuzzle her neck. "I'm going to kiss you everywhere."

His hands brushed along her hips to her waist, moving toward the little silver clasps at the front of her corset. She pushed his arms away. Not now. No explanations. Only kisses.

He sat up. "Or maybe not?"

"No. Yes." Ugh. Her stupid mixed-up brain. "Kiss me," she clarified. "But not… there." She waved a hand over her torso.

Cliff kissed along her jaw up to her ear and sucked on the lobe again until she shivered. "Here?"

"Mmm."

He nudged her legs apart with one knee, his hands settling on her thighs. He paused a moment, then began to tug her skirts higher.

"There?"

"Yes."

Her skirts bunched around her waist. Warm hands ran over stockinged calves up to bare thighs. He tugged her drawers down, exposing the curls of dark hair above her sex. Sabine lifted into his touch, sighing her pleasure at the stroke of his fingers through her wet folds.

He slid down between her legs, his mouth following the path that his hands had traversed. His fingers dipped inside her.

"All the way up there?" he murmured.

"Yes. God, yes. Kiss me, Hartleigh."

"Cliff," he corrected.

"Cliff," she repeated, obediently. She'd use any name he wanted, as long as he didn't stop. He could don that pirate hat again and call himself Le Duc for all she cared. His tongue found her sex at last, and his name morphed into a blissful moan.

Sabine wove her fingers into his thick black hair, keeping his head pinned in place. God, but the man had talent. This was no perfect, professional excavation. It was a wild, enthusiastic treasure hunt, and she couldn't say which one of them was racing to claim the prize.

He teased her clit, curling his fingers inside her, stroking that spot that made her squirm. Her body strained, tighter and tighter, each tiny suck and nibble pulling her more taut, until she hovered nearly at the breaking point, her fingers clenching in his hair, her head tipping back as she let out a groan of agonizing delight.

"Yes! God, Cliff. I... Oh..."

She snapped. The ecstasy of her orgasm swept away all rational thought, the tension inside her unwinding until she was a spent, sated puddle of pleasure.

Her eyes slid closed. Her wildly humming heart began to slow. The soft fabric of the bedding cushioned her, coaxing her into a blissful doze. When was the last time she'd been so relaxed? She couldn't remember, but today she would revel in the sensation.

"Damn, but you're gorgeous," a low voice rumbled.

Sabine stretched, blinked. "Cliff?"

Cliff! Her plan! She bolted upright. She had completely lost control of the situation. Succumbed to his intoxicating touch. But it was over, right? She ought to be satisfied now.

Cliff sat at the foot of the bed, grinning at her as he polished his spectacles with a handkerchief. Sabine's eyes swept over him, little quivers running through her body at the memory of his hands and lips on her. His ardent gaze caused an unexpected burst of shyness, and she tugged her skirts down.

"Why aren't you undressed?" she asked. They were stuck with his plan now, and for it to succeed his needs also required satisfying. Yet he seemed in no hurry. He simply sat there, smiling at her. "Don't you want to finish things?"

He donned the eyeglasses and tucked the handkerchief away. "I was enjoying watching you enjoy yourself."

"I see." Sabine adjusted her clothing, reaching for her discarded drawers. "Well, get on with it. Unfasten your trousers at least, so I can return the favor."

He slid off the bed and rose, but made no effort to undress, instead folding his arms across his chest. "Are you having regrets?"

"No. It was nice."

He grunted. "Nice."

Exquisite. Rapturous. Stupefying. She wanted to do it all over again, and more. She would never suppress her lust while he still looked at her with that heated blue gaze. They needed to finish the job and as quickly as possible.

"Exceptional," she clarified. "I will do my best to reciprocate."

"No, thank you."

Sabine rocked back in shock. "What?"

"I wasn't fishing for favors. I don't want to be a duty to perform. I want you to want it as much as I do." He started for the door. "I'll head downstairs to settle our bill. Take all the time you need."

She watched him disappear out the door, not quite believing what she was seeing. When the door swung closed, she flopped onto her back, staring up at the ceiling. What had just happened?

"What in hell is wrong with you, Clifford Kinsley?" she wondered into the silence.

26

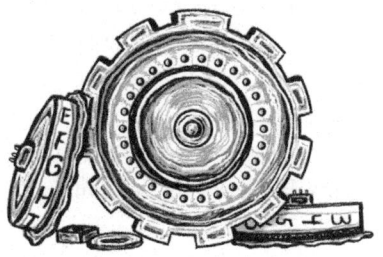

M*ummified Cat, Egypt*

Cliff stared at the two identical labels beside the two small, wrapped bundles. He wasn't seriously going to have to smash through a glass case at a public museum and desecrate an ancient sacred animal, was he? He glanced around the room. The Hunterian Museum in Glasgow was quiet this afternoon. It was empty save for him and Sabine. He trailed a finger over the glass. Maybe there was a latch somewhere to open it.

"Hartleigh!" Sabine called from the next cabinet over. "Get your ass over here. I've found it!"

Cliff turned slowly. That may have been the most words she'd spoken to him at one time since they'd left the brothel the other day. The flight to Glasgow had been long, silent, and awkward. They'd stayed overnight in a secluded cove somewhere along the English coast. Cliff had spent the whole time helping Lola hunt for insects to feed to Lucas and trying to ignore Amy's furious ranting about not going home.

Sabine made a brusque gesture at the exhibit in front of her. "A cat mummy."

"Yeah." Cliff walked to her side, his jaw clenching at the

way she shifted away from him. He peered at the artifact. "There are two more like it over there."

"What?"

He shrugged and pointed. Sabine rushed over to the case Cliff had been examining, scowling at it with hands on hips. "Scheiße." She tapped her foot in irritation "We'll have to unwrap all of them." She tapped on the glass, walked back and forth in front of the case, then paused to look around. "That chunk of rock should work."

The "chunk of rock" was a section of an old tablet, covered in ancient writing. Cliff leapt in front of it, throwing up his hands.

"Whoa, whoa. You can't go smashing things all over the place. This is a museum! These are historic artifacts!"

"Stolen artifacts," Sabine huffed. "The mummies didn't walk here. Someone swiped them from a tomb and pretended he wasn't as much a thief as I am."

"Uh…" Cliff gaped at her a moment. "You have a valid point."

"Of course I do. I'm a treasure hunter. I've sold to museums myself. I know how it all works."

"Fine. But regardless of the methods of acquisition, people still come here to study these objects and learn from them. If you destroy them, you're destroying knowledge."

"Hartleigh's cat mummy is a fake."

"The other two aren't. They meant something to someone. Think how Lola would feel if she'd carefully mummified her beloved spider and placed it in a tomb, only to find out that some treasure hunter was going to come around and tear it to pieces like it was trash."

"The cat owners are dead."

Cliff looked at the ceiling. "Come on, Sabine. Have a bit of heart. It's not a weakness to care about other people."

She flinched. "You don't know anything. I don't have a

heart, okay? Now give me that rock or I'll smash the case with my elbow."

"I'm going to fetch a curator and ask which mummy is ours. Don't smash anything while I'm gone or they're likely to arrest you."

He started toward the entrance, leaving her behind. She would have plenty of time to snatch the mummies and run if she wanted to. She could race back to her ship and fly away without him, cutting him out of the mission and claiming the Heart of Ra for herself. But she wouldn't. It would mean either kidnapping Lola or abandoning her in Glasgow, and Sabine wouldn't do that. She might strive to present herself as a hard, unfeeling pirate, but she was so much more underneath. She had passion. She had affection. And she had a world of pain that Cliff didn't understand but longed to kiss away.

Near the front of the museum, Cliff found a balding man squinting at an open case, muttering to himself.

"Suppose it will have to do," the man sighed.

Cliff wasn't sure what the trouble was. The display of taxidermied fish looked perfectly fine to him. He cleared his throat and the man spun toward him.

"Oh! Didn't see you there, young man. What can I do for you?"

Cliff held out a hand. "Clifford Kinsley, Duke of Hartleigh."

The curator's eyes opened wide, but he shook Cliff's hand. "Welcome to the Hunterian Museum, Your Grace. Such a pleasant surprise to have you here. I am Geoffrey Campbell, collections specialist. How can I be of service?"

"My predecessor left an extensive collection of artifacts, and it has been left to me to ensure they are relocated to suitable homes. As part of this process, I am verifying some of his donations, making certain the correct artifacts are indeed at the places listed in his records."

"Ah, yes. Sensible. I can see you are a great lover of antiquities yourself, Your Grace."

The comment caught Cliff off-guard, and it took him a moment to realize this was the sort of task he ought to have people doing for him. The curator had interpreted Cliff's personal involvement as a sign of his enthusiasm for the subject.

"His Grace is *extraordinarily* passionate about antiquities," Sabine said from somewhere behind him. "He adores museums. Goes out of his way to preserve artifacts and protect knowledge."

Cliff didn't turn around or acknowledge her sarcasm. "Mr. Campbell, please allow me to introduce my assistant, Miss Sabine Diebin. Miss Diebin is an expert in the acquisition and sale of ancient treasures, and is helping me with the cataloguing of my collection."

She made a tiny sniff of disdain, barely loud enough for him to hear.

"Now, according to the records left by the eleventh duke," Cliff continued, "he made a donation to this museum of a mummified cat. Unfortunately, it appears that three such objects can be found here, and I saw no identifying information to tell us which was the duke's cat."

"Oh." Campbell paled. "Oh, the cat. Oh, dear."

"Has something happened to it?" Had they gotten mixed up? Would they have to tear apart all three mummies after all?

"I am so sorry, Your Grace, but that particular mummy was a fraud. A fake. It was no more than a modern replica of the ancient mummies, and, consequently, worthless. It pains me to have to disappoint you, but I hope you understand that this sort of thing can happen to even the most cautious of collectors."

Cliff's entire body went rigid. Had the museum disposed of the piece? After all this time, after evading kidnappers and gun-toting schoolteachers, were they going to be thwarted by a fraudulent cat?

"Of course I understand," he replied, covering his inner turmoil with politeness. "You have my thanks for informing us. This is not the first of the pieces to be other than what it seemed. I'm afraid the duke's mind was not as agile late in life as he may have preferred. Perhaps you might tell us what has become of the piece?"

"Oh, it's in storage. We have a room full of artifacts we can't display."

The tension drained from Cliff's body. The clue hadn't been destroyed. "I'd like to see it."

He didn't ask, just stated. He was getting better at this duke thing. He only had to pretend that everyone he met was an employee, waiting for him to assign them a task.

"Certainly, Your Grace. It would be my pleasure to show you. Please follow me."

Campbell led them through the museum and down a staircase into a dimly-lit basement stuffed with boxes, shelves, and cabinets. He stopped beside a pair of wide cabinets with narrow drawers, frowning at them.

"Your cat should be in one of these, Your Grace," he said. "I cannot remember the exact location. You are free to look around. If you wish to take the artifact with you, you may. Now, if you will excuse me, I must resume my work on the exhibits. I will return to see how you are getting along when I have finished. Enjoy your visit, Your Grace." He bowed and scurried for the stairs.

Sabine began to yank open drawers. "Bugs. Rocks. Broken bits of pottery. So much junk."

Cliff stared at a drawerful of highly colorful butterflies. "I think these are rather beautiful, actually. Someone cared enough to arrange and label them quite precisely. Gives me hope for finding our mummy." He reached for the next drawer down and opened it. "Or not."

The drawer had been crammed full of small mummies. A quick count told him he'd located a full baker's dozen. Cliff couldn't tell whether they were all cats or not, but all thirteen were approximately the same size, and none looked any more or less fake to his eyes.

Sabine swore. "Aren't they labeled at all? I suppose we'll have to start unwrapping."

Cliff held up a hand. "Give me a minute. Why are you so impatient today? We've had no trouble since leaving Switzerland. If no one is chasing us, why the hurry?"

"I want this over. Don't you?"

"Ah. Is it me you're eager to get away from?"

"Unwrap the damn mummies, Hartleigh."

Cliff nodded. He was beginning to understand her. Any time she felt uncomfortable, she fell back on what she knew best: giving orders.

He removed one mummy from the drawer and looked it over. A small, handwritten tag had been affixed to the underside. "'Number 4518. Mummified cat. Cairo, Egypt. Collector: Morton Sykes Abernathy.' Not our mummy, apparently."

One-by-one, they flipped over the mummies and read the tags, until Sabine let out a triumphant, "Aha!"

"Found it?"

"'Donor: Duke of Hartleigh.' And it's even labeled as a fake. How systematic of them."

She hiked up her skirt and drew her dagger, giving Cliff a brief glimpse of that perfect thigh he'd kissed and caressed only days ago. He wanted her now, in the museum, maybe on the floor or up against the cabinets. She'd haunted his dreams the past two nights. Even her standoffish behavior couldn't diminish his desire. He'd seen her in an unguarded, happy moment, and he wouldn't be satisfied until she embraced that side of herself. Preferably while embracing him.

Sabine touched the dagger to the mummy, and Cliff snapped out of his erotic imaginings. "Um, shouldn't we take it…"

Ignoring him, Sabine sliced through the top layer of

wrappings and began to unravel the mummy. Bits of tattered cloth fell to the floor. Layer after layer, she unwound the strips of linen, revealing only more cloth underneath. When at last she reached the middle, the final bit of fabric simply unfolded in her hands.

"I'm disappointed," Cliff said. "He could have at least put some fake bones inside."

"All I care about is the clue." She turned over the cloth. "No writing on this bit. Dammit, are we going to have to search every scrap?"

"Wait, don't move."

Sabine froze. "What?"

Cliff reached for a small strip that had caught in her skirts. He lifted it to the light. A single line had been written on it in the old duke's scratchy handwriting. "Slot four receives rotor number two."

"That's all?" Sabine snatched the fabric from Cliff's hands to examine it for herself. "But what about the settings? Even with the wheels in the right locations, we can't break the code unless we know the initial settings."

"Where's the next bit of wrapping?" His gaze dropped to the mess on the floor. "I guess we should start looking."

They pawed through the ruins of the mummy, finding no other markings anywhere on the cloth. After several minutes, they both sat back with a sigh.

"What have we missed?" Sabine wondered. "I swear we've been through every scrap of wrapping at least twice over."

"I agree. I think we've found all there was to find."

"Your Grace?" Campbell's voice called. "Miss Diebin? Did you find... oh." The curator stumbled to a halt beside the mess that had once been a fake mummy.

"The piece was terribly made, we discovered," Cliff said matter-of-factly. "Completely disintegrated in our hands. We'll have to dispose of the remains, I'm afraid."

"Oh. Uh... Yes. I will have one of the boys tidy up the debris. Is there, er, anything else I can do for you?"

"Yes, there is. Did the duke leave anything else to the museum? Perhaps in conjunction with this sad mummy? Other artifacts? Papers? Records?"

"Nothing I am aware of. I can show you the record books from the time of the donation if that will be of use to you."

"Please."

They left the ruined mummy behind, except for the scrap with the clue, which Sabine tucked underneath her corset. Campbell led them back upstairs to an office crammed with books, binders, and papers. He scanned one of the shelves briefly, pulled out a thick logbook and flipped through several pages.

"Here you are. Mummy donation from the Duke of Hartleigh." He sniffed. "That's odd."

"What?" Cliff asked.

"The object is listed as coming from his personal collection, but above that someone wrote a different location and crossed it out. It appears to say 'London Library.'"

Cliff and Sabine exchanged a look. An instant later, they both grinned.

"Well," Sabine said. "The duchess will be happy."

27

Before the crew had even descended the ladder to lash Die Fledermaus to her moorings, a petite figure vaulted onto the deck and brandished a pistol at Sabine.

"Where is the duchess?"

Sabine surveyed the slight woman from beneath arched brows. The duchess' companion wore a boy's shirt and trousers, but an elegant pair of high-heeled boots. Her dark hair had been pulled back into a simple knot, and her golden skin was tinged pink from her fury.

"Do you hold her hostage?" Luella demanded. "Release her this instant or I will shoot you and all your men!"

"That seems rather drastic," Sabine replied dryly.

"Luella!" Amy came flying up the stairs, but staggered to a halt at the sight in front of her. "Lu? Goodness. You're wearing trousers!"

"Amy!" Luella dropped the pistol and ran to embrace the duchess. "I was so worried."

Amy stroked her hair. "I'm fine, dearest. Merely annoyed. But you. Look at you!"

Luella took a step back, looking down at her clothing. "I know. It's so uncivilized. But I spent so many days fretting and contemplating how I could possibly track you down. When we saw the airship returning at last, I knew I had to do *something*. And it seemed uncouth to storm a dirigible in a dress."

"I had to wear trousers, too," Amy confided. "I had nothing but an evening gown until the crew took me out shopping. It was mortifying."

"Was it? I'd like to see what you look like in trousers."

"Perhaps in private, dearest. Never in front of all these people again. It's fine, perhaps, for a pirate, but a duchess? Never. Now, you must take me home. I am in desperate need of a cup of tea and a long bath."

Luella linked her arm through Amy's and walked her toward the ladder. "I would be delighted to assist you with both those things."

They shared a suggestive look. "I'd hoped you would be. And I need a list of all upcoming events. I want to get Hartleigh married before he and the captain decide they like one another again."

Sabine lowered herself to the ground with a rope, rather than waiting for the other women to clear the ladder, and set to work securing her ship. The task failed to distract her from her own frustrated thoughts. She *did* like Hartleigh. All too much.

He made her want to care. About him, about Lola, about all sorts of people. Sabine had to fight the urge to grin like a fool thinking about how a woman who barely knew how to hold a pistol had brazenly stormed her ship out of love for the duchess. Sabine was surrounded by love—lover-to-lover, father-to-daughter, friend-to-friend. Hartleigh practically oozed love, and it was, oh, so tempting.

Be my friend. Be my lover. Let me close.

She ought to send him away. Or leave him here while she chased after the Heart on her own. He was too much of a distraction. Annoying, confounding, and enticing all at once.

He never listened to reason, and now he had her questioning her every assumption. Given the way she'd been behaving lately, the questioning was entirely valid. She'd been stupidly rash at the museum yesterday, wanting it over with. Wanting away from him. Wanting to protect the sad remnants of her heart.

"You gonna finish that, Captain?"

Sabine blinked and looked up at Hawkes. "Sorry. Yes." She tugged the rope taut and began to tie a knot. "Could you run down to the village and see if you could find a few people to work in the kitchen while we're here? Tell them I expect to stay only a few days this time, but I will pay the full weekly rate."

"Sure thing, Captain. And then I'll be back to take up my butler duties."

"Thank you. I suppose once we're finished sorting the house I'll have to see about hiring a full-time staff. No sense in making the place livable and then not living in it."

Although if Hartleigh were to change his mind about faking his death and remain in the dower house... No, he wouldn't do that. He still bristled every time she used his title. She could retire here, with a big library and a pretty little English garden. Safely far from Redbeard's empire, with the backing of an adoring public. The reclusive ex-pirate.

Suddenly, the life she'd once envisioned as her chance to relax and be free sounded very lonely.

Sabine forced her mind back to her work, checking over every aspect of the ship before she declared everything satisfactory. She'd leave the crew the choice to bunk on Die Fledermaus or to take a room in the house. Her choice had been made long ago. Today she was taking a long, hot bath, eating a proper dinner, and then sleeping in her giant, comfortable, ducal bed. Alone.

She dug the toe of her boot into the gravel of the drive, sending rocks skittering.

Stop thinking about him. Stop remembering his hands and his mouth.

Oh, dear God, his mouth. That dangerous, clever tongue. The goofy grin on his face afterwards, as if she'd just pleasured *him*. She owed him. She owed him and he'd spurned her.

Why did that hurt? She should be happy that he'd asked nothing of her. She should be thankful not to be choking on his probably enormous and demanding cock.

"This is not helpful, Sabine," she scolded herself, storming up the path to the front of the house.

She tugged her small purse from underneath her corset and removed the key to her front door. No one waited inside to greet her. She hadn't even entrusted the key to Hawkes, who should have been opening the house for her. She'd requested kitchen staff, but she'd be drawing her own bath and preparing her own bed. One hundred rooms. One woman.

Which was fine, really. Better than a crowded airship where her cabin was taken by a duchess and a little girl, leaving Sabine to sleep on the floor in Nicole and Ben's room.

She took two steps into the foyer and froze. A heavy silence filled the air. The hall was as empty as she'd left it. No furnishings or statues filled the once-opulent space. The tiled floor was bare of rugs, and the walls uncovered by paintings or mirrors. Nothing obviously out of place.

So why was her skin crawling?

Sabine skirted past the wide staircase toward the most organized section of the house, her sense of unease increasing with every step. She opened the door to the library and pushed the button that turned on the electric lights.

"Gott im Himmel," she cursed.

All her carefully sorted stacks of papers were gone, torn to ribbons, the tables they had sat upon smashed to kindling. Toppled shelves covered the floor, their books scattered and damaged. Sabine dashed to the next room over, finding more of the same. Furniture upended. Papers and artifacts strewn about. She tiptoed over shattered glass and ceramics, climbed over twisted bits of metal. All of Hartleigh's organization, gone. All their hard work, laid waste.

She picked up half of a broken vase and hurled it at the wall. The tinkle of splintering china eased some of her anger, but none of her fear. Her enemies had been here, in her home. Tearing through her possessions, no doubt in search of the key to the Heart of Ra.

The hairs on her arms stood on end. Did they know of the machine? Did they really think she'd be so stupid as to leave it or the coded document behind? She kept the paper on her at all times, and the machine was currently with Hartleigh, who had planned to clean and oil it before setting the wheels.

"Oh, God. Cliff. Lola." Sabine tore from the room, her pounding footsteps echoing through the empty halls.

They'd arrived during daylight hours, on a clear day. Luella's words rang in Sabine's head. *When we saw the airship returning at last…*

Anyone watching the house would know. Would have seen Sabine go off alone, her hands empty. Would have seen Cliff head for the dower house, his arms full of a spider case and a strange wooden box.

No, no, no.

How could she have done this? She *did* care. She'd allowed him to worm his way into her life. And now she'd put him in danger. Again. She'd failed him.

She failed everyone.

Her legs pumped faster.

28

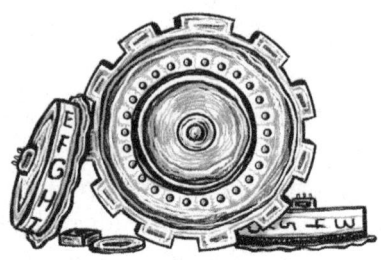

For a split second, Cliff thought Sabine was going to fling herself into his arms and begin to sob.

The next instant, she grabbed hold of his lapels, dragging him toward the study door, and he wondered what could possibly have triggered such a thought. Sabine didn't sob. She fought. If something upset her, she attacked it. At the moment, he couldn't tell whether or not she was attacking him.

"Out, get out," she demanded. "Now. Get Lola. Get the duchess and Lady Luella. We need to leave."

"Whoa." Cliff yanked his coat from her fingers. She tried to grab his arm and he dodged, smashing his thigh against his desk. "Ow. What's wrong? What happened?"

"The house. It was ransacked. We have to go. They could be anywhere. They could be here."

"Ransacked?" He slipped behind the desk to prevent her trying to force him out the door again.

Sabine flattened her hands on the top of the desk, scattering the papers he'd been planning to glance over. He caught one that looked to have come from the US before it fluttered to the floor. He needed to check up on his business. He still wasn't ready to sell. He didn't know if he would ever be.

"Someone tore it apart," Sabine explained, her words sharp and rapid. "Looking for clues. Looking for the machine, maybe. They know we're here. We're in danger. We need to leave now. No arguments. Get Lola. I'll tell the duchess."

"No."

Her fist thumped on the wood. "Goddammit, Hartleigh, why do you always do this? Is it too many centuries of ancestral inbreeding making your brain say, 'I'm a duke and I don't have to listen to anyone but myself'?"

"Show me the house. Then we'll discuss it."

She spun away, her hands clenching. "You are impossible! We need to leave, and I can't leave without you."

"Of course you can."

"No, I can't. You were right. We're friends. I care. I can't leave you in danger."

The corners of Cliff's mouth ticked upward. He stepped around the desk, laying a hand on her shoulder. He tried to turn her to face him, but she resisted.

"I don't think we're in danger. This house is untouched. No one has reported anything suspicious. We're surrounded by Amy's long-time employees and behind locked doors."

"You were kidnapped from a house more crowded than this one."

"Yes. In the midst of a party. A big event full of noise and distractions. This is a normal, quiet day. We can see approaching visitors from quite a distance. Would you like me to set a lookout? Then you can show me what happened at your house and we can determine what to do next."

"You are irritatingly reasonable," she replied. The volume of her voice had dropped, and her words came slower, less panicky. She'd been genuinely afraid. Perhaps his initial thought about her sobbing had been closer to the truth than he'd realized.

"I try to be reasonable. You're the only one who thinks I'm irritating."

Sabine turned to face him. "That seems extremely unlikely. Now, I'm going to explain the situation calmly and then you're going to do as I say."

Cliff leaned back against the desk, crossing his arms. "I'd rather we compromise, but go ahead."

"The house is a disaster. I'm certain they were looking for the Sphinx device, though I don't know if they know exactly what to look for. Many of the papers were torn up, so they may have been looking for a cipher on paper. Regardless, you have the device, and that puts you in danger. Where is it?"

"In the bottom left drawer of the desk. The drawer was just the right size and I wanted it out of sight. Also it's locked in." Cliff patted the small pocket in his waistcoat where he'd put the key. "How did the burglars get in, and did they take anything?"

"How could I possibly know if they took anything from the enormous piles of junk in that house? I didn't see an entry point, but I didn't wait to look. I ran straight here. Anyone within miles would have been able to see us arrive. Anyone watching this house knows we are here and they must know we have the device with us. Do you see why we have to leave at once? We'll get back on the ship and fly off. We'll fly all night to hide our destination. The duchess can give her servants leave to go visit family. Get everyone away."

"What about London and the library?"

"We'll have to sneak in."

Not again. Cliff was fed up with sneaking and lying. It always seemed to land him in trouble. "I have an alternative suggestion."

"It had better involve leaving."

"It does, actually, but not secretly. We pack up our things and we all go to London. Rent a house. Act like we plan to stay awhile. Then we take Lola sightseeing. Visit shops and museums. Let Amy escort us around to wherever she thinks is fashionable. London Library becomes just another stop along the way. We don't appear to be running to or from anywhere. Anyone watching can't tell when we've gotten the clue. We lull them into complacency. Meanwhile, we have the settings for the wheels, we decode your message, and then one night we vanish. Your ship swoops down in the night and whisks us away to get the Heart of Ra and then we go celebrate. You with tons of money and Lola with a special new battery."

Sabine pursed her lips. "What prevents them from attacking us while we're happily sightseeing?"

"They've failed twice to kidnap us. Only you and I know all the clues to use the device, so they need us alive. Most sensible plan to me is to watch us and follow wherever we go."

She considered him for a moment, then shook her head. "No. We're leaving. Let's go."

Cliff jogged to follow as she strode out the door. "Sabine."

"No, Cliff. It's not safe. They'll kill you to get to me. They must know by now."

"Know what, that we're lovers?"

She froze.

"Well, we are," he said. "Or am I misremembering what happened in the pirate room?"

"That was a mistake. It *might* have worked if you had let me reciprocate…"

"I don't want your pity sex," he growled, spinning away and storming back into the study. He closed the door firmly behind him, shutting her and everyone else out.

Dammit, why did he only like women who were entirely wrong for him? Maybe he ought to have been chasing after farmer's daughters like people had suggested. Or maybe he would be best served to go back to his habit of keeping all sexual encounters strictly business. Maybe Sabine's plan had been better than his after all.

He crossed the room to the tiny niche that held the

telephone. He'd call down to the train station at the village and spread the word that due to a burglary all locals should be on the lookout for suspicious persons. He'd instruct the household staff to set an overnight watch, just in case. Then he'd make additional phone calls to arrange for passage to London the next morning and to rent a house for the duration of their stay. If he had time, he'd call Chicago and check up on his company.

He was sitting in his chair, leaning back with his feet propped up on the desk, and listening to a slightly time-delayed update on a new client, when the door flew open and Lola ran at him, a bag slung over her shoulder and her spider cage clutched in her arms.

"Daddy!"

Cliff wobbled and nearly upended himself. "Lo, what's wrong?" He swung his feet to the floor and rose, keeping the phone to his ear.

"Daddy, Miss La Capitaine says it's time to go and maybe there's bad guys coming and everybody is angry and scared and I couldn't find Ralph and she says I have to leave him behind!"

"Uh, sorry," Cliff said into the phone. "Something came up and I have to go. Thanks for the update. I'll call again tomorrow when I'm settled in London." He hung up and hugged his daughter. "Babe, you have plenty of time to find Ralph and pack more than that tiny bag. We're not leaving until the morning. We'll ride a train to London and you'll have a new fancy house to explore. Plus we'll visit museums and libraries and maybe the Tower of London."

"I don't wanna go there. People get their heads chopped off there."

"Hyde Park, then. And we'll go shopping. Find you a toy store. I think you deserve it for being my extra special secret helper."

"What am I helping with?"

Cliff unlocked his desk and removed the Sphinx machine

from the drawer. He opened the box and selected a wheel from the stack. "Open Lucas's cage."

Lola obeyed, her eyes shining with eager curiosity. Cliff shoved the wheel down into the mulch that covered the bottom of the cage, brushing the dirt around until it was hidden from sight.

"Tell no one," he instructed. "Not a soul. Not even Sabine."

Lola nodded gravely. Cliff pocketed a second wheel, then returned the Sphinx device to the desk, leaving the drawer unlocked. He nudged Lola toward the door and they walked out together.

"But, Daddy? Sabine said we were going away on her airship today. Not on a train tomorrow."

"She can go however she likes. You and I are taking a train tomorrow. I've already bought the tickets. I have tickets for Duchess Amy and Lady Luella, also, if they want to come along. Let's go pack your things properly, shall we?"

Cliff had been in Lola's room no more than a few minutes when Sabine walked in. He couldn't see her—he was stuck halfway under the bed, straining to reach Ralph, who, as usual, had gotten his little spider self wedged—but he heard the steady pounding of her boots and the swish of her skirts against her legs.

"Hartleigh! Two wheels are missing. What did you do with them?"

Cliff worked the spider out from its self-made prison, then slid out from under the bed. Sabine glowered down at him, the Sphinx device in her hands.

"I'm keeping one on my person and the other is hidden," he replied.

"Hidden where?"

"I'm not telling. I suggest you take the other two and do what I've done. Then we're equally necessary for the decoding of the machine." He handed Ralph to Lola, who stowed him with the other mechanical spiders, her serious expression giving no hint of their secret.

"I ought to tie you up and force you to go along with me."

Cliff didn't doubt she could do it if she chose. He suspected—he hoped—she liked him too much to try.

"I've purchased a train ticket to London in your name," he said. "I would be very happy if you would join us in the morning. I think we will be safer if you are with us. I understand, however, if you choose another path. Amy and Luella are also welcome to come with us, or to go with you, or even remain here if they prefer."

Sabine stared at him for a long time, then jabbed a finger in his direction and snarled, "If you die, I will never forgive you."

She stormed off.

Lola gave a little tug on Cliff's sleeve. "Daddy?"

"Yeah?"

"I liked it better when Miss La Capitaine wanted to kiss you."

He hugged her. "Me too, babe. Me too."

29

The men trailing them had disappeared from sight. Sabine had a lifetime of experience watching her surroundings and the people around her, but she still couldn't locate them. They were well-trained. Quiet. Competent. Worth every penny she had paid.

A young, middle-class couple brushed by her, on their way into the toy store where Cliff and Lola had been for the past quarter-hour. Sabine could easily have picked their pockets. Even as a child thief she wouldn't have bothered. She'd learned early on to spot wealthier prey.

She took a step further back into the entranceway, tucking her skirt behind her to keep it beneath the small awning. The rain was coming harder now, and people everywhere had ducked into the shops to wait out the storm. Perhaps her bodyguards weren't so good after all. Maybe they'd merely hidden from the rain. Or given up on the boring assignment and taken themselves home.

Wind swirled, flinging fat droplets of frigid rain and biting through layers of fabric. Sabine had turned halfway toward the door when it swung open and Cliff and Lola stepped out. Lola clutched a rag doll dressed as a pirate in one arm. Her opposite hand held a small rubber rat. She let out a powerful sneeze, then wiped her snotty nose on her sleeve.

"It's pouring!" she exclaimed. "Daddy, put Sabine under your coat so she won't get wet." She thrust the doll at him.

Sabine's chest tightened. Lola had named a doll for her? Sabine didn't know whether she wanted to laugh, scoff, or give Lola the biggest hug imaginable. Perhaps all three.

Cliff didn't take the doll. He stepped up to the edge of the awning and opened his umbrella. "I'll hail a cab. Wait here."

He dashed off, leaving Lola, Sabine, and doll-Sabine alone.

"See what Daddy bought me?" Lola asked. "I named her Sabine because she's a pirate like you. She used to be a princess, but I took the clothes off a boy pirate doll and switched them. The store man said we had to buy both dolls because no one wants a boy princess doll, but then a boy near us said he wanted the boy princess doll. *His* daddy said, 'Wouldn't you rather have a pirate or a soldier?' but the boy said, 'I want a princess.'"

The door opened again and the boy stepped out, clutching his princess doll, his face bright with joy. The father followed after, an uncertain frown on his face. Sabine gave him a smile and his expression relaxed. He scooped the boy up, hugged him close, and dashed through the rain to a waiting carriage.

"What an incredible thing it must be, to have a good father," Sabine mused. "Do you know how lucky you are, Lola? Do you think that boy knows?"

Lola sniffled and hugged her pirate. "I don't know. Are some people's fathers bad?"

Hartleigh's well-timed return saved Sabine from an explanation. His trousers were soaked halfway up his calves and splattered up to his thighs, but the umbrella had kept his top half dry.

"I have a steam carriage waiting up ahead. I'll take you one-at-a-time so you can stay as dry as possible." He picked up Lola, settling her on his hip and adjusting the umbrella to cover her completely. "Be right back."

He ran to the vehicle and put Lola inside, keeping her dry while getting himself damper yet. Sabine watched. The cab wasn't terribly far off. She'd been rained on plenty of times in her life. She had no need to wait for him to return. It was silly to wait. They'd end up squashed together beneath the umbrella.

Her body thrilled at the thought of her whole length pressed against him. The last time he'd gotten himself soaking wet...

Before she could even finish scolding herself for fantasizing about that day, he had scampered back, holding out a hand to help her down the two wide steps to the pavement. Sabine's bare fingers closed over his gloved ones. The rain hammered down in torrential sheets, streaming from rooftops, flooding the streets. Cliff didn't even hesitate to shield Sabine with the umbrella, exposing himself to the full force of the downpour.

Sabine knew she should protest. She should insist that she run to the cab on her own, or at least that they share the umbrella. The sheer novelty of the experience kept her mouth closed. Never in her life had anyone treated her with gentlemanly deference.

She wasn't the type to want or ask for help. She sneered at men who offered unsolicited and unneeded advice or assistance. But there was no condescension in Hartleigh's behavior. He knew she could handle far more difficult situations than a rainstorm. He didn't question her intellect or her competence. What he did do was put the needs of those he cared for above his own. He had extended her a courtesy, treating her like a lady.

A lady!

She'd been a thief, a pest, a pirate, an adventurer, a businesswoman, and a heroine, but never just a lady.

"Thank you," she said as he handed her up into the carriage, grateful to be dry and to be seen for herself, as a person, rather than as an untouchable legend.

"My pleasure." He said it as if he really had taken pleasure from walking her through a storm, nonsensical as that was.

He shook out the umbrella and climbed up into the carriage. His clothes were soaked through, his hat a dripping mess. He took off his eyeglasses and tried to wipe them, but even his handkerchief was wet. Sighing, he shoved the smeary spectacles back onto his face.

"Well, Lola," he said. "I'm sorry, but our park visit will have to wait until another day. Even if this rain stops, everything will be mud. Where would you like to go instead? A museum? A library?" Cliff gave Sabine a significant glance.

She shook her head. No. Too early. Redbeard and his allies would be expecting another quick hunt for clues. They needed to take their time for Cliff's plan to work.

"You're going home to change. You're wet to the bone."

He shivered. "I'll dry."

"Yes. At home." Sabine opened the panel between the passengers and the driver and gave the address of their rental house. The carriage hissed and puffed and started down the road, as the rain continued to beat relentlessly down.

With no one wanting to walk and the storm hampering visibility, traffic crawled along the streets like a lethargic slug. By the time the cab rolled to a stop in front of their door, Hartleigh was shuddering like a steam engine about to blow, and his lips had turned a terrifying shade of purple. Sabine pulled him out of the car, up the steps, and into the foyer, not letting him even pause to open the umbrella.

"His Grace needs a warm bath. Now," she demanded of the butler.

"I'm f-fine," Cliff insisted through chattering teeth. He sneezed. "Just need dry clothes."

"A warm bath," Sabine repeated. "Dry clothing, lots of

blankets. Stoke the fire in his bedchamber and have a pot of tea sent up. I'm going to fetch Miss Lola."

She grabbed the umbrella, splashed out to the cab, paid their fare, and carried Lola into the house. Sabine's skirts were damp, but nothing that a few minutes in front of the fire wouldn't fix. She called for blankets and tea, and settled herself and Lola on the floor by the hearth in the front parlor.

"I like pirate tea parties," Lola declared a half-hour later. Her pot was empty, her plate a mess of crumbs and one sliver of salmon she hadn't liked. Sabine-the-pirate-doll sat propped against an unused teacup, the rubber rat tucked beneath her cloth arm. "Are they always this fun?"

Sabine glanced out the window. One of the bodyguards—who hadn't run off after all— caught her eye as he walked by, then ducked beneath his umbrella and took himself out of sight. Good. The house was protected.

"I couldn't say," Sabine replied. "This is my first pirate tea party."

Lola's eyes widened. "Really? Your first?"

"Yes. Most pirates I know don't want to have tea parties." She gave Lola a hand up. "Let's go find your father. He should have joined us by now."

"I thought he was taking a bath."

The exact reason Sabine wanted to bring Lola. In the event he wasn't yet dressed, she wanted a way to check on him without walking in on him naked and starting the spiral of wanting all over again.

Cliff answered when she rapped on his bedroom door. He was no longer turning blue, but his cheeks were pale. He wore a plush dressing gown and no eyeglasses. His hair was tousled, his feet bare.

"Sabine?" He sneezed and wiped his nose with a handkerchief. "Did you need something?"

"We're having a pirate tea party, Daddy," Lola explained, squeezing past Sabine. She sniffled and wiped her nose on her sleeve, then dropped into a curtsy. "Lady Lola and Lady Sabine invite His Grace, the Duke of Hartleigh, to an elegant and dangerous pirate tea party."

"I don't know, Lo." Cliff covered his mouth to hide a cough. "I think you gave me your cold. I should probably keep away from Sabine so I don't..." He sneezed. "Sneeze on her."

Sabine studied him. Watery eyes, red nose. Even in the warm room he shivered. "Hartleigh, you look terrible."

He shrugged. "It's a cold. I'll be fine." He shivered again, a full-body tremor punctuated by a hacking cough. "I'm going to get a blanket."

Sabine walked up to him, laying the back of her hand against his forehead. "Shit. You're burning up, Hartleigh. You need to get to bed. I should never have let you walk through that freezing cold rain without the umbrella."

"It wasn't that c-cold until I had to sit in that cab for f-forty-five minutes."

Sabine made a forceful gesture at the bed. "In bed, Duke. Now."

He gave her a crooked grin. "I wish you would've said that a few days ago." He crawled under the blankets, pulling them tight to his chin. "Still cold."

Lola hopped up on the bed beside him. "Are you sick, Daddy?"

"Yeah, sorry, babe. You'll have to reschedule the tea party. Is Duchess Amy home from her visits? Maybe you can invite her."

"Okay." Lola planted a kiss on his forehead. "Get lots of rest and drink plenty of water. I'll be back to check on you."

Damn, the girl was adorable. Sabine spent the entire rest of the day with her, making up pirate stories, searching the house for secret passages, and periodically peeking into Hartleigh's bedchamber. By evening, Lola had worn herself out, and Sabine tucked her into bed in the adjoining room, leaving the door between the two ajar.

"In case Daddy needs me," Lola murmured.

Sabine kissed her cheek. "Sleep well, little pirate."

You're caring too much, Sabine, she thought, slipping into Cliff's room. He lay still and sleeping, as he had been for the past several hours. *You let yourself befriend them and now you're getting carried away.*

She sat on the edge of Cliff's bed, watching the gentle rise and fall of his chest beneath the blankets. She touched his brow again.

"Still feverish." She pressed a kiss to the spot her fingers had touched. "Be well, Hartleigh. You have a smart, brave, wonderful daughter who needs a Heart. And I need a partner to help me fetch it."

Pirates don't have partners. Cliff and Lola are not your family.

Today they had felt like one, though. A good family, where people loved and helped one another. She was a fool for letting herself linger in that sensation. All too soon it would come to an end. It always did. Someone always got hurt.

She gently closed the door to Hartleigh's room and started for the stairs. Tomorrow he'd wake up feeling better and she could go back to trying not to care.

Now, though, it was time to consult with her night watchmen. No one was getting hurt tonight.

30

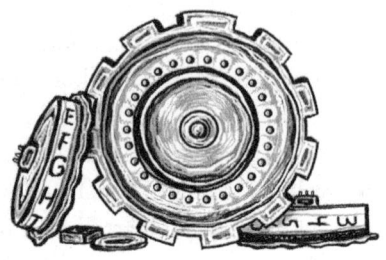

The device clicked and clanked, spitting out another line of nonsense. In deference to Cliff's illness, Sabine had handed over her two rotors so he could play with the Sphinx device. With the caveat that he not "blow anything up again."

Cliff didn't expect to learn anything new, but he was enjoying spinning the wheels into various positions that spelled out words. C-O-D-E. Nonsense. D-U-K-E. Nonsense. L-O-L-A. Now he was just being silly.

He was happily positioning the wheels to spell out naughty words, when a fist hammered on his suite door. Amy whisked into the room before he had a chance to answer.

"Hartleigh. Are you dressed? We have guests. You need to come downstairs."

Cliff coughed, making it sound worse than it really was. "Still sick. Sorry. Don't want to infect anyone."

"You've been in bed for two full days. That's more than enough."

He agreed. Those two days had been miserable. He'd tossed and turned, trying desperately to snatch bits of sleep between coughing fits. He'd been alternately sweating and shivering, half delirious from lack of proper rest, his whole body aching.

Today he was tired still, and the cough lingered, but his fever had broken and he felt well enough to be bored of lying in bed. He'd dressed, but that had sapped much of his energy. Lounging on the sofa in the sitting room under a blanket and fiddling with the Sphinx device was about all he could handle.

"I'm afraid I'm not well enough to leave my rooms. But I'd love another pot of tea, if you don't mind."

"For heaven's sake, Hartleigh, you can't order me to fetch tea! I am a duchess!"

"A duchess by a rather dubious marriage, if you ask me."

"It was a perfectly sensible marriage. He wanted someone to be there for him in his old age, and I wanted a husband who would give me a proper station in life without pressing his attentions on me. We were very fond of one another." She turned toward the door. "Luella," she called, "please send the ladies along. His Grace is lonely and in need of visitors."

Sighing, Cliff closed the Sphinx device and set it aside. "I'm not interested in one of your 'perfectly sensible' marriages."

"Of course not. You're young and vigorous. You want a pretty girl to warm your bed and bear your children."

"I want love."

Oh, hell. Where had that come from? Apparently he'd unburied twenty-year-old Cliff and his fairytale imagination. Or maybe he was stating a simple truth. He wanted the impossible. Knowing you weren't going to get it didn't always stop you from wanting it.

"I will never marry anyone I don't love," he vowed. "Therefore I will never marry."

"One has nothing to do with the other," Amy replied, matter-of-factly.

"In your world, perhaps."

"It's the same world, Hartleigh. You might not like it, but we all have to live in it."

Three young ladies and three older women he assumed were their mothers paraded into the room, circling him like a pack of wolves stalking their prey. One of the young women wore eyeglasses and carried a book. Another wore trousers and a suit coat. The third had her hair cut short. A pair of goggles hung around her neck, and several tools jutted from her wide belt. Cliff glanced at Amy and raised a single eyebrow.

"Your Grace," the duchess announced. "Allow me to present some of the most accomplished, unconventional, and independent ladies in all society."

"Hi," Cliff said, before she could start in with names and titles. He lifted a hand in greeting, then covered a cough. "I'm afraid I'm not in the best health today, so I suggest you all vacate the room before you come down with something. I'm terribly sorry I can't meet you properly. Perhaps another time."

Perhaps never.

"But, Your Grace," Amy said, fixing her icy glare on him, "you said you were tired of being shut up all alone in your suite."

"I was. But as it turns out..." He coughed again, louder and harder. Talking made his throat hurt. "I'm not yet ready for this level of excitement. Please excuse me."

"I knew it," grumbled one of the mothers, just loud enough for Cliff to hear. "I knew your goggle-wearing engineer ways would turn him off. We'll never find a man eccentric enough..."

"I beg your pardon, madam," Cliff interrupted. "Your daughter is a lovely woman who appears to possess both intelligence and spirit, and I'd thank you not to try to crush it out of her. My advice: send her off to college and let her pick her own husband if she wants one." His forceful words triggered a coughing fit, and Amy hustled all the women from the room, babbling apologies.

When the coughing finally died down, Cliff slumped back on the sofa, his chest aching. Perhaps getting up out of bed hadn't been the best idea. He picked up the Sphinx device and opened it, examining the rotors as he awaited Amy's inevitable return. Perhaps the wheels would show patterns of wear that might give a clue to the proper settings.

"You are impossible!" the duchess moaned, barging in without bothering to knock. "I went out of my way to find women I thought you'd like and you didn't even talk to them."

"Sick," he reminded her, not looking up from the wheel he was examining. "I'm thinking of going back to bed."

She sank down onto the edge of the sofa beside him. "One of them would have suited you, Clifford. Maybe you could even have fallen in love."

Her use of his given name made him raise his head. She looked weary, defeated. "Amy, everything will be fine. When this is over, I'll make certain all the debts are taken care of so you and Luella and all your staff can remain in the house without worry."

"When *what* is over? I don't even know what you're doing. Is that machine part of it? What does it do that's so valuable?"

"It's going to lead us to a treasure, but now that I think about it, this machine alone could bring us a great deal of money if sold to the right people."

"A treasure." Her brows arched skeptically. "A treasure and a valuable... typewriter-sort-of-thing."

"Yes. I promise, Amy. I won't leave you penniless. But in return, I'd like you to *please* stop trying to marry me off."

"You need to marry someday or the line will end."

"Then let it end. I really don't care. I'm an American. A Chicago businessman. I make a terrible duke." He fell into coughing again.

Amy smiled at last. "Actually, I think you would make quite a good duke if you let yourself try." She rose and shook out her skirts. "Get some rest, Hartleigh. You look pale and that cough is terrible. I'll order some tea sent up. Good luck with your treasure machine. Keep me informed of your progress."

Cliff eyed the door to the bedroom for a moment, considering a nap. Unfortunately, getting to the bed would require standing up and crossing the room. The sofa wasn't so bad, really. Plus, he did want that tea to soothe his burning throat.

He set the cryptographic wheel back into its slot and adjusted the position, trying to think of any words the duke might have used to encrypt his directions. Nothing obvious sprang to mind. Heart was too long. Ra, too short.

A-M-U-N, he tried, going with the Egyptian theme. He typed the first letter of the mangled line of text Sabine had copied for him from her encrypted letter.

The machine clanked and whirred, the keys suddenly moving of their own accord. Paper spooled from the slot in the side.

"What the hell?"

Cliff held his hands away from the machine as it churned, hardly daring to breathe lest he knock something out of place. When the device at last fell quiet, he ripped the strip of paper off and examined the row of printed numbers and letters.

"My God." He set the machine carefully aside, then threw off the blanket and leapt for the door. "Sabine!" He raced through the halls and down the stairs. "Sabine, are you here?"

He didn't see her anywhere, but he found Amy in the parlor, chatting with two of the young women from earlier. Apparently he hadn't scared them all off.

"Amy, is Sabine here? I need to speak to her at once." He grabbed hold of a chair to steady himself. His legs wobbled and his head spun from the overexertion.

Amy lost none of her cool public demeanor. "Miss Diebin and Miss Lola arrived home from their excursion not long ago, caked in mud. I believe they are both bathing."

"Right. Thanks."

Cliff raced back up two flights of stairs to Sabine's bedchamber. He jiggled the handle, but it was locked tight. He hammered on the door.

"Sabine!" he shouted between coughs. "Sabine, are you in

there? I found something important!" He knocked again. "I think I've found the location of the Heart of Ra!"

The door jerked open and he nearly fell into the room, barely catching himself with a hand on the doorframe. Little colored sparkles danced in front of his vision, obscuring the image of Sabine clutching a towel to cover her naked body.

"You found the location? But how?"

"The machine. I was playing with it. Using that encrypted text you gave me. Putting in settings. It started going all by itself. Spit out a bunch of numbers." He thrust the paper at her. She took it with one hand, her other hand still carefully clutching the towel. "Don't know where it is, but that's definitely a latitude and longitude." The room began to sway. "Whoa."

Sabine looked from the paper to his face. "Cliff? Are you okay?"

"Maybe I should sit down. I feel a little…"

His knees gave out and he toppled. Sabine dropped both the paper and the towel and lunged to grab him. Even naked she still wore that half-armor.

Except it's not armor, his mind slowly registered as she lowered him to the ground. The metal was built right into her skin—an entire half of her chest replaced with cold steel.

The world went black.

31

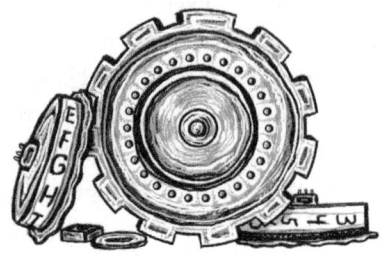

"Sabine." Cliff's arms reached out, hungering to draw her near. Nothing. Empty space.

His eyes flew open in surprise. He would have sworn he could feel her warmth, smell her scent. He blinked several times, forcing his eyes to focus. He wasn't wearing his spectacles.

He lay in a bed, under a thick quilt. That explained the warmth. The bed was unfamiliar. *Her* bed.

Cliff turned his face into the bedding, inhaling. A hint of feminine musk. Fresh, clean soap, tinged with lemon. He could imagine Sabine dragging a bar of it across her creamy skin. Skin that he'd seen all of in that brief instant. He wished the memory brought a clearer image with it.

He didn't sit up, not daring to risk passing out again, but he spent a few moments taking stock of himself. Someone had stripped him down to shirt and trousers. His coat, vest, and necktie were draped across the back of a nearby chair. His boots sat on the floor beside it.

Cliff picked up his eyeglasses from the bedside table where they sat, neatly folded. Sabine had done this, he suspected. With the corrective lenses back in place, he could see more clearly, but another perusal of the room told him nothing new. He was alone, in Sabine's bed, half undressed. His chest still ached from the persistent cough.

His gaze landed on the bell pull. He could ring for assistance. Request some food and drink. Demand to know how he'd gotten here. It seemed a properly duke-ish thing to do. Might as well make some use of his title, since he couldn't seem to do anything for himself yet. His fingers had just curled around the braided rope when the door opened.

"You're awake."

Cliff's hand dropped to his lap. "Sabine."

She was fully clothed, in a dark blue dress topped by a silver corset. Her hair had been done up into a knot at her nape. He caught his gaze lingering on her curves, in an inappropriate attempt to sharpen the blurry memory of her body, and jerked his eyes up to meet hers.

Kinsley, you worthless cad, he scolded himself.

"How are you feeling?" Sabine asked.

"Fine. A bit tired. I haven't tried standing up yet."

"Don't. Hauling you into that bed once was enough."

So she *had* been the one to put him here. She'd probably undressed him, too. The thought sparked a stirring in his groin that he was still too ill to act on.

"Sorry," he replied. "I shouldn't have been running through the house. I was over-excited."

"And then the sight of me fresh from my bath did you in, naturally."

Ripples of arousal raced through his entire body. Dammit, this was not the time!

"Um, right." *Don't look at her. Don't think about her bathing. Be content that your body is giving you positive indications that you are on the mend.*

"That was a joke, Hartleigh. Funny. You're supposed to at least chuckle." She shrugged. "Maybe I'm not good with jokes. Germans have no sense of humor, you know."

Cliff at least cracked a smile at that. "Was that a joke, too?"

She sniffed. "Enough nonsense. While you were in here recovering from your inelegant swoon, I spent some time playing with the Sphinx device myself."

He pushed himself up straighter, grateful to discover that the movement didn't make him dizzy. "And? What else did you find?"

"Nothing. Typing in the text from the coded message produced rubbish. Your setting may have produced a clue, but our treasure map is far from complete."

"Damn. Did you at least look up the coordinates?"

"I did. They lead to a point in South America. In the mountains."

Cliff's eyebrows rose. "South America. That's quite a distance."

"Six days by airship if it's a fast craft in good weather. Could be twice that if things go wrong."

"So it could take up to a month to fly there, find the Heart of Ra, and fly back."

"Why fly back? Once we're there, you'll be closer to California."

"Right." California. Damn. He hadn't thought about that part of his plan in days, if not longer. Finding the Heart had become his only goal.

Primary goal, he corrected, his eyes raking over Sabine once again. He was dying to see her naked again, but not by accident. He wanted her begging him to touch her everywhere, desperate to share all of herself.

She stared back at him, the toe of her boot tapping impatiently. "Well? Are you finally going to ask about it?"

"About what?"

She frowned at him over the top of her spectacles before pushing them securely onto her nose. "This." She waved a hand across the left side of her chest. "That's what's bothering you, isn't it?"

"No." True, he was bursting with questions. What had happened to her? When? Was the metal plate protecting the sensitive organs beneath, or were there further biomechanics under the surface? Was it uncomfortable, or something she hardly noticed? Would she be able to feel it if he touched her there? None of that was any business of his, however, and he wouldn't pry. If Sabine wanted him to know, she could tell him herself, the way Lola had shown off her heart.

"No." She laughed. "Please, Hartleigh. You're staring at me and practically squirming."

"I know. Because I desperately want you in this bed with me, both of us naked and aroused, but it's hopeless because you're not interested and I'm not feeling well. Damned frustrating."

Her lips parted and she stared at him, speechless for a long, awkward moment. "I see." She composed herself. "I suppose that's what you get for insisting on doing things your way. Go back to sleep, Hartleigh. I have outings with Lola to plan for tomorrow and I need you healthy. We're going to the theater two nights from now."

He blinked at her. "We are?"

"Someone noticed that I'm in town and His Majesty King Edward has 'rewarded' me with an invitation to a private performance of some new pirate play—where private means half the royal family and dozens of dukes and things."

"I assume I'm one of those dozens?"

"You are. Go to sleep. Get better."

"Are you going to search the London Library without me?"

"I'm debating it. I'm not certain whether we've lulled our enemies into a stupor or if they're simply waiting for you to make an appearance. They know we're in this together. Good night."

She turned and started for the door.

"Sabine," Cliff called.

She didn't look back. "What?"

"If I'm here, where are you going to sleep?"

"That's none of your business."

He watched her departing backside, wondering how the hell he would ever manage to sleep surrounded by sheets that had hugged every inch of her body.

32

Sabine leaned against the doorframe, watching Cliff fidget with his cufflinks. He was devastatingly handsome, and the exceptionally tailored evening wear only emphasized his trim figure. Her body hadn't calmed down since their brief bout of intimacy, and his candid confession of his desire for her had her lying awake at night. If they didn't return to their hunt for the Heart of Ra soon, she was going to lose what little self control she still possessed.

"Everything is arranged for tomorrow," she said.

He adjusted his necktie. "I assume you mean the library?"

"Yes. I will have guards posted to watch the entrance. If anyone suspicious follows us in or out, or visits during the time we are there, we will know about it. I visited briefly with Lola two days ago, so it will fit right in as part of her 'show Daddy everything he missed' tour."

Cliff turned away from the mirror, fixing his blue eyes on her. "Thank you for looking after her all this week. Every night before bed she's come chattering to me about how much fun she's had. I was afraid after that mess in Switzerland she might hesitate to go anywhere without me, but you make her feel safe and loved and I can't even begin to express how much that means to both of us."

Sabine almost looked away, his gaze was so powerful, but it would have done little good. His voice was thick with emotion and it penetrated down to her bones.

"Thank you," she replied. "She's an amazing little girl." *I adore her. She's crept under my skin and I don't think I can get her out, and I'm terrified you're doing the same thing. Do you know what happens to the people I care about?*

No. Of course he didn't. She hadn't shared, and she wouldn't because that would let him even closer than he already was. And that was far too dangerous.

"She is. I'm glad she has a woman like you to look up to." His eyes drifted up and down, taking in Sabine's elegant opera gown. "You look stunning."

"Thank you. This is my 'meeting with the king' dress, so no short skirts or trousers." Her silky black gown brushed the floor, hiding the boots she wore underneath. The sheer silver overlay added some sparkle and covered her arms and neck well enough to conceal her scars. True, the black corset topping the dress might draw some comment from the more conservative ladies—"Girls these days, turning undergarments into fashion! Shameful!"—but not enough to cause trouble. She would be the Heroine of the Royal Family and not a thieving pirate.

"Dressed up for Dirty Bertie, eh?" Cliff mused. "He'll definitely want to jump you. He's a skirt chaser."

"*Do not* say that tonight. The last thing I need is to have to break you out of the Tower of London or save you from a noose. He's a very popular king. Be respectful."

Cliff shrugged. "I'm an uncouth American."

"You are a duke. Act like one. If you want Redbeard and his lackeys to think we're in town to mingle and party like devil-may-care aristocrats, you need to play the part. You can drink, gamble, and have mistresses, but you *never* insult the king."

His eyes bore into hers. "Very well, then. I'd like a single-malt Scotch and one spectacular mistress, please."

Sabine stared back. "You don't give up, do you?"

"Not easily, no."

She spun on her heel and strode out the door. "Finish your preparations. It's time to leave."

The Countess of Something-or-Other clung to Cliff's arm, peppering him with questions about America and how he was adapting to life in England. She was *so* pleased to find him such a handsome, agreeable man, and Sabine was *so* ready to storm off so she didn't have to listen to any more of the inane fawning.

Cliff caught her eye and gave her a quick smirk, as if to say, *See? Some women do like me.*

She pinched her lips together so she wouldn't scowl and tried to listen to one of her royal rescuees going on at length about her gown.

"It must be a House of Worth design, yes?"

"No," Sabine replied. "It's a Werrington."

The woman frowned. "Pardon?"

"Werrington Designs, by Mrs. Euphemia Werrington Wilson. Look her up. She's brilliant."

"Thank you. I will do that. You are sharing a box with the new Duke of Hartleigh tonight, I hear? You two seem to know one another well."

Apparently this was the polite British way of saying, "So, you must be the duke's mistress."

"Yes. We are neighbors." *And everyone knows we're currently living in the same house and I've been all over town with his daughter.* "We also share a common interest in antiquities."

A bell rang to indicate the performance was imminent, saving Sabine from suffering through any more unpleasant conversation. She made a hasty goodbye and dashed off to her box to take her seat.

Cliff joined her a minute later, sliding his chair so close that his leg brushed her skirt. "You abandoned me. You didn't think I was intending to give in to that woman's flirtations, did you?"

She glanced down at the stage, counting the fluffy white clouds on the painted backdrop to distract her from all the eyes that were staring at them. "It doesn't matter to me what you intend."

"Yes it does."

A heavy silence fell between them, until she looked up at last and sighed. "Fine. She made me jealous. Is that what you want to hear?"

"No, actually. I don't want you to be jealous. I want you to be confident that I prefer you."

"I'm not your One True Love, Hartleigh. You can't win me with a magic kiss."

Although right now she would have given just about anything to have him sweep her into his arms and kiss her senseless. It had been so long since she'd felt his lips on hers and she wanted a taste of him so badly she was starting to question her sanity.

"Watch the operetta," she ordered. "It's brand new and is supposed to be about pirates."

The orchestra took up their instruments, and Sabine gave herself over to the music, her body relaxing somewhat. The stage became the deck of an airship, where the actors sang and danced in celebration of a made-up prince's birthday celebration. The party dragged on. The prince flirted with every woman and bemoaned the fact that now he was of age he would have to marry one of them. Sabine sighed in relief when the pirates attacked at last.

"This isn't very good, is it?" Cliff whispered.

It got worse. The prow of another airship dropped down

from above. Standing on it was a woman in pantaloons with a mass of blond curls piled on her head. She waved a sword like it was a magic wand and began to warble.

"*It is I-I-I, the pirate queen!*" she sang. "*I come to your aid! I come to save you-u-u-u-u!*"

"Gott im Himmel," Sabine moaned. No wonder she'd been invited. This play was some farcical rendition of her own story.

"That's not supposed to be you, is it?" Cliff asked. The horror in his voice matched her own.

"She's blond! And a soprano!"

The ridiculous, trilling excuse for a pirate danced around the stage, slaying enemies with her incompetence, apparently. She nearly swooned when she saw the prince and instead of saving the remaining passengers and fleeing to safety, they sang a ten-minute love duet while supposedly deadly pirates waltzed around them. When the number concluded, the audience burst into enthusiastic applause.

Sabine put her head in her hands. "I have never been more embarrassed in my life."

Hartleigh was using the last traces of his cough to cover near-hysterical laughter. Tears of mirth shimmered behind his glasses.

"Where's your prince, now, Sabine?" he asked, dabbing his eyes with a handkerchief. "He was so madly in love with you."

"He doesn't exist! This is not at all how it happened, and *that woman* is the worst excuse for a pirate I've ever seen!"

The first act concluded with another battle scene, where the pirate queen sacrificed herself to allow the prince and his court to escape. The audience roared their approval as the evil pirate captain dragged her away, bound and gagged.

"I am not leaving this box during intermission," Sabine snarled, her arms crossed over her chest. "I might murder someone if I do."

"I can see why the people of England love you," Hartleigh

said, his laughter finally under control. "They are eating this up."

"It's ridiculous. There were no pirates. It was a storm. I spied a floundering airship and flew to her aid. I did not swing down on a rope shrieking about how I was there to save everyone. I did a careful survey of the ship and her passengers to ensure that it wasn't a trap. Then Nicole maneuvered Die Fledermaus close enough that we could set up a ramp and I could escort everyone off the dying ship before she crashed. I had no idea that among the passengers were two of the king's daughters and half-a-dozen other members of the royal family. I was too busy making arrangements for carrying thirty extra people on a ship meant for no more than ten. We landed as soon as possible and off-loaded everyone. It was only when I saw the papers the next day that I learned I had become some sort of British heroine. Eventually they dragged me before the king to accept a medal."

"A better story. Less melodramatic, though, and there's no prince."

"Thank God."

Cliff leaned toward her, his thigh pressing into hers. He reached to tuck a stray curl behind her ear. "I can offer you a clumsy duke in his place."

Heat flashed across Sabine's skin. She scanned the theater. Most of the boxes had emptied for intermission. No one was obviously looking at her. Could she kiss him without anyone noticing? Did she even care who saw them?

The door behind her opened before she could make a decision. She whirled around in time to see Lord Barton stride into her private box. The woman on his arm was drenched in jewels and was as astonishingly beautiful as anyone Sabine had ever seen. Her sleek, dark curls and perfect olive complexion made even Miss Willingham appear ordinary.

"Hartleigh!" Barton exclaimed. "I thought I spied two empty seats in your box. What luck, eh, old chap?"

Cliff rose from his seat, glowering down at the shorter man. "That's 'Your Grace,' to you."

Barton rocked backward. "Excuse me?"

"I may be a clueless American, but even I know a duke outranks a marquess, and since we are hardly intimate friends, I'd thank you not to refer to me in any sort of familiar manner."

Barton's eyes narrowed. "Why the sudden ill-humor, *Your Grace*? Dukedom going to your head?"

"You barge into my box uninvited and then are surprised when I'm annoyed?"

Barton shrugged. "It isn't as if you could be having a brush with your pirate mistress out here in the open." He paused, lips pursing in thought. "Or would you? Daring, that."

"Get out. You're a pest and I trust you about as far as I can piss. The last time I saw you I ended up kidnapped."

"Ah, yes. Damned shame, that. They should have taken me. I'm one of the wealthiest men in the country, you know, and, well…" He grinned at his mistress. "Lovely Adriana is wearing more than your entire dukedom is worth, from what I understand. It's no wonder they let you go so easily."

Sabine glanced over the rail at the seats below. "Shall I push him over the edge, Hartleigh? He's always drunk, so it'll probably look like an accident."

Adriana let out an offended cry. "Really! Of all the vulgar jests. You may dress like a lady, but you are nothing of the sort."

Sabine almost retorted that it wasn't a jest, but since she wasn't one hundred percent certain Barton was an enemy, she had no intention of actually killing or maiming him.

"Go back to your real seats, Barton," Cliff ordered, waving at the door. "Leave us alone."

Barton only laughed. "Oh, we don't have real seats. We weren't invited. Events are more fun when you pop in unannounced. Have a nice night with your bloodthirsty wench." He took Adriana by the arm and strode out as boldly as he'd entered.

"Asshole," Cliff muttered.

"Spy," Sabine guessed.

"Yes. He conveniently turns up at every event we attend. Do you think he's reporting to Redbeard?"

"Possible. But why? As he said, he's rich. What would he get out of the bargain?"

"No idea. But we'll have to keep an eye on him. And be careful going home tonight."

"I have a guard waiting to follow us home and two watching the house. I'll give them specific instructions to look for Barton tomorrow during our library visit."

"Good."

The people in the next box over returned, ending their chance for further speculation. Sabine watched the stage and fidgeted. Her body hummed with restless energy. Barton's interruption had dampened her lust, though. She could no longer think about kissing Cliff without worrying that an enemy might happen along while she was distracted.

The second act of the operetta was as awful as the first. The enemy pirate sang his own love song, while the warbling pirate queen rejected him with ear-splitting high notes. The prince, meanwhile, gathered an army of redcoats who stomped about to a vaguely patriotic melody. Half the soldiers then vanished so they could reappear as pirates for yet another long battle scene.

Beside her, Cliff had grown tense. She glanced at him. His fingers were clenched, his jaw hard.

"This is insulting," he spat.

"To me? Or in general?" To be honest, Sabine was no longer paying a great deal of attention. She was too busy eyeing the crowd for signs that Barton or anyone else was watching her with particular interest and listening for the creak of the door behind her. She'd even discreetly slipped her knife from beneath her dress for easier access.

"To you. That supposed pirate woman is a travesty. She's

done nothing this entire act but wail and moan for her prince to rescue her. She hasn't even *tried* to escape on her own. She's turned into a helpless ninny. You would have been out of there in a heartbeat."

"I wouldn't have been there in the first place, because I wouldn't have wasted so much time romancing a prince that the enemy had a chance to capture me."

"Very true. And… Oh, for God's sake, now they're kissing instead of fighting."

"Says the man who kissed me while being kidnapped and then again in a secret dungeon entrance."

"Neither of those times involved enemies with swords—" The rest of his words were lost beneath the collective gasp as the entire theater went dark.

33

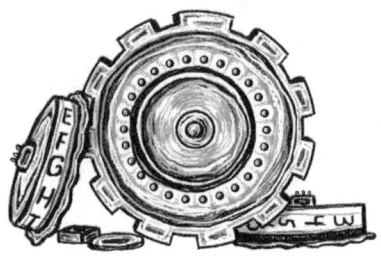

Sabine's fingers clamped down on Cliff's arm, tugging him up and out of his seat. "Stay close," she whispered.

Cliff smacked into one of the empty chairs behind him. Around the theater, points of light began to appear as people struck matches.

"Ow."

Sabine shushed him. The door hinges squeaked and he banged against the doorframe as they stumbled out of the box into the blackness of the corridor. He swallowed another gasp of pain.

"One," he heard Sabine whisper.

"What?" He moved along with her, his feet propelling him forward even as his mind shouted to stop. He braced himself for the inevitable crash into a wall. Or the jab of an enemy knife between the ribs. He shuddered.

"Two."

"Where are we going?" She seemed to have some destination in mind, and he wasn't sure it was "out."

"The safest place in the theater. Three."

"Three what? Can you see anything? I—" He stumbled.

Sabine paused to let him catch his balance. "Almost there. Be quiet."

They walked on for what seemed an extraordinarily long time for "almost there." At last, Sabine stopped and a door creaked.

"Here."

Sabine dragged him through the narrow entranceway of another box, toward a group of people half-lit by flickering flames. In the dim light, Cliff missed the step up and toppled forward, sprawling onto the floor between a pair of startled women.

He winced. "Sorry."

"Your Majesty," Sabine exclaimed. "Are you well? Can I be of any assistance?"

Christ Almighty. Cliff struggled to his feet as quickly and calmly as possible. He'd just fallen on his face in the private box of the King of England. That was probably the sort of social faux-pas that got you permanently banned from the country.

Which could be a good thing. Maybe he was such an embarrassment they'd strip him of his title and send him back to Chicago.

Banishment now, though, would take him away from Sabine and away from the remaining clues to the Heart of Ra. Definitely not so good. He'd have to do his best to apologize.

"Miss Diebin. How good of you to come."

The man who had spoken neither looked nor sounded like the wastrel gossip had claimed him to be. Nor did he seem the angry sort of monarch who would punish a man for clumsiness. Gray-bearded and bald, King Edward had a friendly smile and an avuncular manner. He held a lit cigarette that did nothing to illuminate the box. A man standing beside the king held an oil lamp, and another in the corner of the box shone a flashlight directly into Cliff's chest.

"We are all well here," the king continued. "Nothing but a

power outage, it seems. Unreliable things, these electric lights." His gaze turned to Cliff.

"Hi," Cliff blurted. "Sorry to intrude. I'm…"

"I know who you are, Hartleigh. One can hardly pick up a paper these days without seeing some mention of your name. I would like to talk with you before long. Perhaps after a *proper* introduction."

"Uh, right." Dear God, he was the most awkward, bumbling man in existence. He hadn't expected to feel so stunned to meet royalty. Then again, he hadn't expected it to happen in such an unusual way, either. He was probably supposed to have arranged to be presented to the king long ago, instead of flying all over hunting treasure. "Sorry for being a lousy duke."

King Edward chortled. "Oh, others have been worse, believe you me."

A shadow appeared in the doorway, and both Sabine and Flashlight Man spun toward it, bodies tensed, knives in hand.

"Theater Director Collins with a report for His Majesty," the shadow spoke.

The knives vanished, but Flashlight Man's intense stare didn't waver as the theater director entered. Cliff had a sudden curiosity about how much of his ungraceful fall had been the step and how much may have been someone helping him along.

"Our sincerest apologies for the interruption to the performance," Collins gushed. "There appears to be a problem with the electrical lines coming into the building. Repairs are underway and we hope to resume the operetta shortly. Our staff is lighting lanterns throughout the theater in the meantime. If there is anything we can do to be of service, please let me know."

Cliff spent the next quarter-hour standing stiffly in the corner of the box, behind unknown members of the royal family, or the king's friends, or whoever they were. Sabine stood beside him, in full pirate mode, her body ready for action, her eyes ever searching. Compared to her, he felt like the helpless ninny pirate woman from the play.

The moment the lights were restored, Sabine led him into the hall, but she turned toward the exit rather than their box.

"Move quickly and watch for anything suspicious."

He nodded and followed. They made their way down the stairs and out the theater doors without incident, but were hardly ten yards down the block when a hulking man materialized out of nowhere. Cliff let out a yelp and leapt in front of Sabine, adopting some approximation of a fighting stance.

Sabine laughed. "Nice to see you care, Duke, but he's with us."

"Need a cab, Captain?" the man asked.

A short time later, Cliff and Sabine ascended the front steps of their rented townhouse, while behind them her guards conferred about plans for watching the entrances, windows, and rooftop throughout the night. Every muscle in Cliff's body was clenched. He'd spent the last hour or more waiting for some new catastrophe, certain that enemies lurked around every corner. Even here at home he couldn't relax. What if it had all been a distraction? What if while they were out someone had come looking for the device? Looking for hostages? Looking for Lola? He couldn't relax until he had seen her, here with him and unharmed.

He took the stairs two at a time, a bad idea for someone recently recovered from illness, but he didn't care. Sabine matched his pace, probably expecting him to do something foolish or to faint again. He could explain later.

Two flights up, down the hall, through the door he ran, until he finally staggered to a gasping halt, his eyes adjusting slowly to his dark surroundings. The room was undisturbed since he'd last seen it. Lucas the Spider sat motionless in his cage, guarding the cryptographic wheel that Cliff had once again hidden beneath the dirt. Lola's toys and books sat in messy piles on a small bookshelf. She'd put them away herself, and that was good enough for him.

He walked to the foot of the bed, his anxiety slowly easing. Lola lay peacefully sleeping, the pirate doll tucked beneath one arm. She gave a little sigh and snuggled deeper into her pillow.

Sabine brushed by him, and he jumped. He hadn't expected her to be there, assuming she'd head off to her own room once she saw where he was going. She walked along the side of the bed, then bent and pressed a soft kiss to Lola's brow.

"Sleep well, my little pirate," she murmured, her voice thick with emotion.

Cliff's heart spasmed. Tears stung his eyes. He was destroyed. Utterly, hopelessly laid waste. He gave Lola a kiss of his own, not daring to speak. When he straightened up, Sabine was still there, inches away, watching him. Was it a trick of the faint light, or were her eyes moist as well?

"Sabine," he breathed, his weight shifting to bring him a fraction closer.

"Yes?"

I'm falling in love with you. No good can come of it, but I can't stop it and I don't even want to anymore.

"My room is only ten steps away," he whispered.

He could feel her warm breath on his skin. The scent of her seemed to flow up and around him. She leaned ever so slowly nearer.

"Ten steps too far."

She flung her arms around his neck and kissed him.

34

Hartleigh's door banged closed behind her. Sabine winced. She did *not* want to wake Lola. If anything interrupted this, she was bound to come to her senses, and then she would miss out on the most breathtaking passion of her life.

Cliff kissed her like a man possessed. Like he could never get enough of her and believed this was his only chance to fill his soul with the taste of her. Perhaps it was. This certainly wasn't something they should repeat. It probably wasn't something they should do, period, but Sabine had already gone all in.

She dug her fingers beneath his coat, spreading her palms over shoulders made strong from rowing boats and hefting chunks of machinery. He tugged her closer in response, his hand flat against the small of her back, pressing her into the bulging erection that boldly proclaimed how much he wanted her.

Cliff groaned into her mouth. His tongue swept over hers. He tipped his head, changing the angle of the kiss, pushing deeper, delving for more. Their eyeglasses clanged together.

Sabine reached up automatically to adjust her spectacles,

only to have her hand collide with his. He twined his fingers through hers, breaking off the kiss to grin at her.

"Those probably should be the first thing to take off, but I prefer to see you properly." He kissed her hand, then released it. He walked over to the bedside table to turn up the lamp, then shrugged out of his coat and tossed it aside. "Your turn."

"My turn?" To do what? Kiss him again? Suck his cock? Climb atop him and ride him until she was begging for release?

"I took something off. Now you take something off."

She stalked toward him. "That's not fair. I count six things for you to remove to my four, ignoring shoes and stockings, since I don't know if you mean to count those one-by-one or in pairs."

He licked his lips, his eyes making a leisurely perusal of her body. "I can't be blamed for your choice not to wear anything beneath your dress."

Sabine drew close enough to lay a hand on his chest. She could feel as well as hear his sharp inhalation at her touch. "My turn to take something off?"

"Yes."

She unknotted his necktie and threw it over her shoulder. "There. I took something off."

His answering grin was so filled with naked lust her knees trembled. "So, that's the way you want to play, is it? I guess now it's my turn."

One finger trickled down her arm, from shoulder to wrist, leaving a hot trail of tingling flesh. "What to choose," Cliff murmured. His opposite hand started at her hip, running up along her side, then down to her thigh. "Your ass-kicking boots? Your silken petticoat? Your sexy little knickers?" His hands came around her waist, finding the lacing of her corset. He pressed a hot, open-mouthed kiss to the very top of her neck. "Are you even wearing knickers underneath that dress?"

Sabine trembled in his arms. His touch burned her. His voice melted her insides. She clung to his shirt, swaying as desire spiraled through her. Her corset slipped loose. Cliff popped the busks open and let it fall to the floor. The moment she was freed from the garment, he crushed her against him. Her breasts pressed into his torso, one hard and unyielding, the other soft and supple. His fingers found the buttons at the back of her dress, tugging them loose.

She drew back. "One at a time, Duke. It's my turn."

His eyes darkened into the searing blue of a flame. A pinkish flush colored his pale skin, and his chest rose and fell in heavy breaths. "Okay." He spread his hands at his sides. "Take your pick."

"I think…" She let her fingers hang in mid-air, then dropped them to his groin, tracing the hard ridge of his shaft through his trousers. He twitched beneath her hand and Sabine felt an answering throb between her legs. "I think I'm done with this game." She grabbed him hard enough to make him gasp. "I think I want you in me right now."

Cliff yanked her against him once again. "Do you?" he asked, his lips caressing her earlobe. One finger inched down the back of her dress, flicking each button in turn. "Or are you still trying to hide?" He popped open two more of the buttons, pushing aside the gauzy material of her dress as he kissed down her throat. His lips teased and caressed, gliding over the white slashes of scar tissue that disappeared beneath her now-sagging neckline. "I don't care, you know. I don't care that you're scarred. I don't care that you're biomechanical. You don't have to tell me about it. You don't even have to show me. But you should know that I want to see. I want to touch. I want to worship you as you are."

His palm closed over her soft, fleshy breast, gently kneading. She arched into his hand and he squeezed harder, his thumb rubbing her nipple to a taut peak. The ache between her legs intensified. It had been so long since anyone had touched her like this. Years.

"Cliff," she sighed.

Her dress slipped off her shoulder as his opposite hand continued working the buttons. This was the time when she ought to stop him. She should lift up her skirts and let him take all that he wanted, while leaving her torso covered. She didn't share her trauma with anyone. Her pain was hers, and hers alone. She owed him no explanation, and she absolutely did not want his pity.

The dress slipped further, exposing the top of her chestplate. He pinched her nipple, kissed her bare shoulder, and still she didn't stop him. Why wasn't she stopping him? Cool air low on her back told her the last of the buttons had come undone.

"You're so fucking gorgeous," he murmured, then pulled his hands away.

The dress slithered to the floor. Cliff swiftly undid the ties of her simple petticoat, leaving her standing before him in nothing but her drawers, boots, and stockings.

"Fantastically, fucking gorgeous."

Sabine's heart raced, buzzing furiously beneath her steel chestplate. There was no pity in his gaze. No questioning. Only desire. Her arms reached for him. Her body rocked closer. She needed him now. On top of her and around her and in her. She wanted the full force of his raging passion pumping into her, driving her equally as mad.

She grabbed at the fastenings of his trousers. "This is unfair."

"Completely," he agreed. "Those tiny blue drawers have me close to spending in my pants like a boy." He kissed her hard and spun her around, pushing her down onto the bed. "And since I'd much rather come inside *you*, I suggest we get on with it."

His blunt honesty aroused her almost as much as his roving hands. She shucked her boots and stockings, catching his eye as she eased her drawers slowly from her hips. He made a strangled noise and a button flew from his shirt when he pulled too hard.

He tossed layers of clothing this way and that, scrambling to join her. Sabine's eyes feasted on his body. He was perfect. Disgustingly, enviably perfect. Tall and strong and lean, and still wearing those sexy red eyeglasses. He yanked open the single drawer in the bedside table and flipped open a small wooden box full of condoms.

"Well, aren't you prepared?" she remarked.

He plucked a sheath from the box and slipped it on. "Always."

And then he was on top of her, his cock hard against her thigh, his hands cupping both her breasts, kissing her lips, chin, neck, and moaning her name.

"Sabine. God, Sabine, I want you so bad."

His eager touch sent shivers of bliss coursing through her. Her right breast felt swollen and sensitive beneath his hand. On the left side, she felt only a gentle tickle as he cupped the perfectly rounded metal and thumbed the small nipple. Even that was enough to thrill her. He caressed her as no one had, and there was no shame, no awkwardness. Only desire.

She lifted her hips, spread her legs wider, and he took the invitation. He plunged deep, not wasting time, not bothering to start slowly, matching her own urgency. She arched her back, clutched his shoulders, and when he slipped a hand between them to flick at her clit she cried out in pleasure.

Cliff thrust harder, whispering her name over and over in a strange, erotic mantra. Her nails bit into his skin. She was lost, helpless, overpowered by her body's desperate yearning. The tension inside her burst with the force of a thousand ropes snapping, leaving her dangling for just an instant, then tumbling, falling into a bottomless pool of ecstasy.

Cliff spasmed above her, gasping and groaning as he finished deep inside her. He collapsed, rolled off her, then tugged her into his arms.

Her body stiffened. What was he doing? He couldn't

possibly want more so quickly, could he? She hadn't even recovered herself.

He let out a sigh of contentment and exhaustion. "Goddamn, Sabine. You're incredible. I should get up and wash, but I just want to hold you forever."

Those words should have terrified her, should have made her snatch up her clothes and run for her own room. Instead, her body relaxed, and she snuggled into his embrace. He was warm and cozy, and she liked the smell of sex about him. She could give herself a few pleasant minutes to come down from the high of their wild passion.

The next thing she knew, the morning sun was peeking through the curtains.

And she was still in his arms.

35

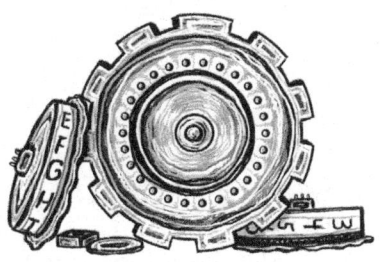

Cliff hopped and cursed, shaking his stinging hand. Punching the wall was one more addition to the list of Really Stupid Things Cliff Kinsley Has Done. Though it didn't rank nearly as high as Sleeping With Sabine Diebin. That one rivaled the time his six-year-old self had decided to row across Lake Michigan to "see how far it went."

He'd thought things would be okay. He'd thought they'd be better than okay, given how peaceful and happy she'd seemed, curled up beside him all through the night. He'd lingered awake far too late, just to watch her, luxuriating in the sweet aftermath of their life-altering union.

If only he weren't the only one altered.

She'd scampered away in haste once they'd woken, which hadn't surprised him. He'd assumed she'd be at least as deeply affected as he'd been. He might not have questioned her scars and her biomechanics, but she'd allowed him to see and touch, and he was certain she didn't do that often.

He'd imagined her reacting in all sorts of ways. His fantasies had involved her sneaking kisses and whispering that she couldn't wait until evening when they could be alone again.

More realistically, he'd expected scowling, cursing, avoidance of his touch. He could have handled any of that. Angry, upset, confused? Fine. The one thing he couldn't take, apparently, was indifference.

"Daddy?"

Shit. Cliff snatched up the pair of gloves that one of the servants had set neatly on the sideboard in the foyer for him—beside a top hat, a billowing overcoat, and a gold-handled cane, for Christ's sake—and tugged them on over his battered knuckles. As someone who worked with his hands, he preferred to go without gloves, but he also didn't want any questions about why he looked like a boxer.

Lola bounced eagerly. "Are you ready to go?"

"Sure am, babe." He swung the overcoat around his shoulders, because he wasn't going to chance getting drenched by a frigid rain again, but left the top hat and cane where they were. Instead he snagged his derby from the hook by the front door and plopped it haphazardly on his head. Much better. He was a perpetually busy, somewhat awkward man of business. Not a duke who attended the theater with royalty. Not a man of sufficient consequence or daring to be the lover of a notorious pirate. "Let's get out of here before someone comes along and tries to make me take that ridiculous cane."

Thank God they had a bare minimum of staff. Too many people hovered as it was, and the last thing he wanted was to have people doing every small thing for him. As a duke he was probably even supposed to have someone help him dress. Which he would only permit if that someone was Sabine and she was helping him look presentable after a torrid embrace in a semi-public location. Dammit.

"What about Sabine?" Lola asked.

"I have no idea what she's doing," he replied, trying and failing to sound as if he didn't care.

Lola gave him a puzzled frown. "Is she angry at you again?"

"I have no idea." *I wish.*

Breakfast had been torture. He'd found Sabine sitting and eating in silence, and when he'd greeted her with a hopeful smile and a "How are you?" she answered him with a dispassionate summary of the plan for the day. No frowns, but no smiles. All business. She hadn't tried to move away when he'd sat next to her, but she hadn't responded to his none-too-subtle attempts to brush against her, either. Every endeavor to bring up a subject not related to today's schedule or the search for the Heart had been deflected or simply ignored.

Purposeful footsteps announced Sabine's arrival. "Good," she said. "You're ready. Lola, put your overcoat on. It's still winter."

Lola obeyed, moving something from her pinafore pocket to the pocket of the coat. Probably a spider.

Cliff stared at Sabine the entire carriage ride, trying to find some indication that she felt any sort of emotion after last night. Her expression was neutral, almost pitying.

His thoughts mocked him, in her voice. *You poor man. You thought that meant something. Wasn't this your plan? One night, then we're done. Satisfied. I'm over it. Why aren't you?*

He would never be over it.

Lola scooted closer to him, and he put an arm around her. His perceptive girl could tell he was upset. "I'm glad you're better, Daddy. We missed you."

"Thanks, Lo. I'm looking forward to seeing everything you want to show me."

That, at least, was true. He would focus on Lola's enthusiastic introductions to all the sights. Try to be normal again.

He didn't see Sabine's guards watching the library, though she'd assured him that they were there and that they had been given instructions to watch for Barton. Cliff walked up the stairs and through the entrance, hand-in-hand with Lola, and was immediately greeted with, "Your Grace! So pleased to welcome you!"

Cliff almost sprang away from the enthusiastic librarian who had rushed to his side. Really, he ought to have gotten used to people knowing who he was and rushing to assist him, but he hadn't. Probably never would. Another reason to remember why faking his death and moving to California was still the best plan.

It didn't feel like the best plan. In fact, it felt like a shitty plan. Like another thing to add to his list of stupid things he'd done. His new favorite plan was to say to hell with everything, kiss Sabine as hard as he could, and fly away in her airship to wherever took their fancy.

Yeah. That was happening.

"Your Grace, we are so very pleased that you have decided to reestablish a membership with us, after the previous duke let his own lapse near the end of his life. The Dukes of Hartleigh have been among our membership since the library opened, you know."

"Ah. Of course. Thanks."

"We've taken the liberty of having the bill sent to your home, where I'm certain it will be taken care of promptly."

Cliff fought off a frown. Wasn't talking about money one of those things that Amy had said was "not done"? Apparently when your dukedom was known to be drowning in debt, people tried to make a point of getting paid.

"Fine, fine," he mumbled, hoping he wasn't spending all that much for a service he'd probably never use again.

"Think of it as paying a small percentage toward the Heart of Ra," Sabine whispered in his ear. She withdrew again quickly, but not before the firm curve of her metal breast brushed his arm.

Memories of the night before swirled through his mind. He wanted to hold her again. Wanted to make love slowly and methodically, exploring her from head to toe. He wanted to caress her soft skin, and the smooth metal that melded with it—cooler than the surrounding flesh, but warmed by the heat of her body. He wanted to trace her scars, to kiss her freckles, to learn every perfection and every flaw and etch them all on his soul.

"Heart of Ra," he muttered. "Let's get on with it."

"Exactly," she agreed, her voice full of the same blunt composure it had had all morning.

"This way, Daddy!"

Lola skipped ahead, thrilled with her role as tour guide, but she didn't dash off as quickly as she would have done only a few weeks prior. Instead, she cast periodic looks over her shoulder, checking that Sabine was keeping pace with her.

Damn. Cliff had been looking for signs of fear and trauma since their wild escape from the castle in Switzerland. She'd crawled into his bed a few times after waking from nightmares, but she'd generally seemed happy and carefree in the house. Having her spider to pet during the day and her doll to hug at night had helped comfort her, he was certain. He'd missed out on all the outings lately, however, while lying sick in bed.

It wouldn't have been obvious to an outsider, but to him it was glaring: Lola was scared to run free the way she once had. The city was full of people, and she'd learned that some of them could be enemies. Not the sort of lesson he'd wanted her to learn when he'd set out for England. That seemed so long ago now. He'd imagined introducing her to new things, new places, new cultures. Letting her dress up like a princess and take tea in a fancy house. What he'd gotten was pirates and treasures and enemies. A mix of the very bad and the very good, and it left him conflicted.

"Come on, Daddy!" she called. She had grasped Sabine's hand and was bounding past rows of books. "We want to show you what we found!"

Cliff wanted to punch another wall. Lola loved Sabine. Felt safe and happy with her. Sabine loved her back, if her agonizingly sweet words last night were any indication. It melted his heart. It fueled that stupid, stupid hope of being a happy little family. Last night that hope had exploded into a giant, raging ball of possibility. He should have known better. He *did* know better. Sabine didn't want that sort of life, and she was making it abundantly clear today. They were over. He was just a passing fancy.

Cliff surveyed the bookshelves as they walked through the library. How were they supposed to find anything in here? They'd been pointed here with no clarifying clues. The information could be hidden in any of thousands of volumes. Was there a codebreaking section, perhaps? Too obvious, probably.

He plucked a book off a shelf at random and flipped through it. Dense text and illustrations of plows jumped out at him. He closed the book and looked at the cover.

Agricultural Technologies of the Late Sixteenth Century.

Well, that would help him sleep at night. He tucked it into his pocket.

"There!" Lola declared, gesturing toward the window ahead.

A half-sized Roman statue stood on a pedestal at the end of the row. Cliff adjusted his glasses and peered at it. It didn't seem particularly exceptional. A sensible decoration to be near classical history or literature shelves. It could have been donated by the Mad Duke, but so could a table, a lamp, a painting, or any book.

Lola scampered up to the statue and turned around, bouncing in place as she waited for him to catch up. As he drew closer, his mouth twitched up into a smile. Then he laughed.

"Huh. Look at that."

"The face looks just like the man in the statue in our garden," Lola declared proudly. "*I* noticed while Sabine was reading books, and she said I was exactly right." She gazed adoringly up at Sabine, who gave her a genuine smile and a conspiratorial wink. A hint of wistfulness flickered in Sabine's eyes as she turned her attention to the statue.

Cliff's heart skipped a beat. A sudden sense of dread churned in his stomach. When the treasure hunt was over and they parted ways, Lola would be heartbroken. Hell, *Sabine* would be heartbroken. She wasn't indifferent. She was acting indifferent because it was the most efficient way to cut him off. She cared, but not the way he did. She knew they would part, knew it would hurt, and wanted to get the whole thing over with. She would break from him as swiftly and fully as possible, *because* she cared. It was like his relationship with Miranda all over again.

"Aw, fuck," he muttered. The urge to smash something swelled inside him once again.

"Daddy." Lola glanced around, looking for anyone who might have heard. "You said that was a bad word."

"Right. Sorry." He stepped closer to the statue, bending to inspect some part of it. Best to get back to work. Do what had to be done. No sense fretting about the inevitable.

Cliff ran his fingers over the marble, feeling for cracks or irregularities that might indicate a hidden clue. The stone was cool to the touch and bore no marks that he could see. Opposite him, Sabine made her own inspection, a slight frown twisting her mouth.

Cliff flattened his hand against the statue. Maybe if he shoved really hard, it would topple out the window and smash on the pavement below. That would vent some of his frustrations and let them find any clue hidden inside at the same time.

"Finding anything?" he asked.

Sabine shook her head.

Cliff took a quick look to check for witnesses, saw none, and squeezed himself behind the statue to check the back. Nothing. No markings, no writing, no seams that indicated that any pieces could be detached.

"Unless he somehow magically sculpted the marble around a piece of paper, I don't think there's anything here to find."

"I agree," Sabine said. "Perhaps in the pedestal."

They both dropped to their knees, inspecting the stone support. That search proved equally fruitless.

Sabine muttered an oath in German. She rapped on the side of the pedestal with one hand. "Could it be hollow? Do you think we could manage to lift the statute or shift it enough to check?"

"Uh, maybe?" He was strong, but he wasn't sure he was *that* strong. He circled back around to the front of the statue and eyed it, trying to decide how best to grip it.

"Daddy?"

Cliff made another check for any onlookers. "Yeah, babe?" He grasped the statue, frowned, adjusted his position, and tried again.

"What does *spiquer* mean?"

"Huh?" This wasn't going to work. He grabbed hold of the statue's arm. Maybe like this.

"Spiquer," Lola repeated. "I don't know how to say it. It's right there."

Cliff paused long enough to look down at where she was pointing. At the base of the statue, as he'd seen on many Roman artifacts and reproductions, were the initials SPQR.

"Oh, God." He took two steps backward, shaking with laughter. "It's a Latin abbreviation," he explained when he recovered. "It stands for the Senate and People of Rome. Means the statue was erected by the Roman government. Or wants to pretend it was, in this case." He caught Sabine looking at him with a raised eyebrow. "What? I went to school. Although apparently I'm still a knucklehead." He laughed again. "Hidden in plain sight."

Sabine folded her arms across her chest. "That does seem very like him."

"Right, then. I vote we go off on the rest of our city tour and try it out when we arrive home."

She nodded. "And if it doesn't work and we need to return?"

Cliff pulled the book from his pocket. "That's why I have this."

Sabine glanced at the cover and raised her eyebrows.

"Dukes are exceptionally interested in this sort of thing," Cliff joked. "Seeing how we have so much land and all."

Maybe she would smile. Maybe she would tease him back. Please, couldn't he at least squeeze out a little bit more friendship before the end?

"You barely own enough land for a vegetable garden, Hartleigh." No teasing. But a comfortingly familiar irritation. Better than nothing, he supposed.

"Good. Because I actually have no plans to read this or any other book on agriculture. I am, however, going to have it checked out in my name so that I have an excuse to return. And because I might as well borrow books if I have to pay to be a member here."

They walked together toward the exit. Sabine and Lola paused to browse the shelves while Cliff veered off to check with the circulation desk about borrowing the book. He grinned at the sound of Lola's voice behind him, stumbling over words as she practiced her reading.

A woman bumped against his arm, startling him.

"Terribly sorry," he apologized hurriedly. She was young, blond haired, and dressed in a flowing, pale-yellow dress. Her mouth was curved in a flirtatious smile.

"Oh, no need to apologize," the young woman cooed. Something jabbed Cliff in the side, and he glanced down to see the gleaming barrel of a tiny pistol. "It was all my fault. Really."

A hand clamped down on Cliff's opposite arm, and his head swiveled. Adriana, Barton's beautiful, dark-haired lady friend, smirked at him from underneath a shabby cap. A plain, faded dress hung loosely around her curves.

"Young man, I do hope you're not flirting with my innocent charge, here. She's a sweet girl. Very interested in books and things. Always searching, you know."

Fear pounded through Cliff's veins. He could no longer hear Lola's voice. With the gun pressing into his ribs and who knew what other weapons at his enemies' disposal, he couldn't even turn to look for her and Sabine. He stuffed the book into the inside pocket of his coat. He'd do what he could to protect them.

"I'm extremely fond of books myself," he replied. "Came here to find a certain one, as a matter of fact."

Adriana steered him away from the circulation desk. "Is that so?"

"It is. And I'll give it to you on one condition."

She laughed. "I really don't think you're in a position to make demands."

"Why not?" he asked brazenly. "You can't really think you can shoot a duke inside a well-known library and get away with it. And my condition is simple. You allow Miss Diebin and my daughter to walk out the front door. Then I'll give you the book."

The pistol dug further into his side. "Or we can simply take it," the blond woman said.

"You won't understand how to use it. It's a code book. You need to follow the instructions. I'll explain the whole thing after you let them go."

The younger woman looked to Adriana for an answer, though her weapon didn't so much as twitch.

"Take him out the back way," Adriana ordered.

36

Sabine nudged Lola around the corner of the bookshelf. "Go find your father." The girl frowned up at her. Sabine gave her another gentle push. "Go. Now. Quickly."

Lola hesitated, then scampered off. Good girl.

Sabine made as if to walk away, then whirled around when she heard her enemy step out from behind a nearby shelf.

"Yvette." Sabine smirked, faintly amused by the momentary look of shock that flashed across the Frenchwoman's features. "Yes, I spotted you approaching. You're not as stealthy as you think."

Yvette glared from beneath her pale blue, beribboned bonnet. The young woman's eyes had become harder and sadder in the years since Sabine had last seen her. Poor girl. She'd never had a chance.

"You've grown up," Sabine remarked.

Yvette withdrew a gleaming dagger from the folds of her skirts. "I'm only three years younger than you, Sabine Thief."

"True, but it always seemed like more." Sabine's eyes darted back and forth, surveying the area for signs of the others she knew must be nearby. "Who else is here? What do you want from me?"

"We want what is ours, and we want the means to decode it." Yvette's gaze skimmed the bookshelves. "A codebook? That makes sense. Good of the Mad Duke to hide it in a library that welcomes women. And, thank *you*, Sabine, for doing the work of finding it."

"Daddy?" Lola's distant voice trembled. "Daddy, where are you?"

Sabine's stomach clenched. "Hartleigh and the girl are innocent. Let them walk out the front door, unmolested, and then we'll discuss the book." They didn't know about the machine. Didn't know what they were looking for. Sabine could use that.

"Daddy?" Lola called again. "Sabine?"

"I don't believe for one second that your duke is innocent," Yvette laughed. She touched one leather-clad finger to the tip of her knife. "Our sisters are… handling him as we speak."

Sabine's world went red. She charged Yvette, pinning her against the bookcase, wrestling the knife from her grip and pressing it to her throat.

"I swear to God," Sabine hissed, "if anyone has harmed him, I will rip out your eyeballs and stuff them down your throat until you choke on them." Yvette let out a strangled whimper. She never had been any good in a fight. "Where is he? And why were they so stupid as to send you after me alone?"

"S-supposed to grab the girl," Yvette stammered.

Sabine swore. Cliff and Lola were to have been hostages. At least that meant they wouldn't kill him. Yet.

She slammed the handle of the knife into Yvette's head. The blow didn't knock her out, but it stunned her enough that she crumpled to the floor. She'd be assumed to have fainted if anyone found her.

Sabine took off in the direction of the circulation desk.

Lola stood not far from it, her eyes bright with unshed tears. Sabine scooped her up and lifted her over the desk.

"You, there," she demanded of the man behind the desk. "You are going to teach Miss Lola here all about how books are borrowed and returned. Don't let anyone else behind that desk."

He stared at her in confusion.

"I'll be right back," Sabine promised Lola. "I think your father got lost in the book stacks."

Please let him be lost in the stacks and not already gone.

Sabine raced through the library, her eyes darting this way and that, her ears perked for any signs of struggle. She skittered to a halt beside a man who was shelving books.

"Have you seen the Duke of Hartleigh? Possibly in the company of a few women?"

The man's eyes opened wide, then narrowed. "No, miss, I haven't."

"Which way to the rear exit?"

"Er, that way, miss." The man pointed. "But it's not for public use."

Sabine was already off running. She tore down the narrow aisles, her footfalls echoing through the steel-frame structure. She saw nothing but books, heard nothing but the sounds of her own body.

"Hartleigh!" she shouted. "Hartleigh, can you hear me?"

A noise made her pause. Footsteps, perhaps? Ahead, and somewhat to the left. She took off. She had just reached the end of the aisle when the crack of a gunshot split the air.

"Cliff!" Oh, God, what had she done?

She flew through the library until the small rear exit emerged before her, daylight slanting through the half-open door. Sabine banged through to the outdoors, flailing as her foot slipped in something wet.

She looked down. A trail of blood led away from the door, into the center of the small, dirty courtyard crammed between the crowded London buildings. Her head swiveled, her eyes darted left, right, up. Nothing. No signs that they'd climbed for the roof or ducked into another building. No airship hovered above to carry them away. The nearby streets would be packed with carriages and steam cars, eager to race away for a coin or two.

"Fuck!" Sabine hammered her fists on the door. Cliff was lost to her. In the hands of her enemies and wounded. She cursed once more, kicked the door, and stormed back inside. She marched straight to the circulation desk, picked up Lola, and carried her out the front door.

"Sabine?" Lola's arms clamped around her neck and her little body shook. "Where's Daddy?"

Sabine couldn't answer, trapped between fury and devastation. She shook her head and clutched Lola tighter.

"Captain."

Sabine's head jerked toward the guard who had spoken.

"Captain, this woman came stumbling out of the library, looking mighty suspicious and saying foul French words." His meaty hand had a good grip on Yvette's arm, and he pulled her toward Sabine. "What do you want me to do with her?"

Sabine bared her teeth in a feral smile. "We're going to take her with us. And then she's going to tell us everything she knows. Isn't that right, little sister?"

"Go to hell," Yvette snarled.

"You first."

37

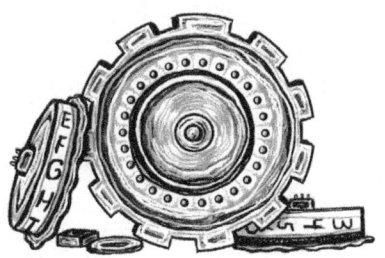

"D<small>RINK</small>?"

"Go fuck yourself."

Barton poured the brandy regardless, sliding the glass across the polished top of his study desk toward Cliff. He leaned back in his towering leather chair and sipped at his own drink.

"Sadly, that's what I will need to do, since you shot my mistress."

"I didn't shoot her, that other woman shot her. Gun went off accidentally when I tried to get away." Cliff shrugged. "She deserved it. She's a bitch."

Barton chuckled. "Of course she is. That's why I like her. We get along famously. But now she's laid up in bed recovering, and who's going to take care of my needs?"

"Some whore with the pox, hopefully."

"Such hostility, Duke. You ought to relax. Try the brandy. We should be friends, you and I. We're cut from the same cloth."

Cliff snorted. "We are nothing alike." He settled back in his chair, folding his arms across his chest, ignoring the brandy.

"Ah, but you're so wrong. We are self-made men. Thrust into positions of rank that had lost their historic power and fortune. My uncle left me less than nothing, and look what I have become. The world is mine for the taking. You are the same. You are heir to a madman. Your title is drowning in debt, yet you wield it as if it were a flourishing dukedom of old. You have a fortune of your own and the skills and ambition to continue increasing it. You scoff at the rules of society and do things your own way without fear or shame."

"You're forgetting the part where you're a heartless, mercenary villain, and I'm not."

"Rubbish. You're hunting treasure with a known criminal. She stole that coded document, you know. She's hardly some innocent damsel. We have similar tastes in women, you and I."

"You don't know Sabine."

"She's a pirate. She betrayed her leader to strike out on her own. She's always on the hunt for new treasures to increase her personal fortune. She's smart, she's ruthless, and she likes to do the naughty with powerful men. What else is there to know?"

She hasn't had an easy life. She's been hurt and she's often lonely. When she's relaxed she can be funny and sweet. She has a big heart, but guards it closely. She's full of passion and life. She wants peace and security, not wealth and fame.

"She's been a worthy opponent, I admit," Barton continued. "Going to see the king when the lights went out was a stroke of genius. Foiled any chance we had to kidnap you last night." He chuckled and took another swig from his drink. "But we did get a good look at your bodyguards, and now you've led us right to what we needed." Barton picked up the copy of *Agricultural Technologies of the Late Sixteenth Century* that he'd taken from Cliff's pocket. "Now. About this book."

Cliff made a pretense of checking his watch. "It's a bit early for a nap, don't you think? If we start to read that, we'll sleep right through lunch, and then we'll be irritable until teatime."

"You think you're funny, don't you?"

"No, I think I'm sarcastic. Funny to some, perhaps, but to you merely obnoxious. You're welcome."

Barton slammed the book down on the desk and leaned toward Cliff, his eyes blazing with anger. "Tell me about the book, Hartleigh, before we have to beat it out of you."

"I don't know about the book. All I did was pluck it off the shelf. Looks horrendously boring to me."

"I don't believe you. You and your pirate whore have been all over, collecting information. You know the secrets, and you had goddamn better tell me, because I do not want blood all over my carpet."

"All right, all right." Cliff let his shoulders sag. "I know how to use the book. But I can't give you what you want. I need to have the book and the coded message together."

"Not a problem."

Barton withdrew a key from his vest pocket and unlocked a drawer in the desk. He lifted a single sheet of paper from the drawer and laid it on the desk. The top third of the paper was covered with handwritten lines of random letters. Cliff sucked in a shocked breath. Sabine's code. Not all of it, but a significant chunk.

"Where did you get that?"

Barton's smug grin widened, and he took a long drink of brandy before replying. "Adriana has many talents outside the bedroom."

"She copied it."

"Just so. Unfortunately, some sneaky little bitch stole the original before Adriana could finish the job." His smirk morphed into a scowl. "And then she bought the damned house right out from under me. Used that bloody hero reputation. At least she's done the work of finding the book for us. Now, tell me how to read my message."

"You've been in this all for yourself from the start," Cliff mused. It finally made sense. Barton wouldn't work for Redbeard. But pretend to work for him to further his own purpose? Absolutely. "You've been offering your services to Redbeard through Adriana. He agrees because you're in England, which is outside his usual area of operations and is a safe haven for Sabine. You get to make use of his machines, the Sisters, and his information. And all the while, Adriana is betraying him."

"I told you we have similar tastes in women." Barton jabbed a finger at the encrypted message. "The book. Or I will begin to take more drastic measures."

"Okay." Cliff dragged the book closer and flipped it open, running his finger down the table of contents.

Shit. What do I do now? How long can I drag this out?

"Each letter has a corresponding chapter." *Thirteen chapters. Two letters map to each chapter. That seems believable.* "So the N that begins the code is chapter…"

"One," Barton interrupted.

"Nine. You didn't think he'd start with A equals one, did you? Nine, from the '90 A.D.' that was inscribed on the reliquary of St. Felicula." The lies began to pour out as an audacious plan came together in Cliff's mind. He pictured the places they'd been and the fake antiquities where the duke had concealed the clues. Why not tell Barton exactly where they'd been and what they'd found? He knew at least some of it already.

Cliff turned the pages slowly to chapter nine. He had no idea what a water-meadow was or how one could devote an entire chapter to such a thing, but the text was usefully dense and incomprehensible.

"Here we are," he announced. "The chapter. Each letter in the coded document then also has a corresponding page." *The hospital and the Greek pot.* "Then a line." *The helmet from the castle.* "And a word." *Cat mummy.*

"Each step gets progressively more complicated," Cliff continued. "The man was a mad genius and probably thought the whole thing was one great mathematical joke. To find the page we need to add our letter to the letters on both sides, then divide by the number of pages. Round to the nearest whole number. Here, A equals four, for the '444 B.C.' inscribed on the fake Greek pot. So our N is a seventeen, plus eight for the E after it, plus zero for nothing in front." He frowned. "That could be wrong and we need to use the very last letter of the message, which you don't have. It won't matter, much, though. We can guess that letter if we solve the others. Back to the formula. Seventeen plus eight is twenty-five. With what appears to be fourteen pages in the chapter, we will get an answer of... one point... eight, approximately. Rounds up to two."

Cliff flipped to page two of the chapter. Barton's eyes had begun to glaze over. Not a fan of mathematics, apparently. Perfect.

"Could I get some paper and a pencil?" Cliff asked. "In order to find the specific line, we need to do a similar calculation, but we need to multiply. And A equals... Damn. What was the third number?"

Barton pushed his chair back from the table. "The Illyrian Institute. What did you steal there?"

"A spider. Eight legs. Right. Thanks."

"If you are trying to dupe me with this mathematical prattle you are going to rue the day you ever heard the name Hartleigh."

"Oh, I already do. I was in this to escape the dukedom, not to find some stupid gemstone, or whatever the hell it is."

A look of surprise flashed across Barton's face before he schooled it into his usual smug smile. He believed Sabine capable of hiding the true nature of the Heart of Ra. Which meant he would believe their relationship to be more casual than it truly was. Good.

Barton rose from his seat. "Here's the deal, Hartleigh. You sit here with that book and my message until you've decoded the entire thing. I doubt your pirate friend will be willing to take up with you again after this, but you'll be free to walk away with your brat and go back to America. If you don't decode the message, or if I find out that you're lying to me, I'll send Barton's Bandits to murder both La Capitaine and the girl. My men are the most experienced housebreakers in all of Great Britain. I don't imagine they'll have any difficulty infiltrating a rented townhouse." He pivoted and strode for the door. "Enjoy the rest of your day, *Your Grace*."

The door closed with a heavy thunk and the lock clicked into place. Cliff clutched the desk with both hands, willing himself to breathe. He had bought himself a few hours, at least. Hours during which he could plot an escape. Hours during which Sabine would be working to find him. He wanted to tell her not to. He wanted to tell her to forget the Heart and just take Lola somewhere safe. He wanted them both somewhere far from all this madness.

Escape. Leave me.

She wouldn't. Whatever claims she may have made in the past, they were partners, and she would never leave him behind. He vowed to find his own way out before she came rushing headlong into danger.

38

"Tea? Coffee?"

Amy gestured at the tray of steaming drinks and delicious baked goods that Hawkes had carefully arranged for just this purpose. Yvette sat perched on the edge of Sabine's bed in the small airship cabin, stiff as a board. Her eyes latched onto the food, however. She'd always been a skinny girl in constant need of sustenance.

Sabine shifted slowly into a more comfortable position, careful not to make a sound. The spyhole was useful for exactly this sort of purpose, but the storage room outside her cabin wasn't the coziest place to sit and watch.

"Coffee, s'il vous plaît," Yvette replied at last. "And something to eat."

Amy piled sweets onto a tiny plate, poured a cup of coffee, and carried both to Yvette. She moved her chair closer to the bed and sat down with tea of her own. She smiled brightly. Oh, she was good at this.

"I'm so sorry to hear that you and Miss Diebin have had a falling out," Amy began. "She can be terribly stubborn and demanding, I'm sure you know." She lowered her voice. "Did you know, she kidnapped me once on this very ship? Locked me in this cabin, just as she's done to you. I was stuck here for days, all because she was too busy rushing around looking for silly clues to allow me to return home."

"That sounds like her."

"She's on some quest for a heart. Sounds like nonsense to me. She's not all bad, though. Lady Luella, my companion, wished for an aerial tour of the city, and as you can see, Miss Diebin was happy to oblige her."

Actually, Sabine had decided the air was safer than the house for the moment, and Amy had been pleasantly eager to assist in a high-skies intrigue. She'd been bored, Sabine suspected, since Hartleigh's illness had thwarted many of her social plans.

"I don't like heights, personally," Amy continued. "I'd much rather stay here, in this pleasant little cabin with good food and a charming companion. Tell me, how do you know Miss Diebin? She called you 'sister,' but you are French and she is German, so that cannot be."

"Sworn sisters. Daughters of Redbeard. We gave our oath to be his eyes and ears and his helping hands, but she betrayed that vow."

"Oh, dear. She *is* so terribly independent, isn't she?"

"Oui."

Yvette had an independent streak of her own, Sabine remembered, and she hoped it would work for her here. Yvette had always been the tag-along, the younger sister, the one who helped out on mission after mission but never led one of her own. Never trusted. She disregarded rules too often and didn't do as she was told. It had happened again today, when she confronted Sabine instead of snatching Lola.

"Well, I'm certain you and your 'sisters' are better off without her. No sense in fighting amongst yourselves. You'd never get anything accomplished. Mmmm. These biscuits are delightful, don't you think?"

"Yes, thank you." Yvette sipped at her coffee while Amy patiently waited for her to speak again. "I wish we could do without her, as we had done for years. But then she came and stole the document."

Amy leaned in. "The secret to the treasure? She stole it?"

"Yes."

"How awful!"

"We had to pursue her to reclaim it, but she'd taken refuge here in England. The British sky navy is hostile to many outsiders."

To Redbeard, for murdering British citizens, Sabine corrected. *They never pursued me with any great diligence.*

"How on earth did you come to be here, then?" Amy asked.

"Adriana had made a particular friend in Paris who was a British citizen."

Adriana. Sabine's spine straightened. Barton's mistress. She was a Daughter of Redbeard? It all made sense. Sabine could have predicted Yvette's next words.

"She moved to England with him, and invited a number of us to visit, with the hope that we would be able to locate the stolen document and return it to its rightful owner."

Sabine had to smother a snort. Cliff was the rightful owner. That document should have remained with the duke's other papers, and would have done if one of his solicitors hadn't stolen it and spread news of the Heart of Ra throughout the criminal world. Redbeard had offered him payment for the document and then promptly killed him.

"It sounds like a terrible misunderstanding," Amy sighed. "There must be something you can do to halt this ridiculous feuding."

Sabine left her to continue playing the compassionate duchess and slipped out of the storage room. She walked the few feet to her cabin door, paused for a moment, then made several heavy footsteps to mimic stomping through the hall. She unlocked the door and strode in without knocking, scowling at the cozy scene in front of her.

Amy gave her a cheerful smile. "Sabine, how nice of you to come below to join us."

"You know Lord Barton, don't you?" Sabine asked abruptly. Yvette didn't flinch, but her eyes widened, just for an instant.

"Yes, a bit," Amy replied. "We are not friends, but I have met him at many a party. He is in town, I believe."

"He is. He and his charming companion came by our box at the theater just last night to chat."

Was it really only last night? Good Lord. Since sitting through that awful show at the theater she'd invaded the king's box during a power outage, Cliff had taken her to unparalleled heights of sexual bliss, she'd slept more soundly than she had in years, they'd found the last clue to the Sphinx machine, and Cliff had been kidnapped. All in less than twenty-four hours. Damn.

"I was thinking I might like to visit them," Sabine said.

Yvette did flinch this time, and Sabine turned a triumphant smile on her. "Is there a problem with that, Yvette? Are you afraid if I go they'll find out all about your latest mistake?"

"If you go, you'll find nothing there," Yvette lied. "They had nothing to do with this."

Sabine stalked over to her, glaring down. "They took Hartleigh, and he may be wounded. I will not rest until I have found him. You can either confirm who took him and where he is, or I will report your failure to them and to Redbeard, including how much you've divulged to the lovely duchess here."

"Who's going to believe a traitor like you?" Yvette spat. Much of her anger, Sabine suspected, was self-directed. She'd made too many mistakes and she knew it.

"I'm willing to offer you a deal," Sabine said calmly. *This is it, Yvette. How much of that independence do you really have?*

How much have you longed to escape your subordinate role? "You tell me what I want to know and you can join me. I have only one mission, and it's for you and you alone. Because you're the only one who can do it."

Wariness warred with eagerness in Yvette's pale eyes. "Tell me what the mission is."

"Not until you tell me where Hartleigh is."

"At Barton's. Adriana and Gretchen went after him. You're to surrender the document and the method to decode it if you want him back."

"You're all making quite the assumption about how much he means to me."

Yvette sniffed and tossed her hair. "Don't be silly, Sabine. I saw the way you reacted. I can see those clenched fists right now." Her laugh was a high trill. "The street thief is in love with a duke. C'est mignon."

"I'm not..." Sabine cut herself off. Denying it was exactly the sort of thing someone would do if it were true. "That's irrelevant. I want the address and everything you know about the house."

"I know plenty. Much more than the others think. I *do* watch and listen."

"Redbeard should have made you a scout. You're good at flirting and you read people well. But that's not why I need you. I need you because you can fly an airship."

Out of all the Daughters of Redbeard Sabine had known, only she and Yvette had been insubordinate enough to learn that particular skill. Women didn't fly his ships, or work on them in any capacity. He kept a strict division of labor: men operated the ships and did all physical work. They learned fencing, marksmanship, and hand-to-hand fighting. Women were his spies and thieves. Knives and small, concealable firearms were all they trained with. His men were brawn, his women brains.

Sabine had chafed at such arbitrary restrictions, teaching

herself to use a sword and pilot a ship. She'd bribed the men to give her lessons, or snuck off during missions to practice on small, stolen vessels. Yvette had been the only one to join her. Sabine had thought of her as just a little sister, but she wasn't. She was a fellow rebel.

"I can fly as well as any man," Yvette declared.

Sabine nodded. "Your task is this: steal an airship that could be mistaken for mine. When I leave London, you will do the same. We will go at a busy time and fly in different directions to cause as much confusion as possible. After that, you are free to do as you please. Take the ship and go anywhere. Build your own crew or simply see the world. And if you want future jobs, simply keep in touch, Captain."

Yvette's face lit up with joy, and Sabine couldn't suppress a grin. Victory. And all it had taken was to give the girl what she'd always wanted: a chance to prove herself.

Sabine took a seat on the bed beside Yvette. "Now, tell me everything. The house, the people in it, what they might have done with Hartleigh. Leave nothing out."

Yvette squared her shoulders and nodded.

39

Sabine shifted the unwieldy bag of rags to her opposite hip and continued her unhurried walk down the street. No one glanced twice at the ordinary woman in a tired gray dress and a sagging cap. She counted the houses, marking her target well ahead of time.

Barton owned a fancy house in Mayfair, but it was nothing more than a showpiece. His real work was conducted here, where the neighbors would ask no questions and the staff was well-paid and close-mouthed.

The building was a pretty, brick terraced house, four stories tall and well-maintained. The windows on the lowest floor were barred, to keep criminals out—or prisoners in. If Cliff was well enough to pose an escape risk, he would be there. If his injuries were severe, he could be anywhere. The memory of the blood-stained ground flashed in Sabine's mind and she shivered.

The street was narrow, and the buildings cut off much of her view of the sky, but Die Fledermaus was up there somewhere, ready for her part in this rescue. Sabine took another small step.

Walking at the pace of an average person was almost painful, but her usual fast, powerful strides would give her away.

Which of these windows hold spies? she wondered. Barton and the sisters had to have a lookout. They would be expecting Sabine to stage a rescue. She'd crafted her plan with that assumption.

A shadow crept over the street, the oblong shape too regular to belong to any cloud. Her helpers had arrived. Sabine continued her methodical walk, sparing only a brief, curious glance at the dirigible blotting out the sun. *None of my business. I have work to do. Need to put bread on the table.*

The airship dropped lower, hovering directly above Barton's residence. Ropes unfurled. A small, ceramic container fell overboard, shattering on the street below. The contents burst with a thunderous crack.

Sabine covered her mouth with a handkerchief as smoke spread over the area. Up above, a woman in trousers and a high-necked, long-sleeved shirt descended through the haze. A single gunshot obliterated a fourth-floor window, and the woman swung inside.

A second smoke bomb fell. Inside the house, two more explosions sounded. Sabine rushed through the fog, her disguise abandoned. She scurried down to the basement entrance, pulled a small, square device from her pocket, and positioned it above the lock. It vibrated beneath her hand, scratching and clicking as it worked the tumblers faster than any human lockpick could hope to achieve. She'd bought it from an American engineer for one hundred dollars, and it had proved its worth many times over.

The lock popped and Sabine slipped inside, letting the handkerchief drop from her face and abandoning her fake bag of laundry. She tossed the cap aside, ripped off the tear-away skirt, and drew her knife. The doors around her were closed, the hall empty. Light and noise filtered in from the kitchen beyond. Sabine scampered up the stairs.

The ground floor appeared deserted. The haze from the smoke bombs outside blocked out the sun, leaving the main hall lit only by a few dim bulbs. A faint clamor rumbled upstairs. That part of the plan had gone well.

Sabine peeked into the drawing room. The furnishings were costly and too elaborate for her tastes, but suited to a flashy couple like Barton and Adriana. The room was unoccupied, and her quick look around didn't reveal any obvious places to imprison a man. She moved on.

The large dining room at the back of the house also had its door opened, but a smaller room off to the right was closed. Light shone through from the crack beneath the door. Sabine grasped the handle. Locked.

Her pulse quickened. Cliff! If he was inside, she could have him free in under a minute. She again pulled out her lockpicking device and pressed it securely to the lock. The entire door shifted. She jerked her hand back in alarm. Several seconds ticked by, but no one emerged from the room. Sabine reached out and gave the door a shove. The door toppled inward, crashing to the floor.

Sabine leapt through the empty doorframe, knife in hand, ready to battle whatever enemy lay in wait. She saw the improvised weapon coming at her out of the corner of her eye and dove to avoid it. At the same moment, her attacker yanked it away, stumbling back in surprise.

"Sabine?"

"Cliff!"

He dropped the crystal decanter to the floor, allowing the contents to dribble out onto the carpet without comment. Sabine picked herself up and appraised him.

"You're not wounded." Her clenched muscles sagged in relief.

He grinned. "No. You came to rescue me. Naturally."

"Yes. But you seemed to be getting out on your own."

He lifted a battered letter opener. "I removed the hinges."

Her eyebrows rose. "With a letter opener."

"I dismantle junk for a living. I have used many peculiar things to pry apart other things." He dashed over to a desk that was covered with papers, most of which appeared to be mathematical calculations. "How much time do we have?"

"None."

Cliff picked up a pencil and wrote something on the bottom of a page covered with letters written in all capitals. Random letters.

"Scheiße. Is that my code?"

"Part of it. I'll explain later."

Cliff added more letters to the section at the bottom. Sabine peered at the paper, trying to read the squashed-together words.

GREETINGSMYNOBLEHEIRIHAVEEN
TRUSTEDYOUANDONLYYOUWITHTHIS
MESSAGEANDTHEMEANSTOREADITI
HAVECONCEALEDTHEHEARTOFRAIN
SIDEAWOODENBOXBURIEDBENEATH
THEFLOORINTHEMAUSOLEUMOFAUGUS
TUS…

He finished before she could get through it, then he grabbed her free hand and started for the door. Together, they dashed into the hall and out the front entrance. Smoke still obscured their vision, but much of it had lifted into the air, hiding the dirigible and her distraction on the upper floor. Sabine led Cliff down the street, not daring to release his hand, lest he trip or turn the wrong direction. She ran to the end of the block, turned left, then the next right, then left again. Away from the smoke, she could once again see blue sky. And there, blocking a portion of it, was her ship. Rope ladders unfurled, dropping down to their predetermined meeting place. Cliff and Sabine scrambled aboard and Die Fledermaus rose into the air, leaving London a play town full of moving dolls below.

"You're not wounded."

Sabine sounded skeptical this time, not relieved. Cliff poured himself a glass of brandy that he was ninety-nine percent certain hadn't been poisoned and lowered himself into Sabine's cozy armchair. Lola clambered up into his lap and snuggled against his chest. He tried his best to ignore the little furry legs that reached out of her pocket and brushed against him.

"Not at all," he replied. "Adriana wasn't so lucky. Barton was bemoaning the fact that she would be unable to provide him with intimate companionship while she recovers. He may be the biggest ass in the world, but he seems genuinely attached to her."

"Romantic entanglements are peculiar things."

Cliff looked straight into Sabine's luminous brown eyes. "Yes. They are."

She didn't flinch. "Tell me everything."

"Everything." *Well, let's see. First I could say that I love you. Then I'd tell you how insanely happy it made me that you came to rescue me. And how absolutely furious it also made me, because I don't want you putting yourself in danger.*

"Barton. Adriana. The papers all over the desk. What did you learn?"

"Adriana was copying the coded message, intending to go after the Heart behind Redbeard's back. You stole it before she could finish. She and Barton are still in this for themselves, but pretending to go along with Redbeard. They didn't know about the device and thought the book I had on me held the key to deciphering the message. I made up a bunch of mathematical nonsense that sounded complex enough to have been planned by the duke, and Barton insisted I sit down and decode his part of the message. So I did. The papers you saw were various math problems. Only the first few were even real. I stopped when I realized I could just write random numbers because no one was going to look that closely."

"And the message you wrote beneath the code? Did you send him in the wrong direction?"

"Nah. I didn't think he'd trust me. I wrote, 'Greetings, my noble heir. I have entrusted you and only you with this message and the means to read it. I have concealed the Heart of Ra inside a wooden box buried beneath the floor in the Mausoleum of Augustus in Rome. The location is marked by a small plaque that reads, "Rot in hell, Barton."'"

Sabine laughed. Damn, did he love that sound. He wished she would laugh more often. She deserved more happiness in her life.

She rose from her chair, all business once again. "Right. No time to waste, then. Let's decode the message properly." She knelt on the floor beside the bed, reaching beneath it and pulling out the Sphinx device. She set it on the desk and opened the box. "The fourth wheel, if you please."

Cliff frowned at her. "Don't you need the other wheel as well? The one I hid?"

"No, I have that one. Just hand over the one you've been carrying on your person."

"But, how…"

Lola giggled in his arms, pressing her face into his shirt. "Miss La Capitaine and you both tried to hide them in the same spot!"

"Either we're both brilliant or we're both fools," Sabine said. "Take your pick. Now, can I have the last wheel?"

"Um… yeah. One moment." He stood up and set Lola on the floor, then turned his back to the ladies to unfasten his pants.

"You hid it in your trousers?" Sabine blurted.

Cliff hurriedly freed the wheel from its less-than-comfortable hiding place and fastened everything back up, his face flaming. "It seemed safer. If I'd left it in a pocket, Barton would have it right now."

"How did I not know this already?" she asked.

Cliff thrust the wheel at her, wanting the conversation over before he had to start fielding extremely awkward questions from Lola while Sabine watched and listened.

"I suppose you undressed yourself, didn't you?"

Lola eyed them both with the puzzled suspicion only a child could have. She knew there was something between them, but she didn't understand it. Explanations were already forming in Cliff's mind.

"Can we get on with it?" he asked. *I do not want to have to explain sex to Lola in front of you.*

Because surely Sabine would have her own input on the matter. It would be perfectly rational and clinical. And then he would be left to explain that there could be—often were—emotional aspects to it all. Which would leave him openly confronting the fact that while his emotions were absolutely involved, Sabine's might not be. He couldn't do that. Not yet. He was a coward.

Sabine made a pretense of wiping the wheel clean with a handkerchief, then placed it carefully into the correct slot. She placed the three remaining wheels, then turned each one to the correct initial setting.

"It seems it's now my turn to fetch something from beneath my clothing." She began to unbutton the saggy, gray blouse she wore, not bothering to turn away. Underneath, she wore her favorite bright green corset. She unclipped the top busk and withdrew a folded piece of paper.

"Maybe pirates should sew pockets into their underthings," Lola suggested.

"Good thinking," Sabine replied.

She opened the document on the desk, not bothering to refasten her clothing. Cliff had a perfect view of the swells of her breasts, the gleaming top of her chestplate, and the scars that ran up the left side of her neck. He couldn't say whether she was teasing him or if she simply didn't care anymore, now that he'd seen all of her.

She typed an N, then an E, deliberately punching in each letter of the random code on her document. The apparatus whirred, printing out the corresponding letters. Cliff leaned over the desk, watching the paper slowly spool from the slot, his heart pounding. This could be it. The answer to the Heart of Ra. An easier life for Lola and the end of their wild chase. His eyes began to pluck words from the stream of letters.

> *To my unfortunate heir. You have my deepest apologies for the mess I am surely leaving you. In recompense, I am giving you, alone, the secret to my greatest and worst invention.*

"My God, we did it," Cliff blurted. "We've decoded the document!"

Sabine pushed him aside. "Stay back. I don't want to mistype anything."

Cliff backed away, bringing Lola up beside him so she could watch the discovery unfold. "We did it, Lo," he whispered. "We've solved the mystery of the treasure. Pretty soon we'll go dig it up just like real pirates."

She beamed up at him for a moment, but then her nose wrinkled and the corners of her mouth turned down. "But what happens after? Do we have to go to California?"

"Um…" Shit. He still hadn't planned beyond retrieving the Heart.

Lola's bottom lip trembled. "I don't wanna." She stared up at him, cheeks coloring and small fists clenching. A tear trickled down her cheek. She pulled away and tore from the room.

"Lola."

Sabine's hand clamped on his arm before he could follow. "Let her go, Hartleigh. Give her a moment to be angry at you."

Cliff shook her off. "I can take care of my own child, thank you." *Stay out of it. You're already too close, and it's all going to go to hell.*

Something hard flickered in Sabine's eyes. Pain? Regret? "I remember what it's like to be a little girl. She has so little control over her own life. She's tough. She'll be okay. Give her a chance to vent her frustrations."

"Fine," Cliff sighed. He couldn't even put up a fight. Couldn't push her away, even knowing the end was near. He'd dug himself a pit that was too deep to climb out of. God, he wished he could cry and run off like Lola had done. "Let's finish the code," he said, gruffly.

Sabine resumed her careful typing and the words continued to print. When at last she finished, she tore off the paper, pushed her spectacles firmly onto her nose, and began to read.

To my unfortunate heir. You have my deepest apologies for the mess I am surely leaving you. In recompense, I am giving you, alone, the secret to my greatest and worst invention. Since you have come this far, I know you are both capable and determined. I only wish I knew your heart. Though you may do with the Heart of Ra as you please, I beg you to use it only for good and not allow it into the hands of any who may misuse its power. Retrieving the invention requires two parts: the coordinates of the area where it is buried and a map showing the precise location. Reset this Sphinx device to retrieve the coordinates. The sun-king will show you the way. As for the map, you may find it concealed at the base of the fountain in Forsyth Park, Savannah, Georgia, US of A. Blessed journey, my heir, and remember, the Heart of Ra holds but a fraction of the strength of the heart of man.

"Dammit!" Sabine cried.

Cliff flinched. "What's wrong?"

"Damn! Shit! Bloody fucking hell!" She continued on with a string of curses in languages that he didn't understand.

"Sabine, what's wrong? What's the problem?"

"Fucking Savannah is the problem! Of all the goddamned places…" She threw the paper down onto the desk and sank heavily onto her bed. "Just my luck."

"Why is Savannah a problem? It's an easy stop on the way to the Andes."

"I'm wanted there." She flopped onto her back and stared up at the ceiling. "For murder."

40

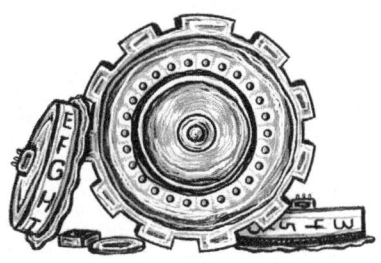

Land! Merciful God, he could see land!

Cliff leaned so far over the rail, gaping at the beautiful sight before him, that a hand grabbed hold of his coat and hauled him back down.

"You'll break the Captain's heart if you tumble to your death, Duke," Nicole scolded.

"I won't be a duke down there," Cliff replied, keeping his thoughts focused on the shoreline and not on Sabine. "That's America. I can be ordinary Cliff Kinsley."

"Hmph. You don't blend in as well as you think you do."

"I'm ordinary enough." He wouldn't be in the papers. People wouldn't know who he was. And hopefully enemies wouldn't be chasing him down.

He'd spent far too much time over the past four and a half days staring through the lens of a telescope, looking for other airships, watching for any signs of hostility. Landing would be a relief, and not only for that reason.

"Lola! Come see! We're nearly there. We'll be back in America before you know it."

"Okay." She didn't even look up from the treasure map she

was drawing. She'd been quiet since the day they'd decoded the document, even after he'd sat with her and promised that once they found the treasure they would decide together what to do next. He worried she was still angry with him.

Frustrated, he fetched the telescope again and stood watching the land creep ever nearer. The journey was almost over. He would be able to stop feeling so damned useless. Flying through the night, the crew worked in shifts. Constantly busy. Keeping the ship safe, clean, and on course. He'd sat around and done... nothing.

"I'd like a look, if you don't mind."

Cliff jumped, then stepped aside and handed the spyglass to Sabine. "It's your ship."

"Mmm. Not for long."

What did she mean by that? She loved this ship. He'd hardly spoken a word to her in days because she'd been working non-stop. She piloted the ship, did repairs and maintenance, cooked up meals in the kitchen. He'd even seen her swabbing the deck. He'd offered to help, but she'd said only, "You're a passenger."

Sabine lowered the telescope and handed it back to him. "We'll be arriving soon. In Savannah, this is not my ship. I am not and never have been a captain or even a crewman. She belongs to Nicole and Ben. They are merchants based in Jamaica. I am only a passenger. Your wife. I'm quiet and shy of strangers. We came from Europe, where we were visiting my family. Soon we will be boarding a train home to... You're the American. Tell me where we should be from."

"It has to be Chicago. I sound like I'm from Chicago."

"Chicago, then. We are here for one day only, just to see the town before we leave. Can you handle that?"

"Probably. Do I get to sleep with my wife?"

"Don't be an ass, Hartleigh."

"Resentful husband in a sexless marriage, then. I'll flirt with the waitresses when we go for dinner."

"You will not. We are a loving family."

He turned from the rail to look her in the eye. "We'll have to talk to one another, then. You know, act like we like each other."

Sabine put her hands on her hips. "I *used to* like you." She spun and stalked away.

Cliff stared morosely over the rail, letting the minutes tick by as Die Fledermaus drew nearer to the shore. She was right. He was an ass. He was so damned frustrated with the days of hardly talking and not touching. Her resistance to even acknowledging what had passed between them did nothing to suppress his desperate wanting. Desire didn't care how impossible a future would be. No wonder Lola was avoiding him. He probably radiated bitterness.

Sabine was knowingly putting herself in danger by going to Savannah. She was probably scared and angry and had every right to be. Cliff didn't doubt whatever crime she had committed there was justified. Something bad had happened to her. And he'd offered her nothing but his own petulance.

Damn. He owed her an apology.

Cliff crossed the deck to where she stood, her arms crossed over her chest, lost in her own thoughts and memories.

"I'm sorry."

She nodded, but didn't respond.

"Very sorry. I've been frustrated and worried, but it's no excuse. I've been selfish. Your concerns far outweigh mine and I should have been thinking of you instead of dwelling on my own problems. I will do my best to make amends. What can I do to help?"

Sabine sighed. "I don't need any help, Hartleigh."

"I know."

Her head whipped around to look at him, brown eyes wide with surprise.

"You're so strong and so competent," he said. "You always

have been. I love that about you. But I'm offering to help anyway. That's what friends do. So, what can I do to help?"

She turned away again. "Just play your part."

"I can do that." He stepped closer, speaking in low tones. "And if you want anything—someone to talk to, a hug, another night of mind-blowing sex—you only need to ask." Her head moved in the tiniest of shakes, and he sighed. "I know, I know. You're over it."

"Over it?" This time when she turned, she stepped nearer, closing almost all the space between them. "You think I'm over it?"

Cliff shrugged. "Isn't that why you've been trying to ignore me? Because you're not interested?"

"Not interested." Her chuckle carried no humor. "Hartleigh, I can hardly stand to touch you, but it's not because I'm not interested. It's because if I give you any encouragement at all, you might start dragging me off to have your way with me and I'd allow it."

Cliff lifted a hand to her cheek. His thumb grazed her lower lip and it trembled. "I fail to understand how that is a bad thing."

"It's a dangerous thing. You're much too close already."

"No." He bent his head to hers. "I don't think I'm nearly close enough."

Her lips parted almost before he kissed her. He plunged inside, a satisfied growl rumbling deep in his throat as he finally claimed the treasure he'd been coveting for days. She melted beneath him, content to let him lead as their tongues danced and their bodies met. Her arms wound around his neck, his around her waist, and they clung to one another, each the other's anchor. If they drowned in the passion, they drowned together.

"Sabine." Cliff groaned her name as he kissed along her jaw. Damn that high neckline that blocked him from the beautiful column of her throat. "Sabine, maybe we should go downstairs."

"Below, Hartleigh." He liked the breathy quality of her voice. "You don't say 'downstairs' on a ship."

"Wherever. Let's go there." He tugged her, and she hesitated only a moment before following.

"Lola will have questions."

"Mmm-hmm." It was difficult to walk and kiss at the same time. Questions were beyond anything his brain could comprehend. Later. He'd explain later.

A high-pitched keening sound shocked him out of his fog of lust. He and Sabine parted, looking for the source of the noise.

Cliff's eyes widened in alarm, taking in the giant creature hurtling at them. "What the…?"

The pointed beak of the flying mechanical bird speared into the ship's hull with a shuddering crack. An instant later, the beast exploded.

41

S*MOKE. FIRE. PAIN.* No. Sabine fought the panic rising inside her. This wasn't the same. She wasn't wounded. She could stop this.

She scrambled to her feet. The moment that bird dragon *thing* had detonated, Cliff had knocked her to the deck, shielding her with his own body. He'd yelled at her to stay down and had run to get Lola.

Another horrific screech reverberated through the air. A second bird speared the balloon above her. Air hissed from the damaged segment. The ship lurched and dropped several dozen feet as Nicole swung her into an emergency maneuver. Too late. Die Fledermaus sank, slowly, but inexorably.

The birds rained down upon them, screaming their hideous battle cry. Three, four, a dozen. Some of them missed, plunging into the ocean, but not enough. Too many more punctures to the balloon, and they would plummet hundreds of feet to the water below.

Sabine covered her ears against the piercing cries. This was a classic Redbeard attack. He didn't just want you captured or dead. He wanted you wailing in terror, watching helplessly as the end came.

Another bird-dragon struck above her, and a section of the envelope erupted in flames, so hot that she flinched away.

Smoke. Fire. So hot. Surrounding her. Choking her. Searing agony spreading over her skin.

"Sabine, get down!"

That voice. The memory wavered. This was now, not then. She had to save him. It couldn't happen again. Not again.

She ran to the voice, reaching to pull him toward the hatch, to hide him away from the fire and the smoke, but he grabbed her first and she toppled into his arms.

"Stay down. Cover your head."

Her head shook rapidly back and forth. "No. I can't. I have to fly the ship. We have to escape."

"The ship's doomed. Nicole is taking us down, can't you feel it?"

A chunk of flaming debris fell from the sky and she flung herself over him and the little girl he held. "No!" An ember landed on her arm and she screamed in terror. "No!"

Sabine leapt back to her feet, racing for the helm. "Get away!" She grabbed for the wheel, only to find the firm hands of her engineer clamping down on her. "We have to fly! We have to get away!"

"Sabine," Ben's quiet voice murmured. "Sabine, it's too late. Sit down and hold on. It will not be pleasant when we hit the water."

"Take everyone to the cargo deck," Nicole ordered. "Prepare to launch the boat."

Another hand, even bigger and stronger, grasped her arm, steering her through the smoke. She could see nothing but the flickering flames. Somewhere, metallic screams still echoed through the hazy sky. Dying. They were all dying.

The big man led her down, down, lifting her into a low,

wooden vessel, where the man with the small girl waited for her.

"Take care with her. She's not fully with us right now."

"I will," the man with the girl promised. He helped Sabine into a seat, then took her hand and placed it in the hand of the little girl. "Stay here. Hold on to each other. I will be right back."

Sabine's eyelids fluttered and her pulse began to slow now that she was away from the smoke and the flames.

"Cliff?" she asked. "Hartleigh!" But he'd already dashed off, and she couldn't desert Lola.

Lola's fingers gripped like iron. Her opposite hand moved back and forth, stroking a very patient spider in a motion of self-comfort.

This is the end. This is death.

It was better than the last time, and worse. She wasn't alone, the last survivor, her internal anguish as great as the pain of her flesh. But this time she would see it. She would watch them die.

The ship cracked and convulsed, wood splintering as it slammed to a sudden halt. Above, the sounds of twisting metal and snapping beams punctuated a steady patter of debris raining down on the ceiling. Cliff darted back into the room, leaping into the boat, a bulging sack in his arms. Hawkes followed on his heels, and a moment later the rest of the crew clambered into the small craft. Ben pulled a lever, and the last undamaged section of the hull gave way, launching the escape boat into the waters beyond.

"I'll drive," Cliff said, climbing to the back of the boat and starting up the engine with practiced hands. The boat sliced through the waves, speeding toward land that seemed dangerously far away and held dangers of its own upon arrival. But only for her.

Reach it, she chanted in her head. *Reach it, reach it, reach it*. The others would be safe on land. They could melt into the crowd or hop a train to a new life.

Her eyes fell on the sack. "What did you fetch?" she asked, needing the distraction.

"The Sphinx device," Cliff replied. "In case we need it again. Lola's doll and her spiders. Her luxene. A medical kit. And your first edition copy of *A Study in Scarlet* with the handwritten note from Sir Arthur himself that you kept so nicely on your shelf."

Sabine gaped at him. If she'd been anyone else, she'd have burst into tears. As it was, she simply sat, unmoving. A single drop overflowed and dribbled down her cheek.

42

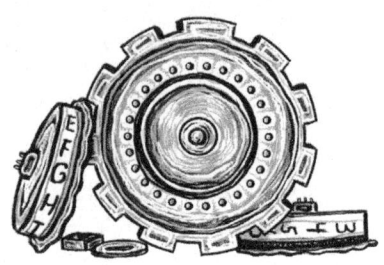

Cliff's boots sank into the white sand. Fresh sea air filled his lungs. Overhead, the sky was a brilliant, cloudless blue, and in front of him the Atlantic sparkled like diamonds. The beauty of it all broke his heart. Sabine deserved torrents and howling winds. Something to scream her pain to the world, since she wouldn't or couldn't do it herself.

"I lost my treasure map." Lola's arms clamped around Cliff's waist, and he gave her a reassuring squeeze.

"I'll help you make a new one," he promised. Strange, the things one clung to to cope with such shocking and sudden loss. Half-a-dozen times since they'd made land he'd reached up to adjust his hat, only to realize he wasn't wearing one. He had no particular attachment to the hat, yet he mourned the lack of it.

Lola was silent a long moment, then drew back and looked up at him. "What if I don't want to be a pirate anymore?"

"Be whatever you want. A princess, a doctor, a squirrel."

She giggled, just a tiny laugh, but an encouraging one nonetheless. "Can I be a duke, like you?"

"Sure. We'll find a remote island and claim it as our own duchy. You can be Lola, Duke of Spiderhaven."

She fell silent again, her head tipping to lay against his side. "Will Sabine live there with us?"

Cliff's muscles clenched involuntarily. He had a whole arm free. In an ideal world, Sabine would be tucked beneath it, comforted and comforting, not standing on her own at the water's edge, waves lapping at her boots. She looked like a lost soul, prepared to fling herself into the ocean, hoping its depths would be kinder to her than the world above had been.

"I saw you kissing her," Lola said when he didn't reply. "Slobbery, yucky kissing. You touched her with your tongue."

The accusatory tone made him wince. He didn't know if she simply found the kissing distasteful in itself or if she was jealous that he'd bestowed his affection on someone other than her. Perhaps she wasn't even certain.

"It's not yucky to grownups."

She raised a skeptical eyebrow.

"Sabine likes my kisses," he promised. "I wouldn't kiss her if she didn't want me to."

Lola's eyes followed his, taking in Sabine's hunched shoulders and crossed arms. "She's sad."

"I know, baby. We're all sad."

"But she's the saddest."

Out of the mouths of babes... "You know what she needs?"

"More kisses?"

"A hug." Many hugs. A lifetime of hugs. Affection, love, and compassion. He yearned to give her all that and more. If he tried anything right now, though, she'd turn away, pull further within herself. She hadn't spoken even to her crewmates since they'd clambered out of the boat. He couldn't touch her. But Lola could. "A big, big hug from a little girl who loves her."

"I'm eight tomorrow. I'm not little."

Tomorrow. Jesus. In all the madness, he'd entirely lost track of the days. His to-do list was becoming increasingly unmanageable: hide from pirates, find treasure map, arrange new transportation to South America, help Sabine recover without seeming condescending, throw improvised birthday party.

"A big, big hug from a girl who will be officially big *tomorrow*."

Lola nodded. She walked across the beach, her expression grave, her shoulders square. At the last moment, she broke into a sudden run, flinging herself at Sabine, who reacted just quickly enough to avoid toppling onto the wet sand.

Cliff followed slowly, giving them both time to adjust to the awkward embrace. Sabine remained stiff and didn't speak, but she draped an arm around Lola, giving her a gentle pat.

"Don't be sad, Sabine," Lola said. "Lots of pirates lose their ships. You can steal a new one. Or I can ask Daddy to buy me one for my birthday and you can have it."

Sudden tears welled in Cliff's eyes, and he brushed them away with the back of his hand. Hell, yes, he'd buy her a ship. He'd buy her five ships. But that wasn't what she needed. Sabine could afford to buy her own ships. She couldn't buy love. Cliff could only hope that she would accept it when it was offered freely.

He walked to stand beside her, saying nothing, looking out at the wreckage of her airship as it came apart in the waves. Wisps of smoke still curled into the air from sections of the burnt hull. It could have been so much worse. They were stranded, with little more than the clothes on their backs, but they were alive. All that mattered to him was right here.

He curved an arm around Sabine, resting his hand against the small of her back. For a moment she remained frozen, and he thought she might pull back or push him away. Then she relaxed beneath his touch and turned into him, letting her head fall onto his shoulder and splaying a hand across his chest. He brought her closer. Lola snugged up between them, grasping Cliff's other hand.

Alive. Together. Not one of them spoke. The sea breeze toyed with their hair and their clothing. Waves rolled gently onto shore, their soothing music an eerie contrast to the destruction that was steadily sinking into their depths.

"I'm sorry."

Cliff twitched, stunned that Sabine had been first to break the silence.

"I hope you mean sorry we're all stranded here, and not sorry it was your fault," he replied. "Because it wasn't. Yvette's ship was a good match for yours, and you mixed the two up thoroughly before we left. We had a fifty-fifty chance. It was as good as we could hope for."

Her fingers clenched on his clothing. "Sorry I didn't help." Her words were sharp, angry. "Sorry I did *nothing.*"

"You were scared. It happens."

"I was *useless!*"

She started to pull away, but he tightened his grip. "Sabine. You were terrified. Your body reacted in a way you didn't like. Sometimes that happens. Because you're human. You're not a machine that does the same thing over and over."

She twisted in his arms, yanking on the front of her bodice, tearing the buttons loose to expose a simple corset and the top of her chestplate. "I am. I am a machine. Look at me. I don't even have a heart! Only a pile of gears. But I might as well be a piece of your scrap, for all the good I did you!"

Lola stared at Sabine's chest. She lifted a single finger to touch right between her breasts, where flesh met metal. "Miss La Capitaine," she whispered, her voice trembling with awe. "You're just like me."

"Yes. We're both broken and put back together."

Lola took a step back, frowning. She put her hands on her hips. "Daddy says I'm not broken, I'm beautiful. I think you're beautiful, too."

"So do I," Cliff murmured.

Sabine pushed against his chest, and he relaxed his grip,

letting her go. She'd taken more comfort from him than he'd expected. He'd keep trying, but he wouldn't overwhelm her.

"Sir! Ma'am!"

Sabine spun back into his arms at the sound of the unfamiliar voice, hiding her damaged bodice. Her hand slipped between them, working at the buttons that hadn't come off. "I'm your wife," she hissed. "I'm shy."

The man who had called out jogged toward them. "Sir! Were you-all the passengers from the crashed airship? Is anyone hurt? Shall I send for a doctor?"

"We're unharmed," Cliff replied, "but we've lost most of our possessions and are in need of a room for the night. I would appreciate it if you could point us to a quiet hotel where my wife and daughter might recover. And then, perhaps, a shop where I might gather a few personal items."

"And a telephone," Sabine whispered.

"Ah, and I will need the use of a telephone, as well."

"My pleasure, young man. Come this way and I'll call you a carriage to drive you into town. Are there other survivors hereabouts?"

"No one else was aboard the ship other than the crew, and they are all accounted for. I believe they are making their own arrangements." *Back to the plan. Not our ship. We were only passengers.*

"Good, good. I am happy to hear no one was harmed. Dangerous things, these dirigibles. Please, come with me."

They followed the man away from shore, pausing only to pick up the sack with their few possessions. Hawkes handed it over with no more than a nod, then he and the others walked off in the opposite direction. Plan in motion, despite the lack of a ship.

Cliff walked silently, holding Lola's hand, his other arm still around Sabine. She was all business, once again, moving on from her pain and sorrow, the way she must have done her entire life. God, was she strong. He desperately wanted to be the one who held her and supported her, so that every once in a while, she didn't have to be. Her firm stride and the serious set of her jaw were at odds with the shy, helpless woman she was playing, but she stayed close to his side and neither flinched nor drew away when he let his hand slide soothingly up her back. For now, that was enough.

43

He was going to kill her with patience. That was his secret.

Sabine slowly undid the remaining buttons on her bodice and hung it in the wardrobe, trying to resist the urge to turn and look at him. She would have to find a new dress tomorrow. She could only get away with, "My dress was damaged in an airship crash," for so long, and the more attention she drew to herself, the better the chances that someone in town would recognize her.

She hung her skirt, as well, before loosening the laces of her corset. She could sleep in her shift, the way she usually did onboard ship—at least during peaceful times when she wasn't merely sleeping in her clothes, ready to jump back to work at a moment's notice. Nightgowns were reserved for her rare bouts of lounging around at home. In these surroundings, however, she felt strange without one.

A "quiet hotel" had conjured up images of small, plain rooms, perhaps with the feel of a country inn. Instead, they had been escorted to this den of luxury. Everything was beautiful and expensive: plush carpets, ornately papered walls, a wealth of electric lights. It struck her as the sort of place the president might stay if he came to town.

The high four-poster bed had heavy curtains and embroidered coverings. It was wide enough for all three of them to sleep comfortably. Lola had already built herself a fort from the vast number of pillows. To be perfectly honest, it reminded Sabine of the bed in her duke's palace back in England.

An odd burst of longing swept through her, and it took several seconds to recognize it for what it was. She was homesick. She had put a great deal of her hard-earned money into the purchase of that house. The first home she'd ever owned. The only place in the world aside from her ship that had ever been *hers*. With Die Fledermaus at rest beneath the waves, it was her only home.

Sabine closed the wardrobe as methodically as she'd done everything else, then finally turned back to face the room. She had nothing left to occupy her.

Cliff wasn't staring. In fact, right now he was holding Lola a foot off the ground so she could reach the washbasin and brush her teeth. His eyes flicked briefly to Sabine, however, moving quickly up and down before he glanced away. He was watching her. Waiting.

Lola spit and rinsed her mouth, and Cliff set her down. She smoothed her hands over her shift, a plain cotton garment much like the one Sabine wore.

"Daddy? I don't have my blanket sleeper. What am I going to wear to bed?"

"You can sleep like that. We'll shop tomorrow."

"But..." She frowned down at herself. "But my feet aren't covered and it's not warm and fuzzy. What if I get cold?"

"You won't get cold, Lo. It's warm in Georgia, and I'll be right next to you."

"What will *you* wear to bed?"

Sabine raised her eyebrows at him and his cheeks colored. "My clothes, I guess," he replied.

She looked him over, mentally undressing him, feeling her body warm at the memory of what lay beneath. Their eyes locked, his darkening to a deep blue. He licked his lips and her right breast tightened in response. Damn him.

"Okay." He grasped Lola around the waist and lifted her up to sit on the bed. "Fuel, then bed."

Sabine sat on the long sofa, perching on the edge as she watched Lola open her chestplate and fill her small reservoir of luxene with practiced hands. No complaints, no fussing, no difficulty. Cliff glanced at Sabine multiple times throughout the procedure, watching her watching. Continuing to say nothing.

"Sabine, do you need fuel, too?" Lola asked, her gaze anchoring on Sabine's chest.

Sabine unfastened the top button of her shift and crossed the room. "No. I'm different." She took a seat beside Lola, not looking up at Cliff, though she knew he was watching with interest. She pressed carefully on her chestplate, and the access panel popped open, revealing the clockwork inside and the small winding key.

"I wind it every night," she explained, turning so Lola could get a good look. "It can run for longer. As many as three days and nights, I'm told, but I've never tested that. It's easier and safer to keep to a routine of winding every night."

"Wow."

Sabine let Lola watch the winding process, then closed the panel, rebuttoned her shift, and gave Lola a nudge. "Into bed with you."

Lola bounded across the room to bid goodnight to Lucas, who sat at the bottom of a glass jar filled with sand and beach rocks that Lola had produced from her pockets. She retrieved her Sabine doll and a pillow from her fort and scrambled into the bed.

"I still miss my footie sleeper," she complained. "My feet are cold."

Sabine gave her a kiss goodnight. She couldn't help it. The girl was so full of spunk and vivacity. Innocent and adorable, but smart and strong. Sabine had always had a tender heart for children, even hard as she'd had to be to survive.

Cliff made no secret of the fact that he loved her for it. She rose from kissing Lola to see him beaming at her, his expression so full of naked adoration that it should have sent her running for the hills. She shrugged off the urge to fling herself into his arms and returned to the sofa, picking up her book and pretending her body wasn't tingling.

He closed the curtains around the bed and sat on the opposite end of the sofa. He had no book, no newspaper, nothing to keep him occupied. Sabine stared at the words on the page in front of her, determined not to look up.

He waited. Not moving. Not speaking. Hardly even looking. His patience seemed limitless. And it was driving her absolutely insane.

Minutes crawled by. Sabine read the same paragraph three times, comprehending none of it, despite the fact that she had this book nearly memorized. Across the room, Lola's squirming had quieted as she fell into a well-deserved sleep.

Cliff stole a glance in Sabine's direction, his gaze drifting down to the dark pink of her nipple, barely visible through the thin fabric. He grinned, then looked away.

Sabine slogged through another page before shutting the book and setting it aside.

"Please, just ask," she sighed.

"Ask what?"

"Anything. Any of the million questions you're dying to hear me answer. The murder here in Savannah. How I got these damned biomechanics. Why Redbeard hates me so much." She shrugged. "I guess I don't need to answer why I went looking for the Heart of Ra."

"That one is rather clear, yes. Thank you for showing Lola. It means so much to her to know someone like her."

"So ask something else. Do it. Or, if you can't ask invasive personal questions, at least ask me for sex. Which I assume you want from the way you keep eyeing my tits and licking your lips."

"How about I ask you about your extremely lengthy phone call this evening?"

"Ah. Yes. I telephoned my friends in Scotland. Charlie is an airship designer. He's going to fly here with a new ship for me."

Cliff's brows knit together. "That's quite the friend."

"He owes me a favor."

"I see."

"You're not going to ask about that, either, are you?"

He settled back on the couch, stretching his legs out in front of him and lacing his fingers behind his head. "I've decided it's better for everyone if you tell me what you want to tell me in your own time and of your own free will."

"But then I'll never tell you anything."

His mouth curved into a half smile. "I don't think that's true." He closed his eyes. "I will give Lola another quarter of an hour or so to sink into a nice, deep sleep, and then I'm going to bed myself. If I fall asleep, nudge me."

"I was twelve years old when I left home," she blurted, the need to unburden herself suddenly bursting through the dam inside her. "I'd been hiding money for years. My father became angry if I didn't bring home as much money as I had the previous day, so I learned to hide the extra on any days I did well. One day he did something unforgivable."

Cliff opened his eyes and gave her a small nod of encouragement.

"He… I had a brother. Only a baby. I planned to take him with me and raise him as my own. Until I came home to find that…" She took a measured breath. "My father had traded my brother away to someone for two bottles of liquor and a gold pocket watch."

"Christ." Cliff gazed at her, but didn't reach for her. "The bastard."

"Yes. I like to believe the people who took my brother were good. That he is happy. But my heart was broken. I ran away."

Cliff nodded and she continued.

"I had thought to flee to Vienna, because it sounded glamorous. I didn't even know how to get there. I made it from Berlin to Munich, where for the first time in years I was caught pickpocketing. Not by a victim. By a man named Schanbacher, a criminal king who within the next year would make himself infamous as the pirate Redbeard.

"I thought I'd found my place in life. He recruited older girls and young women, all whip smart and with talents such as thieving and spying. He called us his 'daughters' and we bonded like blood sisters. I wasn't alone.

"Even so, I didn't put my full trust in him and his organization. I did what I'd always done: earned money and pocketed small amounts for myself. A jewel here, a coin there. I was a good thief, always doing well, but never the best. Never drawing unnecessary attention.

"The older I grew, the more I realized it wasn't the life I'd hoped it was. Redbeard is a tyrant. His ships run on fear. He avoids hiring men who might outsmart him so he can always be the leader. He adores intelligent women, but still believes himself above them, knowing he could physically overpower them. I began to plot my eventual escape. When I was seventeen, he ordered me along on a plan that involved killing innocent people. I refused. I gathered my money, ran away to France, bought a piece of shit airship, and started pirating."

"Good for you," Cliff applauded. "You're a hell of a woman, Sabine Diebin."

Sabine crushed the fabric of her shift in her fingers, staring at the wall, unable to meet his eyes. "There's more."

"You don't have to tell me now."

"You need to know. What happened here. About the murder. Why you are in danger by being with me."

"Only if you want to tell. Only if it helps you. Sabine, you're pale as death and your fingers are about to gouge holes in your lovely shift."

She relaxed her grip, finally allowing herself to look at him. She realized her mistake at once. His eyes weren't ice-blue now, but the soft velvet of a new spring flower. She didn't move when he inched closer.

"It's not lovely. It's plain and ordinary."

"Lovely," he insisted. "The only way it would look lovelier is in a puddle on the floor."

She put a hand to his chest. "You did not just say that. That stupid, overused seduction ploy is *not* going to work on me."

He moved again, bringing his thigh up against hers. "Yes it is. Because you know I meant it. I'm used to hiring professionals, Sabine. They don't care what I say. I'm not good at romancing. But I am good at saying the honest truth, hackneyed though it may be."

Her hand lifted to his cheek, her thumb brushing over the trace of dark stubble that had grown since morning. "You *are* good at romancing. Much, much too good." She dropped her hand back to her lap. "You should go, you and Lola. Leave, before I get you killed."

"Not happening."

The arm of the sofa prevented her from backing away, so she shoved him instead. "You saw what happened today. You could have died, and it would have been all my fault."

"It would have been Redbeard's fault for attacking us. And my presence on that ship was my own choice. You didn't force me. I chose to undertake the journey with you. And I'm not going to change that decision. I don't desert the people I love, Sabine."

"Don't say that word."

"Which word? The?"

She shoved him again, and he toppled off the sofa, arms flailing.

"Ooof. I love you." He didn't bother to get up, remaining on the floor in an awkward heap, his spectacles askew.

"Stop it."

"I love every bit of you. From the tip of your perfect nose to the soles of your ass-kicking boots, I love you. I love your strengths and your flaws. I love your mechanical heart, and the fathomless depths of human kindness that flow from it. I love the way you come apart in my arms, and I love the way you will defend me to the ends of the earth."

"Cliff, please."

He sighed. "Stopping. Sorry."

He picked himself up and sat beside her again, but she turned away, fighting tears. "You make me so angry."

"I certainly never meant to do that."

"Yes, you did. You're always pushing. Even when you don't say a word, you're pushing, pushing, pushing. I hate it so much. I hate that you're good and kind and care about the feelings of others but won't let yourself be trampled on. I hate that you put others first without being weak. I hate that you make love look like a good, powerful, beautiful thing. I hate that you make me want it."

"You should want it. You deserve it. And it's yours. You stole my heart, my darling pirate, and I don't want it back."

Sabine turned to face him. He was so close to her. So horribly, wonderfully close. Her hands clamped down on his shoulders, dragging him in for a kiss.

"I hate how much I want you."

His fingers moved to the buttons of her shift. "I know. Love is terrifying." He pushed the garment down her shoulders until it fell to her waist. He grinned at her bare torso, then reached one hand to stroke the gentle slope of her metal breast. "Can you feel this?"

"Yes." She closed her eyes as his feather-light touch moved in a slow caress. She could sense the pressure of his fingers in each place they touched, sending faint vibrations through the chestplate and into her body. "It tickles a bit."

"Do you like it?" His thumb brushed over the small steel nipple.

"Yes."

He cupped her other breast, his hands moving in parallel. The contrast between her deeply sensitive flesh and the subtle sensations beneath the metal brought every nerve in her body roaring to life. She pressed into him, twisting to bring him closer.

Not good enough. She squirmed from his grasp long enough to reposition herself sideways on the sofa, legs splayed. He dragged her shift and her drawers down her legs and dropped them onto the carpet.

"A puddle on the floor. What did I tell you?"

She jabbed him in the ribs. "Jackass." Her gaze darted to the bed. "What about Lola?"

"She won't wake up." He swiftly crossed the room to fetch a blanket, which he deposited on the floor beside the sofa. "And in the unlikely event she does, we'll simply cover up."

Sabine watched him strip off his clothes. His movements were efficient, but unhurried. She had plenty of time to change her mind. Plenty of time to remind herself why he was best kept at a distance. Plenty of time which she spent admiring the hard planes of his chest and the eager jut of his erection.

Her whole body quivered. She was wet for him, and her skin tingled in anticipation. He knelt between her thighs, his hands resuming their patient exploration. Slowly, he lowered himself down atop her, his lips finding hers.

She rocked her hips into his, grinding in a rhythmic dance,

sighing at the feel of his cock sliding against her, rubbing over her slick folds, teasing her clit. The pace of her thrusting increased, drawing a groan from deep in his throat.

"Fuck," he gasped.

"Yes, Cliff, please," she begged. "I want you inside me."

"The damned condoms sank with the ship," he growled.

"Then you'll have to be careful," Sabine replied. "Unless you want Lola to have a baby brother or sister."

Cliff froze.

He did want that. Oh, God, he did, and he wanted it badly. She could read the helpless longing in his wide, blue eyes. She knew that look. Had lived it. The yearning for the impossible.

She pulled her spectacles off, fumbling to set them on the table behind her, then kissed him ruthlessly, doing all she could to make him forget everything but the here and now. She spread wider for him, moaning her satisfaction into his mouth when he entered her.

"Sabine," he whispered as he thrust. "Sabine, I love you."

She clung to him, letting him carry her away from the earth to a place where nothing existed but the two of them and this pure, honest pleasure. She convulsed around him, and he jerked free, coating her inner thigh with his sticky seed.

Sabine clasped her arms around his neck, holding him to her, ever a thief, stealing this precious moment when he was hers.

I love you, too.

Sabine awoke before dawn, curled up beside Cliff in the enormous bed, her body warm and relaxed. She pressed a kiss to his cheek, but he didn't stir. She let her fingers wander over him, only for a moment, tracing his hip and the muscles of his arm, gently ruffling his thick, black locks.

"I love you," she whispered. She looked past him at Lola, the Sabine doll clutched in her arms. "Both of you."

She slipped from the bed, dressed quickly, and opened the door, hesitating for only a moment.

"I love you so much."

She stepped into the hall, the door slipping softly into place behind her. The click of the lock echoed like a death knell in her ears. She would finish this alone. It was the only way.

44

Four damn days.

Four days of worrying, wondering. Four days of frantically checking the papers for news that a wanted murderer had been captured or that a mysterious woman had been found dead. Lola's birthday had been a tearful disaster, and things hadn't improved since.

Cliff chucked the extra slice of bread out the window and watched the birds fight over it. His wife was in bed with a cold, he'd told the hotel staff. She wasn't to be disturbed, but she wasn't poorly enough that she needed a doctor. He'd had food brought to the room for her to maintain the fiction, and then he'd had to either eat it himself or dispose of it.

The ruse was probably a waste of his time and effort. Sabine's friend the airship designer could arrive at any moment now. She'd be off after the Heart of Ra, and he'd never see her again. He could hop a train to San Francisco and send word that the Duke of Hartleigh had died in an airship crash.

"My dear Duchess," he composed aloud. "It is with deepest sympathies that I must inform you of the tragic demise…"

He let his words trail off and yanked the window closed,

drawing the curtain. No sense letting anyone get a glimpse of him. Savannah was a small city, and outsiders stood out. If gossip spread about him, it could bring Redbeard's minions right to his door. Assuming they hadn't already left town in pursuit of Sabine. She'd already retrieved the map from the hiding place in Forsyth Park. He'd checked the morning she'd left. She had no reason to stay in town and several good reasons to leave. She could await her replacement airship elsewhere.

"You'll make Duchess Amy sad," Lola said. She sat on the floor, watching Lucas crawl around. Nothing else seemed to hold her interest anymore. "She likes you."

"I know. I like her, too. I'd like to see her and Luella again, and find out how the household is faring. I never finished cleaning up all the junk in Sabine's house. It needs to be sold if we're to pay off the debts." He ran a hand through his hair. "I'm not in a place where I can leave all that behind. I have responsibilities."

Lola nodded. "Will Sabine go back to her house? After she finds the treasure?"

"I don't know, babe. I wish I did, but I don't know why she left when she did or what her plans are. I can only guess."

Cliff paced the room, fists clenching and unclenching in frustration. These past few days he'd imagined there'd been a chance she would return. She was merely hiding elsewhere to protect them, and would show up at the door when her ship arrived, announcing that it was time to leave for the next part of their journey. Now reality stalked him, waiting to pounce with its bad news.

"I'm going to lose her, dammit," he growled. "I'm going to lose her because I haven't done enough. I haven't searched hard enough. I'm out of time, and she's gone and I'll never know…"

Never know if something terrible has happened. Never know if she finds the Heart of Ra. Never know if she really loves me.

"Daddy, be careful!" Lola snatched Lucas up off the

ground, cradling him protectively. "You almost stepped on him."

"Sorry, Lo. I'm making this worse for you, aren't I? God, I'm such a wreck. I don't know what to do. I don't know how to find someone without being obvious that you're looking for them. Especially if they don't want to be found." His head snapped up. "She was wanted here. A known criminal."

Cliff paced back to the window and parted the curtains just enough to peer out. "She must have worked in the area. Probably smuggling. Taxes on spirits are high and Savannah is a thirsty town. Plus, with the temperance movement flourishing, the number of customers wanting to buy their drink in secret will be on the rise." He drummed his fingers on the window pane. "And if she smuggled, she needed contacts. Safe havens. A way to move the merchandise undetected. Where would a pirate hide in this city?"

"Captain Flint died in Savannah," Lola said. "He lived at a pirate inn where he died of rum, remember? Maybe Sabine went there."

"*Treasure Island* is fiction, babe, but yeah… that's exactly the sort of place." He jerked the curtains closed and spun around. "I have an idea. Let's go shopping."

· · · ⚙ · · ·

"Avast!" Lola cried, though with somewhat less gusto than when they had begun two hours ago. She stabbed the air with her wooden sword.

"You like pirates, boy?" the white-haired woman asked, leaning on her cane as she peered at Lola.

"Girl," Lola corrected. She flipped her pigtails. Only her long hair indicated "girl" to most observers. Her new outfit consisted of a tricorn hat, tall black boots, a pale blue military-style jacket, and a pair of gray trousers. She looked adorable.

Unfortunately, everyone they'd met had called her a boy.

Cliff was one raised eyebrow away from a, "Most of the pirates I know are women and they're damned good at it," rant.

"A girl pirate," the woman replied in a slow drawl. "We had one of those, a few years ago. Nearly burnt down the entire airfield, then killed a woman in broad daylight."

"Will you tell me pirate stories?" Lola asked, following the script as she had done four times previously. Cliff leaned against a tree, feigning disinterest. "Do pirates still live here?"

"Your sort of pirates came here long ago," the woman replied. "Horrible villains, they were, murdering and kidnapping. Not what any young lady should speak of."

"I like speaking of it. Do they have secret hideouts in caves? Or hidden treasures in the cellar?"

"Word is, they would sneak through tunnels with their rum and stolen loot. But those pirates died out long ago. These days it's the dirigibles that bring trouble. Smugglers and thieves zipping in and out in their wicked flying machines. They're a plague, child, and you'd best stop believing those fool stories that glamorize them."

Cliff gritted his teeth in frustration. He'd cooked up this ridiculous scheme for nothing. Five pirate conversations and not a single clue.

Lola sighed her own frustration. "But I like those stories. They have secret hideouts and treasures and ghosts."

The woman shook her head. "Those ghosts are the only real truth, girl. The old inn on Broad Street is full of them. Angry men done in by other angry men. You stay away from the ghosts, child." She looked directly at Cliff. "Tell your daddy to take you home to your dolls."

Cliff held out a hand to Lola, his heart thumping in his chest. A lead, at last. "Come on, Lo, we should be going."

It only took one brief question to get directions to the inn. As Cliff expected, the directions came along with, "But you don't want to take a child there. Full of whores and thieves." Since he was looking for a thief, that suited him just fine.

The pirates' inn was a ramshackle wooden structure occupying a corner lot. Years of wind and rain had cracked and warped the wooden siding, and several shutters hung loose or were missing altogether. Heavy drapes covered windows, blocking prying eyes from the goings on inside. Above the entrance a sign swayed in the wind, its painted depictions of food and drink faded to ghostly outlines.

"Wow," Lola gasped. Her fingers tightened on Cliff's hand. "There prob'ly *are* ghost pirates here."

"I'm only interested in one pirate, and I hope someone here can help us find her. Let's go."

Cliff strode into the building, pausing a moment just inside the door while his eyes adjusted. The room ahead of him was wide and crammed with tables. Men of all races and ages packed the seats, accompanied here and there by women in revealing clothing. More women moved between tables, serving food and drinks.

The lights overhead were electric, but dim and recently fitted to the building. Bare wires crisscrossed the ceiling and ran down the walls. A rumble of sound filled the room, but quieter than he would have expected for such an establishment. The men were talking, but many were keeping their voices down. Exchanging secrets and passing information.

Cliff spied an unoccupied table near the right hand wall. He would need to walk halfway across the room to reach it. His stomach tightened at the thought of wandering into this nest of possibly armed criminals. But someone here would know Sabine. He felt the certainty in his gut. He squared his shoulders, drew Lola close to his side, and strode toward the empty table, wielding the only weapon he possessed.

"Well, aren't you Mr. High-and-Mighty?" a gray-bearded patron remarked as Cliff passed by. "With your fancy suit and your shiny shoes."

Cliff had owned nicer suits. He'd had to buy this one off the rack and it didn't fit quite as well as he liked, but it served his purposes. It showed him to be a man of wealth and power, one who wasn't afraid to march into a room of pirates, head held high.

Hopefully no one could tell he really *was* afraid.

He took a seat at the open table, positioning Lola between himself and the wall, where she was safest. Cliff didn't truly expect that anyone here would harm a child, or do more than rough him up a bit. The men here liked to keep a low profile, and that meant not attracting unnecessary attention.

A waitress wandered over, leaning one hand on the table. "You lose your way or something, Yankee?"

Cliff gave her a winning smile. "How did you peg me for a northerner before I even opened my mouth?"

She laughed. "Only a Yank would be fool enough to wander into this place wearing a suit like that. You might want to check your pockets and see how much money you've lost."

"I don't have any money," Cliff replied. "Spent it all on the suit."

A man at the next table over laughed. Cliff glanced his direction and almost jumped. The man looked like Ben Palmer. This man had a moustache, and his face was a bit thinner than Ben's, but the resemblance was unmistakable. Cliff looked quickly back to the waitress, not wanting to stare.

"Well, how are you gonna pay for your drinks, then?" the waitress asked. She turned her gaze to Lola. "Or is the little pirate boy paying?"

Lola slammed her hat to the table. "I. Am. A. Girl!"

The waitress flinched. More men laughed.

"Girls can be pirates, too," Lola insisted. "I have a friend who is a real girl pirate. So there."

"A cola for my fierce girl pirate, please, and bourbon for myself. On the rocks." Cliff dug a coin out of his pocket and spun it across the table.

The waitress picked up the gold coin and frowned at it. "What's this? English money?"

"It's a half sovereign. It should more than pay for anything we order today. A cola and a bourbon, if you please."

She shrugged and left, leaving Cliff and Lola alone at the table, half the eyes in the room staring at them.

"Problem, gentlemen?" he asked. "Haven't you heard of the Mad Duke of Hartleigh?"

He met the eyes of the men around the room, refusing to flinch, conjuring up every bit of ducal pride Amy had tried to hammer into him. Most of the men glared in return, but a few shrugged and glanced away. Cliff let his gaze return to the man who resembled Ben.

"Mad Duke?" the man chuckled. His voice was similar to Ben's, as well, his accent Jamaican. It couldn't be a coincidence. They had to be related. Brothers—or cousins—perhaps?

"Indeed." Cliff gave him a nod before looking away. That man could be his key to finding Sabine. "So, Lo, what do you think? Piratey enough for you?"

"Not enough girls," she complained.

As if in answer, the front door opened and a pair of women entered. They wore boots, snug trousers, and loose tops. Identical pouches at their hips could have held anything: weapons, money, the bones of their enemies.

Cliff pushed his chair closer to Lola. All day he'd been watching the women around him, certain Redbeard's minions were prowling the streets of Savannah for him. He'd spotted nothing unusual, but he was no spy and the Daughters were trained for stealth and deception. A pair of female pirates appearing so soon after his own arrival was entirely too coincidental.

A knot twisted in his gut. He should never have come here. He was completely out of his element. Maybe Sabine had been right after all. Maybe he should have stayed where he was and let her handle it all on her own. Because if he'd led Redbeard to her, he'd never forgive himself.

45

"Damn you, Hartleigh," Sabine muttered under her breath. The irritated words did nothing to squelch the joy that had radiated throughout her body at the sight of him. He'd come looking for her. He wouldn't give up on her. On them. So endearing. So foolish.

She edged closer to the transparent mirror. He was magnificent, sitting there meeting the glares of smugglers and thieves, refusing to cower or flinch. Every inch the duke. Sabine knew him well enough, though, to see the tension in his posture.

An old smuggler took a seat at Cliff's table and they began to chat. Sabine couldn't hear what they were saying, but the way Lola leaned in, her eyes wide, suggested ghost stories. This old place was full of them. Stories, that was. Not ghosts. The strange noises, mysterious sightings, and sudden disappearances had nothing to do with pirate hauntings and everything to do with the secret tunnels leading out to the river.

Sabine turned her gaze from Cliff to the two Sisters who

had followed him here. She recognized them from previous encounters, but didn't know their names. Part of Redbeard's trusted personal crew, hired after she'd struck out on her own.

They sat calmly with their drinks, their heads close together as they talked privately, no different than most of the men in the room. Not preparing for an attack, as far as Sabine could tell, but watching. Hoping Cliff would lead them to her, probably. Which meant the sensible thing to do was to leave before anyone knew where she was going.

Love and sensible did not go well together.

"Damn you, Hartleigh," she muttered again.

"Anything else I can get for you?" the bubbly young waitress asked, whisking Sabine's empty plate from the table.

Sabine smiled at her. "No, thank you, Betsy. But I do have a favor to ask of you."

"Of course." Betsy Hale knew of this small, secret back room because she was the owner's daughter. But she served the few patrons allowed here because she was smart and dependable. She'd grown from a gangly teen to a woman in the years since Sabine had last seen her.

"I need you to carry a note to Mr. Palmer in the main room."

Betsy's light brown cheeks reddened to a shiny copper. Apparently she'd also developed a crush during those years. "Of course, miss."

Betsy fetched pen and paper and Sabine scribbled a short note.

When hell breaks loose, get Hartleigh and the girl out.

Good enough. He'd know who had sent the note and which tunnel she meant him to take.

Next step: a distraction. Sabine leaned back in her chair and stared out through the mirror. Cliff had three hardened criminals sitting at his table now. His rash bravado and implication of wealth had earned him respect. The smugglers and pirates assumed he was looking to buy, and they wanted him for a customer.

The moment Betsy appeared in the main room, Sabine hopped up from her chair. She slipped out through the hidden door and wove her way through the back rooms to the kitchen, where she donned a cap and apron like the serving girls all wore. The kitchen staff raised eyebrows at her, but no one said a word.

"You'll be paying for anything you destroy," Mr. Hale commented as she passed by.

"Naturally," Sabine replied. They weren't friends, but they shared a certain mutual trust. She'd kept him flush with tax-free liquor for a number of years, during the heyday of her piracy.

She found a tray and piled it high with mugs of pale ale and bowls of piping hot stew. Her target—a regular patron she remembered only for his bad temper—was seated between Cliff and the pirate women. She considered the angles and her paths in and out of the room, then hefted the tray and backed through the door, pushing it open with her backside as she'd seen many of the girls do.

The Sisters weren't looking. Serving girls were part of the backdrop here, and Cliff was their focus. He noticed, though. He glanced up as she entered the room and his body went completely rigid. Their eyes locked. The tray in Sabine's hands trembled. So many questions lurked in those eyes of his. Questions she had no time for. She gave a tiny shake of her head.

Too late. People had noticed his sudden agitation. She had no time to walk closer to her target or prepare her offensive.

She balanced the tray on one hand, scooped up a bowl of stew, and hurled it across the room. It landed square in the center of the hot-tempered pirate's table, splattering him and all his companions with the scalding broth.

He sprang to his feet with a roar and Sabine flung a mug

at him. The man at the near side of the table also rose, just in time for the mug to strike him on the back of the head. The men the next table over burst out laughing.

That was all it took. The room erupted into noise and fisticuffs. Mug-head lunged at one of the laughers, and they went down in a heap, knocking into several other tables and sending drinks flying. The angry pirate stalked toward Sabine, punching and pushing anyone who got in his way. A flurry of retaliatory fists slowed his speed to that of a three-legged tortoise.

Sabine continued throwing food and drink around the room, aiming for anyone who looked angry. The Sisters had figured out who she was, but struggled to make their way to her through the melee. Sabine hit one of them in the face with her last bowl of stew. The woman howled in pain, striking a bystander as she flailed. He tackled her.

That's my cue to leave.

Before Sabine could turn toward the door, the table in front of her overturned, and she skittered back to avoid being hit. The angry pirate shoved the table aside. Blood trickled from his nose and he bared his chipped and yellowed teeth.

"You! You'd better run, bitch," he snarled.

A chair crashed down on his head, and he crumpled. "No one touches her," Cliff vowed.

Sabine locked eyes with him again for only an instant before James Palmer ushered him and Lola out the door.

The bolt slammed into place, locking the hatch closed above them.

"Hey, wait!"

The man who looked like Ben gestured down the long, low corridor. Sparse electric lights hanging from a single wire lit the brick tunnel. "This way."

Cliff tried to reach for the hatch, but the man blocked him. "Sabine's still up there."

"She will take her own way out. Do not worry. She knows this building almost as well as the Hales do."

Cliff didn't move.

"Yes, you are stubborn. I can see why you give her trouble." He gave Cliff a push. "We must go. This tunnel is known, and the lock will not take long to pick."

"What? Then why..." The man pushed Cliff down the tunnel ahead of him, and Cliff sighed and went, keeping Lola close.

"I am James Palmer," the man said. "La Capitaine's favorite person in Savannah." He flashed a mischievous smile.

"Palmer. Then you *are* related to Ben?"

"Brothers. We pirated together for many years. But he likes the air, and I like the land. I found a home in Savannah, and he found a place with La Capitaine. We made a fine team, with her ships and my friends on land. We had many successful years before the attack."

The attack. The event that had left Sabine scarred and in need of biomechanics? Did Palmer know the details? Cliff had to bite his lower lip to keep from asking. This was not the way to find out. He needed Sabine to confide in him, and going behind her back would not earn her trust.

"Um, Daddy?" Lola tugged on his sleeve and pointed.

Cliff's slick new shoes skidded on the bricks as he pulled to a sudden halt. Up ahead, the tunnel ended abruptly in a jumble of broken bricks and dirt. Wherever it had gone in the past, it certainly didn't reach there anymore.

"Don't panic," Palmer said, motioning toward the ceiling. Tiny wisps of sunlight filtered through what looked to be a metal grating covered with vines. "For me." He paused and bent down, running his fingers along the brick floor. "And for you."

The floor vibrated. Cliff jumped back as a section lifted

from the ground, then flipped open to reveal what looked like a small elevator at the top of a deep hole.

"Down you go," Palmer said. "The lower tunnel will take you beneath the river and then up to the airfield on Hutchinson's Island. It is close to half a mile. Your lady will await you there, I imagine."

Distant noises echoed from the corridor behind them. Cliff climbed into the elevator and helped Lola down after him. "Thank you," he said.

Palmer nodded. "My pleasure. Happy to work with La Capitaine again, even if only for a day. Good luck." He ran his fingers across the bricks again, and the hidden hatch began to close.

Lights came on the moment the hatch closed completely, and the elevator descended deep beneath the ground. At the bottom, it opened into a cylindrical concrete tunnel, reinforced by steel ribbing every ten feet. A flat cart looked to be connected to a track running along the bottom of the tunnel.

"This is her smuggling tunnel," Cliff marveled. "She would have unloaded her cargo and sent it along here, under the river, right to the people who would distribute it." He circled around the cart and found a panel of simple control switches. "Hop on."

The cart drove slowly, but silently, and turned what would have been a long, boring walk into a long, boring rest. Lola leaned against him and rehashed everything that had happened at the inn. The barroom brawl had excited her more than frightened her, thankfully, but she was sensible enough to finish with, "I don't think we should go there again."

The far end of the tunnel had an elevator identical to the one near the inn, and they quickly found themselves standing in a small, square room with a mechanical door in the ceiling. Cliff pulled a lever, and the heavy metal plates began to shift, the clanking of the gears sounding much too loud in the small chamber. He climbed up out of the hole into the middle of a thick clump of bushes, then reached down and pulled Lola up after him. He kicked the lever and the door closed, hidden away beneath the dirt. He saw no way to open the tunnel from this side. The smuggling operation required a team effort.

Cliff and Lola pushed their way out of the bushes into the sunlight. Dozens of airships covered the grassy lawn in front of them, many unloading cargo. The closest ship, a beautiful small craft with a ladle-shaped hull and a round blue balloon, stood no more than fifteen yards away. A red-haired woman in a very low-cut dress was stepping down from the ladder built into the hull. A mechanical snake hung around her neck like a scarf.

The woman turned just in time to see Cliff and Lola step out from the cluster of shrubs. She started, then smiled.

"Oh!" she said in a distinctly British accent. "You must be Sabine's duke. You're cute."

46

Sabine limped to the water's edge and bent to scrub the blood from her hands. This city was the bane of her pirating career. She was never coming back. Not for anything. Tragic, how a place of such beauty, with its sweeping beaches, curving rivers, and trees dripping with lush Spanish moss, could bring her nothing but pain and death.

Or near death. Redbeard's spy had still been alive when Sabine had left her, and there was a chance someone would get to her on time. If not... she'd brought it upon herself when she'd attacked.

She'd been good—just figuring out which exit Sabine had taken and following her had required skill—but not good enough. The Pirate's House boasted an array of swords, not all of them decorative, and Sabine had grabbed one on her way out. Maybe if Redbeard allowed his female employees to study swordplay, the woman would have stood a chance. For tonight, Sabine was glad he didn't.

Sabine's head spun as she rose, and she had to wait for the wave of dizziness to pass before she walked on. She jogged as best she could on her aching knee. Her enemy had gotten in a solid blow right on the kneecap, and it would probably hurt for days. Beneath her skirts, the hastily tied-on sword banged against her leg. The ache in her side had dulled somewhat, but the wound was still sticky with blood. She'd get it checked out at the airfield. She was leaving tonight, whether Charlie had arrived or not.

"You going across the river?" she asked a man sitting beside a small boat, smoking a cigarette.

He blew out a ring of smoke. "Not planning on it."

Sabine pulled out the remainder of the coins she'd pickpocketed over the last few days. "Can I change your mind?"

He grinned, stubbed out the cigarette, and accepted the bribe. "You sure can, miss. Hop aboard."

The rapidly fading sunlight and Sabine's dark dress hid most of the blood stains, but if the man noticed, he didn't say anything. Her bribe was big enough to keep him silent for now. If anyone came along asking questions later, she'd be long gone.

Across the river, merchant dirigibles drifted slowly to the skies, taking advantage of the weather as they departed for long, overnight journeys. Other ships rested in the field, their cargo loaded or unloaded, silently waiting for morning. These were the quiet hours in the airfield. The smugglers wouldn't be out until well past dark.

Sabine remained silent during the river crossing and as she limped across the airfield in search of her crew. Even the air felt heavy tonight. Too many old memories pressing down on her. Too many new ones adding to their weight.

The sight of Charlie's speedy little sloop lightened her heart and her step. They'd arrived. And the ship beside his…

Sabine almost stopped walking to gawk at it. Gorgeous. The hull was of dark, polished wood, with a gray ovoid balloon, and a sturdy, but artistically carved rail. She was larger than Die Fledermaus had been, but still small enough to fly with a crew of four or five.

Sabine picked up her pace, hoping this was the ship meant for her. Her knee twinged and the wound in her side stabbed, but the promise of a new ship pushed her through the pain.

"Captain." Charlie tipped his hat to her as she raced up. "Good to see you. What do you think of her?"

"She's astounding. I'll pay whatever you're asking."

"Well, in that case…" Charlie gave her a grin. "Actually, she's pretty sparse on the inside, so you'll want to bring her to get fancied up when you can. But she has room for a family of four and a crew of ten, and a wee bit more cargo space than you had in the past. Two functioning water closets and a shower."

"Perfect. Has my crew seen her?"

"What, you mean my crew that has mysteriously increased during the course of the day? Yes, they're on board. I believe they've already inspected her from stem to stern."

Sabine stepped closer and lowered her voice. "And the duke and his daughter?"

Her mechanical heart hitched in her chest. They were here. They had to be here. Palmer would have found her if anything had gone wrong.

"On The Kestrel with Effie."

Sabine let out a relieved breath. "Thank God. You don't think you could…"

"Fly them back to England? Not a chance. His Grace would probably leap over the side of the ship trying to catch you. He's been frantic with worry. The man's crazy for you, Sabine."

"I know. I…" *Want to keep him safe. I want him never to leave my side. And there's no way to do both.*

"Sabine!"

She turned toward The Kestrel at the sound of her name. Effie hopped to the ground, skipping the last few rungs of the ladder and bounding across the grass. Cliff and Lola scrambled down after her. Sabine's aching muscles relaxed at the sight of them, unharmed.

"Sabine, it's so good to see you," Effie called. "I brought you a few dresses, since you'd lost everything. They're not all your usual style, but... Oh!"

"What?" Sabine glanced down at herself. She'd stepped into a pool of light cast by the ship's lanterns. Her dress was smeared with much more blood than she'd realized. "It's not mine," she replied. The pain in her side intensified, just thinking about it. "Not all mine."

Her knees trembled. Now that the rush of the fight had worn off, her body had begun to protest. Her head swam. She took a deep breath to steady herself.

"Sabine!" Cliff pushed past Effie. "My God, what happened?"

She waved him away. "I'm fine. I should sit down. Rest."

He walked straight up to her and scooped her off her feet. Her skirts tangled and the sword dangled awkwardly from her hip.

"Lower the cargo hoist and fetch a medical kit," Cliff demanded.

Charlie grabbed for the handholds running up the side of her new ship and scampered up to do Cliff's bidding. Sabine squirmed in his arms.

"Put me down."

"No."

"I'm fine." She winced as her wiggling sent another jolt of pain through her. "A few stitches at most."

It wasn't just the wound, though. She hadn't slept much the last few days, nor had she been eating right. Hiding out wasn't really the healthiest way to live. But she'd gotten by.

"I've been through a lot worse and you know it. I'll walk myself to bed, have some food and drink. I can handle it. I don't need..."

"Shut up," he snarled, sounding so unlike his usual self that her mouth dropped open in shock. "Just shut up."

The cargo hoist hit the ground and he stepped onto it, nodding his head at Lola to tell her to join them.

"I know you don't need me," he continued as they rose into the air. "I know you're fierce as Boadicea and twice as deadly. Hell, you probably wouldn't ask for help if you'd cut off your whole damn arm. But, goddammit, Sabine, tonight, just once, you're going to let someone take care of you, okay? Give me one night. One single night. And then I won't ask anything of you again."

What was he even talking about? He was being ridiculous. He'd be back to making demands tomorrow. Probably of the silent, stare-at-you-until-you-give-in type. Sabine was too exhausted to protest, though, especially in the comforting embrace of his arms. She let her head fall onto his shoulder as he carried her across the deck and down to the captain's cabin.

As Charlie had warned her, it was unfinished. The walls were bare wood and uncovered lightbulbs hung from the ceiling. The built-in shelves were only half-complete, and not a stick of furniture had been brought in.

And yet someone had turned it into a home.

A pile of blankets on the floor had been carefully spread out and smoothed down to serve as a bed. A small, glass spider home sat beside a second, smaller bedroll, where a pirate doll lay propped on a pillow. The dresses from Effie were neatly folded in a corner, and topped with a few simple grooming items. Cliff's and Lola's personal effects rested nearby, also neatly stowed. The Sphinx device made a makeshift bedside table, Sabine's Sherlock Holmes novel sitting atop it.

Cliff placed her in—or on, more accurately—the bed and began stripping off her clothing without a word. He found the map to the Heart of Ra tucked beneath her layers and laid it atop her book without even looking at it. Sabine never saw who took away her ripped and blood-stained dress, but she didn't expect to ever see it again.

"Good." The word rushed out of him on a heavy breath.

"You weren't lying about it not being your blood. Who on the crew has experience with stitches?"

"They all do. But Hawkes is the neatest."

"I'll fetch him."

Five simple stitches sealed up her wound nicely, and by the time they were complete, the ship had launched, carrying her away from the memories that cut much deeper than any knife could.

Cliff returned to her side the moment she was patched up. He wiped her clean of blood and grime, propped her up with pillows and towels so she could sit comfortably, brought her food and drink, and even undid her mess of a hairdo, combing it out with gentle fingers.

Sabine closed her eyes as the brush ran through her hair, teasing the tangles free and smoothing it down. No one had ever brushed her hair for her, that she could remember.

"You're good at that," she murmured.

He chuckled. "Of course I'm good at it. I have an eight-year-old daughter. I do it every day." He divided her hair into sections and began to weave an intricate braid along one side of her head. "You should see what happens when she tries to brush it herself."

"I missed her birthday." Sabine's eyes flew open, seeking Lola, but the girl was already in her makeshift bed, lulled to sleep by the sway of the airship. "I'm so sorry. I'll make it up to her soon. Get her a special treasure for her heart."

Cliff's lips brushed her neck. "You should wind yours."

"Yes."

Sabine hadn't dressed after her stitches, and it took her only seconds to open her chestplate and ensure that she would keep ticking for another several days. Cliff finished a second braid, set the comb down, and then settled himself against the wall, lifting her into his lap.

"You were lucky," he murmured, running his fingers over

the long scratch at the bottom of her chestplate. "Between the ribs of your corset and this, you were spared serious damage."

"It wasn't luck. I use my metal body as armor. As much as possible I protect my right side and leave the left exposed."

He twitched, then his arms came around her. "That's why you always put me on your right. I thought it was because I can't walk in a straight line."

"No. Left side faces the enemy. Anything I'm guarding goes on the right."

"You've been protecting me, all this time."

"Yes."

"And you've trusted me from the start."

Sabine had to think for a moment. "Yes, I suppose that's true too. If I'd thought you likely to stab me in the back, I would have done things differently."

He kissed her again, the softest, gentlest kiss she'd ever felt. Her eyes closed once more, and her limbs became boneless in his embrace. How could such a tiny thing hold such immense power? Here and now she would have given anything to stay this way forever.

"Thank you for this," he murmured.

"Thank *you*," she replied. Her worn-out body surrendered, welcoming sleep's embrace.

Soft. Warm. Loving.

Fire. Smoke. Pain. The liquid fire covered her, eating away at her flesh, tearing the life from her body. She screamed, the sound coming from outside her body, where the fire consumed all she loved. Coming from him.

No!

"No!"

"Sabine!" Strong arms hugged her to a firm chest. "Sabine, I'm here. It was only a dream. You're safe."

She gasped for air. Sweat trickled down her back. Slowly,

the trembling in her limbs began to ease. She shifted out of Cliff's arms and lay on her back, staring at the ceiling.

"They've been bad since Die Fledermaus went down," she said. Her voice was soft and still a bit shaky, but she continued. "A little mixed up now, between the two events. And sometimes you're there."

"Want to talk about it?"

For the first time in her life, she did. "Redbeard plays a long game. He'll take opportunities as he sees them, but if he doesn't succeed, he'll pull back. Wait. He will be just as satisfied to revenge himself upon me in five years as he would be to do it now.

"Four years ago, my own career was flourishing. I flew goods between Europe and the Americas, the best smuggler in the world. I had a fleet of four fast ships, run by trusted lieutenants, such as the Palmers and Hawkes. I had just commissioned Die Fledermaus to be my personal craft, and I was recruiting new crewmen to take over the running of the ship I had been using. Among them was a former Daughter of Redbeard, a woman about my own age named Victoria.

"That was my greatest joy and triumph, to bring others out from under his clutches. To show them how much better life could be when we worked together, making decisions as a group and valuing all the skills we possessed without judgment.

"My ship was crewed entirely by Redbeard's former workers, four women and two men, and they were my world. My friends, my family, my lover. I adored them all with everything in me."

Tears trickled down Sabine's cheeks, unchecked. Cliff made no move to wipe them away or to embrace her, but his arm pressed into hers, reminding her that he was there. Ready. Listening.

"Savannah was one of our most profitable locations. We were preparing to leave, flush with cash and some lovely new things we'd purchased with our earnings. The crew were already aboard. I always did the final check to make certain nothing was left behind. I was preparing to board when I saw Victoria coming down the ramp with two of the airfield cargomen. I knew immediately something was wrong. She smiled and told me they'd just loaded the last box.

"Everything past that is a blur. I pushed past them, somehow, running for the deck, screaming for the rest of my crew. The explosion obliterated half the ship. I don't—" She swallowed back a sob before continuing. "I don't think they suffered, but my heart was destroyed in an instant. The blast knocked me to the deck and everything around me was smoke and flame. The explosion had spattered gobs of thick, burning liquid everywhere, including across the left side of my body. I just lay there, weeping in agony, wishing that death would take me as my world burned down around me."

A long silence fell. Sabine stared up at the unadorned ceiling, listening to the hum of the dirigible's engine and Lola's steady breathing.

"Do you want me to hold you now?" Cliff whispered.

In answer, she rolled over, burying her tear-stained face against his chest. He cradled her, his hand stroking over her back, strong, but soothing.

"I don't know who found me," Sabine said, "but I woke hooked up to a machine in the office of a biomechanologist. She told me if I wanted to live I would need a mechanical heart. I agreed. As soon as I was able, I hunted down Victoria and stabbed her straight through her own traitorous heart, right in the middle of the street. I spent the next year doing nothing but harassing Redbeard and causing as much trouble as possible. Charlie's ship? We stole it from Redbeard. Killed six of his men and lost none of ours, though Charlie lost his eye, and one man lost a hand. Eventually I went back to pirating, because it didn't matter. My heart was shattered beyond all hope of repair. Nothing could bring them back. Nothing could heal me."

"I'm so sorry," Cliff whispered. "I would take away your pain in an instant if I could."

"I know."

She clutched him tight, breathing him in, soaking up his warmth and his love. She would never be whole, but he filled some of those gaping spaces inside her.

Sabine woke with a start. The ship had landed. But where, and why? She bolted upright, surprised to find herself alone in the pile of bedding. Where was Cliff?

Her eyes scanned the room, homing in on all the sudden wrongness. No spider house. No dolls. Only her own clothes. A small, handwritten note beside the bed. She snatched it up.

My dear Miss Diebin,
I can't even begin to tell you how sorry I am for all the strain and worry I have heaped upon you. I have involved myself where I am not qualified to be, and it has brought you pain, misery, heartache, and even danger to your person. I am flying back to England with Lola. We will see to the cleanup of the house and have it finished before you return. If you wish to sell, I'll take it off your hands, but if you wish to stay, I will not hassle you about it. I expect to settle elsewhere, as I will be returning to my business and spending much of my time in Chicago. You may keep the Heart if you wish. We will get on well enough as we were. I wish circumstances were different, but as it stands, I cannot bear to be the cause of any future trouble, stress, or danger for you. As of now, please consider our association severed.

Yours,
Hartleigh

47

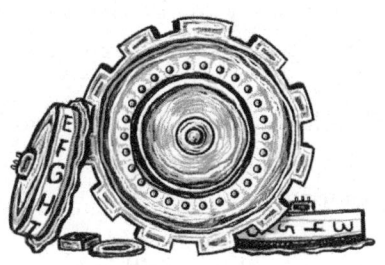

"I won't! I won't! I hate you!"

"Lola, for God's sake," Cliff groaned, trying to dodge flailing legs in order to pull her to her feet. The heel of her boot caught him right in the shin, and he hopped back, grimacing in pain. "Babe, please listen."

God, he must look like the world's worst father. Lola had never been one to throw many fits, and she hadn't done so at all since she was three. Now, here she was, having an all-out tantrum in the middle of the Key West airfield, while dozens of upper-crust travelers looked on in horror.

Cliff circled his daughter, searching for any sort of opening where he might reach down and grab her without injuring either of them in the process. He didn't think his chances were especially good.

"We're leaving," he said sternly. "I'm sorry you don't like it, but it's what we need to do."

"I won't!" she shrieked again, battering his already sore leg with her small fist. "You're stupid! Stupid!"

"Fine."

Cliff sucked in a breath and braced himself, bending to

grasp her by the waist and haul her to her feet as she kicked and screamed and lashed out. He stood her upright, but didn't release her. Lola grabbed his hand with both of hers, trying to pry it off of her.

"Let me go! Let me go!"

"I do not want to carry you kicking and screaming onto an airship, but that's exactly what I'm going to do if you don't stop, do you understand?"

She pushed on his hand again. "Let me go."

"Are you going to throw yourself on the ground again, kicking and screaming?"

"Yes!"

Well, at least she was honest. "Then I can't let you go."

"No," she pouted.

Cliff relaxed his grip, slowly pulling away in case she flopped again. When she remained standing after a few seconds, he straightened. "Now, do you want to talk about this before we get on the ship?"

"No." She crossed her arms over her chest. "You're stupid. Stupid, stupid, stupid."

It was difficult to refute her when a big part of him was saying the same thing. He took another deep breath. "I'm sorry, Lo, I really am."

"No you're not. If you were sorry, you'd stay. You'd marry Sabine so she can be my mommy."

"I'm trying to help Sabine. I'm trying to protect her."

Lola turned away, pulling Lucas from her pocket and petting him, the way she often did these days when she needed comforting.

"Babe, I led bad people to her because I wouldn't listen. I wouldn't stay away like she wanted and she got hurt because of that. I can't keep doing that to her. It's not right."

She remained facing away from him, arms tight to her chest, saying nothing.

"Just because you love someone doesn't always mean you

can be together. Sometimes the only thing you can do is let them go."

"I won't," Lola said, quietly but firmly. "I don't want to go. And Lucas doesn't want to either." She spun and tossed the spider into the lap of a woman who sat nearby, resting atop her traveling trunk.

The scream carried clear across the airfield and probably all the way back to Savannah. "Get it off! Get it o-o-o-off!" She flailed at the spider at the same time as a man lunged to grab it, and he howled in pain when her nails met his skin.

"It bit me! It bit me!" He hopped in a circle, cradling his hand. "Call a doctor, the monster bit me!"

Cliff moved closer to the chaos, cringing at the shrieks that stabbed into his ears. *Do I just sweep him off her skirts? Or lunge and grab?* Even here in the US, he would make headlines. *So-called duke attacks travelers with man-eating spider, gropes innocent woman.*

Another man intervened before Cliff could cause a scandal, grabbing the bottom of the woman's skirts and shaking them until Lucas toppled to the ground.

Thank God. Cliff bent down, prepared to scoop the spider into his hands and then give Lola a thorough scolding.

A large boot flew past his head, smashing to the ground atop the spider. The snapping and crunching made Cliff's stomach heave.

"No!" No. Not her spider. Not her beloved pet. "Oh, God, no."

The boot lifted away to the sound of a satisfied, "Much better."

Cliff grabbed for the wretched, squashed insect. He'd hold a funeral. He'd weep with her. His baby. His poor, heartbroken baby.

"What the…" His fingers touched fuzzy legs and a crushed exoskeleton. No guts. No insides. No spider. He'd been mourning an abandoned shell. She'd tricked him. She'd tricked everyone. Cliff shot to his feet, furious at her, at himself, and at the whole damn world. "Lola Ann Kinsley, you…"

The blood drained from his face. She was gone. He whirled in a circle, looking everywhere, desperate, terrified.

"Lola!"

Nothing. Nowhere. She was gone. Cliff darted this way and that, pushing people aside to look behind them, clambering over heaps of trunks, screaming her name.

"Lola, goddammit, where are you?"

A hand clamped down on his arm. "Sir, I need you to calm down," the porter said, his no-nonsense tone and iron grip brooking no arguments.

"My daughter is missing," Cliff pleaded. "Let me go. Help me, dammit."

"You're spewing foul language in front of women and children," rebuked the man who had been "bitten" earlier.

"Your sensitive ears matter more than *my child*? Go to hell."

"She should be with a governess. A firm hand. A good thrashing for disobedience. You brought this upon yourself, spoiling her as you clearly do."

Cliff pulled out of the porter's grip, trying to calm himself before he punched someone. He stormed off, fuming in silence. He had to think. Where would she have gone? Back to the ship? Was it even there anymore? The crew hadn't put up a fuss when he'd asked them to drop him at the nearest port. He'd assumed they'd fly off again immediately.

Cliff rushed back to where he'd disembarked. His heart sank at the big, empty space before him. No ship. No Lola. He fought the urge to fall to the ground and cry.

"Okay, okay." He put his head in his hands. "The ship's not here. Where else would she go? She's a smart kid. She'll want to hide until the ship I was hoping to board takes off."

He began a slow scan of the airfield, looking for potential hiding places. A distant ship rising into the air made his breath catch. If someone had kidnapped her…

"I will hunt them down and break every bone in their body," he vowed.

"Rather bloodthirsty for a man 'not qualified' to be a pirate."

Cliff spun around. "Sabine?"

"No one else is harebrained enough to go after you." The words were flippant, but her eyes blazed and her cheeks flamed. She was furious. "How could you?" she shouted.

"I—" He blinked at her, not fully certain he wasn't hallucinating. She'd come after him? Joy. Sorrow. Panic. Confusion. His brain couldn't process all the conflicting emotions. "Lola's missing," he blurted.

Sabine paled. "What?"

"She distracted me with a fake spider and disappeared. She didn't want to return to England."

Sabine's eyes darted this way and that, surveying the area much as he had. "Smart girl. We'll find her." Her voice carried a slight tremor, but her body remained braced for action. "Let's start from where she disappeared. Look for tracks. If there aren't any, we can spread out. Cover more ground."

"Right." Tracks. He hadn't even thought of that. "This way."

Together they jogged back to the scene of the spider incident. The area was well-trampled from the feet of travelers and smashed down by luggage. Cliff could see no way to track Lola, but Sabine's background as a thief gave him some small hope. Maybe together they could do this.

"I was standing here," he explained. "When she threw the spider skin, I turned, putting her behind me, right there by… It's gone!" His head swiveled around, confirming it. "The bag with all our things is missing."

"Lola took it," Sabine guessed. "She would never leave that pirate doll of hers behind."

"Then she can't have gone far. She can't run lugging the bag."

"If I were doing it, I would run from one pile of luggage to the next. She'll be harder to catch when she's on the move, and if any adult spots her, she says she's playing a game. Most likely she ran that way, away from you."

They raced to the next closest pile, where a teenaged porter in an ill-fitting outfit hauled trunks as big as he was onto a cargo hoist.

"Have you seen a little girl?" Cliff asked. "Black hair done up in braids, dark gray dress probably covered in grass stains, carrying a canvas bag?"

The boy only shrugged.

Cliff and Sabine split up, each running toward another potential hiding place. Nothing. Cliff raced onward, his heart sinking further with each passing second. The whole horrible morning replayed in his head. Why hadn't he explained better? What could he have done differently? He was a menace to everyone he loved. He ran on, not knowing what else to do.

The bag caught his eye and he was careening toward it before his conscious thoughts even processed what was happening. "Sabine!" he shouted. "Over here! Lola! Lola, are you there?"

He couldn't take his eyes off it. The bag sat atop a mechanical cargo lift, at the edge of a big pile of luggage. Stacks of trunks beside the lift provided convenient steps for an agile girl. A perfect hiding place.

"Lola!" Cliff flew across the field, heedless of anything but that one bag.

The lift shuddered and began to rotate. Lola's head popped up from the pile. "Daddy!" she cried.

"Lola! I'm coming!"

His foot caught on something, and he fell flat on his face, sending the wind rushing from his lungs and his glasses tumbling into the grass.

"Daddy! Help me!"

Cliff grabbed for his spectacles, struggling to his feet as the lift spun, cutting off Lola's path to the ground. A steam truck pulled up and the lift tipped, dumping the cargo and a shrieking little girl into its bed.

"Lola, hold on!" Sabine shouted, streaking into view from off to Cliff's right.

They converged on the truck as it hissed and belched, pulling away from the lift.

"Give me a boost!" Sabine yelled.

Cliff didn't need clarification. He knelt, spreading his hands to make a stepping stone. The instant her boot hit his palm, he hurled her upward with as much force as he could, sending her flying up and into the back of the departing vehicle.

The bag with his belongings hit the dirt, followed only a second later by a furious pirate with an armload of sobbing girl.

"I'm sorry. I'm sorry. I'm so sorry," Lola wept.

"You are in so much trouble, Little Miss Lola," Sabine growled, her hands moving in soothing strokes over Lola's back even as she scolded. "You scared the shit out of us."

"I know. I'm s-sorry."

Sabine released Lola into Cliff's arms, and he clasped her against him. "Oh, thank God. You're safe, babe, you're safe. Don't you ever do that again." Tears of relief trickled down his cheeks and dripped from his chin. He hugged her tighter.

"D-don't squish Lucas," she cried.

Cliff stepped back, keeping his hands on her shoulders. "Do you understand, Lo, how worried I was? I thought I'd never see you again."

"I'm s-sorry. I didn't want to go. I didn't want to never see Sabine again."

Sabine sniffed. "As if I would let my best cabin girl get away. You knew better. You've got some sense in your head." She glared at Cliff. "But you..."

He didn't flinch from her angry gaze. He could take it. He could take anything now that they were all here together. "Me."

"You left me!" she raged. She dug a hand into her pocket and brandished the note he had written "You wrote this! *This!* How could you?"

He sighed. Everything he'd done since he'd awoken felt

both rash and wrong, no matter his motive. "I was trying to help." He wasn't sure if he was explaining to her or to himself. "You were right to want to get rid of me. I'm so sorry I didn't listen. I've been foolish and careless, and I hurt you and let others hurt you, and I was only trying to make it right. I know it was cowardly to leave a note, but I didn't want—"

"You signed it with your *title!*"

Cowardly and callous. "I, uh... thought someone else might read it, and thought it would be better—safer—if it sounded like I wasn't so... ardent."

She slapped the note against his chest, and a shiver of delight raced through him. Even her fury thrilled him, after thinking he might never feel her touch again.

"It is splattered *with your tears*, you oaf!"

"You oaf!" Lola echoed, wiping her dripping nose on her sleeve.

Cliff had no reply. He couldn't even shrug. It had nearly killed him to leave, and he didn't think he'd have the willpower to do it a second time.

"We are partners!" Sabine shouted, not removing her hand from his person. "You do not abandon your partner!"

Cliff gave in to his selfish desires and inched closer. "I thought pirates didn't have partners."

"Well, this one does! And I'm not going to let you wander off and leave me to find the treasure all on my own. It's not my treasure, it's *our* treasure, and it's for Lola. You didn't honestly think I would keep it for myself?"

Lola peered up at the adults. "The treasure is for me?"

Cliff covered Sabine's hand with his own. "No, I didn't think you'd keep it, even though I told you to. I imagined you barging through my door with the Heart of Ra in your hand, shouting, 'Hartleigh! What the hell am I supposed to do with this?' And then I imagined sweeping you into my arms and kissing you." He sighed and disentangled himself, stepping safely out of her reach. "And then I stopped imagining and told myself to quit being selfish and leave before I got you killed."

"Did you ever think maybe you should've asked me if that was what I wanted?"

"He didn't ask me, either," Lola huffed.

Cliff crossed his arms and scowled. "You'd made it pretty clear what you wanted. How many times did you try to send me and Lola away? And who did the leaving in Savannah?"

"I was trying to protect you."

"And, as I have already stated, *I* was trying to protect *you*."

Sabine sighed heavily. "I was wrong, okay? You were right and I was wrong. I thought last night made things different. You came for me. You weren't giving up. You were there for me all night."

"You don't need me, Sabine."

"But I *want* you. Dammit, Hartleigh, I don't care if it's stupid or foolish or dangerous. I want you and I want you always. We're better together. I'd rather have a short life with you in it than a long life thinking about what might have been."

Cliff cracked. He opened his arms and let her fling herself into them, gathering her close, breathing her in. He'd already proven himself incompetent with words, so he simply held her. Lola joined the embrace, and they stood locked together in the warm sunlight and the gentle breeze. Together. Family.

"I think we've missed our flight," he murmured.

"My ship's down at the other side of the airfield," Sabine replied. "I told them to go stock up on supplies, since I didn't know how long our search would take."

He pressed his lips into her hair. "Or were you preparing for the possibility that you'd have to track me all the way to England?"

She tilted her head up and caught his mouth in a bruising kiss. "I would hunt you down anywhere. Now let's go find a Heart."

48

"Captain?"

Sabine yanked the blanket up to cover her naked body. Dammit, why now? Snatching time alone had been almost impossible during the days since they'd left Florida, and now when they finally had a moment together...

Hawkes pounded on the door again. "Captain, I think you need to see this."

Cliff burrowed beneath the bedding, finding sensitive skin and sucking hungrily. "Tell him we need half an hour."

Sabine slid reluctantly from his arms. "Maybe this is it. Maybe we've reached the coordinates." She planted a kiss on his cheek. "We can celebrate after."

He sighed and rolled over. "It's probably another storm that we'll have to go out of the way to avoid."

Sabine hoped not. Inclement weather had slowed their progress to a crawl. Days of thick clouds blanketing the mountains and heavy rains had made flying treacherous and pinpointing their location difficult. This morning the sun had come out—prompting Lola to run up top to play—but they had no guarantee conditions would remain favorable.

"I'll be right out," Sabine called.

She slipped into the little black dress Effie had designed. Functional hooks, laces, and buckles ornamented the bodice, and the skirt had useful slit pockets, but it was otherwise entirely unlike Sabine's usual style. Low cut with tiny cap sleeves, it left swaths of skin bared to onlookers. All her worst scars were visible, as well as the top of her chestplate, inviting rude stares and ruder questions. She'd had no intention of ever wearing it in public until she'd worn it in front of Cliff.

He'd gaped for a moment, then grinned at her, eyes shining with undisguised lust, and said, "Damn, Sabine, you're the sexiest fucking pirate who ever lived."

She was now reconsidering her fashion choices.

Sabine pulled on a pair of dark gray hose—the skirt only barely hit mid-thigh—and her usual rugged boots, then headed for the deck. Cliff stumbled after her, unable to walk and button a shirt at the same time.

"Ah, Capitaine!" Jules called. "Come! See!"

Sabine and Cliff hurried to the rail where the navigator stood with Lola, holding her tight as she peered down at something.

"At last we have been able to maneuver through these mountains and reach your coordinates. We were puzzled that the numbers had led us to this place of nothing, but then as we flew closer…" He gestured for them to look over the rail.

Sabine stepped beside Lola and followed her gaze down.

"Bits of wall!" Lola announced. "There's a secret city in the jungle!"

Sabine stared. There below her, in a saddle between two rocky peaks, evidence of a by-gone civilization poked through tangles of greenery. Her eyes traced the overgrown structures. A wall here. A corner of a building there. Terraced slopes, carved from the hill by human hands. A city, once alive, now ravaged by the forces of time and nature. It took her breath away.

"Jesus," Cliff swore. "That's your map. How did he ever find this place?"

"I don't know. But we need to go down there." A strong gust of wind buffeted the ship. "I don't think we can land."

"No," Jules agreed. "Nor can we hover for long. The wind is picking up and the sky in the distance is not as fair as that above us."

"We'll have to go now. Only Hartleigh and myself. The rest of you remain with the ship. Circle nearby and watch Lola. I'll need a signal flare, tools for digging, and a bag of provisions. We may be some time, trying to walk through all that vegetation."

The clouds had already thickened by the time Sabine and Cliff stepped off the cargo hoist and into the ruins. Sabine unfolded the map and checked that her sword hung properly at her hip. She'd need it to cut through any particularly obstructive plants. Cliff adjusted the small bag of provisions he'd slung across his body.

"Here goes nothing," he said.

They started off, side-by-side, heading for a high point where they could survey the area and locate their position on the duke's treasure map. Cliff stepped carefully, watching the ground as he walked.

"You should have a specialist look at your eyes," Sabine suggested. "A biomechanologist, perhaps."

"Why?"

"I don't think you see straight, even with the glasses. You tilt your head frequently, and you walked straighter when wearing an eyepatch. Maybe it's not something fixable, but it can't hurt to try."

"Are you saying you don't like me clumsy?" he teased.

"Actually, I love you just the way you are, but I wouldn't be upset if you were able to make small changes that could make your life easier."

He hooked an arm around her waist and dragged her in for a sudden kiss. "I will never forget that you first said you loved me on a mountain top in the Andes with a sword strapped to your waist. It's the most romantic thing I can imagine."

"You're ridiculous."

"Mmm. And you probably love that too."

She did. She let him sneak one final kiss, then paused to orient herself with the map.

"Here. This looks like that steeply terraced section off to the right. Which makes that bit of wall ahead of us this." Sabine jabbed a finger at the map.

"I agree. Which means that other section of wall..." He pointed. "Is here." He dragged his finger over the paper.

"Putting the treasure ahead and a tiny bit to the left!"

Sabine raced through the bramble, leaping from high areas to lower ones, matching landmarks to the lines on the map as she ran. Cliff crashed noisily through the undergrowth behind her, occasionally swearing, but never giving up. She loved his awkward stumbling. She loved his determination to keep working at tasks that didn't come easily to him. She loved every damn thing about him, and the thought that she got to keep him forever made her dizzy with glee.

Or maybe that was the altitude.

"Not long now." She slowed, checking the map carefully against the ruins surrounding her. "Follow this wall here." She drew her sword and hacked away at some branches clogging her path. "Then we should be able to climb down." She hopped over a wall to the ground below, twigs snapping beneath her boots.

Cliff landed beside her and leaned over her shoulder to look at the map. "So our treasure should be..." He scanned the area, one finger extended, then suddenly froze. "Well, look at that. Nineteen hundred and two. Someone left us a convenient date."

Sabine ran to the wall where the date had been carved, her whole body shivering with excitement. "This is it! This is the X." She examined the ground at the base of the wall, kicking aside bits of rock and stick with the toe of her boot. "Time to dig."

Cliff opened the bag and produced a pair of spades, handing one to Sabine. They knelt, plunging the trowels into the earth, laughing and exchanging smiles as they worked.

"No wonder you like treasure hunting," Cliff said. "This is like being a kid again, digging on the beach, hoping to turn up the shiniest rock, or maybe even a penny that someone once dropped."

"It won't be so fun once we've been digging for forty-five minutes with no results."

"Don't be so pessimistic." Cliff thrust his spade deep, and it clanged on something hard. "That sounded like metal."

Dirt and leaves flew as they tore into the earth, uncovering the object concealed beneath. A square metal box emerged, speckled with rust spots, but whole and sealed. Cliff wedged his trowel beneath it and levered it loose. Sabine grabbed for it, lifting it out and setting it on the ground between them.

"Would you like to do the honors, Duke? After all, it's going to your daughter."

"You should open it," Cliff replied. "You began the quest. You should finish it."

Hands trembling, Sabine unfastened the latch on the front of the box. She took a deep breath and lifted the lid.

For a moment, they both stared at the contents, dumbfounded.

"Son of a bitch!" Cliff swore. "If the bastard wasn't already dead, I'd kill him! Another clue? After all this?"

Sabine removed the single piece of paper from the box and unfolded it, hands still shaking, though now with anger and frustration. Her eyes swept over the paper. Pictures, not words jumped out at her. Diagrams. Carefully numbered and labeled.

"Oh!" Her heart buzzed in her chest as her pulse jumped. "Cliff, this is it!" She spread out the paper in front of him. "It's not a device, it's a design! These are the plans for creating the Heart of Ra. Everything. Measurements, diagrams, lists of all necessary parts. We can make two—for Lola and for me!"

Cliff embraced her, crushing the paper between them. "My God, Sabine, we did it! We'll hire an engineer, work with the best biomechanologists in the world. We'll make both my ladies indestructible."

She pushed him away and carefully smoothed out the paper. "Not if you ruin the plans, we won't." She gently refolded her treasure, unlaced her bodice, and tucked the paper into a special hidden pocket. Effie thought of everything. A quick retying and she stood up, brushing the dirt from her skirt and trousers. "Bring the box. Peculiar as Hartleigh was before you, he might have meant that to be important, too."

Cliff collected the spades and stashed them away before picking up the box and rising himself. "Looks like a wholly ordinary box to me, but can't hurt to be safe." He kicked the loose dirt into the hole. "It'll be obvious someone dug here, but since this place doesn't seem to get many visitors, I don't think anyone will care."

"Who's going to come here except to study the ruins? They'll be digging anyway."

"Good point." He put the box in his right hand and held out his left to her. Sabine twined her fingers with his. "Let's hike back up to higher ground and signal. I can't wait to show Lola."

Sabine looked up to the sky. "Just in time, too. The clouds are getting thick and that definitely looks like rain."

The trek back up took more effort than their wild run down to where the treasure had been buried, but Sabine's heart was so light that the burning in her muscles felt glorious. She scrambled up to the top of a wall and set her flare. Her ship would be here in no time. In a week, they'd be home. They would still have to consider the problem of Redbeard, but in England they would be safe. Especially after they reported all they knew about Barton and his Bandits to the authorities.

Sabine found herself a comfortable spot and sat down beside Cliff, leaning on his shoulder, happy simply to be with him. Pirate partner, lover, beloved.

A metallic grinding noise above made her look up. Out of the clouds dropped the most warlike balloon she could have envisioned. The envelope was red as blood. Giant thorns protruded from all sides of the metal creature that hung below. A pair of enormous pincers jutted from the front, and a barbed tail swayed behind. As the landing craft drifted down, the thorns opened, sprouting three pairs of segmented, insectoid legs that settled on the ground. The tail rose, then stabbed deep into the earth, anchoring the balloon in place. The scorpion's snapping claws spread apart, making way for a tall, swaggering man with a long white beard. Three hulking men followed, swords at their hips and malicious grins on their faces. They spread out to flank their leader.

"Ah, my wayward daughter," Redbeard said, baring his perfectly reconstructed teeth. "So good of you to lead us to the treasure." He drew a revolver. "Please hand it over, or I'm afraid your darling duke will meet his end here on this lovely mountain."

49

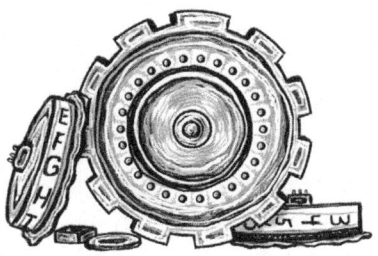

Cliff was moving before the pistol even swung in his direction, scrambling to the top of the wall, treasure box in hand. Behind the wall, the ground fell away, a craggy slope of eroded terraces and broken rock. He dangled the box over the edge. Droplets of rain splashed him as the sky darkened.

"You shoot me, this tumbles down the mountain with me, and you'll never see it again," Cliff threatened.

Redbeard studied him with narrowed eyes before lowering the revolver to point at Sabine, who stood on the ground below, sword in hand.

"And if you shoot her, I throw it, then kill you."

Redbeard gave a slow, disappointed shake of the head. "Your lover thinks he's clever, daughter. You can't help but chase the clever ones, can you?"

"How do you get Sabine to spread her legs?" taunted one of Redbeard's goons.

"Let her catch you reading a book!" chortled the man beside him.

"Unfortunately for the two of you, it doesn't work if you're holding the book upside down," Sabine retorted.

Redbeard motioned to the two men. "Go get him."

As the men came at him from both sides, Cliff inched along the top of the wall, mind racing, considering his options. The rain came down harder and the wind whipped at his clothing. He glanced to the sky, but saw no sign of Sabine's ship. His foot skidded on a patch of wet moss and he teetered.

"Stop!" Sabine shouted. She took a deliberate step forward. "I'll make you a deal. You let us go, unharmed, and we'll give you the Heart of Ra."

The two goons slowed, looking to Redbeard for instructions.

Cliff let the box slide down to his fingertips. "Might want to listen to her. The rain is making things slippery."

Redbeard's men froze, glancing at one another. One of them shrugged. Redbeard remained unflappable.

"You're bluffing, daughter," he sighed, sounding so much like a disappointed parent that Cliff shivered. "You wouldn't give up a treasure so easily. Not after all you've done to find it."

Sabine took another step forward. She kept her body at an angle, the left side closer to her opponent. She was primed for attack, but her chestplate couldn't protect her from the power of that revolver.

"He means more to me than the Heart. Let us go and we'll hand it over."

Redbeard smirked. "Thank you for clarifying. Grab him."

Cliff shuffled along the wall, but the two men were converging quickly. He could stall no longer. He glanced down at the precipitous slope behind him, then back to Sabine. The men lunged. Cliff took a deep breath and jumped.

Sabine looked back just in time to glimpse colliding bodies toppling over the wall. A scream of helpless terror echoed from the mountain peaks, only to be drowned out by the sharp bang of a nearby thunderclap.

"Cliff!" His name tore from her throat. *It wasn't him. It wasn't him. He's alive. He's well.*

She willed it to be true. To believe anything else would render her unable to function, and she wouldn't allow that to happen. Cliff had given her time and removed two enemies. He needed her to defeat the others. Somewhere in the skies above, Lola needed her.

Another clap of thunder shook the air, making Sabine look up. The rain was steady, but not a downpour, and the clouds weren't the heavy gray of a thunderstorm. Her stomach turned over. Cannonfire. Redbeard had allies in the sky.

"You have a high-altitude ship," she guessed. It explained how he had followed her so stealthily. She rarely flew more than a mile high. A ship that could conceal itself high in the clouds could watch from above, especially with good telescopes.

Redbeard grinned that horrible, smug smile she'd come to despise. That smirk of condescension. The tyrant, sneering at his inferiors. The silent lackey standing at his shoulder mimicked the smile, though not as effectively.

"I do. Exquisite vessel. Enclosed, pressurized deck. Painted a mottled white and gray to blend in with the clouds. Large cargo doors underneath to release my landing balloon and other devices."

Those bird bombs that had destroyed Die Fledermaus. He would pay for that.

Another cannon blast sounded. "Thirty guns," he added.

A bead of sweat trickled down Sabine's back. Fledermaus Zwei had no guns. She would need to flee. She was fast, especially stripped down as she was. Any ship large enough to hold the scorpion balloon and thirty guns would be lumbering. Sabine's crew could escape. *If* they left her and Cliff behind.

They were too loyal. They would run, but only to hide, waiting for a chance to return and rescue their missing crewmates. Sabine admired them for it. In their position, she would do the same thing. No man left behind. Perhaps she had never truly been a proper pirate.

Redbeard made a little beckoning motion with his pistol. "Hand over the Heart of Ra, my dear, and perhaps we can make arrangements to spare your friends."

"Hartleigh has the Heart. You saw it in his hands." *He is alive*, she told herself once again. *He is alive and waiting for you.*

Redbeard considered himself too civilized to snort, but his abrupt huff of laughter sounded suspiciously like one. "Now, now, daughter. We are not fools. We both know you would never trust him to carry your treasure."

"I would trust him with my life," Sabine vowed. She had trusted Cliff with her heart, and that was the riskiest of all.

Redbeard sighed. "I should have put a stop to this fondness for men when you were still a girl. By the time you started trading your favors for piloting lessons, it was too late."

"I paid for the piloting lessons with jewels," Sabine retorted, taking yet another step forward. "It was the sword fighting lessons that I bought with sex." She lunged and her sword flashed, smacking into his hand hard enough to throw him off balance. Another flick of her wrist and the gun went flying. "They were a bargain."

Redbeard danced backward, out of the way of her blade. Still agile for a man of sixty-ish years. The taciturn lackey drew his own blade, a rapier better suited for gentlemanly fencing competitions than battle.

Sabine parried his attack easily, despite the longer reach of his thin blade. They both regrouped, swords at the ready, watching one another. Sabine shuffled around to put herself between Redbeard and the gun. As long as she could keep the contest to swords only, she could win this.

Her opponent moved gracefully, and his fighting stance appeared relaxed and confident. He'd had formal instruction. Good. She knew how to handle that.

She slapped his blade hard with the flat of her cutlass,

doing no damage to either him or the sword, but disrupting his technique. His scowl of annoyance made her smile. She repeated the attack.

The lackey took a step backward, setting himself up to thrust at her with his longer weapon. Sabine simply backed away, edging closer to the pistol. Redbeard realized what she was doing and darted toward the gun, but a vicious slash forced him back. Sabine hadn't fought multiple opponents at a time since the raid three years prior that had liberated The Kestrel, but she'd learned early on how to fend off two and three attackers at a time. Franz, her teacher, had been a good lover and an even better instructor. Since the day he'd died in the blast that had left her scarred, she'd done her best not to think of him, but today his memory brought her comfort. He lived on in each step she took and each slash of her blade. And she *would* do him proud.

Redbeard drew a dagger from the scabbard at his hip, moving toward Sabine's left, away from his rapier-wielding minion, trying to flank her. Sabine continued to retreat, keeping most of her attention on the fencer. A short blade on her armored left side was by far the lesser threat, even with Redbeard as her opponent.

Twigs snapped beneath her feet. Larger branches poked at her arms and legs. She darted behind a bit of shrubbery and the rapier stabbed ineffectually into the leaves. The fencer swore. The thick vegetation hampered him far more than it did Sabine.

Redbeard made his move, circling around her left side in a wide path, then running for the gun. Sabine whirled to stop him, leaving her right side vulnerable to attack as she did so. The fencer lunged and the rapier bit into her upper arm, but she hardly registered the pain. Preventing Redbeard from reaching the gun was all that mattered.

Before she could make her next move, a flying chunk of

rock whizzed past her head, striking Redbeard on the shoulder. He stumbled.

"I warned you not to touch her," Cliff snarled. Blood dripped from his temple, mud soaked his clothing, and he held his left arm clutched tightly to his body, but he was alive and standing. Sabine didn't even try to pick up the gun. She ran at it at full speed and kicked it toward Cliff. He scooped it up with his good hand and joined her, facing down their enemies together.

"Where's the box?" Sabine asked.

"Gone. I lost it when I fell. Sorry. One of the thugs went with it. The other fell further than me, but he's climbing." Cliff clutched the pistol with both hands, grimacing when he moved his left arm. He aimed at Redbeard. "I think it's time you all let us go."

Redbeard looked to his sword-wielding minion. "Get them!" he ordered. He whirled around and ran for the scorpion balloon.

The fencer charged. Cliff pulled the trigger. The man stumbled, staggered, then fell, clutching his chest.

"Go, go!" Sabine shouted. "Don't let Redbeard get away! He's got a ship up there."

Cliff ran alongside her, but his face had gone pale. "Shit. Sabine, I think I killed him."

"Good. He was going to kill us. Hurry! The tail is pulling out."

The scorpion's legs began to fold up. The claws twisted and snapped, barring the way into the vehicle. Sabine darted forward, spinning and dodging, but had to pull back before the sharp metal clamped down on her.

"Dammit!"

"I've got this," Cliff called. He had stopped several feet out of range of the claws, holding the gun and taking careful aim. He fired once, twice. A hissing noise rose from one of the claws and it ground to a halt. "Clifford J. Kinsley. Scrap metal and recycling. I can dismantle anything."

"I fucking love you." Sabine grabbed his uninjured arm, and together they clambered over the frozen claw and into the landing vehicle just as it began to rise.

Insect-like appendages aside, the scorpion balloon was a simple airship, with a basket of metal mesh perhaps six feet long on a side. It had no seats, no cargo. Nowhere to hide. Redbeard stood at the far side of the basket beside the vehicle's small control panel. Between them, the burner hung down almost to the level of Sabine's head, its flame popping and hissing as it heated the air of the balloon.

Sabine leveled her sword at Redbeard. "Surrender."

His gaze flickered back and forth between her blade and Cliff's gun. He knew he was outmaneuvered, but he remained as cool as ever. He glanced upwards. "Really, daughter, do you think my crew will treat you nicely if you harm me? We are rising to my ship right now. Perhaps if you turn over the *real* treasure to me, we can come to an arrangement."

Sabine remained silent for a long moment, assessing this man who had spent his entire life amassing wealth and power by any means. "I could give you five Hearts of Ra. It wouldn't matter. You'll never be satisfied. All you crave is more, more, more. You will never understand what a real treasure is."

She knew, though. She'd found hers in a clumsy American duke and his feisty daughter. She needed nothing more.

Sabine thrust her sword back into its scabbard and unfastened the top of her bodice. "The Heart of Ra isn't a device," she said. "It's an idea. Some scribbles on paper. And I think I'd rather see it destroyed than in the hands of anyone like you."

She ran at Redbeard, whirling around when he raised his dagger, taking the strike right where her armor was strongest. With a flick of her wrist, she tossed the paper into the flame of the burner.

Redbeard screamed in rage, grabbing for the hilt of her sword. Sabine stomped on his foot, threw her elbow up into his chin, and hammered down on the arm that was drawing her sword. The cutlass spun to the floor and she dove for it. Redbeard leapt at her, dagger raised, but Sabine was faster. She rolled, sprang to her feet, and brought the curved blade down on his exposed neck.

He collapsed, choking, gurgling.

"That's for everyone I loved."

Her enemy fell silent and still.

50

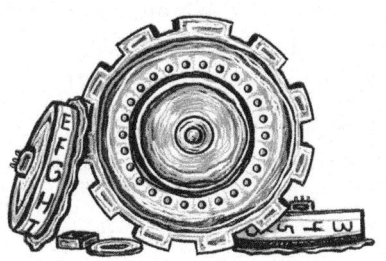

Cliff heaved the body overboard and let it tumble to the ground below. The bastard didn't deserve anything more than that.

"You okay?" he asked Sabine.

She stood by the controls, touching nothing, pale and silent. The balloon rose steadily into the air.

"They have thirty guns," she said at last. "Pirates don't give up when their leader dies. Someone will step forward and take charge. Lola and our crew will be in danger as long as that ship is in the air."

Cliff placed his hand against her back. His limbs still trembled a bit. He'd shot a man. And nearly toppled down a mountain. But he and Sabine were both alive. That was all that mattered.

"What do we do?"

"What all good pirates do. Board the ship."

"And then?"

"Then we either disable it or take it over. Preferably the first. A high-altitude ship large enough to carry thirty guns must have a crew of a hundred. That's half Redbeard's organization on one ship. We'll work by stealth. Stay low, out of sight when the bottom hatch opens to allow us in. Once inside, we look for a way to damage the ship. Then we open the hatch and fly out again."

"Why not just run and leave them behind?"

"If they discover we're commanding this craft, they'll shoot us down. And this can't fly fast enough to escape."

"Okay. Take the ship down, then. If they have cannon, they'll have gunpowder. We can set it off."

All color drained from Sabine's face and she trembled, but she nodded.

Dammit. They couldn't set off an explosion or start a fire inside a ship. He'd seen what had happened when Die Fledermaus went down. If Sabine froze or panicked, she might never make it out. And even if she did, the trauma would be overwhelming. He'd find another way.

They sat on the floor of the tiny airship as the scorpion-shaped basket swayed in the wind. The constant rain plastered their hair to their skulls and soaked through their clothes. Cliff's handkerchief was too wet to wipe the droplets from his glasses anymore. He tucked them into a pocket. If he got a headache from trying to focus, he'd live with it. Sabine simply smeared the droplets around with the hem of her skirt and pushed the water-streaked spectacles back on her face.

"Sabine?"

"Yes?"

"What did you burn? I'm assuming you didn't actually destroy the plans for the Heart of Ra."

"No. I burned your letter. I didn't want to look at it ever again, because you are *not* leaving."

He squeezed her hand. "No. I'm not."

A shadow formed above them, too dark to be a cloud. Metal ground against metal. Sabine stood up and manned the controls to steer the landing craft into the ship.

"Keep that gun ready," she said. "The hangar shouldn't

need more than a few people to anchor the balloon, but we need to be prepared for anything."

Cliff's fingers tightened around the grip of the revolver. His left arm throbbed with pain. He'd wrenched it badly while grabbing branches to prevent himself from tumbling down the mountain, and both his wrist and elbow smarted.

The ascent into the hangar seemed interminable. Sabine dropped down beside him, putting a finger to her lips. Outside the scorpion, men shouted directions as they moored the landing craft. Cliff counted three distinct voices.

"Don't shoot unless absolutely necessary," Sabine whispered. "We want to bring them down silently if possible."

The hatch banged closed beneath them. "All clear, Captain," a man called.

Sabine charged. The man was down before he even knew what had happened. Cliff followed, revolver at the ready, but she needed no assistance. Within seconds she'd dispatched both the other pirates. Damn, but she was remarkable.

She came to stand at Cliff's side, breathing heavily. The only sign of distress was the slight tremble of her lower lip.

"I don't like killing," she murmured. "No matter how well deserved."

"I know. It'll be over soon." He nodded toward the opposite end of the chamber, where a dozen of the bomb birds sat tied to the floor. "If we point those straight up, they'll plow into the decks above and tear the ship apart."

She nodded, her jaw clenched.

"I want you to open the hangar and launch the balloon," he said.

"What?"

"I'm going to set those off. There's going to be fire and smoke, and you shouldn't be here for that. You leave in the balloon and as soon as it's done I'll lower myself out the hatch and you can pick me up. We can set up a rope for me right now."

Sabine grabbed his arm, her fingers clenching around

his biceps. "Are you insane? I can't leave you here! What if something goes wrong?"

"I can do this. I promise. This ship is going to go down hard and fast. The balloon needs to be out and ready to flee immediately. I can't do that part. But you can."

Tears welled in her eyes. "Damn you, Hartleigh."

"I love you, too."

She released him and took a step back, taking a deep breath. She extended her hand. "Partners."

He grasped her hand and shook. "Partners." He leaned in and kissed her with all the love in his heart. "Tie me up an escape rope and then get the hell out. I'll be right behind."

Cliff raced across the hangar, making a quick assessment of the bomb birds. They were well-designed. Simple to use. He pulled levers and spun dials, aiming them up at the heart of the ship. Mooring lines fell to the floor as he unfastened hooks and kicked away ballast bags.

He glanced back at the scorpion craft. The top of the red balloon fell from view, the hatch dangling open. It was time.

The first bird took off at an angle, smashing into the side of the hangar and bursting. Cliff covered his head as debris rained down. He launched the next and the next. His ears rang with the noise of the explosions. Smoke filled the chamber and chunks of flaming wood tumbled from the deck above. Cliff raced from bird to bird, setting them off as rapidly as he could manage. He missed one or two, but he wasn't stopping to go back. He ran for the hatch, diving beneath the smoke and grabbing for the rope that Sabine had left him. Slipping the loop around his waist, he tumbled out into the air below.

He was falling. Falling into nothing. Far, far below were plants and trees and jagged rocks, rising toward him. Too fast. He'd never stop. Not until he stopped hard enough to end it all.

The rope jerked him to a sudden halt, sending pain streaking through him. Miles and miles of nothing hung below him, waiting. The rope shuddered. It slipped. He spun helplessly, slipping inch by inch. A slow, unending death.

A hand grabbed his foot, pulling. Hard metal mesh scratched against his legs, then his belly. The rope snapped. He tumbled, landing on solid ground. Cool metal pressed against his cheek.

"Would you stop screaming? You're safe now."

Gentle arms wrapped around him, helping him sit up, and a beloved face smiled.

"Sabine." He crushed her against him.

"Yes, love, that's better. I much prefer you to sigh my name than to scream it in mortal terror." She wiggled from his arms and went to the controls. "You did well, partner. Now let's go home."

"Home," he agreed. Sabine had been right from the beginning. The dukedom, with its problems and responsibilities and heaps of clutter, was a part of him now. England had become home, as much as Chicago was. He could live in either place, or both. He would probably never be a proper duke, but he wouldn't run away from the title, either. After all, it had led him to his pirate. And wherever she lived would always be home.

51

I'M HOME!

Sabine wanted to jump for joy. Riding down from Fledermaus Zwei on the cargo hoist took an absurdly long time, but she suffered through it for the sake of her loved ones. Cliff still suffered from height anxiety after his wild jump from Redbeard's dirigible. He shied away from the rail and paled every time he even looked at the rope ladder. He'd happily scooped a sleepy Lola into his arms and declared that they needed to ride down instead. Now he stood rigidly in the exact center of the lift, hugging his daughter tightly and looking anywhere but down.

The last rays of sunlight glinted off the windows of Sabine's mansion, bathing the area in a warm, orange light. A ridiculous home, certainly, with its unusably numerous rooms and its piles of the old duke's eclectic collection, but it was hers. She couldn't wait to get inside and bury herself beneath the blankets of her unnecessarily large bed.

The lift touched down and Cliff let out an audible breath. He climbed right over the rail, not bothering to wait for Sabine to open the gate, and strode off in the direction of the dower house, his long legs carrying him swiftly across the lawn.

Sabine ran to catch up. "Where are you going?"

Cliff stopped, frowning at her in puzzlement. "Home. I need to put Lola to bed."

Sabine's heart sank. That big bed wouldn't be so cozy after all if she had to lie in it alone.

"Where did you think I was going?" he asked, his brow still crinkled in confusion.

"I'd hoped you might want to stay with me at my house. I know it's a mess and I haven't any servants, but the bedrooms are clean and I'd… I'd like us to be together."

"So would I. I suppose I assumed you'd come to my house. That was presumptuous and insensitive of me. I apologize."

"Yes, you are clearly a terrible person, Hartleigh."

His mouth curved into a winning smile. "So, your house." He changed direction, moving swiftly toward the massive Hartleigh ancestral home.

"It's the only house I've ever owned," Sabine explained. "The first time I've ever had a *place* that I could return to. My childhood home and the houses I lived in with Redbeard's daughters were places to rest my head, but I lived there at the will of others. Here I come and go as I please. It's *mine*."

"Then I'm honored to be invited to share it."

"I'd like you to have half. I'll draw up a contract. Fifty-fifty ownership. I want it to be *ours*."

Cliff's arms were full with Lola, but he moved close enough that he brushed against Sabine. "What's more than honored? Overwhelmed? Laid low? Awestruck?"

"'Happy' is good enough."

They tucked Lola into bed in the chamber that had once been reserved for the Duchesses of Hartleigh. It had been one of the first rooms Cliff had cleared out, and it was now completely empty except for a bed.

"Imagine it filled with dolls and wooden swords and terrariums full of spiders and frogs," Sabine whispered.

Cliff squeezed her hand. "She wants a scorpion now."

Sabine grinned. Towing Der Skorpion had slowed their journey by two days, but Lola's joy at having a craft she could learn to fly had made it all worthwhile. Sabine was nearly as excited to begin lessons as she was.

"Our room is right through there." Sabine led Cliff through the adjoining door into the master bedchamber. While not as bare as Lola's new room, it still lacked many furnishings. It needed a cozy sofa where she could curl up with a book, or where they could make love if they were bored of the bed. Someday, this house would be perfect.

Cliff started stripping immediately, dropping his clothing on the floor as if he actually had a valet to pick everything up for him. Sabine found herself stopping to watch, marveling again at how stunningly handsome he was. She wondered if perhaps her interpretation of handsome had been warped, if he looked better to her than an identical stranger would. Probably. He was her Cliff, and his internal beauty shone like a thousand suns. Maybe that was how he could stare at her scars and call them beautiful. Maybe he saw the same in her. She shimmied out of her dress, enjoying the way his eyes darkened with each layer that peeled away.

They climbed into bed from opposite sides, reaching out to touch hands across the enormous gulf that separated them. Why did anyone need a bed this large?

Cliff's fingers stroked hers, moving in little whorls across her skin. Tiny vibrations of pleasure raced up her arm. He edged closer, his caress sliding along the back of her hand, over her wrist, slowly up to her elbow. Every nerve in her body buzzed with excitement, and she scooted closer. Bit by bit they inched together, until his hands found her torso and his lips met hers. At last. The kiss, the joining was like magic.

She wrapped an arm around him, drawing their bodies flush, sighing at the heat of contact.

His hands mapped her curves, cupping and squeezing. She rubbed her thigh against his cock and he groaned at the friction. A moment later, he broke their kiss.

"I'm sorry I still don't have any condoms. I'll have to go into town. You'd think a serviceable airship ought to come stocked."

Sabine laid a hand on his chest. "Cliff. I think we need to talk."

"That doesn't sound ominous at all." He pulled away, once again leaving a large gap between them in the enormous bed. "What have I done wrong?"

· · · ⚙ · · ·

Cliff cursed himself silently.

He'd been irresponsible. All through their days on the airship he'd been pulling out dangerously last-second, and he hadn't made much effort to offer suggestions or alternatives or ask her what she preferred. That had to be the trouble. He hoped it wasn't anything worse than that.

"You haven't done anything wrong," Sabine replied.

His tense shoulders sagged in relief. "Thank God. I had a sudden terrible fear that you'd realized you didn't actually want me in your bed after all."

"Don't be absurd. But if we're to live together, we need to discuss family."

Family. His heart jumped so hard he thought it might bust out of his chest. She was his family. Him and Sabine and Lola. Legal or not, "proper" or not, they were a family. He didn't give a damn what outsiders might think or say.

"Do you want more children?"

"Yes," he blurted, almost before she had finished asking. He'd dreamed for years of having siblings for Lola, of more wild, adorable creatures climbing on him, begging to hear stories, shouting for Daddy. Fatherhood had been his single great joy until Sabine had brought a second love to his life. Now he hoped to add to his collection of titles: Scrap Collector, Duke, Father, Husband.

"But it's okay if you don't," Cliff rushed to add. He would not lose her over a hypothetical future. Children and marriage meant nothing if he didn't have Sabine. "Lola is enough, if that's what makes you happy."

Sabine skimmed a finger along the bottom edge of her chestplate. A band of scar tissue about two inches wide marred the skin beneath. "The biomechanologist who patched me up offered me a choice: a bigger plate with less scarring and more protection or one that stopped right here so it wouldn't interfere if I ever wanted children. At the time I couldn't imagine a future that would involve any sort of family, but some part of me must not have lost all hope." She closed her hand over his. "Thank you for finding that part. Forget the condoms. Maybe we will make Lola into a big sister someday. And if not, we are enough."

They embraced again, holding one another close, sharing tender, loving kisses. It was enough. They were enough. The future would be what it would be. They would try for a baby and he would dream of wild pirate children. They would be intimate and passionate and love one another. Someday he'd work up the nerve to ask her to marry him. Whatever happened, they would be happy together.

Sabine rolled onto her back, taking him with her and wrapping her legs around him. "Make love to me, Cliff. Make me forget that our bodies do come apart sometimes."

He laughed and nuzzled her neck, dragging his tongue across her salty-sweet skin until she trembled. "Oh, I'll make you come apart, love. Don't you doubt it."

He eased his way into her, loving the feel of her hips lifting to take him in further, her muscles clenching around him. God, she was heavenly. All heat and moisture and throaty moans. His eyes slid closed and he surrendered to the pleasure, riding wave after wave of her ecstasy, reveling in the thrill of her sighs and shudders. When she cried out his name, he let the last of his control slip away and thrust deep, joining her as he lost himself.

52

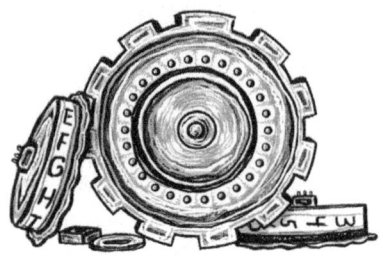

One month later

"Kinsley. Have a seat."

Cliff lowered himself into the chair, assessing the man across the desk. Once again he was struck by the casual confidence Evan Tagget exuded. Tagget was short and slight, but he didn't sit in a high chair or in any way attempt to make his physical presence more imposing. Everything he owned was of the absolute highest quality, but none of it was flashy. Today, his hair was mussed, his sleeves rolled up, and his shirt stained. He looked like he'd come straight from his workshop. Cliff respected a man who wasn't afraid to get his hands dirty.

Tagget fished in the pocket of his vest and produced two tiny cylinders, each no more than an inch long and half that in diameter. He set them in the center of the desk, along with a small piece of paper with a name and address written in precise, loopy letters.

"I modified the design." Tagget pulled out a cigarette and touched the head of a small dragon that sat on the desk. The mechanical creature spewed a gout of flame. Tagget lit the cigarette and leaned back in his chair. "The original plan was unnecessarily powerful. These batteries are smaller and will still last well beyond the lifespan of any human."

Cliff picked up one of the cylinders. "You're absolutely certain? This is my family we're talking about."

Tagget smirked. "Really, Kinsley. You came to me with plans for a device that I could sell for millions or turn into a bomb as easily as I breathe. And *now* you don't trust me?"

Cliff had to admit he'd hesitated at first. But Tagget had refunded the money of everyone who'd once purchased the tainted Dynalux luxene. His replacement company, Pure-Lux, had a stellar reputation. And Tagget Industries was the best engineering company in the world.

"The batteries will work," Tagget declared with absolute confidence. "I've given you the name of my biomechanologist. He's the best, so don't go to anyone else. Your daughter and your mistress will have hearts far better than your own sorry human one."

"Thank you." Cliff tucked the paper and the tiny Hearts of Ra into his innermost pocket. They would remain on his person until he arrived home. "How much do I owe you?"

"No charge."

"What?" Cliff leaned over the desk, staring at Tagget, certain that must have been a joke.

"I'm a philanthropist, or haven't you heard?"

Cliff had heard. It's what had ultimately tipped the scale in Tagget's favor. Word was he'd lost millions of dollars in business deals over his choice of bride. Most of the rest of his fortune he was slowly parceling out to women's rights foundations and schools for poor and underprivileged children. And he seemed happy about it.

"I'm willing to burn the plans, as you suggested," Tagget said, gesturing with his cigarette at the fire-breathing dragon. He pulled the now stained and crumpled design from a drawer and spread it on the desk. "Feel free to do it yourself. My improved design, however, exists both in my brain and in my personal notebook. There will be others who need these batteries. My new biomechanics division will manufacture and distribute them through my medical fund." He tapped his chest. "My own biomechanics have saved my life. No one should die when we have the technology to save them, just because they can't pay like I did. What do you say, Kinsley?"

Cliff rose from his seat and extended a hand. Tagget did likewise.

"I'd like to contribute," Cliff replied.

Tagget smirked again. "I thought you might."

Sabine's tea had gone cold and Lola had eaten the last biscuit. Sabine contemplated remarking on both those things, but to do so would interrupt Amy's oration. Which was rude. Since the point of this exercise was to familiarize herself with the peculiarities of upper-class British manners, being rude seemed counterproductive.

More importantly, Amy might start the whole reading over if interrupted, and Sabine wasn't about to sit through this twice. She yawned.

Amy sighed and set the book down. "You can't yawn. Ladies, whatever rank, do not yawn."

"I was bored."

"Ladies do not become bored either."

Sabine rolled her eyes. Amy noticed but responded only with a forlorn shake of her head.

"What if they're tired?" Lola asked. "Can they yawn then?"

"No. They politely excuse themselves and retire to bed. A lady may claim headache or illness if no other reason for departure can be reasonably cited."

"So lying is fine, but honest boredom is not," Sabine scoffed. "Sensible. My tea's cold. How do I get a new pot in a ladylike manner? Or is it okay to scowl and reprimand the help?"

Amy picked up her gloves and tugged them on in a calm, unhurried manner. She rose from her seat and arranged her skirts. "I think we are done for today. I will have to reevaluate my planned lessons. It seems I was not suitably prepared for the magnitude of this task."

"Amy, dear." Luella rested a gentle hand on her lover's arm. "You don't have to make her a perfect duchess. He's never going to be a perfect duke. Truthfully, it would only disappoint people. They're all enjoying the scandal."

"Well, this looks shockingly domestic," Cliff's deep voice intruded. He strode into the room. "Ladies at tea in the parlor? Maybe I have the wrong house."

"Daddy!" Lola leapt from her seat and raced across the room to embrace him.

"Nope. Not the wrong house." He held out an arm to hug Sabine and gave her a kiss. "I have treasures for you both."

Lola did a little dance. "Yay! Treasure!"

"Any news since I've been gone?" Cliff walked to the table and poured himself a cup of the cold tea. He took one sip, then pushed it away.

"I'm damned glad you didn't go to San Francisco, because there's just been a massive earthquake," Sabine replied.

"I heard."

"Closer to home, your report about Barton and his house and activities have led to the capture of the gang that styled themselves 'Barton's Bandits.' Barton and Adriana themselves have vanished, along with a great deal of money. My guess is we'll never hear of them again."

Cliff nodded, pursing his lips. "Good. There was news circulating in Paris that you should be aware of. Talk of Redbeard and a marauding all-female crew. I'm a bit concerned that someone has taken over what he left behind. Someone has stolen a great deal of cargo in the last two weeks, but the ship is reportedly too light and fast to be caught."

"She might be terrible at some things, but she's an excellent pilot."

"What?"

Sabine grinned, wiggling with excitement the way Lola often did. She'd been waiting to tell him this story. "Yvette. She's adopted the name Redbeard and used it to recruit her own crew. She's his perfect heir. Friendly to us, and she's his natural daughter."

Cliff's eyebrows lifted behind his red-rimmed spectacles. "She is?"

"That's why she was allowed to be a Daughter, even though she was disobedient and a terrible spy. She was his biological daughter, by a young French prostitute—who later made a name for herself. You know her as Madame Séverin. She must be a proud mother now."

"Damn. Small world."

"Isn't it?" Sabine threaded her arm through his. "Let's get out of this silly room so you can show us the treasures."

They walked out to the garden together: father, daughter, and mother. Maybe. Hopefully. Lola wasn't calling Sabine "Mommy" yet, but the other day she'd asked, "Do you have to marry Daddy to be my mommy?" Sabine had stammered something noncommittal, caught entirely off-guard.

"So," Cliff began, letting the word hang for a moment before continuing. "Treasures number one and number two: tiny Heart of Ra batteries." He showed off one of the miniature devices, then carefully tucked it away. "We'll schedule a date to travel to Cambridge where we've been referred to a biomechanology specialist. No more fueling or winding."

Lola whooped. "Me and Sabine are going to be exactly the same!"

Cliff beamed at her. "Treasure number three." He reached into his large outer pocket and produced a small mechanical scorpion, which he handed to Lola. "Tagget Industries special. She will respond to your voice."

Lola hugged the tiny bug-dragon, plopped down on the ground, and began to shout commands at it. Cliff and Sabine walked on, hand-in-hand, laughing.

"Where's my second treasure, Duke?" Sabine demanded in mock annoyance. "Don't I deserve a voice-controlled monster, too?"

"Yours is... smaller." He stepped back, staring into her eyes, shifting nervously.

Sabine's every muscle tensed. Her heart vibrated. Cliff pulled out a tiny box and opened it. A pair of matching gold rings sat on the velvet. One for each of them.

"I want to marry you, Sabine," he said, half-whispering. "If that's not what you want, that's okay. But I wanted to at least have some symbol of what we are to one another."

Sabine gently lifted the smaller of the two rings, her hands shaking, her eyes watering. Etched into the gold were the words, "Mein Schatz. My treasure." She burst into tears.

Cliff slipped his own ring onto his finger and drew her into his arms, resting his head atop hers as she sobbed into his chest. "What do you say, love? Will you marry me? Or will we remain as we are forever and ever?"

Sabine wiped at her eyes. "Yes, I'll marry you. I'll be a terrible duchess. Amy was trying to give Lola and me lessons on how to be a proper lady, and we'll never take to them. But I don't care in the slightest."

"Nor do I. And I think pirate duchess sounds brilliant."

Sabine kissed him, long and deep and lingering, until a small child wedging herself between them broke them apart.

"*Now* will you be really my mommy?" Lola asked.

Sabine hugged her. "Yes. Absolutely. Your daddy and I can get married today, even. We'll all fly up in my ship and I'll declare us married."

Cliff frowned. "Um..."

"You don't like that idea?"

"I don't hate it, but I was hoping for something more public. Maybe a fancy church, flowers, bells ringing. Lola in a beautiful dress leading the way for you while I stand by the altar weeping tears of joy. Lots of newspapermen with cameras."

Sabine laughed. "Admit it, Hartleigh, you're a romantic."

Cliff shrugged. "I suppose I am."

"Very well, I accept. You can have your fairytale." They kissed again and this time Lola applauded. "And as we say in Germany, 'and if they haven't died, then they are still living today.'"

"I like the American way," Lola replied. "And the duke and the pirate lived Happily Ever After. The End."

EPILOGUE

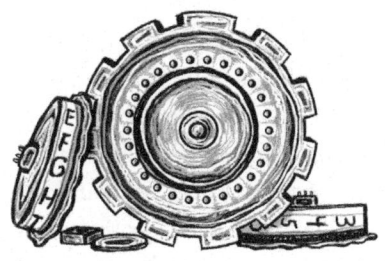

Chicago Tribune, July 30, 1911
Yale Expedition Discovers Lost Inca City

Historian Hiram Bingham of Yale University has confirmed the existence of a previously forgotten city of the Inca Empire high in the Peruvian Andes, at a site known as Machu Picchu. Mr. Bingham notes that the site possesses many fine buildings and high quality stonework. Future expeditions are planned to excavate and further explore the area. While Mr. Bingham is officially the first to bring this discovery to the Western World, there is some question as to whether others reached the site before him. Markings found on a wall indicate that another explorer may have visited in the past, and the nearby remains of a crashed airship testify to the grisly end of an earlier failed expedition.

England, January 1912

"AVAST!"

Cliff dodged the wooden cutlass and continued dismantling the automatic rotating clothes rack he'd removed from the wardrobe. It was hopelessly broken and probably had never worked well in the first place, but it contained some saleable parts. With luck he'd have it apart within the hour and they could be done with this house by dinnertime.

"Surprise!" shouted a second young voice from his opposite side.

They always tried to flank him. Cliff twisted to avoid the point of his daughter's blade, then dropped his screwdriver and grabbed both children by the sword arm.

"Got you, you little mischief makers!"

Something jabbed him in the back and he yelped.

"The Duke of Hartleigh is our prisoner," intoned a serious voice. "He will be held captive until a ransom has been paid."

"Et tu, Lola?" Cliff released the twins and raised his hands in the air. "Very well, I surrender."

The younger kids whooped as Cliff turned around to face his traitorous teenager.

"I thought you were working today. Shouldn't that put you on my side?"

Lola shrugged. "This house is boring. Nothing but papers. I'm sick of papers. Playing was more fun. Pay up."

Cliff dug into his pockets and jingled the handful of nuts and bolts he found. "Here's the ransom for you. Go get it." He scattered the shiny scraps across the room.

"Treasure!" Max shouted. He and Ilse scrambled to gather up as many little pieces as they could find. Cliff wouldn't tell them, but sometimes when he needed a part he went poking through their treasure chests.

"Junk," Lola muttered. "I demand a higher price. A piece of candy, at least."

"When do I ever carry candy? Some little pickpocket would swipe it."

Lola waved her toy sword in a lazy but well-practiced motion. "I suppose you'll have to remain my prisoner forever then."

Cliff looked past her to the doorway. Sabine shimmed sideways through the entrance, her arms full with an enormous portrait.

"I'm not worried," Cliff said. "Your mother will rescue me."

"Again?" Sabine set the portrait down and propped it against the wall. "Found that behind the big tapestry in the library. Everything's down from the walls now. What am I rescuing you from this time?"

"Lola is holding me for ransom. Demanding candy."

"Or money," Lola suggested.

"Mommy!" Ilse came tearing across the room, her hands full of metal bits. "We have the treasure! Look! I found the biggest, sparkliest one!" She proudly held up a gleaming cap nut.

Max pouted. "Hmph. Well, I get to be a duke someday." He stuck out his tongue at his sister.

Cliff stepped between them before he had to listen to another "dukes are stupid" argument. Six years in and he was still learning both the perks and the responsibilities of his title. Explaining all that to a five-year-old was impossible.

"Titles are no more than words," he said instead. "What matters is that you all learn to work together as part of the family business or you study hard and find your own way to contribute to society. Being born with money doesn't mean you get to be a lazy good-for-nothing. Not in this family."

"Yeah," Lola agreed. "Let's all get to work and finish this house so we can go back to Chicago." She picked up Cliff's discarded screwdriver and took over where he'd left off.

Sabine slipped an arm around Cliff, leaning on his shoulder. "Give her a few more years and she's going to run Kinsley Metals."

"I know." Lola was good with machines. She had a knack not only for dismantling them but for fixing them. He probably should have left the broken clothing rack to her in the first place. His British business of buying estates from impoverished nobility then sorting and selling the contents didn't suit her nearly as well as the Chicago scrap metalworks. He loved both equally. He would never tire of salvaging discarded machines. Finding peculiar devices, valuable art, or interesting books in dusty English attics was his own personal treasure hunt.

Max grabbed another screwdriver from the tool chest and jabbed at the broken machine, watching his big sister and copying her. Ilse chose a wrench and wrapped it around a hopelessly rusted bolt. Cliff and Sabine left them to play, turning to examine the artwork she'd brought in.

"It's hideous," she said. "I doubt anyone will want it."

Cliff cringed. "Yikes. Is that a dog? Or a... fox, maybe?"

"I'm more concerned with why her arm is twisted in an entirely unnatural position and yet she's smiling. This is why I'm glad you've always hired photographers for our family portraits. If we look bad, it's our own fault."

Cliff gently touched a section of one portrait where the paint was flaking off. A chunk cracked and fell away, revealing part of another image underneath. "We can have it looked at, just in case it was painted over something more valuable. Otherwise, you're right, no one will want it. Also the frame is rotting. We may as well remove that and dispose of it now."

Sabine grabbed a section of the frame and ripped it apart with her bare hands, grinning. "Destruction is fun. It was wise of me to find a husband who makes a living at this. Prevents me going back to piracy. So far."

"Well, that and the fact that it's difficult to fit a grand piano on an airship. I can't imagine you giving up your music lessons."

"I could take up a more pirate-worthy instrument. The fife, perhaps."

"Too shrill." He pried apart one corner of the frame. It broke so easily he wondered if the wood had already been rotten when the frame was made. "You could sing sea shanties."

"Swift may our dirigible fly," she sang in a high, clear voice. "O'er valleys low and mountains high."

Cliff added his baritone into the mix. "Someday when the treasure is mine, I'll take my love and go."

He began to launch into the first verse when Sabine seized his arm. "Wait! Don't move."

Cliff froze. "What?"

She reached across the painting and plucked something from the underside of the piece of frame Cliff held. "Someone was hiding papers in this awful piece of art."

Cliff tossed the wood aside and moved close to Sabine as she carefully unfolded the paper. It was yellowed and dry and it crackled as she opened it.

"Hoo-boy," he breathed. "Is that what I think it is?"

The children dropped their tools, rushing over to view the discovery.

"Definitely a treasure map," Sabine declared. "And this symbol in the corner matches what's on the cover of that strange old atlas we found in the library."

Cliff wrapped an arm around his wife, letting his fingers slide across the slight bump of her belly. "Are you feeling up for some adventure?"

"I'm a pirate. I can handle anything."

"What do you say to a family holiday?"

She turned to kiss him, then beckoned to the children to join their embrace. "We'll probably find nothing. But it's the journey that matters. I'll never turn down an adventure alongside my own personal treasures. Let's go."

Cliff kissed her once more. "Aye, aye, Captain."

THE END

Sea Shanty

Chorus:

> Swift may our dirigible fly,
> O'er valleys low and mountains high.
> Someday, when the treasure is mine,
> I'll take my love and go.

Verses:

> The strange, old duke had finally died.
> The search for an heir ranged far and wide.
> They combed the American countryside,
> To a man in Chicago.

> The dukedom was awash with debt.
> The new duke said, "This is what I get?
> I'll find a way to get out of it yet.
> Though how I do not know."

> His neighbor was a pirate lass,
> With an airship, swords, and lots of sass.
> He turned to her for help. Alas!
> He feared she would say no.

> She thought for a time, then said, "You see,
> I'll help you fake your death and flee.
> But pirates never work for free,
> So a debt to me you'll owe."

> "I seek a treasure beyond compare.
> Come help me find it, if you dare."

The duke looked at the pirate fair
And said, "All right, let's go."

So duke and pirate off they flew,
But their treasure hunt may find friendship too.
And even lead to a love that's true.
If fate declares it so.

About the Author

AWARD-WINNING AUTHOR CATHERINE STEIN believes that everyone deserves love and that Happily Ever After has the power to help, to heal, and to comfort. She writes sassy, sexy romance set during the Victorian and Edwardian eras. Her stories are full of action, adventure, magic, and fantastic technologies.

Catherine lives in Michigan with her husband and three rambunctious kids. She loves steampunk and Oxford commas, and can often be found dressed in Renaissance festival clothing, drinking copious amounts of tea.

· · · ✦ · · ·

Visit Catherine online at
www.catsteinbooks.com
and join her VIP mailing list for a free short story.

Follow her on Twitter @catsteinbooks,
or like her page on Facebook @catsteinbooks.

Also by Catherine Stein

Potions and Passions

The Earl on the Train - Book 0.5

How to Seduce a Spy - Book 1

Mishaps & Mistletoe -
A Holiday Novella -Book 1.5

Not a Mourning Person - Book 2

Once a Rake, Always a Rogue - Book 3

Love at Second Sight - Book 4

Sass and Steam

Love is in the Airship - Book 0.5

A Shot to the Heart - Book 0.75

Eden's Voice - Book 1

What Are You Doing New Year's Eve? -
A Holiday Novella - Book 1.5

Priceless - Book 2

Arcane Tales

The Scoundrel's New Con - Book 1

The Spinster's Swindle - Book 2
Coming Fall 2021

Other Books

Mating Habits - Book 1

Idle Nature - Book 2

Available at your favorite online retailer.
www.catsteinbooks.com

· · · ✦ · · ·

Thank you so much for reading.
If you enjoyed the book and are so inclined, I would love for
you to leave a review. Happy readers make an author's day!

I love hearing from readers,
so feel free to contact me on social media, or email:

catherine@catsteinbooks.com

Made in the USA
Las Vegas, NV
16 September 2021